"I'll stop at nothing to protect ye."

Her eyes searched his, looking for something he hoped she found. "And what have I done to earn such a champion?" she whispered on parted lips.

"'Tis nothing ye've done, Amelia, and it can never be undone." He bent to kiss her again. She fell back on the bed, taking him along with fistfuls of his shirt in her hands.

Feeling her beneath him made him hard as steel. He wanted her, throbbed for her, and he was tempted to tear away the two flimsy layers of wool between them, spread her wide, and sink deep.

But she was untried and untouched. And though every nerve ending on his body burned for her, ached to be her first, he didn't want her to regret anything.

"I fear if I take ye, I won't let anyone else ever do so." It was a statement of truth that pained him as it left his lips.

"And I fear," she whispered into his hair as he bent his head to her throat, "that if ye take me, I will never be satisfied with anyone else."

Highlander series book. This fast-paced tale of political intrigue populated by sensual characters with deeply rooted senses of honor and loyalty is spellbinding...Top-notch Highland romance!"

—*RT Book Reviews*

"A winning mix of fascinating history and lush romance...Readers will be captivated by the meticulously accurate historical detail...and Connor and Mairi's searing passion."

—*Publishers Weekly* (starred review)

"[A] must read...Paula Quinn weaves romance, suspense, and history into a story that unleashes a smoldering desire within the heart of the reader. A breathtaking romance full of history and heart-melting Highlanders."

—NightOwlReviews.com

"This series is one hit after another and I enjoy it more with each book...Paula Quinn keeps her books historically accurate, which adds to the depth."

—GoodReads.com

Seduced by a Highlander

"*Seduced by a Highlander* is sparkling, sexy, and seductive! I couldn't put it down! Paula Quinn is a rising star!"
—Karen Hawkins, *New York Times* bestselling author

"Top Pick! An engrossing story brimming with atmosphere and passionate characters...a true keeper."

—*RT Book Reviews*

"Scottish romance at its very best! Deliciously romantic and sensual, Paula Quinn captures the heart of the Highlands in a tender, passionate romance that you won't be able to put down."

—Monica McCarty, *New York Times* bestselling author

"A rich tapestry of love, rivalry, and hope...the simmering passion made for very heated scenes...I can't wait to read more of the family in future books!"

—TheRomanceReadersConnection.com

"Five Stars! Reviewer's Recommended Award Winner! Paula Quinn went above and beyond my expectations...With a hero to make a heart sigh and a heroine who can match the hero wit to wit, this story is one I highly recommend adding to your bookshelf."

—CoffeeTimeRomance.com

Ravished by a Highlander

"Deftly combines historical fact and powerful romance...There's much more than just sizzling sensuality: history buffs will love the attention to periodic detail and cameos by real-life figures, and the protagonists embody compassion, responsibility, and unrelenting, almost self-sacrificial honor. Quinn's seamless prose and passionate storytelling will leave readers hungry for future installments."

—*Publishers Weekly* (starred review)

*The Seduction of
Miss Amelia Bell*

Also by Paula Quinn

The Seduction of
Miss Amelia Bell

PAULA QUINN

FOREVER

NEW YORK   BOSTON

Forever
Hachette Book Group
237 Park Avenue
New York, NY 10017

www.HachetteBookGroup.com

Printed in the United States of America

First Edition: March 2014
10 9 8 7 6 5 4 3 2 1

OPM

Forever is an imprint of Grand Central Publishing.
The Forever name and logo are trademarks of Hachette Book Group, Inc.

The Hachette Speakers Bureau provides a wide range of authors for speaking events. To find out more, go to www.hachettespeakersbureau.com or call (866) 376-6591.

The publisher is not responsible for websites (or their content) that are not owned by the publisher.

ATTENTION CORPORATIONS AND ORGANIZATIONS:

Most Hachette Book Group books are available at quantity discounts with bulk purchase for educational, business, or sales promotional use. For information, please call or write:

Special Markets Department, Hachette Book Group
237 Park Avenue, New York, NY 10017
Telephone: 1-800-222-6747 Fax: 1-800-477-5925

To my Hero... You never fail

Acknowledgments

Thank you, Dan, Samantha, and Hayley. I love you.

Cast of Heirs and Their Subjects

Edmund MacGregor ~ *eldest son of Colin MacGregor and Gillian Dearly*

Lucan MacGregor ~ *eldest son of Tristan MacGregor and Isobel Fergusson*

Darach Grant ~ *eldest son of Finlay Grant and Leslie Harrison*

Malcolm (Cal) Grant ~ *eldest son of Connor Grant and Mairi MacGregor*

Lady Amelia Bell ~ *niece of the 2nd Duke of Queensberry*

Sarah Frazier ~ *her handmaiden and best friend*

The Duke of Queensberry ~ *her uncle*

David Pierce ~ *captain of the duke's garrison*

John Bell, Baron of Selkirk ~ *her father*

Millicent Bell, Baroness of Selkirk ~ *her mother (the duke's sister)*

Walter Hamilton, Earl of Seafield and Lord Chancellor of Scotland ~ *her betrothed*

Ladies Eleanor and Elizabeth and Anne ~ *her sisters*

William Buchanan ~ *Buchanan chief*

Janet Buchanan ~ *William's sister*

The Seduction of
Miss Amelia Bell

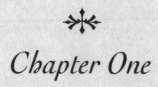

Chapter One

Edmund MacGregor crept along the hall of Venus's Flower, a small brothel on Barkley Lane, and unsheathed his claymore. If he was correct, several members of Parliament were inside these rooms, helpless with their hose around their ankles and their moral values cast to the four winds. Colin MacGregor, his father and the greatest spy in the three kingdoms, had taught him that it was always better to catch victims unawares and desperate to save their lives. One gathered the most information that way.

And Edmund needed information.

He heard a woman scream down at the other end of the long, poorly lit corridor and held his breath, knowing that his cousin Lucan had just burst into the room she shared with Lord Aimsley of Cambridge. The Highland invasion had begun.

They raided often, he and his MacGregor and Grant cousins, invading everything from brothels to grand balls. They'd even managed to convince several MacKinnons and MacDonalds to join them on a few excursions to the Lowlands and had succeeded in postponing Scotland's union with England twice. They were feared throughout the kingdoms, but no one knew their true identities. They were outlaws, belonging to a clan almost utterly extinct and hidden in the clouds.

Edmund kicked open the door in front of him. From the bed, a woman screamed, her shriek followed by two more from the other prostitutes throughout the brothel. The man who shared this woman's mattress paled when he saw the hooded Highlander coming toward him. Edmund's smile remained hidden beneath the black linen covering his face. He raised his sword over his shoulder. "Lord Sunderland. A pleasure to finally meet ye."

The terrified man pissed the bed that the savage would have the knowledge of his identity. Aye, Edmund knew who the patron was. Respected baron, member of Parliament.

He moved around the bed and pointed his blade at the naked nobleman. "Who else needs to put their name to the act? Ye have five breaths to tell me or I'll take the life out of ye here and now."

The baron squeezed his eyes shut and whimpered. Edmund took the moment to flick his eyes toward the woman, breathless and afraid, in the bed next to his victim.

"I don't know which act you speak of."

Edmund moved behind him and pulled him up by the hair. "Then let me be more precise." He positioned his blade across his captive's throat and waited patiently for the nobleman to cease his hysterics. "Who else needs to sign the Union with England Act, the one that will put into effect the Treaty of Union, which will join the three kingdoms and enslave Scotland to England?" He pressed the edge of his blade deeper, wishing Sunderland hadn't already signed. There was no longer a reason to kill him. "The act ye and traitors like ye were bribed by the Duke of Queensberry to sign. *That* act." He bent to Sunderland's ear and whispered, "Yer time is running out."

"Only a few," Lord Sunderland cried. "The Duke of Roxburgh, the lord chancellor, and Queensberry himself!"

Only three and it would be done. Edmund's stomach sank. Were he and his cousins too late? Could they succeed now? He closed his eyes and called upon his fierce determination to see this through. He'd done it before. He could do it again.

"When?" He drove the blade deeper still, drawing a trickle of Sunderland's blood. "When will it be completed?"

"In one month!" the baron cried.

One month until the bastard traitor, the Duke of Queensberry, had all his signatures and brought the act before both Parliaments. The Treaty of Union would be enacted soon after that and Scotland would become part of the new Great Britain.

One month to plan the abduction of the man in charge of procuring the rest of the needed votes. They wouldn't kill him. That would only postpone the treaty until England found someone else to do it. This time, they would do it differently. Many would tell Edmund it was impossible, but he wouldn't listen. He would do whatever needed to be done for Scotland. He would give up anything, including his life, to save his adopted country from further subjugation to England.

"Don't kill me!" the baron whimpered.

"Give me a reason not to," Edmund said over him. "Ye sold yer homeland for a wee bit more than Judas received."

"No! No! I'll help ye!"

When Edmund received the information he needed to move forward, he released his prisoner. He watched the baron trip over his feet on his way out of the room, trying to dress as he went. Edmund's jeer mixed with Lucan MacGregor's when his cousin met him in the hall.

"What did ye learn?"

"They need only three more names. We have a month to stop them," Edmund told him.

Luke shook his head slightly, but he didn't give voice to the doubt that they could do it. "I didna get much more than that from Aimsley."

"I got a wee bit more," Edmund went on as they walked together. "After Sunderland begged me to spare his life, he told me that there was soon to be an announcement."

"Aye?" Luke pulled down his mask and waited.

"The Duke of Queensberry's niece is to be betrothed to the lord chancellor. They will both be in attendance in Edinburgh at the same time."

"Kill them?"

Edmund shook his head. "We'll discuss the details later with the others."

"Aye," Luke agreed. "Should we take the rest of the place? The mistress told me that there are three other noblemen upstairs."

Edmund would rather ride straight for Edinburgh, but he knew his cousins were weary from the trek from Skye to Stirling. They needed a night of drinking and warm, soft bodies to encourage them in their fight to save their country. "Aye, let's drive them out and have the place to ourselves fer the night."

They caught up with their cousin Malcolm a little while later in the parlor with three women in his lap.

"Where's Darach?" Luke asked, his mask tucked into his belt. He accepted a cup of warm wine from a woman with an even warmer smile.

"He's takin' what Lord Lincoln left behind. Bastard might even be makin' the earl watch. Now that I think on it, I dinna' remember seein' Lincoln leave."

Edmund didn't doubt that Darach would do such a thing. He raised his cup with his two comrades and they toasted, while wine and women flowed, to their enemies' defeat. They had a task to see to, and see to it they would. Tomorrow they would set pace toward Edinburgh in an effort to save Scotland, her rights, and her beliefs. But tonight they would drink and enjoy laughter and warm bodies.

Reining in his mount, Edmund fastened his gaze on the magnificent skyline of Edinburgh in the distance. Though he'd seen it many times before, the sight of it never ceased to captivate him. He loved the Highlands, they were his home, and his passion to save them drew him to the capital city like the North Star on the Holy Night.

"We should arrive at Queensberry House just before dawn."

Edmund cut his glance to Luke, the least talkative of their scant troupe. Most of the time, the others welcomed his silence, preferring it to the sharp edge of his tongue and the zeal of his views on the kingdom and all that was wrong within it. Luke was passionate about what he knew, and the man knew a hell of a lot, thanks to his father's affinity for books. Whenever Edmund grew bored on their journeys, he counted on Luke to stimulate the conversation. He was ready for something with a bit more bite after listening to the previous topic of interest between Malcolm and Darach.

"Ye have our thanks fer the information, Luke. We haven't traveled to Edinburgh enough times to figure that out fer ourselves."

Lucan lifted his head to return Edmund's caustic smile—and with a glint in his eyes that fired the golden hues within, accepted the challenge. "If ye expect me to apologize fer thinking the rest of ye too dull-witted to sense time, ye'll have to do something more than discuss the shape of a lass's bosoms fer the last four leagues to convince me."

"Has our crude speech offended yer delicate sensibilities, Luke?" Darach Grant, the youngest among them at nine and ten years this spring, leaped into the fray, unfazed that Luke was the largest among them. "If ye expect *us* to apologize fer enjoyin' what is as yet unfamiliar to ye—"

"'Tis unfamiliar to ye, as well, whelp." Malcolm Grant, cousin to all three and Edmund's closest friend, laughed. "The only bosoms ye've tasted were yer mother's when ye were a babe."

"And that was what," Luke quipped, "almost a month ago now?"

"Aye," Darach told them with a sinister curl tipping the edge of his lips. The lad never backed down from any man, or any number of them. "'Twas aboot the same time

I proved to yer fair Colleen MacKinnon that some men are better at certain skills than others."

Luke tossed him a deprecating smirk before freeing a pouch of water from his saddlebag. "Being quicker at a skill doesna necessarily make ye better at it, lad. I just hope ye didn't get her accustomed to it."

They shared laughter, and Edmund was thankful, much as he'd been for the whole of his life for these men he'd grown up with. Men who could take a punch as well as throw one. Men he loved like brothers, though his bond with them was not forged in blood. Edmund wasn't born a MacGregor. In fact, he wasn't even Scottish. He'd been adopted into the clan when he was almost four, raised as a son to the man he loved more than any other, Colin, his father. He shared much in common with his cousins, especially their love of Scotland, their home on Skye, and their hatred of the renewal of laws against their name.

"I'd prefer if we ride into Edinburgh and complete our task as MacGregors and Grants," Darach said a little while later. "We havena' had a decent fight in over three months."

"There'll be plenty of fighting soon enough," Edmund told him. He turned in his saddle and whistled, bringing a large, gangly four-legged beast galloping toward him, long tongue dangling out of the side of its mouth, tail wagging. "Today we enter Edinburgh as noblemen. We must not deviate from the plan." Edmund wouldn't let them deviate. He'd thought long and hard on what they should do. Harming their enemies would do no good. There were plenty more. The only way to save Scotland was to dissolve the treaty. And there was only one hope of getting that done. They would enter Queensberry House as guests in disguise and take the duke's niece, leaving nothing in their wake but a ransom note. Once they had the girl, they would bring her to Malcolm's family holding, Ravenglade Castle, in Perth. She would be released only after the duke and the chancellor denounced the union.

"'Tis now or never," he continued. "We must stop the union."

Things were dangerous enough for the MacGregors since William of Orange renewed the proscription against them upon his ascension to the throne almost a score years ago. Few MacGregors ever left the shelter of Camlochlin in Skye. It wasn't that they were afraid. They were simply content, certain that the consequences of losing their Parliament would not reach them so far north.

Edmund wasn't as sure about their continued security, nor was he content to sit around in Camlochlin ignorant to the laws being passed against his countrymen. He preferred to ride with his cousins into England's tawdry brothels to gather information from their enemies while their noble heads were absent of wig, and their arses of hose. Defiant plaids swinging about their brawny knees, they made their points at the end of a claymore.

The act would soon be signed. They knew who, they knew where, and now they knew when. They weren't foolish enough to thunder to Parliament's doors and expect to take on the Royal Guard. They were skilled, but none were good enough to fight an army. No, they had to stop the Duke of Queensberry and the Lord Chancellor of Scotland without bringing outright war to their kin.

"I want to give bein' a Gordon a go this time aroond."

"Nae, Darach," Malcolm said, "I hold a Huntley title. I should be a Gordon. I know more aboot them."

"Ye were a Gordon the last two times, Cal," Darach argued. "I'm tired of ye winnin' all the lasses because of yer title."

"Darach," Malcolm issued with a slight curl to his lips and a flash of twin dimples, "my name has nothin' to do with it."

"Och, fer hell's sakes," Lucan said, "don't get him started up again about his 'many attributes.'"

Malcolm tossed his rakish grin to him. "Luke, unlike in yer case, if I dinna' boast of them, others will."

Luke laughed shortly. "Part of yer predicament is that ye think so."

"What predicament is that, cousin? That I dinna' wish to follow yer ancient ideals and long-dead values? That I believe there are too many women to settle fer just one?"

"Remember that bard in Inverness who sang aboot our Miss Bell?" Thankfully Darach veered off the topic with a flash of mischief lighting the green of his eyes. "He sang of how she was lookin' fer a husband, but none would have her because ill fortune is said to follow her. We are no' afraid of such folly, are we, lads? One of us could court her," he suggested, without waiting for an answer to his query. "Imagine Queensberry's reaction when he learns that after we took her fer ransom, one of us planted our seed in his garden."

Lucan cast him a repugnant look and then shook his head at the heavens. "Why did we bring him again? He's as senseless as Malcolm."

"He looks the most innocent," Edmund reminded him. "Folks are less afraid of us when they see him and his angelic features."

Darach immediately took offense. "I dinna' look angelic. Ye're the one with them golden waves springin' over yer eyes, Edmund."

"Ye haven't a hair on yer pretty face, Darach," Malcolm reminded him while he passed him on his horse. "And it doesna' look like any whiskers will be showin' up anytime soon."

"Don't fret," Edmund amended, not wanting to rile Darach up before they reached their destination. "I said ye *looked* innocent. Everyone here knows ye're a deviant miscreant with horns beneath that bonnet ye wear."

And everyone knew Darach was just that. But those who knew him best, like Edmund and the others with them, knew that hidden deep beneath his rough veneer, Darach enjoyed reciting deeds and facts, much like his father, Camlochlin's beloved bard, Finlay Grant. Oftentimes, when he thought he went unnoticed, he sang. The men found no fault in the desires his heritage spawned. If Darach wanted to someday be a great bard, they would not see him as less than a warrior. Darach could play the pipes better than anyone Edmund knew. And he could fight better, too.

"By the way," he added, looking the lad over with a closer eye, "make certain ye change into yer Lowland attire before we get there, and don't ferget, ye cannot wear yer bonnet over yer wig."

"I dinna' want to wear a wig...or hose," Darach complained. "They make me hot and itchy."

"We don't have invitations to the celebration," Edmund reminded him. "After we find another way in we will mingle. We can't do that in our plaids. Just wear the wig and quit yer grumbling."

"Are ye my faither now?"

Edmund tossed him a wry look, barely discernible in the moonlight but audible in his voice. "Why? D'ye want me to sing to ye before ye lay yer head down tonight?"

"If ye sang like my faither," Darach countered, "ye would likely have a wife by now, or a betrothed...or someone's warm body to lay *yer* head down on at night besides that mongrel dog of yers."

Edmund smiled—more at Malcolm rounding on his younger cousin. He watched, wearing the slightest satisfied grin when Malcolm shoved out his fist and knocked Darach clean off his horse.

Edmund's shoulders tightened around his ears at the loud *thunk* of Darach's arse hitting the dirt.

The other reason they liked having the youngest Grant along on their excursions was because he had something to prove, and there were none better to help him prove it than his three companions. They helped make a man out of him.

Edmund didn't participate as often as his Scottish kin did, but he enjoyed a bit of sport as much as the rest of them did. For now, though, he had a task to plan and see through. He would do what had to be done to stop the signing. Of that, he had no doubt. Scotland depended on it. According to Lord Lincoln, the duke was away from the castle, so this was the best time to go in and take what was his. The four of them would have no trouble taking all of Queensberry House down if they had to. The challenge of avoiding that scenario was more exciting to

Edmund than tossing his sword around and hacking off the fingers of men who loved to point them. Thankfully, most of the men who rode with him agreed.

"The lad speaks true." Luke rode up beside him while Darach leaped back to his feet and swore oaths at all three of them.

"About what?" Edmund asked with a bit of a drawn-out sigh. He knew what his cousin meant. They'd had this conversation a hundred times before.

"When d'ye think ye might start looking fer a wife and quit fighting Scotland's battles?"

"Someone needs to do it, Luke. We're being swallowed up by England. We're about to lose our Parliament. The nobles tell us about the advantages of a political union with England, declaring that 'tis in our best interest fer peace and wealth. But 'tis the Protestants who will gain security in the realm, and we, the Catholics, who will lose all our rights. As MacGregors, have we not lost enough already? Our name is once again denied us and forbidden from being spoken. Everything our grandsire fought fer has been lost once again."

"Aye, I know this, but we're safe in Camlochlin."

"Fer how long?" Edmund asked him. His cousin couldn't answer. " 'Tis not just about us, Luke. Scotland will suffer. Sir George Lockhart of Carnwath is openly against the union and has stated that the whole nation appears against it, but Queensberry and Lord Chancellor Seafield and their commissioners—all bought and paid fer—don't listen. Other negotiators to the treaty have observed that 'tis contrary to the inclinations of at least three-fourths of the kingdom. But petitions from shires, burghs, and parishes have all but been ignored." He set his determined gaze toward his destination. "Someone must make the men in power listen."

Keeping his horse at an even pace with Edmund's, Luke smiled at him. "Ye're not Scottish."

"It matters not. Scotland is my country." Edmund glanced at him and scowled. "What the hell are ye still smiling about?"

"Ye're more committed to Scotland and her sovereignty than most men who were born here. Fer ye, 'tis a choice to adopt her ways, and ye have. 'Tis an honorable thing, Edmund. I'm proud to call ye my kin. Unlike I am about those two."

"Och, hell, Luke," Darach complained, back in the saddle and riding up behind them. "Ye're not goin' to start in with all yer honor and knightly virtues drivel, are ye? Cal's correct aboot ye."

Luke laughed softly, letting Darach pass him. "Ye would do best to learn some of the drivel if ye ever mean to sing in Camlochlin's halls."

Darach swore something about singing that was lost on the wind as he kicked his stallion into a full gallop.

The dog that traveled with them had been Edmund's from the moment it left its mother's body. Ears perked at Darach's furious departure, the beast merrily joined in the chase, catching up quickly with its prey.

"Sometimes," Edmund said over Grendel's loud barking and Darach's subsequent shouts for the mongrel to let him go, "I think Darach enjoys having his arse removed from his saddle several times a day."

"Aye," Malcolm agreed, taking Luke's place beside Edmund and watching the commotion ahead. "He's the source of every silver hair on his mother's head."

Edmund laughed and then cringed a little at the oaths spilling from Darach's lips, so unlike the eloquent poetry his father produced.

"Grendel!" he called out to the monstrous hound running away with Darach's bonnet between his teeth and Darach losing ground behind him. "Good boy!"

Malcolm cheered the dog, then turned to his best friend. "If only we could get Grendel to close his jaws around Queensberry's throat. After the duke shyt his breeches we could convince him not to sign."

Edmund shook his head and smiled, watching his dog run in wide circles while Darach chased him. "Grendel wouldn't harm a fly," he said, his smile fading. "'Tis me whom the duke should fear."

Chapter Two

I swear on m' dead mother, 'twas longer than m' forearm."

Lady Amelia Bell stared, eyes wide, her mouth gaping slightly at her best friend, who was sitting across from her on the bed, and then the two burst into laughter.

"'Twasn't humorous when I laid m' eyes upon it," Sarah Frazier confided, her green eyes bright with wickedness. "I felt like Eve when she first spied the serpent in the garden. I wanted to run, but the temptation was too great."

Amelia gasped behind her palm. "Oh, Sarah! That is positively blasphemous!"

Sarah shook her head and flicked a lock of auburn hair off her shoulder. "Ye concern yourself overmuch with what others think."

"I don't!" Amelia charged, removing her hand from her mouth to fold her arms across her chest. "Save fer my father's poor sake," she added as an afterthought, always plagued by the troubles she caused him. "Do ye think I would sneak through the gardens to come and hear all yer sordid secrets if I cared what others thought? Ye know what my mother or uncle would do if they found out."

"Aye," Sarah agreed with her, falling back onto the mattress. "I don't know which would anger them more, the topic of our conversations, or that ye sometimes spend yer nights in the servant's quarters."

"Both." Amelia yawned and stretched out beside her.

"But still ye come."

Turning to her, Amelia took her hand and held it to her cheek. "Ye have always been my dearest friend. I will never let my uncle's title or my mother's rigid intolerances stand in the way of that. I will do what I believe is right."

Sarah's smile softened against the flickering light of the twin candle flames and then faded. "Do ye believe that marryin' the chancellor is the right thing then?"

Amelia looked away and shook her head. "It's the right thing to do fer my parents, Sarah. My mother—"

"Yer mother is as much an insufferable snob as yer betrothed. Amelia, ye will not be happy as Walter Hamilton's wife!"

Amelia knew her friend was correct, but what could she do? Bring disgrace on her parents yet again by rejecting a marriage proposal from the chancellor of Scotland? Her mother would never forgive her and her father, well, he never blamed her but wasn't it bad enough that she was the reason for every gray hair on his head? "My sisters did not want to marry their husbands, Sarah. We are not afforded any silly notions of love. It is the price we pay fer nobility. Marrying the chancellor will help my father earn him the respect of many nobles and make him less beholden to my uncle. So that is what I must do, whether I want to or not."

"But I don't want you to leave Queensberry House, Amelia." Sarah's eyes glistened as the fears she'd tried to deny spilled forward. "Whatever will I do without ye when ye go to Banffshire with yer new husband?"

What would Amelia do without *her*? They were inseparable, friends since they had learned to take their first steps and stumbled straight for each other. Amelia's mother had tried to keep them apart, scolding Archie the smith for not keeping a tighter rein on his child. But the truth of it was that Lady Millicent Bell was too occupied with kissing her brother the duke's arse and trying to find suitable husbands for Amelia's three older sisters to do anything truly drastic about her youngest daughter's friendship with a servant. As the girls grew older, the hammer came down a bit harder, mostly due to Sarah's less than modest behavior. But if it wasn't for her friend's sometimes crude tales of her affairs, Amelia would know absolutely nothing about the marriage bed. Her sisters certainly would never share their knowledge about what a man enjoyed in his bed.

"Do not worry over my betrothed, Sarah," Amelia promised, heartbroken to be leaving Sarah, as well. "I will use what ye've taught me to convince Walter to send fer ye."

Sarah didn't look convinced as she swiped a tear off her cheek. "I wish ye were a servant with me, Amelia. Then ye could choose your own husband. I wish ye could persuade yer father to choose someone else. Is there nothin' we can do?"

"The betrothal celebration is tomorrow—rather, today," she corrected looking toward the window. "Besides, there is no one else who has offered for me." Thanks to what her mother called her imprudent nature, there was no one else interested in her hand. Amelia did her best to avoid it, but misfortune seemed to follow her everywhere she went, in everything she did, beginning when she was a child and she dropped her uncle's only son on his head. She had wanted to carry the tiny babe, but her request was denied. Undaunted, she'd lifted him from his cradle anyway. The babe didn't die after the terrible accident, but he grew mad. Mad enough to cause his father to lock him away for good and her mother to forever blame her for everything that went wrong in their lives after that.

And, of course, she hadn't intended to leave her embroidery on Walter's chair when last he visited. She had no idea how the needle came to be sticking straight up, poking a three-inch hole into his buttocks.

She certainly hadn't meant to douse four of her uncle's men with dirty water last week. She hadn't wanted Sarah to have to clean her shoes after she'd stepped in horse manure, so she'd cleaned them herself and tossed the water out her bedroom window. How was she to know her uncle's men were directly below?

Things just went awry when Amelia was around. She didn't like it any more than anyone else did, but she tried not to let it concern her to the point of distraction. She often failed.

"All will be well, Sarah, ye'll see." She patted her friend's hand and did her best to mask her apprehension and misery. She didn't want to leave Queensberry House, to be married to a man she barely liked simply to appease her mother's desire to see her last daughter bound to a man of wealth and position. She didn't want a life filled with no choices, full of obligations, a life without her dearest friend to help her forget her duty. But she would not bring her father further shame by refusing his choice of husbands before the entire realm. "The hour grows late and I must soon be off. Tell me more about the notorious rogue of Ayr, Lord Thomas Lamont, and his colossal...attribute."

"Well." Facing her best friend, Sarah snuggled deeper into her pillow and lowered her voice to a whisper. "He's Scottish, ye know. I tell ye, Amelia, God looks favorably upon the Scots. They tend to be better endowed than the English, and know more about how to use what they've been given." She grinned, her apprehension over losing her friend banished by Amelia's full attention.

"Did it pain ye?" Amelia asked, bringing her fingers to her mouth to stifle her audacious question, though no one was there to hear it but Sarah.

"Aye, but he was a gentle lover."

Amelia closed her eyes and sighed wistfully while Sarah went on to describe her tryst with the Scottish nobleman. Would Walter be a gentle lover? Would she please him enough to bring a smile to his face hours afterward, the way Lord Lamont smiled when he spotted Sarah earlier today? She imagined her life with Walter. Would she ever find happiness with him? Her mother assured her that she would—if she worked hard at being a lady of grace and dignity, warmth and intelligence. Amelia didn't particularly care for being those things. At least, not in the way her mother meant, which was, stand around and look pretty and keep her mouth shut. Amelia wanted love and the kind of passion that came without restrictions, the kind her father told her about in his stories of courtly love. But it wasn't to be and she had learned to accept it.

She began to drift off to sleep, content to dream about the life she wanted. But the truth quickly dawned on her and she opened her eyes before she fell fully asleep. She sat up. Her betrothal was being announced tonight. She had to return to her room before her nursemaid Alice arose and found her missing!

"Sarah." She shook her friend, not sure if Sarah was sleeping or not. "I must go." She slipped out of the bed and rushed toward the door. "'Tis almost dawn! I shall see ye at the feast." Reaching the door, she pressed her ear to the wood, listening for the sounds of anyone in the hall. She pulled on the handle and turned to cast her friend a lighthearted smile before she left. "I will try not to laugh if I run into Lord Lamont today."

Amelia's bare feet treaded lightly over the flagstone path leading to the main house. The garden was silent save for the cry of robin hatchlings demanding to be fed somewhere within her uncle's carefully pruned trees. The fading moonlight cast deeper shadows along the arcade offering concealment beneath the high stone canopy from her nightly visit to the servant's quarters. Normally, the garden was the safest route back to the house, but today the servants would be busy scurrying to and fro preparing for the festivities. Guests would be arriving from all over the kingdom for the weeklong celebration commemorating her uncle's success at almost procuring Scotland's vote in favor of the Union with England Act, and her betrothal to the Lord Chancellor of Scotland. Rooms had to be aired out and food had to be cooked. Indeed, some of the cooks were already about their duties, for the aromas of baking bread and smoky venison permeated the air.

She quickened her pace and muffled a screech when her toe dashed against the base of one of her mother's beloved statues. Amelia glanced up and swore an oath at Neptune. There were ten of them lining the inside wall of the arcade, each meticulously placed between tall stone columns to appear framed within the arcade's depressed arches, all life-size and carved in stone, all naked, or close to it, and ridiculously muscular. There was Zeus, Heracles, Apollo, Neptune, Apoxyomenos, the Dying Gaul, Hermes, Aesculapius, even a nude Caesar.

Paul Tolson, Queensberry House's resident pastor, detested Millicent Bell's affinity for Greek gods, but Amelia knew her mother's devotion had less to do with pagan deities and more to do with the male physique. Amelia didn't share her mother's appreciation of bulging sinew and sheer brute strength. She much preferred a man like...him.

The sun began its lazy ascent over the garden, swathing the statue at the end of the arcade in warm hues of pale rose and gold. A replica of Michelangelo's *David* stood sublime, supreme over the others. His posture was relaxed, exuding confidence, his grace divine before his battle with Goliath. His sling tossed casually over his shoulder depicted a man who used faith and cleverness, not brawn, to battle his enemy. Moving to stand below him, Amelia's gaze drifted appreciatively over the sleek contours of his legs, so finely formed they made her heart flutter. Refined and vigilant, his body stood in absolute composure, conscious of his power to face his greatest enemy. Aye, she thought, backing up to sit for a moment or two on the marble bench before him, there was no man more perfect than *David*.

She knew she should make haste, but looking at David's statue made her contemplate her future. Oh, how she wished for a man like David to come rescue her from her fate. A strong warrior who would never let harm befall her, even the harm she might bring upon herself, someone who wouldn't force her into the sort of rigid life she was born into. How would she ever find happiness at Banffshire? Would her mother let her take *David* along?

She was so sleepy and lying down with Sarah had only made her more tired.

Her feet were cold, so she tucked them under her on the bench. She should have worn her slippers when she stole across the gardens earlier to be with Sarah. She sighed, thinking how angry her mother would be if she saw Amelia in such a disheveled state. She would just have to make certain that her mother never discovered her secret rendezvous with Sarah. She smiled at the beautiful face cast in stone and closed her eyes.

She dreamed she heard a dog barking somewhere in the distance.

Chapter Three

Edmund and his cousins had attended many balls and gatherings without invitations in the past. This one was nothing new, save that there were more guards at Queensberry House and more nobles attending that might recognize Edmund or one of his cousins from a prior raid. They would have to enter the house with stealth and then blend in.

Leaving Grendel and their horses in a nearby stable, they crept across the garden lawns behind the house, using trees and the veil of darkness to hide their approach.

Edmund saw her as the sun began to spread its gossamer beams over the arcade, her back to him, locks of rich chestnut spilling to her hips as her head tilted upward at a statue of God's warrior, David.

Silently, he signaled to the others to hold back lest she see them. He watched her, waiting for her to leave the arcade, but she remained still. In the silence of the earth poised on the brink of waking, he thought he could hear her breath, quickened by the view that captivated her. Who was she? What was she doing out here alone, clothed in her nightdress? His gaze followed her when she sat on a bench facing the sculpture.

He waited, counting his breaths while she remained motionless, her head resting against the column beside her. What was she doing? he wondered, when Malcolm tossed him a questioning look. He didn't want to frighten her. One scream and she would alert the guards to their presence.

After twenty more breaths, he realized the lass must have fallen asleep. Leaving the cover of a thick apple tree trunk, he motioned for the others to breach the doors on the eastern wall. While they hastened forward, barely making a sound, Edmund made his way toward the arcade, crouching low when the heavy doors creaked open. He raised his palm to Lucan, who'd stopped to wait for him, gesturing for them to go on ahead of him. Edmund wanted to see her face, hoping it might convince him that she was made of flesh, and not an angel traipsing around in the dawn, waiting for her god to awaken. She piqued his curiosity. She enthralled him as it seemed *David* had enthralled her.

Stepping into the arcade, he glanced first at the statue, and then at her. His breath stalled in his chest. The sun's gentle amber glow lent its radiance to her startling beauty. Lush, long lashes smudged cheeks of smooth velvet. Plump, rosy lips parted on a transient breath, as if she were waiting to be kissed in her dreams. Thick sable hair tumbled loose about her shoulders. One lock caressed the curve of her jaw, tempting him to touch her before she vanished with the night. He let his eyes linger over the delicate symmetry of her features, unable to steal himself away. She was slim of form, with breasts fashioned perfectly in size to fit into his palms. Her hands were small, as were her bare feet. The last brought a smile to his lips.

The full sight of her aroused him, sparked a desire he hadn't felt before.

Like one of God's divine, serenity emanated from her slumbering features. Who was she dreaming about? He turned, severing his gaze from her to look at Michelangelo's *David*, and then toward the various kings and gods lining the wall, all bulbous muscle and fearsome scowls, evidence of their might. But it was this lissome warrior garbed in naught but a flimsy sling and a knit brow that had earned this lass's worshipful appreciation.

He returned his attention to her, unable to keep his eyes off her. Was she a servant stealing a few moments before her daily duties to feed her dreams? He stepped closer, bending to her to inhale her scent, to bask for but another moment of his own, mayhap to nourish something lacking in his dreams as well. Something that until this moment, he didn't think he needed. He wondered what color her eyes were beneath the spray of her heavy lashes, and if they would recognize the power of his purpose, as she recognized David's. He was tempted to kiss her brow, her lips, so close now that her breath warmed his chin. But she would wake and scream, seeing a stranger poised above her. Pity, for he wanted but one taste of her, to imprint on his mind the memory of something sweet, something passionate, before going into battle.

"What in blazes is keepin' ye?" Malcolm's hushed voice echoed throughout the canopied arcade. "Edmund?"

Angling his head, Edmund glared at the head poking

out of the open door. A strangled gasp pulled his attention back to the lass before he could move away.

She did not scream as his eyes fell upon her again. She remained motionless, save for her bosom rising and falling hard beneath his hovering shadow. Her eyes were deep, rich mahogany—the color of warmth and gloriously huge and sparked with terror.

He brought his finger to his lips, begging her for silence before he moved away and disappeared into the castle.

Amelia bolted to her feet. Her heart beat a riotous litany in her breast. Clutching her chest, she counted out nine breaths in an effort to get a hold of herself. On the tenth, her eyes darted to *David*. "I was dreaming," she said, more to herself than to it. She had to have been, for no mortal man could scorch a soul with the heat of his gaze alone. Like sapphires caught between light and shadow, his eyes had glittered as they moved over her, scalding her nerve endings, robbing her senses. A dream.

But his scent still lingered all about her. She inhaled, filling her senses with the fragrance of dew and leather. She pulled in a deeper breath, closing her eyes this time. Who was he? A guest who had arrived early, mayhap? A very bold guest, carved from the gold God used to pave heaven's streets.

Her heavy lids flew open. Guests! Dear God, she had fallen asleep!

Hiking up her skirts, she dashed for the doors, giving no more thought to the man whose whispered name had awakened her from her dreams of *David*. *Edmund*.

She reached her room, taking three steps at a time, and

leaped into her bed. No sooner did she close her eyes than her father entered, toting Amelia's breakfast on a tray.

"Good morning, love," John Bell greeted her. "Alice is busy so I thought I would bring ye yer..." He looked up and stopped, looking at her. "Ye're deathly pale!" He laid the tray on a nearby table and went to the bed. "Are ye ill, Mellie?" He covered Amelia's face with his fingers. "Ye're clammy and short of breath. I'll get one of yer mother's physicians."

"No, Papa!" Amelia clamped his wrist as her father moved to leave. Lord, she hadn't expected to see him so early. "I'm not ill. I am...anxious about my future, that is all." She concentrated on slowing her heart rate. When her father's expression turned sympathetic, Amelia knew she had taken the right path. The last thing she wanted was a dozen of her mother's physicians crowding her bed. Lady Selkirk had a different physician for every ailment, which was a good thing for her, since she suffered with most of them.

"Are ye certain that's all it is?" he asked, resting on the edge of the bed and running the backs of his knuckles across Amelia's forehead.

"Aye, I barely slept." It was the truth and she truly was anxious about her future.

"Don't fret over yer marriage," her father said, scooping up Amelia's hand and bringing it to his lips. "Ye will be happy."

She thought about her conversation with Sarah. She could never ask her father to go back on his consent and try to find her a different husband. Even though the betrothal wasn't officially announced, everyone knew. Her father would be shamed if they backed out now. She didn't love Walter at all. Oh, she knew love was irrelevant but damnation it would have been nice to have some feelings for the man who would be her husband. She knew little about the chancellor save that he turned up his haughty nose to Sarah. "Will I, Papa? Will I be happy?"

"Why do ye ask?" He searched her gaze. "Has the chancellor offended ye in some way?"

She wished Walter had offended her so she could answer truthfully. But accusing her betrothed of something he didn't do was not only wrong, but quite dangerous to her father. "Nae, Papa, he has been kind."

He relaxed his shoulders and allowed an indulgent smile to spread across his lips. "What ye're feeling happens to most new brides…and grooms." He winked at her. "But ye've no reason to fear."

"Did it happen to ye, Papa?"

He nodded and smiled, remembering. "It did. I didn't know yer mother. I didn't know if she was comely or had two eyes or one."

Amelia smiled into his rich, mahogany eyes, loving him more than any man alive. "Did yer heart belong to one already, Papa?"

He shrugged his shoulders, still broad even in middle age. "My heart belonged to many. But that's of no concern. Yer mother turned out to be one of the bonniest women I'd ever seen. We wed and had ye girls and we remain together to this day."

But did he love her? Amelia didn't have the courage to ask him.

"Ye do care fer Walter, do ye not, Mellie?"

She blinked at him. He'd never asked her that question before. Would her answer make a difference? She didn't get a chance to find out, since her bedroom door opened and her nurse plunged into the room. When she saw Amelia's father, she apologized for her interruption and backed out.

"Alice," her father called, stopping her departure. "Come back. I was just leaving." He stood up and brushed off his coat. "I will see ye tonight at the celebration, love." He bent to kiss the top of Amelia's head, then turned and smiled at Alice before he left the room.

"We have a lot to see to today, sweeting." Alice came in and went straight for the windows to pull open the curtains. "Finish yer breakfast and let's get on with the rest of this miserable day."

Amelia sighed and snuggled deeper into her pillow. She didn't want to get on with it as much as Alice didn't want to.

"I know, gel," her nursemaid agreed after hearing Amelia sigh in her bed. "But at least yer husband will die someday and ye'll be freed from the subjugation of his will. This treaty will stay in effect forever, and England will always come out on top."

"I know ye're unhappy about the treaty with England, Alice. But I'm sure everything will be well with ye."

"Of course, 'twill, my joy," her nursemaid agreed, turning to smile at her.

"I thank God each night for ye, Alice," Amelia told her, loving her like a mother, "and fer Sarah, too." She yawned. "Fer had I been raised by my mother, I fear 'twould have been her that I took after. I would not care about the consequences of my own actions...or words...and Walter would be enough fer me."

Alice appeared before her and pulled the coverings off.

"I love ye like my own, but there's no time to ponder such things."

"But there must be time," Amelia pressed. "I don't want to leave my bed yet. Please Alice, just a few moments. Sit and chat with me."

Her nurse scowled at her but gave in easily. "Ye look worn out and exhausted," Alice said upon closer inspection. "Were ye awake all night with Sarah again?"

"Well, aye, I was. The time escaped me. Truly."

"Gel, if yer mother discovers ye..."

"I know." Amelia buried her face in her pillow, hating that her friendship with Sarah was forbidden. Amelia knew that if her mother discovered them together, Sarah might get sent away for it. So Amelia did her best to make certain that her mother didn't discover her. Until early this morning, when she fell asleep in the garden. Today, someone had seen her.

"Alice." She sat up in the bed. "Have any of the guests arrived early?" Mayhap if her nursemaid knew him...

"Only Lord Lamont and two of his men."

Lord Lamont! Of course! The man in the garden was one of Lord Lamont's men! Chewing her lip, Amelia picked at a speck of dirt on her nightdress. Dare she speak his name and rouse Alice's curiosity as to how she knew it? She had to. She had to know who he was. "Of Lord Lamont's men, are any of them called Edmund?"

"I don't believe so." Alice threw her a probing look. "Why do ye ask?"

Indeed, why *did* she ask? She couldn't tell Alice that she'd been careless and fell asleep in the garden and that when she woke up there was a beautiful man watching her sleep.

"Sarah mentioned him."

Alice thought about it for a moment. "There's the baker yer mother hired from Ayr. He arrived yesterday and has been preparing his cakes all night."

Was the man in the arcade the new baker? No, Amelia shook her head. Bakers were rotund little men with flour staining their noses. Weren't they? They weren't tall and broad shouldered, with jaws dusted gold and chiseled by a master sculptor, or golden hair that curled at their napes and seemed to absorb all the light in the garden. Oh, she would never forget waking and looking into his eyes, of feeling terrified and enthralled at the same time, so thrillingly aware of a man's potent power.

Alice spotted Amelia's gown hanging over a chair and left the bed to get it. She held up the gown for inspection. The pale lilac fabric shimmered against a beam of sunlight spilling in from the window. The gown was lovely, boasting a long, pointed bodice and satin petticoat, and, in keeping with the fashion as her mother insisted, voluminous three-quarter-length sleeves, pleated at the dropped shoulder and cuffs.

"Oh, look at these wrinkles! I'll have to have them smoothed out. Oh, and your sisters have already arrived with their husbands and insist upon working on yer hair. I bid them time to wake ye first."

"That was thoughtful of ye," Amelia thanked her. "I'm not certain I could bear listening to how difficult their journey was to get here, or how the weather just doesn't suit their delicate constitutions. Lord, and if I have to sit through one more tale of how disagreeable Eleanor's unborn babe is in her belly, I will scream."

"I know, love," her nursemaid replied, folding the

gown carefully over her arm. "That's why I didn't let them come up. Now, let's go. Chatting's over. We have too much to do to get ye ready fer tonight."

"Alice?" Amelia asked while she dressed. "When will my ill fortune end?"

"Everyone has a season, gel."

"But seasons are supposed to end."

"As will yours," Alice promised.

Amelia smiled at her. "Aye, it will. I think I would prefer it if Sarah worked on my hair today. She knows better than anyone how to get the tangles out." She was in no hurry to see her sisters and have to endure Elizabeth's clicking tongue every time she put a question to her, or one of Anne's disapproving glances if Amelia dared laugh too loudly.

She wondered if Edmund had arrived with one of her sisters' groups. Edmund. The thought of seeing him again today at the ceremony made her heart accelerate just a little and she chastised herself for it. She belonged to someone else, a man who had agreed to take her despite all her shortcomings. Mayhap she would tell her father's bold guest what she thought of him for frightening her senseless while she slept. Then again, mayhap it would be more prudent not to speak to him at all, to simply forget him, put him out of her thoughts and occupy her mind with Walter instead. Lord, if she did that, she just might fall asleep again. It wasn't that Walter was dull... Well, in truth, he was. Did he care for her? She doubted it, since he had never professed it to her.

"I'll send for Sarah and see what I can discover about a guest called Edmund," Alice said, heading for the door with Amelia's gown in her hand.

Prudence, Amelia, she warned herself as her mother had on countless occasions. *Get your head out of the clouds and cease being so troublesome to yer poor father.*

"Nae, Alice. Ferget I mentioned him. I'm to be married soon. It's time to get my head out of the clouds."

Chapter Four

The celebration was in its second hour, and there was still no sign of Amelia's living statue. There was no sign of her betrothed either. It was announced to Amelia's father that the roof in her soon-to-be new bedchamber in Banffshire had fallen in. The betrothal would have to be postponed along with the announcement.

Amelia shifted in her chair at the high table and groaned softly. The sound drew a critical glance from her sister Anne, but Amelia didn't care. Her arse was bloody killing her. She had a terrible ache in her temples from the pearl-encrusted pins Sarah had woven throughout the thick knot at the back of her head. She could barely keep her eyelids up but was too afraid of snoring to let them close, even for an instant. Falling asleep in her chair, in front of her uncle's noble guests, would surely send her mother into fits. And what would the mysterious Edmund think of her if he found her slumbering yet again, and during her postponed betrothal feast, no less?

She'd put no queries about him to her father, but she had spoken with Sarah about him, and commissioned her friend to discover who the stranger was. Sarah was more than happy to oblige, but so far, she had found out nothing. Edmund had not arrived with Lord Lamont, or any guests who'd arrived thereafter.

He had to be someone! she told herself, sweeping her eyes over the myriad of faces below. She found Sarah standing over the table of a French count visiting from Anjou. Arching an elegant brow, Amelia shook her head playfully when Sarah shot her a whimsical smile over her shoulder. How was it that her friend looked so alert and vivacious after staying awake all night?

Dear Sarah, born a servant, with the freedom to behave as she chose. No one cared how the daughter of the smith spent her days—or her nights. Amelia sighed, bringing her cup to her lips. She envied Sarah, though had *she* been born to a serf, she still would not toss herself into the bed of any man who smiled at her. Edmund's sun-gilt face flashed before her. No matter how decadently carved his lips were.

"John." Her mother leaned forward over the empty chair at Amelia's left. "You did tell the chancellor to make haste at Banffshire, did you not?"

"Of course I did, Millicent." The clip of annoyance in his voice did not deter her mother from expelling a long-suffering sigh. And why should it? Her father scowled more often than he smiled. Save when he caught Amelia's eyes. Of his daughters, she was favored. And she knew it.

"Of all the dreadful days for the roof to collapse!" Millicent huffed and sent her husband a heated look. "I hope you're happy, Amelia."

"She had nothing to do with it, Millicent. Ye sound as mad as yer nephew shackled below stairs."

Amelia closed her eyes, wishing the night would end.

"That's a horrible thing to say, John. Especially tonight! How could my brother allow the chancellor to go and leave our daughter to sit here alone like a forgotten waif at her own celebration?"

"Yer brother is not here either," John reminded his wife. "This celebration is for his accomplishments as well as our daughter's betrothal. Ye would think he would have postponed his trip to Roxburgh fer a few days at least."

Amelia caught Sarah's attention below and rolled her eyes, signaling that it was going to be a torturously long evening. Her parents argued often. Amelia wondered if they were happy together. She didn't think so. She barely, if ever, saw them share affection. The story her father told her this morning was only a small part of their life. Millicent often complained about marrying beneath her station. The marriage, much like Amelia's, was a forced one thanks to the affection of Millicent's father, the first Duke of Queensberry, for the Bell family. After Robert Bell, Amelia's grandfather and a soldier in the Royal Army, saved the duke's life on a hunting excursion, the duke promised his daughter to Robert's son. Millicent never forgave him.

"My brother is securing the last of his support of the union. He has every reason not to be here."

"And Seafield thought it necessary to see to the repairs himself, Millicent. The ceiling did fall in their future bed-chamber, after all."

Amelia's cheeks flared as red as the claret swirling around in her cup. *Please don't let them begin a discussion of my bedchamber*, she prayed silently. Veiling her eyes beneath her dark lashes, she brushed her gaze across the hall. No burnished-haired masterpiece come to life was in attendance.

God help her troublesome soul, she rebuked herself. How could she be so curious about another man when her considerate husband-to-be had dashed off to prepare a safe new home for her? And worse, why had the mention of her bedchamber instigated her curiosity? She was reprehensible. Walter Hamilton, Earl of Seafield, Lord Chancellor of Scotland, wasn't so bad, really. With his raven mane and intense cobalt blue eyes, he turned many ladies' heads at court, just not hers. He worked hard at pleasing her uncle, and he did so because he cared for her. He must. So what if he was dull and tedious, not to mention sickeningly snobbish. Lord, she didn't want to marry him. Sobbing into her supper wouldn't help, especially after her father had gone to so much trouble making certain the food was all fresh and prepared by master cooks. She couldn't run away and she couldn't refuse. But oh, how she wished she could.

"It could have waited a few days, John." Her mother slapped her palm softly against the table. "I don't care what room it was."

Thank God. Amelia yawned.

"Millicent, fer the love of God, do not vex me about this any longer. I have enough to keep my mind occupied wondering how much this celebration is going to drain what is left in the coffers."

"'Tis my brother's coin. Why should the cost of all this concern ye?"

Amelia slipped her hand over her father's and gave him a sympathetic pat.

"Everyone here thinks the chancellor changed his mind," her mother continued, lowering her voice to a whisper when Lady Josephine Hartington glanced at the table. "They whisper that perhaps he has decided to wait for a more sensible wife. They all know what she's like since that unfortunate incident at the Earl of Clare's wedding last spring."

John's crimson face proved that that particular event was scored forever in his brain.

Dear God, if Amelia hadn't had Sarah to laugh with her about the incident when she returned home, she would have wept for a month. Alice tried to convince her that it wasn't her fault, but even so, Amelia was sorry for ruining the earl's second wedding.

It happened on the morn of the ceremony. The earl's dashing young son, Lord Albert, had invited her to go riding. Of course, she'd accepted, which, according to her mother, was her first error in good judgment. The ride across the English countryside was invigorating, innocent, and quite safe. She was an excellent rider, and Lord Albert had been a perfect gentleman. They'd even made it back just before the wedding. But, as circumstances often went in Amelia's case, catastrophe was lurking somewhere just inches from her horse's hooves. To this day, she had no idea what had startled her mount into a full gallop, or why the beast had refused to slow down, despite her best efforts. She was almost thrown, and would have broken her neck if she hadn't been holding on for dear life, when the mad stallion vaulted over a row of slack-jawed guests. Amelia had given the reins one more desperate yank as her wide eyes met the earl's horrified ones. The only thing left to do was squeeze hers shut and

pray that the earl, his bride, and their priest moved the
hell out of the way.

They had. No one was injured, save for her father's
name. Thanks to her, the name Bell had become syn-
onymous with disaster. Amelia was sorry for it, for her
father's sake. She was sorry for it all.

"Enough." John's dark gaze over Amelia's head
warned his wife that she had finally succeeded in exhaust-
ing his patience. "Any man would count himself among
the fortunate to be given our daughter, sensible or not."

Her dear father. He loved her despite her faults.
Amelia turned to him and smiled softly, bringing happiness to his face for the first time that evening. Whatever
would she have done without him in her life? When he
leaned in and kissed her forehead, her eyes welled up
with tears. "I love ye, Papa," she whispered softly enough
for her mother not to hear.

"And I ye, dear one."

Content, Amelia rested her elbow on the table and
dropped her chin into her palm, oblivious to one of the
pinned curls dangling from her temples plopping into her
soup. Heavens, she was beginning to lose feeling in her
legs. How much longer was this celebration going to go
on? She closed her eyes. Just for a moment.

"What if the chancellor doesn't return for her?"

John Bell swore to himself that if his wife went on
about this for one more instant he would get up and
leave her sitting here alone. "The chancellor will return
by morning," he muttered. "The guests aren't going anywhere."

"It is not the morning that concerns me, but tonight,"

Millicent said out of the corner of her mouth. "Tonight the betrothal was to be announced."

"By the saints, woman! Have ye no bloody . . . ?" His half whispered oath was cut off when his son-in-law the Earl of Bedford stepped up to his chair and tugged his sleeve.

"What?" John asked and lifted his ear from Bedford's lips. "Where?"

His son-in-law pointed and Amelia's father rose to his feet to peer at a man standing at the far end of the hall engaged in quiet conversation with another man he'd never seen before. "Ye are certain he was introduced as Lord Huntley?"

"I heard the introduction myself. Malcolm Gordon, Earl of Huntley."

"And the man with him?"

"Edmund Dearly, Viscount of Essex. They travel with a Campbell and a Drummond, as well."

John cast a glance at his wife. He didn't recall seeing their names on the invitation list. Lord, he hoped no one had insulted them by forgetting to add them.

"They are coming this way." John straightened his shoulders and smoothed his coat, readying himself for an introduction.

"Ye do know that Huntley's family is distantly related to the queen, do ye not?" Millicent asked, fixing her hair.

Adjusting his wig, John offered his guests an amiable smile, but the Viscount of Essex flicked his eyes to the only person still seated in her chair at the dais.

Suddenly, sickeningly, John peered down at the top of Amelia's head. He visibly cringed when a small snore escaped her lips. Struggling to retain his pleasant demeanor while his guests stared at her, he yanked her to her feet.

* * *

Amelia came awake rather sharply, but it took a moment for her head to clear completely, and for her to realize she'd been asleep in her chair. But even that mortification was nothing compared to what she felt when she looked at the men standing before her.

"Lord Huntley, Lord Essex," her father's voice cracked when he called out. "Welcome to Queensberry House. We were not expecting ye."

Forgetting her drooping curl, Amelia's eyes opened wider. Her Edmund was Lord Essex? His friend was Lord Huntley? And she'd fallen asleep in her supper? She ached to peek up at her father, to somehow beg his forgiveness.

"Perhaps if we had been invited..." Edmund's...Lord Essex's voice was a deep, sensual blend belonging to both England and Scotland. The smooth and steady sound of it danced across her ears, invading her thoughts.

"An oversight fer which I would beg fergiveness." Her father bowed.

Amelia flicked her gaze to Edmund as he strode forward. This was twice now she'd awakened from her dreams to find him in her world.

He was real. But whatever she had found enticing about him before had vanished with the dawn. He stood now, with full authority squaring his shoulders, and cool unyielding indifference hardening his features. Was he just another power-hungry nobleman then? Would he punish her father for his error?

He lifted his palm to her father. "No need fer apologies. Lord Huntley and I prefer to remain discreet. Isn't that correct, Huntley?"

"'Tis," his friend agreed, smiling at Sarah when she appeared with a tray of wine. Heavens but he was so roguishly handsome Sarah almost dropped her tray. With eyes dipped in fathomless shades of blue and green and a dimpled grin that could make an angel fall from heaven, he was temptation incarnate. Like a wolf on the hunt, his eyes followed Sarah's departure, forgetting, or not caring about, the conversation going on in front of him.

Remembering that Sarah was no angel, Amelia returned her attention to Edmund.

He'd been discreet all right—a shadow skulking about the garden between night and day. Amelia's eyes widened with alarm. The garden! She swallowed suddenly. Her gaze darted to her father. Would the viscount tell her father that he'd found his willful daughter sleeping outdoors alone while the sun rose?

"Is the duke in attendance?" Essex asked, barely looking at her. "We had hoped to offer him our well wishes on his success with the union."

"Alas," her father said, turning a miserable glance at his wife, "he has been called away to Roxburgh."

"Unfortunate," Essex said. The frost in his eyes hardened his quick smile. "I would give my accolades to the Earl of Seafield then, as he is the duke's right hand."

"Again—" Her father cringed to his bones at the sound of her mother's slight groan. Poor man, Amelia thought. Her mother was never going to stop complaining about this later. "I regret that he has been called back to Banffshire to repair the roof of his wedding chamber."

Essex raised a golden brow. "Ah yes, I had heard rumor that the earl was to be betrothed."

"That he is," her father informed him. "To the most beautiful lady here, in fact."

Lord Essex slanted his gaze to her before her father identified her as the bride and set Amelia's heart to racing. She could barely breathe watching those diamond-hard eyes grow warm on her. Tonight he wore a powdered periwig that gave him a more noble appearance than an ethereal one. Shadows danced across the chiseled angles of his sun-bronzed face and his heavy brow, adding depth to his smoky blue eyes.

His clothes were even finer than Amelia had first thought in the garden. He wore a scarlet embroidered justacorps with a matching bow tied beneath his aristocratic chin. The cuffs of his poet's shirt beneath were crisp and white as if rarely worn. He wore hose over his breeches, boasting strong, muscular calves. His shoes were polished and bowed, as was the fashion.

He moved more like a panther than a peacock, though; agile, quiet, and dangerous. Yet he'd walked among them all day, unnoticed. Discreet.

He came to stand directly in front of her table and angled his face to her. After an endless moment of silence and a frantic prayer from Amelia that he wasn't deciding how best to tell her father of her nightly romp, the husky dip of his voice fell across the hall. "Am I to assume this is the prize the earl has won?"

Amelia didn't know whether to feel flattered or insulted at being called such a thing. While she was trying to decide, something cool and wet slithered down her bodice. She looked down to find her soup-soaked curl dripping over her breast, staining the fine fabric of her gown.

Oh, damnation, could this evening get any worse?

Chapter Five

Could his fortune get any better? Edmund's gaze lingered over the lass rubbing her palm over her bosom. This was the lass for whom they'd come. The slumbering angel from the garden who'd lingered in his thoughts all day was the duke's niece, and with both her uncle and her future husband gone—the duke no doubt procuring the third signature—she was free for the taking.

Almost free.

"Ye assume correctly, Lord Essex," Baron Selkirk said, moving closer to his daughter. "May I present my wife, Lady Selkirk, and my daughter Lady Amelia Bell."

Amelia. Edmund said her name over and over in his head. Beautiful, just like her.

Thankfully, he wasn't moved by pretty faces. He was here for a purpose. Nothing had changed. Nothing would sway him from his plans, not when it came to Scotland, not for the land that had breathed new life into him as a boy. Miss Bell was the loveliest lass he'd ever beheld, but Scotland held ownership of his heart.

Still, that didn't mean he couldn't charm her witless

tonight. Since the duke and the chancellor were both absent, Edmund could take his time with the plan, enjoy it…her, a little. If he played this right, he wouldn't have to force her to go with him and she might not hate him so much in the morning. She piqued his interest by sleeping in the open in her nightdress, barefoot and vulnerable beneath the permanent gaze of the greatest warrior who'd ever lived. Asleep again at the foot of her father's chair, at her own celebration. He'd expected the duke's niece to be more elegant and proper; what he got was a peculiar soul arrayed in mystery and mischief. Getting her to trust him tonight shouldn't be difficult, but it would be pleasant.

"An honor to meet ye, Lady Selkirk." Edmund bowed to Amelia's mother first, then to her. "Miss Bell, yer beauty is honored in song by traveling troubadours, but the splendor of yer countenance was grossly underexaggerated." His eyes smoldered beneath their glacial veneer as she raised her eyes to his. "Ye are lovelier than anything I have ever dreamed."

Miss Amelia Bell could make a man happy, Edmund thought, basking in the delicate smile she cast upon him, in the sensual sway of her hooded gaze—like horses racing on the moors. Seafield, traitor to Scotland that he was, did not deserve her. Edmund knew seducing her out of Queensberry House would be an easy task when her lips parted on a suspended breath before she addressed him.

He vowed that before the night was over, he would kiss that mouth.

"Do ye speak such painted words to all the ladies ye meet, my lord?"

He smiled, delighted by her boldness and the glint of humor in her eyes. "None have heard me speak so."

She graced him with another, more genuine smile that brought a soft groan to Malcolm's throat. Edmund shared the sentiment but remained silent about it.

"Well then," she continued, oblivious to her mother's horror above her, "as far as dreaming goes, I share yer sentiment."

"Amelia!" Clutching one hand to her chest and the other to her chair, the Baroness of Selkirk gaped, appalled at her daughter. Her husband downed his wine and glanced heavenward before he stepped to his wife's side and held her upright. But it was Amelia who needed rescuing, Edmund thought as a flurry of whispers arose from the crowd behind him. Her smile vanished and she looked away from him.

"My lord." Lady Selkirk pulled his attention away from her daughter. "You must excuse her. She is…"

"Delightful," Edmund finished for her, and caught the slight inhalation of breath that lifted Amelia's bosom beneath her chin.

"If ye would excuse me," she said in a low voice to her parents. "I need to use the…" She darted another mortified look to Edmund, then to her mother's scandalized expression. "I would like to freshen up."

"Go," her father allowed, sounding as disparaged as his daughter.

Edmund's gaze followed her lithe figure as she made her way from the table and disappeared through a doorway to his right. A moment later, a serving lass with hair the color of sunset followed her. She was the same lass Malcolm had eyed earlier. He moved after her now, sharing a nod with Edmund and no words to the baron.

"Lord Essex." Selkirk's gravelly voice pulled Edmund's attention away from the exit. He turned to find the baron had also left his seat and had come to stand at his side.

"I will have our finest chamber prepared for ye and yer men. With so many guests attending, I'm afraid we have no rooms to spare for yer privacy. In the meanwhile"—he reached up and rested his hand on Edmund's shoulder—"please share in our feast, if not yet a celebration, and tell me some news of England." He motioned for a server to bring him two cups of fresh wine. "We are all delighted about the treaty. 'Twill help us recover from financial disaster."

"Ah, ye stand on the English side then," Edmund replied vaguely. No revelation there. Scottish barons kissed the same English arse as the dukes and earls did. They sold their country and their daughters for the highest offer.

Traitors to so much.

"Do yer daughter and the chancellor share affection?"

"Pardon me?"

Edmund spared him an impatient glance. "Are they in love?" In his line of duty he asked questions. He needed to know how the chancellor felt about Miss Bell. If he would keep his name from the treaty for her.

"I . . . I believe so," her father said. "The reason he isn't here has nothing to do with my daughter, but with his desire to see his holding fit fer his bride."

"Of course," Edmund replied with an easy smile that did not reach his eyes. "So then, she is pleased about the marriage."

"Most certainly."

Helpful to know that she agreed with the rest of her family, Edmund thought, while his eye caught the return of the auburn-haired servant at the doorway. She looked toward the table at Lady Selkirk, who was sharing a word with a lass who resembled Amelia, save for her pinched lips and swollen belly, then hurried back in the direction from which she came. This time it was Lucan who'd caught sight of her and took up his steps to follow her. Malcolm was nowhere to be seen, likely catching the eye of some other lass who wasn't busy spying for her mistress.

When Amelia finally reappeared, she, too, looked toward the table, then decided against returning to it. She headed off in the opposite direction.

"He loves her."

"What?" Edmund turned to her father.

"The lord chancellor," Lord Selkirk repeated. "He loves my daughter. He's assured me of it."

"I'm pleased to hear it," Edmund told him. Loving her meant that the chancellor would do as they ordered while she was in Edmund's custody and not sign.

"Even her accursed ill fortune has not deterred him from seeking to win her favor. Alas, she has driven off more suitors than I can count." He sighed, catching sight of her across the hall. "But they were fools. All but Lord Seafield. He has…"

Edmund stopped listening when Amelia's path was intercepted by a stern-faced lord who looked older than her father, but was still fit enough to pose a threat. "Who is that man speaking with yer daughter?"

Her father peered around Edmund's arm to have a look. "That is Lord Bedford, my Eleanor's husband. She is expecting their first child within the next…"

When Bedford clutched Amelia's arm, Edmund left her father's side without hearing the rest.

He didn't rush to her side, but advanced quietly, seeking to catch a bit of their conversation, which seemed to be growing more heated each moment.

"I will return to my mother in a moment, Bedford," Amelia insisted, pulling on her arm for him to let go.

"She insists that you return now." He yanked her forward. "Before you crash into a candle stand and set the house aflame."

Amelia dug her heels into the floor, and with a flick of her lashes, her dark eyes scored his flesh. "Do ye manhandle my sister, as well?"

"There is no need." He leaned toward her and practically growled in her face. "She is not undisciplined as you are, and does as she's told."

"What a pity for ye then," she said, somehow regaining her complete composure, or seeming to. The fire in her eyes still burned, igniting Edmund's blood.

Her brother-in-law laughed, a haughty, lordly sound. "Where is the pity in having a dutiful wife?"

"She ends up with a terribly bored husband," Edmund said, reaching them.

Bedford turned, startled by his sudden appearance. "Lord Essex."

Edmund clasped his hands at his back and tipped his head. "Lord Bedford," he greeted pleasantly. "I'm certain that as tempting the prospect of being dragged across the length of this hall is fer Miss Bell, she would not be averse to me escorting her back to her mother."

"Of course, my lord." Bedford released her with a smile and scurried off.

Edmund could feel her eyes on him. He'd felt them surveying him from the moment he'd spoken, driving him mad with the desire to look at her. When they were alone, he finally did. He kept his breath from falling short.

"Ye robbed these good people of at least a se'nnight of gossip." Her voice was a light, teasing caress that made him doubt it was her beauty alone that provoked his thoughts of kissing her senseless.

"How thoughtless of me," he said and crooked his arm, offering it to her. When she accepted, looping her arm through his, he cut her a smirk that twinkled in her eyes and escorted her to the opposite end of the hall, away from the table.

"I really must apologize for what I said earlier," she told him while they walked.

"So there *have* been men more comely than me in yer dreams then?"

She glanced up at him and her smile was made all the more stunning by its lack of guile. "Well, I do sleep quite frequently."

"And in odd places," Edmund agreed, surprised at the ease with which she spoke with him, smiled at him. There was nothing coy or calculating about her, and Edmund found himself wanting to trace his fingers, his mouth, over the soft blush that spread across her cheeks. Once he took her prisoner she wouldn't want to kiss him, and he wasn't the kind of man who forced himself on a lass. If he was going to taste the sweet honeyed nectar of her lips, it would have to be tonight.

"I'm terribly sorry for being asleep during yer arrival." Her blush passed as quickly as her repentance. "I barely had a chance to shut my eyes since meeting ye in the garden this morn."

"Ye're not sleepy now, are ye?"

"Nae." She giggled. "Why?"

"Because I intend to spend the night dancing with ye."

She cut him a look from beneath the sooty sweep of her lashes. "That would be lovely but my card is already full. 'Tis my mother's doing. A ruse to make the other hens believe I am sorely desired."

She didn't need a ruse, Edmund thought to himself when she leaned a bit closer into his side and tilted her lips to his ear. He bent his head to hear her. "In truth, I was hoping to steal a moment alone with ye to discuss our early meeting, and then there ye were, and here we are now. I would call that a fortunate thing, wouldn't ye?"

"I would." His gaze moved over the beguiling curves of her profile.

"What I wanted to ask ye was not to mention finding me in the arcade to my parents. It would vex my mother terribly to know that I was"—she paused, and veiled her gaze from his—"wandering about the garden at such an ungodly hour."

Edmund was surprised to find that he was curious about what she had been doing there. He didn't ask though. It wasn't pertinent to his cause, so why bother wasting thought on it? In the morning she would hate him for taking her from everyone she loved, including her betrothed. Tonight, he intended on winning her favor and perhaps something more. After they had her, he wouldn't have to speak with her again.

"Why do ye sleep in the garden when ye know yer mother disapproves?" He crooked his mouth at her. "Are ye rebellious then, Miss Bell?"

"Not particularly, my lord," she answered. "I simply don't agree with her reasons why I shouldn't."

Edmund smiled at the limp lock of glossy chestnut hair dangling off her shoulder, reminding him of Selkirk's comical expression when he saw his daughter asleep in the soup.

She cast him a worried look and he winked at her to let her know he saw nothing wrong with her way of thinking.

"So ye will say nothing?"

"Upon pain of death, ye have my word."

She gifted him with a grateful grin and then turned to leave him almost before he could stop her. She paused and turned back to him.

"Did a troubadour truly mention me in song?"

He gazed down at her and thought how many ways his uncle Finn could describe her. "He did."

"And what did he say?"

If anything else were at stake besides everything he believed in and loved, he would have had a hard time keeping his hands off her once he got her out of here. She was close enough to kiss right now, if he just dipped his head to the right angle.

"He said ye were lovelier than a rose in winter, more radiant than one of God's own angels dreaming at dawn."

The soft blush across her nose accentuated the shimmer in her large sable eyes when they looked up at him. "Are ye sure 'twas me he sang about?"

He smiled, caught completely off guard by her candor. He was tempted to brush his thumb over her jaw, her lips, to tilt her face to accept his mouth.

A moment passed between them when Edmund ceased to see or hear anyone else but her. She smiled as if sharing his thoughts.

"How did ye know what I was thinking earlier?" When

he didn't answer right away, she clarified. "With Bedford, about being bored with his dull wife?"

"Because 'twould be dull and tiresome fer me."

Their eyes met again and so much passed between them in the space of that breath that Edmund felt exposed and open more than ever before. He looked away first, afraid that if she looked hard enough, she would see his secrets, his true purpose for being here. But everyone had secrets, didn't they? Even this tantalizing angel. He could see them plainly in the shrouded slant of her gaze, the mischievous tilt in the curl of her lips. What were they? He wanted to discover them all but he would discover nothing if she was dancing with everyone else.

"What is it about Michelangelo's *David* that captivates ye so?"

This time, she remained by his side, her dance card forgotten. Tempting her to disobey her mother and using King David to do it was likely a sin, but Edmund would repent of it later.

"He was the perfect man."

"Ye know much about him."

"I read the scriptures," she told him, picking up her steps again and following him toward the garden doors. "He was fearless and faithful, and..." Her voice trailed off and she blushed again. "Tonight I dreamed that he came to life."

He laughed and shook his head. "I am nothing like him."

"Oh?" Leaning her back against the wall, she tossed him a look filled with whimsy. "Ye don't go about slaying giants then?"

"As a matter of fact"—he leaned in closer, tempted to

kiss the smile from her lips—"I'm hunting a giant right now."

When she giggled, he decided not to let her go tonight. To hell with her dance card. Wanting to be alone with her, he swept her out of the hall and into the garden. Concern marred her brow for only an instant before it was replaced by moonlight.

"We should not be alone."

"We're not alone, my lady. Yer champion is but a few mere feet away."

She looked over her shoulder at the statue of *David*, then turned to him when he took her in his arms. He didn't try to kiss her, though the battle was not easily won. Music from inside wafted through the windows and blended with the song of the crickets and Edmund wanted to dance with her. He held her gently, indecently according to the day's standard way of dancing. He didn't learn these steps in any nobleman's hall, but in the brothels spanning Scotland. She didn't object, but breathed rapidly against him when he swayed with the melody.

"What form of dancing is this? 'Tis scandalous." She didn't sound offended.

He grinned, loosening his hold to look at her. "'Tis the new dance of Spain."

She gave him a doubtful smile. "Heads would roll if people danced like this in Spain."

"France, then." He laughed when she gave him a playful shove.

"I should scream."

"Why?" He leaned down, smiling. "Does what we're doing feel dangerous?"

She laughed softly against him. "Aye, it does. With

me, every day is dangerous. Tempting fate by stealing these moments with ye will likely end in some kind of catastrophe."

"Then why do ye do it?"

"Do ye truly wish to know?"

He did and he nodded.

"Because these moments are fanciful and fleeting. Ye remind me of the dreams I had as a child, the ones that sometimes still haunt me. I would risk stealing them, but nothing more. I am no longer a child."

"So fancy is only fer children then?"

She shrugged her delicate shoulders and then laughed with him.

Edmund accomplished his goal of keeping her to himself for the night. They danced long into the hours and with each moment he spent with Miss Amelia Bell, he knew that if she wasn't the duke's niece, the chancellor's future wife, and a treaty supporter, she could be something meaningful in his life. He had to be extremely careful with her and not let her anywhere near his heart.

Chapter Six

What did I tell ye about the Scots? They're a virile lot."

Amelia felt the blood rush to her cheeks at what else Sarah had told her about them.

They sat on Sarah's bed, careless of the lumps in the thin mattress poking into their backsides, or the dim light of the single candle obscuring their vision. They had eagerly awaited the end of the night, when they could shed their positions in society, be themselves, and share their secrets, although Sarah's were far more titillating.

"But Edmund is not Scottish."

"Accordin' to his friend Lord Huntley, yer Edmund was raised in Scotland. So he might as well be a Scot."

Whatever he was, he was the most divine man Amelia had ever laid eyes on. She closed her eyes, wanting to shout and dance and twirl with joy atop Sarah's rickety bed. She wasn't sleepy or weary, though she'd spent most of the night dancing with Edmund alone in the garden. She'd told him that her dance card was full, but it wasn't. In fact, there were no names on it at all. At first, she hadn't cared that no one wanted to dance with her, but she felt mortified to let Edmund know that. That, and she hadn't thought it the best idea to spend the entire night dancing with him when he suggested it. A full dance card should have chased him off, but it hadn't.

In the end, she was glad it hadn't. She was grateful to him for stealing her away so cleverly, for being a gentleman and keeping his word. One of them, at least. He hadn't tried to kiss her. She wished he had, but was glad he hadn't. She wasn't under any illusions that there could ever be something with Edmund Dearly of Essex. She was to wed Walter. She hadn't forgotten her duty. Nothing had changed. She wasn't free to marry whom she wanted, but she could think about it. She could pretend for just one night that things were different, that they *could* be different. And what a magical night it had been. Edmund made her laugh and he asked her questions that made her think instead of constantly trying to make her blush with flowery words he might or might not mean. Heavens, but he didn't need words. Not when he looked at her like he was hungry for more of her. Not something his eyes could behold, but something deeper. No other man had ever looked at her like that.

She'd wanted to kiss him. Oh, but she ached with a desire to be held in his arms, kissed until she lost her breath, and her logic. She'd been spending a lot of time contemplating her wedding night with Walter. Now those images were replaced with Edmund. And they came alive and heated her belly. So, she was fanciful. The only one who disapproved was her mother, and tonight, just tonight, Amelia didn't care what her mother thought of her.

Her dreamy smile vanished and she opened her eyes.

"Ye didn't take Lord Huntley to bed, did ye?"

Sarah rolled her eyes at her. "Honestly, Amelia, I just met him this night."

"Did ye?"

"Nae." Sarah shook her head. "He chased Lizbeth Cameron and her gigantic bosoms around most of the night. I think I even saw him flirtin' with the duke's wife. When he did speak to me, his friend Mr. Lucan Campbell kept appearin' at our sides to discuss some piece of artwork, which, of course, I knew nothin' about. I confess that one frightens me a bit with those piercin' wolf-colored eyes. I found them on me fer most of the night. He has a look about him like he's eager and able to spill blood, and a lot of it. But enough about the others. Tell me of yer Edmund! Och, Amelia, he *is* handsome. Ye were certainly correct about that. Was he terribly upset about findin' ye unchaperoned in the garden at dawn? I thought he might have pulled ye away to admonish ye."

Amelia shook her head. "He was quite wonderful about it." Her breathlessness did not escape Sarah's notice. "He isn't stuffy at all. He vowed never to speak of it."

"My, but I like him better fer ye already. D'ye think yer father would—"

"Sarah." Amelia stopped her before she went any further. "My fate is sealed. Please don't make it any more difficult. Besides, Lord Essex isn't interested in me as a wife. And after all he's likely heard tonight about my 'incidents,' I'm certain he cannot wait to leave Queensberry House."

"Oh, what a bucket of nonsense!" Sarah exclaimed, pounding her thigh. "Every man in the Great Hall wished he was sittin' at yer side at that table tonight, includin' Lord Essex! Ye are the loveliest woman that ever graced this house."

"Sarah, don't be ridiculous. Did ye see my hair? I fell asleep in my soup!"

Sarah's mouth curled into a smile. "Aye, and he called ye delightful. I heard him."

"Aye, he didn't flinch when my mother made apologies fer me."

"Ye like him then."

"Of course I do. Who wouldn't? But he is leaving in the morning and I am going to be the wife of one of the most powerful men in Scotland."

"But Amelia, think of what Lord Essex has hidden in those snug hose!"

Amelia's cheeks went up in flames before both women burst into laughter.

Later, when they lay on the bed staring at the flickering shadows along the ceiling, arms flung over their heads, Amelia's thoughts were filled with Edmund. "Sarah?"

"Aye?"

"What is it like to kiss a Scot, well, an Englishman who was raised in Scotland?"

"'Tis verra' nice, and verra'...indecent," Sarah answered in a voice deep and drowsy.

The thought of Edmund kissing her indecently stirred Amelia's blood. "Tell me how they kiss, won't ye?"

And Sarah did, leaving little to Amelia's imagination.

"Walter has never put his tongue into my mouth," Amelia confided when her friend was done.

"Of course he hasn't. He's as dull as wet grass."

Amelia smiled at the ceiling. When Sarah's breath

grew slow and even a few moments later, Amelia pressed a kiss to her dearest friend's forehead and left her bed.

Edmund sat in the shadows of the Duke of Queensberry's garden and waited for Amelia to return from wherever she had gone. To meet her lover? The thought didn't sit well with him, but he told himself it was because it meant that things weren't so good between her and the chancellor, and if the chancellor didn't care if she was kidnapped, he'd sign the treaty and all this would be for naught.

That's what Edmund told himself.

He waited for her like a thief in the night, ready to steal her away from the people she loved, eager to begin the process of winning this battle for Scotland.

Eager to see her, to speak to her again. He'd sincerely enjoyed the night he spent with her and the more times she smiled at him, laughed with him, opened up to him, the more he hated the idea of using her as a pawn. She was nothing like some of the other noblemen's daughters he'd met in the past. He wished she were haughty, like her mother and her sisters. It would make what he meant to do easier. But she seemed to genuinely care about her uncle's servants and her father's well-being.

He hadn't kissed her. He'd promised himself that he would. But now, feeling drawn to her like he did, he decided it was best that he kept his mouth and his hands off her.

He'd been untruthful to women before in his quest for information, but he'd never gone out of his way to make them trust him, believe that he was someone he wasn't.

He was no courtly, pure-hearted warrior sent from heaven to battle giants with a sling. No, he used innocent women to win his war.

But there was no time for regrets. He must carry out his and his cousins' plan and save his kin, his clan, his countrymen from suppression. Nothing would stop him. Not even the slight flip of his heart when he saw her entering the garden in her nightdress, humming to the stars.

Amelia glanced up at the stars strewn across the warm violet sky. She was late again—or early, depending on how one looked at it. She didn't care. No one would miss her if she slept a few extra hours. As she made her way across the arcade, she cursed her ill fortune that a man like Edmund came into her life merely to remind her how dull her days were going to be with Walter. Edmund, who thought an obedient, ever-dutiful wife was tiresome. *Stop it, Amelia*, she chided herself. *Ye're going to be wed in a month.*

She blinked, trying to adjust her vision as she approached the statue of *David*. A shadowy figure of a man moved away from it, as if stepping out of the stone carving to become flesh.

"Ed...Lord Essex, ye startled me." She groped at her night robe as he stepped into her path. The fragrance of earth and leather flirted across her nostrils, going straight to her head. She stepped back. He moved closer. "Whatever are ye doing out here?"

"I had trouble sleeping and came here to seek my dreams."

The smoky cadence of his voice above her head sent a

warm tremor down her spine. She tilted her face and his breath fell upon her lips.

"A lover?"

"What?" She blinked slowly, enraptured by his close-ness, his height, his scent enveloping her. Every other thought fled her mind, save one. She wanted to kiss him. Just once to help her remember during her marriage to Walter what something passionate felt like.

"Are ye meeting a lover, Miss Bell?"

Her head cleared instantly and she moved back, then skirted around him to head for the doors.

"Amelia." His uneven breath as she passed him stopped her.

She didn't look at him before she spoke. She didn't want to see the censure in his eyes when she told him the truth.

"I was meeting with someone whose friendship I treasure. She is frowned upon by my mother, and so our friendship is forbidden." She didn't want to be talk-ing to him about this. Not him. She picked up her hem and left, but he followed and reached her in two long strides.

"Why is it forbidden?"

"Because she is a servant," she blurted, not slowing her pace. "Ye may have noticed her in the Great Hall. Sarah is difficult to miss. She's quite lovely; red hair, dancing green eyes, a kind heart." Dear God, why was she trying to convince him that Sarah had no faults other than her station?

"I did notice her."

Her heart faltered, as did her steps. "Ye did?" she asked, turning to look up at him. She loved Sarah, but the thought of Edmund taking notice of her made Amelia want to weep.

"Aye, she followed ye when ye left the table and then hovered about fer most of the night. One of the men I traveled here with has been speaking of her all night, which is part of the reason I couldn't sleep."

"Lord Huntley." Amelia almost sighed aloud with relief.

"Nae. Mr. Campbell."

"I see." She slipped her gaze from his. "And did he speak kindly of her?"

"Aye, I feel like I know her already," he said, and the teasing lilt in his voice drew a smile to her lips.

"And our being friends?" she asked apprehensively, but now she had to know. "What do ye think of that?"

"If ye're asking me if I approve of yer being friends with a servant, I find no fault in it. Where I live we don't have servants. We are all equal, save fer our chief."

Amelia stared up at him. She meant to say something to him about his kindness, but the sun began to break over the horizon and bathed the rugged angles of his face in its warm light and tempted her to promise her life to him, if only she could. Aye, she knew it was madness and had she opened her mouth she likely would not have pledged herself, but God help her, everything about him was so beautiful, so kind, and where in blazes did he live? No servants? She wanted to go there.

"I will say nothing to yer parents," he promised, thinking her afraid that he would. "Ye have nothing to fear from me, Amelia."

His eyes drew her closer. They were intense, warm blue embers mirroring her thoughts, devouring her, as she did him. He wanted to kiss her, and if she remained still but a moment longer, he was going to—and she was going to let him.

"I should go."

"Aye," he agreed roughly. He took her hand in his and brought it to his mouth. "But don't."

His breath felt warm against her knuckles, his finely carved lips, firm yet tender. She cursed her station in this life and the duty that bound her. She wanted to explore all the feelings Edmund ignited in her. She wanted to feel what his mouth was like, if his kiss would be indecent or chaste, like Walter's. He didn't want her to go, but how could she stay? If they were discovered out here, alone...

He didn't seem to care about consequences when, still holding on to her hand, he pulled her in close enough to cover her with his size, his honeyed breath. "Grant me just a few more stolen moments, Amelia."

Her name falling from his mouth sounded rich and so very warm. She wanted to grant him whatever he wished. But another scandal would end her father. So she pulled away, trembling with an unfamiliar ache she didn't think she could resist another moment in his company.

"I must go," she said again and broke free of him.

She didn't go far when she turned and looked at him standing there next to *David*. Her first error. She would never forget her night with him. She didn't want it to end. Not yet. No one would discover them. Just one more stolen moment and she would be satisfied. Hiking up her nightdress, she ran to him, into his arms.

He met her halfway and cradled her face in his hands. His kiss was open, hungry, and raw with need, sending fire straight to her belly and below. He played with her mouth, tasting her lips, devouring her tongue to taste her more fully. As their kiss deepened, he cupped her nape in one palm and her back in the other and hauled her closer to his hard, supple angles.

Her heart beat furiously at the scandalous passion of his embrace. He enveloped her like smoke, molded her limp, yielding body to all the tight, hard planes of his own. She groaned against him, certain that no man, especially not the chancellor, would ever kiss her like this again.

Finally, and with languorous reluctance, he withdrew. Amelia watched his eyes drift open, the residue of passion still smoldering within their depths. It made her head spin. Oh, she couldn't marry Walter. Not after that!

"Come away with me," he whispered, not letting her go.

"Away?" She giggled against his mouth. "Where would we go at this hour?"

"Ye'll see."

"All right then, I . . ." She didn't remember much after that, only a cloth coming over her face, Edmund's cool blue eyes looking down at her, and a single thought.

She knew something terrible would happen for behaving so recklessly with him. She was right. He was kidnapping her! The lying, scoundrel bastard.

Edmund lowered an unconscious Amelia into Darach's arms. Just for a moment, he let his gaze linger on her face, the smudge of her lashes resting on her cheeks. He ignored the battering of his heart against his ribs. He liked her. He'd wanted to kiss her and he did. Now it was over and time to get serious about what needed to be done. He wished there was another way.

There wasn't. He would stay his course, steady and relentless, seeing his duty to Scotland through. Nothing would stop him. He was born to do this and no mere lass would get in the way.

"Follow the road to Canongate," he told Darach. "Luke will meet ye there."

"What aboot ye?"

"I must leave the letter fer Queensberry and Seafield. Once that's done, I'll retrieve Grendel and catch up with ye. I don't know where Cal is, but he knows the plan. He'll be there."

Darach nodded and hefted Amelia over his shoulder.

"And Darach," Edmund called out before Darach left the garden. "If she awakens before I get there, reassure her that no harm will come to her, aye?"

Darach nodded again, then left without another word.

Edmund watched him go. He would make certain that no harm came to her. She was a valuable pawn in Edmund's cause. But there was more to it than that. He'd kidnapped her. Now she was his responsibility. He hoped he didn't regret it.

All that was left now was to pen a note to Amelia's uncle and one to her betrothed. If they wanted to see her alive again they should disband their commissioners and publicly denounce the Treaty of Union. He would be in touch with them after that about her return. He would write it in French just to throw them off and keep them guessing for a while.

He smiled as he headed for the duke's study. Soon, Scotland would be liberated.

Chapter Seven

Edmund narrowed his eyes on his troupe waiting for him in the distance. He was glad for the dawn and the light it afforded. He could see Amelia sitting straight up in Darach's saddle. What would he say to her? How would he explain what he'd done? Why he'd done it? Would she understand, when her own uncle was the one rallying for the act to be signed? Her father had even fooled himself into believing Scotland would be better off in subjugation to England. Then again, mayhap Edmund was being too kind. Mayhap all John Bell cared about were his coffers and that was why he'd secured a wealthy husband for his daughter.

Edmund gritted his jaw. What did he care about the lass and whom she married? He planned on never seeing her again when this was all over. Still, the memory of her sweet lips, her soft yielding body against his, her easy laughter…

He shook his head, trying to rid his thoughts of the memory.

Grendel, cantering at his horse's side, took off at a full gallop when he heard Lucan's voice. In the early dawn Edmund saw Amelia recoil at the dog's approach. He called out and Grendel screeched to a halt and returned to him.

"Where the hell is Cal?" Luke asked when Edmund reached them. "We need to be away from here before the sun comes fully up."

Edmund nodded. Damn Malcolm for doing whatever he was doing instead of being there with them. Edmund would have words with him later. Right now, he set his eyes on Amelia. The fury in her gaze almost made him look away.

"I know ye're—"

"Please." She held up her hand, then grimaced with pain and cradled her hand in her lap. "Do not speak to me. I've heard enough lies from ye fer one night."

"What is the matter with yer hand?"

When she didn't answer him, he turned to Darach, then to Luke.

Luke answered first. "She refused to let me relieve her of Darach."

"I didna' even know she was hurt." Darach shrugged. "She tried to take a bite out of me and leaped from m' horse."

"I didn't leap," Amelia corrected him sharply. "I'm not a fool. I fell off when I—"

She squealed with either surprise or fright, or both, when Edmund reached over his saddle, fit his hands under her arms, and swung her onto his lap.

"Let me have a look."

"Get yer hands off me!" She tried to push him away

with her good hand. When he didn't budge, she swung at him, missed, and almost tumbled to the ground.

Grendel leaped up and snapped at her.

"What in God's name is that thing?" she screeched, lifting her face away from the beast's dripping fangs and wedging herself deeper against her captor.

"A dog. He doesn't like it when anyone tries to strike me. Now give me yer hand and quit being stubborn."

"I will not give ye my hand. These two were discussing what needs to be done with it and I'll not let ye touch me."

"Amelia."

When he spoke her name, she looked up at him and her eyes glistened large and bright in the soft luminance of the morning.

His heart broke a little for her, for what he'd put her through, and for what he was about to put her through. He wanted to protect his country. That didn't make him a heartless rogue.

"Yer fingers need tending. It must be done."

She closed her eyes, fighting back the tears threatening to spill out. Silently, she held her hand out to him and squeezed her eyes tighter. When he touched her, she startled and opened her eyes. "Wait! Make me sleep like ye did before."

"I have nothing left. What I had, I stole from one of yer mother's alchemists."

She cast him a sour look, then closed her eyes and readied herself again. He took her hand gently and examined it. Two fingers needed readjusting. He knew the pain would be intense and he hated having to do it.

"There's Cal," Darach informed them, peering over

Edmund's shoulder. "It appears he has someone with him."

Amelia opened her eyes to look and Edmund drew her close and popped one finger back in place, and then the other. He did it quickly, ignoring her first cry. When she buried her face in his chest to muffle another cry, he cupped her head in his hand and held her closer, more gently than he thought he could ever touch anyone.

"There now, lass," he whispered into her hair. "'Tis all done. Fergive me. Fergive me, Amelia."

She shook against him, sobbing quietly and soaking his shirt. He turned his mount away from Darach's and Lucan's watchful eyes...and came face-to-face with Amelia's handmaiden, Sarah.

"By the saints!" Luke shouted, bringing his horse close to Malcolm's. "What the hell were ye thinking bringing her?"

Edmund had to agree. "Cal, bring her back," he warned, while the woman in his lap and the one in Cal's reached for each other and began a high-pitched dialogue Edmund did not understand.

"Nae time. The guards are wakin'. We'll be discovered."

Lucan whirled on Edmund. "This is madness. Fighting fer Scotland is one thing, kidnapping lasses and bringing them to Ravenglade is something entirely different. There's nae honor in this."

"'Tis too late fer integrity, Luke," Malcolm told him, his arm looped around Sarah's middle as if he meant to keep her forever. Edmund knew him better than that. "We have our kin to think about, brothers and sisters we dinna' want enslaved by England's laws. We're doin' the right thing."

"And what does this fair lass have to do with our duty to Scotland or our families?" Luke asked him, pointing to Sarah.

Malcolm smiled and shrugged. "Verra little, I imagine. She's here to keep me in good humor."

Edmund glared at him. He loved Malcolm like a brother, but sometimes the frivolous Highlander thought entirely with his groin and not with his head. "Malcolm, ye can saunter into any village or tavern from here to Perth and have a dozen lasses at yer beck and call. Why her?"

"Och, Amelia, what have they done to ye?" The handmaiden looked up at Edmund and shook her head like a disapproving mother. "Ye did not have to kidnap her, ye brute. She was pinin' fer ye all night."

"Sarah!"

Sarah cast her friend an apologetic look.

"Ye see how they care fer each other?" Malcolm pointed out. "That could work to our advantage if the lady here"—he motioned to Amelia—"tries to escape or warn her uncle."

"Remind me to beat yer head into something hard when we reach Ravenglade," Luke said, then turned his horse away.

"What's done is done," Edmund said, knowing that if this was going to work, his kin needed to stay calm, determined, and focused. The last thing they needed was another woman to distract them, but it was too late to bring Sarah back. "We need to go before discoveries are made."

"Why?" Amelia asked as they rode away from Edinburgh. Her soft voice drew Edmund's attention to her. He gazed down at her profile, aimed straight ahead. He fought not to regret what he'd done. "Why did ye kiss me and then cover my face with a poisoned rag? What kind of barbarian does such things?"

Hell, what could he say? She didn't shout at him this time. He wished she would. She sounded defeated and betrayed, and he felt like a cad because he was responsible for it.

He leaned down closer to her ear so she would hear him. "I would speak with ye about it later, when we make camp and..."

She turned in the saddle, and he closed his arms around her to keep her from falling again. "I am in my nightdress, ye bastard!"

"Undress is the fashion, lass." He wanted to tell her how completely ravishing he found her with her hair loose and tumbling down her creamy, gauze-draped shoulders.

She shook her head at him. "I was terribly wrong about ye."

He knew she'd be angry with him. But he still didn't like it. "Aye, ye were."

"I would know yer intentions now. Do ye intend to force me to lay with ye?"

"What?" His eyes opened wide. "Nae, of course not."

She turned away, refusing to look at him. He hated himself for thinking it, but there had to be another way to save Scotland. "We have no such heinous plans fer either of ye. This is a purely political move against the duke. Unfortunately, ye were caught in the crossfire."

"My uncle?"

"Aye."

"Ye're kidnapping me to get to the duke?"

"Or yer betrothed. We wish to stop them from signing the Treaty of Union." He might as well tell her everything.

"I see, so this is about the signing, and nothing else. What happened between us tonight was just…"

Her voice went so soft he almost didn't hear her and leaned in closer. A breeze swept a few loose tendrils of her hair across his face. He inhaled the scent of her. Wildflowers. Honeysuckle, mayhap.

"…a clever deception to get what ye wanted. None of it meant anything to ye."

He thought about dancing with her, laughing with her, kissing her. "That isn't entirely true."

She turned and looked at him now, allowing him to see the disappointment and hurt in her eyes. "Nothing ye say can be trusted. Is yer name even Edmund Dearly?"

He shook his head. He would lie no more. It was best if she knew the truth about everything from the beginning. Besides, he was proud of who he was. He would never deny his name. "I'm Edmund MacGregor of the clan MacGregor."

Her eyes widened on him. "The *outlawed* clan MacGregor?" When he nodded, she narrowed her eyes on his wig. He quickly pulled it off and released a tumble of golden waves over his eyes.

She snatched the wig, slapped him with it, and then threw it to the ground, where it was promptly seized by Grendel and torn to shreds.

"Speak to me no more, Edmund MacGregor," she warned. "I want no more lies passing my ears."

Edmund was relieved not to have to explain anything else at present. There would be enough time for that later.

They rode for a few more hours with Amelia twisting to look for Sarah over her shoulder—about as many times as Luke glanced back at the ginger-haired servant. Edmund should speak to his cousin about his obvious attraction to her. These women weren't here for sport or for anything deeper. They all had to keep that in mind.

Still, it hooked him in the guts just a little when Amelia continued to refuse him a word and twice, when he would have spoken to her, she stiffened in his arms as if the mere sound of his voice repulsed her. He understood. He'd kidnapped her. She had every right to hate him. He left her alone and let her sleep against his chest for a little while.

They stopped later that day to eat and make camp on the outskirts of Perth. Sarah seemed more excited to be in the company of infamous ruffians than frightened by them. Edmund let the women sit together while they ate. He didn't worry that they would run. They were about nine leagues from Queensberry, a long way back by foot. From his place standing against a tree, he watched them share words, heads tilted together while they watched the men in return. Edmund tried to hold her gaze when he caught Amelia's eye, but she looked like she would rather shoot him full of musket balls than give him an instant of her attention.

"It feels good to be back in my plaid."

Edmund looked at Malcolm, who was bending to pluck an apple from his discarded saddlebag. "I ask ye this as a friend and a brother. Do not break the handmaiden's heart."

Malcolm looked up at him, straightened, then tossed the apple up in the air and caught it again. "What concern is she of yers?"

"She is Amelia's dearest friend. Ye should not have brought her along."

Returning with firewood, Lucan paused on the other side of Edmund and joined them. "I agree."

"Steady, Luke, nae harm will come to her," Malcolm promised. "She might have heard us speakin' aboot keepin' our ransom at Ravenglade. I dinna' want the duke's and the chancellor's men at the doors of m' castle. It took m' grandsire years to repair and m' father more years after that."

"Ye might have mentioned that earlier," Luke told him.

"Speaking of Ravenglade," Edmund said. "Everything is ready fer us there, aye?"

Malcolm nodded. "Aye. I've kept on a few of our servants to help keep the place livable between m' visits. Chester, m' steward, still resides there, as well, to keep the Grants' affairs in order. Och, and ye'll be happy to know that I was able to find Henrietta, m' parents' auld cook. I thought she left fer France after we moved to Skye, but turns oot, she was still livin' right here in Scotland. We'll be eatin' good tomorrow, lads."

"Dear Henrietta," Darach groaned, stepping out from behind a tree and replacing his bonnet where his wig had been. "The thought of her cream puffs and tarts makes my innards quaver like a virgin's—"

"I was speaking more in terms of yer guardsmen," Edmund said, cutting Darach off. "Damnation, Cal, do ye ever think in terms of battle and protection, or is yer head filled only with thoughts of women, food, and comfort?"

Malcolm flashed them all his best smile. "What's wrong with a satisfied cock, a full belly, and a soft place to rest my arse?"

Edmund and Lucan shared a tedious look. Why did they expect more from him?

Catching their reaction, Malcolm laughed and gave in. "I hired a dozen mercenaries to guard the castle until our arrival. Does that make ye both feel better? Though the only trouble we may run into is from the Buchanans. Those bastards will never give up their claim to Ravenglade from the time of m' uncle Connor Stuart's days with the traitor James Buchanan."

"And we'll continue to make their clan smaller," Edmund promised with a clap to his friend's back. "We'll rest here tonight and travel the rest of the way at first light."

"What are we goin' to do with a pair of lasses?" Darach complained. "We canna' stay at Ravenglade forever. I want to go home and those two will likely do nothin' but complain all the way to Skye."

"Let me offer up a suggestion." Malcolm bit into his apple as sinfully as Adam might have done in the garden. "I say we build a nice fire, promise them the world, and give them the best fu—"

"Malcolm. Watch yer damn mouth," Luke warned.

Edmund remained silent in the middle of them, letting them fight it out the way they usually did. He loved them both, but Malcolm was the first child he'd ever played with when he arrived at Camlochlin so many years ago. And while he shared much more in common with Luke, he forgave Malcolm more easily than the others did for his faults.

"Fer once, remember that they're ladies, aye?" Without another word, Luke walked away. He dumped the firewood on the ground a few feet from the women and then squatted to get the fire started.

"He's been verra' sour lately." Malcolm turned to give Edmund a curious look. "Have ye noticed?"

"Aye." Edmund nodded. "Ye know how he feels about treating lasses carelessly." And it would seem especially Sarah. Luke had spoken about her almost the entire night before they left Queensberry House. Edmund hoped his cousin wasn't beginning to fancy her, since Malcolm was most likely going to use her for his pleasure and then leave her alone.

"We didn't come to Edinburgh to bed lasses or to lose our hearts to them," Edmund reminded his friend.

"Who the hell said anything about losin' our hearts to them?" Malcolm asked and laughed at the preposterous notion.

Edmund continued on. "I'm beginning to believe that taking Miss Bell was unwise. Visiting the fairer sex in their homes or their beds is one thing, kidnapping them and then riding to Perth and possibly farther with them is another."

"Aye." Malcolm sighed. "I agree with ye there. The wench is likely to fall in love with me, especially after she sees the grandeur of m' castle. I will be stuck with her fer God knows how long."

Edmund closed his eyes and said a silent prayer that Sarah didn't fall in love with Malcolm and that Malcolm would gain some clarity about not being the perfect delight of every woman in the three kingdoms.

"I think ye should just leave Sarah to Lucan fer now. He'll keep her safe and—"

"What would ye think aboot me ridin' with yer bonny Amelia the rest of the way?"

"Malcolm—"

"'Twould benefit all of us when ye think aboot it. The gel is angry with ye, if ye'll recall."

"Put it out of yer mind."

"At least if something happened between the two of us, there would be less consequence, seein' how I'm no' a MacGregor."

"I think she fancies ye, Cal," Darach chimed in. "I saw her lookin' at ye twice now."

Malcolm flashed his dimples at Edmund. "Ye see? We could—"

"Nae, we couldn't," Edmund cut him off. "Don't bring it up to her. In fact, don't speak to her." He walked away before he said something he might regret later, like *touch her and I'll break yer neck.* And before he had time to ponder why he might have said it. He looked in her direction and realized too late that his feet were leading him straight to her. He wished she smiled when their eyes met. She didn't; in fact, she cursed him in two different languages when Grendel reached her first and dropped a filthy, saliva-drenched, shredded wig into her lap and wagged his tail at her.

Chapter Eight

Amelia wanted to be afraid of the man, or rather, the small group of men watching her and Sarah at the end of the clearing, but she was just too damned angry. She'd been duped, and duped mightily! Now, because she'd allowed herself to be charmed by a handsome smile and a few flowery words, the Treaty of Union might not get signed. Her uncle would be furious! Her mother would blame her—and rightly so! Her uncle said the Union with England Act was historic. History could be changed and it was all her fault. Oh, if she had a pistol she would shoot Edmund MacGregor where he stood watching her. He took her from her family to use her as a pawn. Walter's proposal would likely be withdrawn and she would end up a miserable spinster. How was it, she lamented, that everything she did caused catastrophe? Was it so terrible that she was so desperate not to think of her forced marriage to the chancellor that she trusted a stranger? She supposed it was, when the stranger turned out to be an enemy of her uncle…or betrothed. And what did he intend on doing to Walter, or to her uncle for that matter? She'd heard terrible tales about the MacGregors and what they were capable of. Would he try to harm Walter, or her family, if he didn't get what he wanted? He'd kidnapped her and was holding her for ransom. Dear Lord, what were his plans? She had to find out. And what could she do to stop them? Nothing as long as she remained in captivity. She'd tried to talk to Sarah about escaping but her friend warned her not to be so foolish. These were MacGregors. They would surely chase her and Sarah down and kill them where they caught them if the girls tried to make a run for it. And where would they go? How far away were they from Edinburgh already? A few times Amelia had to fight back tears. Tears for her father and the idea that she might never see him again. Tears that once again, because of her, his name would be shamed, perhaps even going down in history as the father of the fool who botched the Treaty of Union. She wanted to rant and rage against her captors, one in particular, for deceiving her with such ease, but when he stepped out from behind the trees donned in his Highland attire, she could barely remember her name, let alone what she wanted to say to him. She struggled to remember that she hated him and why.

In her father's hall he'd looked handsome and commanding in his justacorps and hose but out here, surrounded by thick trees and a backdrop of azure sky, he was nothing short of glorious to behold. Draped in soft, flowing wool that fell to the tops of his kneecaps, he stood like a bronze god holding court over lesser mortals. He spread his crystal blue gaze on her and she stopped breathing.

But he'd deceived her. He charmed her, danced the night away with her, swept her off her feet, and then kissed her—oh, how he'd kissed her—and it was all a ploy to get to her uncle. She hated him for making her smile at him like a milkmaid too dimwitted to recognize a wolf. She felt foolish for having liked him so much, for thinking so highly of him when he was nothing but a snake, a man who could not be trusted.

"Heaven help us, Amelia," Sarah whispered close to her ear. "Have a look at them. We've been abducted by four Highlanders! Look at those swords! They're so long and deadly. We are goin' to need to be strong, dearest, or they'll have our skirts over our heads in no time."

Amelia was quite certain her best friend had just purred. "Sarah"—she turned to face her fully, stunned that her friend could think about them with desire—"do ye ferget that they kidnapped us? We'll be fortunate if they don't kill us! They only care about stopping my uncle. What if my uncle won't be stopped, not even fer me? What value will we be to these four Highlanders?"

Satisfied by Sarah's low whimper that she'd scared her sufficiently, Amelia returned her gaze to the men gathered together by the trees. They certainly looked dangerous enough to be a threat to her and Sarah's well-being. Purposefully, she kept her eyes off Edmund, too hurt by him to want to ever look at him again.

She shifted her gaze to Lord Huntley, Malcolm Grant, probably the most lethal one among them. He'd smiled at her twice while they rode and Amelia went powerless against the flash of deep dimples and sultry turquoise eyes eclipsed behind broad strokes of chestnut and gold.

No women were safe against that one.

From him, she moved on to his cousin Darach, the bastard who let her fall off his horse and jam her fingers. She hadn't tried to leap from the saddle. He released her when she bit him and let her fall without offering a hand. He possessed all the arrogance of a prince and the guileless beauty of an angel.

Deadly indeed.

Finally, she surveyed the last one, who was trying to start the campfire. She'd heard the others call him Lucan. The one Edmund had said mentioned Sarah. He was the tallest of the four, with a sleek tail of dark hair tied at his nape and bare, muscular arms. He'd seemed angry all day and hadn't spoken a word to either her or Sarah.

"I never saw a pair of eyes that color before," Sarah said, following her gaze across the camp. "They are like sunsets against the dark, harsh plains of—"

"They kidnapped us. They lied to us. Aye, they're pleasing to look at, but do we trust a frame just because it's sweet?"

"Hush. He's comin'."

Amelia turned to see who her friend meant and was greeted by a large white set of fangs, drool, and a ball of what was once a pure white periwig. She didn't realize she'd spoken, or even what she'd said until Edmund leaned down to pluck the wig from her lap where his monster of a dog had dropped it, and offered her the barest trace of a smile.

"Grendel is a male," he corrected her foreign oath, his potent gaze level with hers. "I think he likes ye. He doesn't usually share."

"Neither do I," Amelia retorted, pulling herself together while he straightened above her, "but if he doesn't stop drooling on me I might just share my last meal with the both of ye."

He ordered his mongrel to heel, then eyed her lap. "How is yer hand?"

"Better. Ye have my thanks fer that at least, scoundrel."

He quirked his mouth into an infuriatingly handsome smile, then turned his attention to Sarah. "I don't think we've been properly introduced. I've heard much about ye."

Sarah blushed and grinned at Amelia. "Amelia is too kind."

"Not always," Amelia corrected her and glared at her captor. "Why do ye think my uncle or the chancellor will do as ye command? Do ye know how long they have been preparing fer this union of kingdoms?"

He scowled and Amelia slanted her gaze to Sarah to discover if she was the only one breathless by the man's anger.

"They haven't been preparing longer than Scotland has been fighting fer her independence."

"Ah, ye're a patriot." She shook her head at him. "I would think ye MacGregors had little love left fer the country that continues to try to strike yer name from memory."

"'Twas not the land but the men who feared us that made us outlaws. Men like the late William of Orange. Men like the duke and the man ye're going to wed."

"Those men had and still have good reason to fear ye," she argued, rising to her feet and pulling Sarah with her. "From the moment King William claimed the throne, Highlanders opposed and fought him. They used barbaric tactics to—"

"By the divine right of kings," Edmund interrupted, his eyes hardening on her enough to make her take a step back, "William held no claim to the throne."

"A purely Catholic belief," she managed, determined not to let the power of his gaze unsettle her.

"One I'm certain the MacDonalds wished had been upheld when William sent the Campbells into Glencoe to massacre them because they did not offer their allegiance to him by the appointed deadline. Seventy-eight were killed. More than forty of them were women and children. Do not speak to me of barbaric."

Amelia had been a young child when the massacre was ordered, but she remembered her father speaking with her uncle about it a few years after it happened. Her uncle had taken the king's part and voiced no remorse for those lost. The children, he had said, would only have grown up as Catholic Royalists, trained to fight against the king.

It had sickened Amelia then, just as it sickened her now.

"Fergive me fer using the term so blithely. What happened at Glencoe was tragic and I in no way condone such a thing—or any cruelty fer that matter."

"Of course." His expression softened, granting her absolution easily.

"Mr. MacGregor." Sarah thankfully interrupted before Amelia had time to think about the way his locks fell to his brows, creating shadows in the cool indigo of his eyes. Or did they only appear with the trace of his smile? "Is Mr. Grant wed?"

He blinked his gaze to Sarah. "Nae."

"Betrothed?"

Amelia could have kicked her. She closed her eyes and said a silent prayer that her best friend left Mr. Grant alone.

"He is not interested in becoming either of those

things," Edmund told her. "Ye'd do well to keep a good distance from him. He's been known to leave many broken hearts in his wake."

Sarah actually laughed. Amelia almost wept. "Och, I've been known to do the same. I doubt he—"

"Sarah." Amelia interrupted her. Her friend could not honestly be serious in her interest in a man who had helped kidnap them. "I think it best if ye leave Mr. Grant to…"

She let her words fade as Sarah sauntered away to cut across the clearing and loop her arm through Malcolm Grant's. In the center of the clearing Lucan finally sparked an ember. The sudden flames that rose up startled Amelia and matched his eyes while he watched Sarah walk off behind the tree with Mr. Grant.

"Our conversation bored her."

Amelia shook her head at Edmund's observation and tried to think of some defense to offer for her friend's rudeness. "She isn't bound to worry about the condition of things. I envy her."

She felt his eyes on her and looked up at him.

"What do ye worry about, Miss Bell?"

"Besides being alone in a forest with four men who seek to use me to hurt my uncle and my soon-to-be husband?"

"Ye will come to no harm. Ye have my word."

She laughed. "In addition to everything else ye are, ye are, first and foremost, a liar. Ye've already brought harm to me, Mr. MacGregor. Think ye no one saw us dancing? I blame myself fer my scandalous behavior, and because of it, this will be considered my fault. Ye have no idea what my father and I will be put through. I hope my uncle and Walter do sign the treaty, despite yer threats, because if they don't, it will be worse fer me when I am returned."

He stared at her for a moment, his jaw tightening around something he wanted to say. Something she guessed might not be kind. He looked away instead, pausing to think on his words.

"Worse fer ye?" he asked quietly. "Do ye know what it means fer my country if they do?" He didn't give her time to answer. "It means that there can never be another Catholic on the throne. The United Kingdom of Great Britain will become a Protestant kingdom and some of us will lose our right to pray as we see fit. We will lose our ancient independence and be swallowed up by England's gaping jaws, just as Wales was."

For an instant, he almost gained her sympathy. She caught herself quickly though. "Ye waste words on me, Mr. MacGregor; no matter how passionately they fall from yer lips, they fall on deaf ears. I am acquainted with yer silver tongue in the most hurtful of ways."

He had the decency, at least, to lower his eyes and avoid her gaze.

"I understand yer anger," he told her. "Ye are entitled to it, but my cause is important to me and unfortunately, ye are the only one who can help it presently."

Presently, she didn't give a damn about his cause, or any other cause where she was used as a pawn to gain advantage. But she was curious about his passion for it.

"If the union is so bad why do Scots sign?"

"After Scotland attempted and failed to become a world-trading nation, many noblemen lost everything. England promised them a return in coin for showing no more resistance to the treaty."

Amelia took it all in. Aye, it might be unwise to join with England, but it didn't change the fact that he'd kissed her and emblazoned the indelible memory of his mouth forever into her heart. And then he covered her face with a rag and snatched her away.

"Ye took me from my life. Do ye think I can fergive ye fer that?"

His expression didn't soften on her. "Nae, I don't. But I'm not asking fer yer fergiveness."

Oh, she hated him! "Then we have nothing more to talk about, Mr. MacGregor."

"There is one more thing, Miss Bell," he said. "Do ye love him?"

"If I say I do, how terrible does that make me fer kissing ye?"

"If ye say ye do," he countered quietly, "how terrible does it make me fer wanting to kiss ye again anyway?"

Saints help her and her traitorous body for the quiver through her belly and the breathless fluttering of her pitiful heart. She didn't look at him but shielded her gaze beneath her lashes. "I don't think Walter will go against my uncle and all of his supporters by renouncing the union."

"Then he is a fool."

She lifted her eyes to his again, hoping that his meaning wasn't threatening. She didn't want anyone to die because of her. Not even Walter. His solemn, sincere expression convinced her that it wasn't.

"If ye were mine," he told her, "I might be tempted to give up everything to keep ye."

Amelia's heart swelled with something that made her mouth go dry and her palms grow moist. He couldn't mean it. Hadn't he spoken pretty words to her last eve, all to get her away from her uncle and Walter? He deceived with the casual ease of the devil himself. He'd stood in Queensberry's Great Hall and boldly presented himself as a lord from Essex when in truth he belonged to an outlawed clan.

She offered him a frosty smile. "As I said, Mr. MacGregor, ye waste yer words on me. Do well fer both of us and spare me no more."

He drew in a deep, thoughtful breath, then smiled before he left her. "As ye wish."

Chapter Nine

Edmund watched her from over the embers sparking above the flames. In the wavering firelight she looked like she had stepped out of his dreams; shimmering, warm, luminescent. She kept her fingers coiled around Sarah's while her friend sat beside her and shared conversation with Malcolm and Darach. Edmund thought she might be trying to keep her friend from running off with Malcolm and doing things she might regret in the morning. She was, he decided, a good friend. When Luke sat on the other side of her, she offered him a practiced smile that turned more genuine in an instant when he smiled back at her.

Edmund shifted in his spot, fighting a natural instinct to get up and go to her. She didn't need his protection from Lucan, and he sure as hell had no claim over her. Part of him regretted taking her. If this brought her or her family shame, he was truly sorry. But he couldn't…he wouldn't turn back now. He'd never considered giving up his cause. He wouldn't begin now. He would do well to remember that, no matter how her laughter, her kiss, her last words, pricked at his thoughts.

He didn't want her to hate him. If things went as planned they would be together in Ravenglade for some time. No use in spending that time fighting with her. She'd made it clear that she didn't want to speak with him. Could he change her mind, soften her up just a bit?

He studied her when she answered a question Luke put to her. He watched the way she veiled her eyes beneath her lashes, avoiding contact with him the way one did when she had secrets she feared might be revealed in her gaze—or because the sight of him repulsed her. Before long though, Luke's naturally charming disposition coaxed her into what seemed to be a very enjoyable conversation. She even let go of Sarah's hand.

Leave it to the knight in shining armor to break the stone.

Edmund could have sat where he was and watched the different nuances of her smiles for hours, remembering how her lips felt against his...but women fell for Luke fast and it wouldn't do for any of them to form attachments that would only have to be broken later.

He got up, not really knowing what to say before he covered the distance of the two steps it would take to reach her. He'd lied to her, stolen her away from her home, her family. She had every right to never forgive him. He would handle her anger with the respect she deserved and he'd failed to give her. He ran his fingers through his hair and paced before the fire. What the hell was the matter with him? She wasn't the first lass he'd found to his liking. So what that her winsome smile played on his memory like a siren song beckoning him to follow her and win back her favor. Aye, the curl of her lips, the tilt of her nose, and the depth in her gaze made him want to take up painting to try to capture her image forever.

He stopped his pacing and almost laughed out loud at himself. What the hell was he thinking? She was his enemy's niece and he wasn't some love-starved lackwit. He was the son and grandson of two of the most fearsome warriors the three kingdoms had ever known. He sure as hell wouldn't grovel to a woman.

He was about to turn back to his previous place by the fire when Luke stopped him.

"Cousin, ye look perplexed and a bit agitated. What is it?"

Edmund's gaze settled on Amelia when she finally looked up at him. What did he see in those large sable depths? Hurt, insult, anger. He'd tricked her into liking him, trusting him, giving a tiny piece of herself to him, and then he'd stomped on the scant moments of happiness they shared. "Tell me the secret of making the lady smile. I've tried to no avail."

"There doesn't seem to be a secret," Luke told him. "The lady smiles quite easily."

"Aye?" Edmund asked, finally sitting beside them. "The memory of it fades in its absence."

"Ye kidnapped me, Mr. MacGregor," she pointed out a bit tightly. "Before Lucan's comforting assurances that none of ye will harm Sarah or me, I sat frightened fer our lives. Did ye expect smiles then?"

Edmund didn't think reminding her that he'd already made the assurance would make a difference. "Nae, of course not, Miss Bell. But now that ye've been properly comforted, mayhap ye will grace me, as ye did last eve, with a smile."

"Last eve, ye were someone else."

Looking a bit uncomfortable that he may overhear something he didn't need to know, Luke leaned forward and addressed Edmund. "Let us return then to the topic that made her smile, cousin, aye? We were speaking of Henry Purcell."

"Ye have probably never heard of him," Amelia said tersely. "He was an English composer who, while including French and Italian elements in his music, became famous for his distinctly English form of Baroque music." She cut him a side glance accompanied by a barely concealed smirk. "Fergive me. 'Tis careless of me to think ye know what Baroque is. Shall I explain?"

Edmund smiled at her. "Let me think. Does it not originate from the Portuguese word *barroco*, meaning 'malformed pearl'? Is it not also a style of composition in music that is marked by expressive dissonance and elaborate ornamentation?"

She looked so bonny in the firelight, her lovely lips parted and her extraordinary eyes large with stunned surprise and a wee bit of irritation. "That...that sounds correct."

He hadn't seen this side of her. He was pleased to find her spirited and saucy. "And as fer Purcell," he went on, turning his attention to the flames rather than grin at her with the satisfaction of knowing what she thought he didn't know. "He wrote many musical dramas while holding royal appointments in Westminster and serving three kings. Some of his most notable works include *King Arthur* and my personal favorite, *The Fairy-Queen*."

"Blasphemous," Lucan said, feigning disgust. "No drama is better than *King Arthur*."

"Ye know my affinity fer Shakespeare, Luke." He turned back to Amelia. "Although *The Fairy-Queen* was more a masque than an opera, the libretto, written by an unknown author, was based on William Shakespeare's *A Midsummer Night's Dream*."

She narrowed her eyes on him and sized him up with curiosity sparking her eyes. It made his blood sizzle. "Ye think ye're quite clever, do ye not, Mr. MacGregor."

"Call me Edmund, please. We are not strangers and are in the company of friends."

She ignored his most charming smile. "What else are ye keeping from me?"

He held out his arms. "Ask me what ye would know."

He got what he wanted. She smiled at him, though it was a smile hardened by a cool edge. "If only I could get the truth out of ye, I might be tempted." She turned to Lucan. "Ye tell me. Ye, I trust."

Lucan bowed in his sitting position and did so impressively. Edmund rolled his eyes. His cousin took honor and knightly duties a wee bit too seriously.

"He speaks four languages," Luke began. "English, Gaelic, French, and Spanish."

She stared agape at Luke, then turned to Edmund and asked him in French if this was true. *"Est-ce vrai?"*

"Non, il avait oublié l'italien."

"I am corrected," Luke acknowledged. "He speaks five."

"I spent my days as a babe learning from my mother how to read in different languages," he explained. "There was little else to do."

"Why was that?"

He smiled at her firelit face. "Why was what?" He didn't realize he'd spoken aloud.

"Why was there little else to do?"

His smile remained as he looked into the crackling flames and contemplated telling her. He hadn't thought of his days before Camlochlin in years. When he recalled his childhood, he always saw himself surrounded by men, women, and children who loved him. "I wasn't born in Scotland, but in England."

"So, this is not even yer country then."

"Aye, 'tis. 'Tis my country by choice. The land of my heart because it pulled me from a dark, dreary mire and taught me how to live. I would give my life fer Scotland, fer my kin."

"Do ye have brothers or sisters?"

He nodded. "I have a brother, Kyle, who is the same age as Darach, and a younger sister, Nichola. Everything I do, I do fer them, too. I'll not have them live their lives afraid to proclaim their name or their faith."

She nodded, her eyes gleaming with hues of deep chestnut and warm sable. He felt like he had when they first met, captivated, a little distracted. He thought it a good sign that her smile had softened at some point during his short tale. She was enjoying his honesty and he found himself wanting to tell her more.

"And yer father?" she asked him. "What did he teach ye?"

Edmund's smile widened, thinking of the man who raised him. "He taught me how to be brave and compassionate and how to fish."

Her smile softened for just an instant before it faded into something less friendly. "Intelligence, bravery, and a good fisherman...such nice qualities. Pity honesty is not among them."

Sitting close by and apparently catching their conversation, Darach laughed and Edmund remembered why so many inhabitants of Camlochlin took joy in beating the youngest Grant senseless. "His faither taught him that particular trait, as well. Colin MacGregor was a master at deceivin' folks when he was a spy fer King James."

Edmund reached for a piece of dried meat left over from supper. He called for Grendel, then tossed the meat to Darach, close to his face. Very close. Grendel nearly snapped off Darach's ear when he leaped for it.

"Ye're goin to wake up one day," Darach warned, pale faced, "and find that mongrel thrown into the nearest loch."

"Ye would have to touch him to get him in the loch," Edmund reminded him. Darach never touched Grendel, save to push him off when Grendel tried to play with him.

"Ye're correct. He's even uglier than his faither, Aurelius."

"Watch yer mouth," Edmund warned, half serious. "Leave Aurelius out of this."

"Who is Aurelius?" Amelia asked.

"A dog," Darach informed her. "This mongrel's sire."

Grendel sat on his haunches, barked in Darach's face, then commenced panting, his large brown eyes never leaving the young Highlander.

Darach tried to ignore the beast but finally conceded and got up and left. Lucan also left them and followed after Malcolm and Sarah when they would have wandered into the shadows beyond the trees. He stopped them, pulling Malcolm to the side. Edmund watched for a moment, making a mental note to speak to both his cousins. But not now.

"So yer father is a spy?"

He turned to Amelia and did his best to keep his thoughts off kissing her in the soft glow of the moonlight, beneath the shadow of Michelangelo's *David*. "Was."

She shifted her legs beneath her and folded her arms around herself. "He must have been exceptional at deceit in order to have served the king."

"Are ye cold, lass?"

"Just a bit."

He sprang to his feet and retrieved a blanket from his saddlebag. He returned to the fire and draped the blanket around her shoulders. She thanked him, cutting her gaze to his but offering him no more smiles.

"Did ye learn how to lie to others so easily from him?"

Edmund wasn't sure if he wanted to laugh or beat Darach senseless for mentioning his father and his prior service to the king.

"My father did what he believed was best fer the kingdom, as I do. And he didn't lie to me or my mother once he decided to save us."

She turned to him now, her profile shimmering against the firelight. "What did he save ye from?"

Would she look down her nose at him if she knew he was born a bastard? His parents had always told him there was no shame in his heritage. They certainly never made him feel anything but adored and accepted. Sometimes though, he did feel set apart, an emotion he'd created himself. Mayhap it was the driving force of his passion to offer something back to Scotland for what she did for him. He owed her and the MacGregors something.

He smiled at himself. He wasn't a bastard and she

wouldn't look down on him. Not this lass, who defied her parents because her best friend was a servant.

"My mother bore me out of wedlock and as punishment her father sent her off to live in seclusion with her cousin the Earl of Devon at the edge of the Dart estuary."

Her eyes narrowed on him and he immediately found himself enjoying the intelligent glint in them. Edmund wondered if her future husband appreciated his spirited soon-to-be wife.

"The Earl of Essex's nephew is the Earl of Devon," she pointed out. When he nodded, she folded her arms around herself and studied him. "So ye weren't being completely untruthful back in Edinburgh, then. Yer mother is the daughter of Lord Essex?"

"Aye, but I hold no title. I haven't seen my grandfather since I was a babe of four." He told her of Colin MacGregor and how the man who became his father had taught him how to fight monsters in the night and to trust that no matter how big or powerful those monsters were, they could be vanquished with courage, determination, skill, and an army of kin at his back.

Before he knew how, hours had passed and Amelia Bell knew more about his life than any lass before her. Even the ones living in Camlochlin.

"Yer monster is the Treaty of Union, isn't it?" she guessed later when his voice finally grew quiet.

"Aye."

"Will ye do whatever it takes to stop it?"

"Aye."

"Even kill my uncle or the chancellor?"

He flicked his gaze to the fire. He didn't want to lie to her again.

When she laid a trembling hand on his arm, he looked
down at it. "I would ask ye to be merciful and honorable
and promise me that ye will not kill them."

How could he promise her that? If things came to
fighting, he intended on living. He was surprised at how
much she loved the chancellor that she would beg for his
life. The way they had danced, the way she held him,
kissed him…she couldn't love the chancellor as much
as she claimed. Then he realized that she hadn't claimed
anything. Her father had.

"I will try fer yer sake not to let it come to that."

"Ye have my thanks fer that." Her voice was quiet and
she rose to her feet. "Good night, Mr. MacGregor."

"Good night, Miss Bell," he answered, watching her
walk away.

Chapter Ten

He's a strange one," Sarah whispered beneath the thick woolen plaid she'd been given to keep her warm for the night.

"Mr. Grant?" Amelia whispered back. She guessed if she were giving her full attention to Sarah, she would have known whom her friend was talking about. But her full attention was occupied somewhere else.

"Nae, Lucan MacGregor." As if speaking his name held some intangible power over her, Sarah pushed the edge of her blanket down around her neck and swept her gaze down her nose and over the clearing, seeking the one of whom she spoke.

Amelia allowed herself to do the same, since Sarah was already looking and all. The truth was she hadn't been able to get Edmund out of her thoughts since she left him over an hour ago. She was still angry as hell with him for deceiving her, kidnapping her, and setting her life to ruin, and she hated herself for finding such interest in his life, but she couldn't forget how utterly thrilling it felt being held in his arms that night while they danced. Or how deliciously scandalous it felt kissing him.

Getting a slanted, slightly distorted glance at him sitting around the fire with the other men wasn't going to help her unwelcome obsession with him, but she wanted another look at him just the same.

He laughed quietly—thoughtfully, she realized, when he turned his head to look at where she lay with Sarah. She yanked the blanket back over her face and held her breath.

"He knows we were not asleep, Amelia."

"It doesn't matter. If they see us watching them they will think we fancy them."

"What's so terrible about that? Ye fancy Edmund," Sarah accused.

Amelia's mouth fell open. "How can ye think that? Sarah, he kidnapped us!" she protested in a hushed tone. "Do ye realize what my mother will say? Or if the Highlanders have their way, how I will disgrace my father? Not to mention they may still kill us and leave us by the side of the road! How can ye think I could fancy him?"

"Don't be a fool, Amelia. They aren't going to kill us."

"They're Highlanders, Sarah! Who knows what they will do? Well, Edmund is not truly a Highlander. But the others are."

Sarah pulled the blanket down past her eyes and examined the clearing again. "Och, my love, but Edmund is a Highlander, and nothing less."

Try as she might not to, Amelia had to peek.

He sat at a certain angle that positioned him directly under a thread of pale silver moonlight. It gave him the appearance of being carved from marble. In contrast, the golden firelight softly defined the cut of his classically masculine profile and illuminated the burnished waves about his forehead like a halo.

She turned to her friend. Did Sarah see it, too? He was simply breathtaking. She had to quit looking or his memory when she left him, if she lived, that is, would haunt her. She buried herself back under her blanket, but he was still with her. She thought about the story he'd told her of his upbringing. The MacGregors had given him much; freedom, vast heather-lined meadows of it. He'd smiled when he spoke of his very first friendship with a puppy called Aurelius that taught him loyalty and steadfastness. She envied his adventures with Malcolm and Lucan—though Lucan's family had remained at their ancestral Campbell Keep in Glen Orchy for a number of years after William took the throne. He'd grown to manhood with the sons and grandsons of great warriors. Scotland and the MacGregors had given him much indeed. It was no surprise that he was so passionate about saving them from England.

He still looked like *David*, sublime, unconquerable, unafraid of giants...or monsters.

Walter and her uncle had an army behind them, but then, so had Goliath. What would happen when they came together? Who would die? Of course, she didn't want her uncle or Walter to perish. She didn't love Walter. But she didn't want Edmund to kill him. There had to be a way to save them but she couldn't think of anything now. Not with Edmund in her head...and a cold, wet nose in her back.

"I am not afraid of ye, Grendel," she whispered, pushing him away. "Give me some room," she demanded when he didn't budge.

Honestly, what kind of beast was Grendel? Edmund had told her that he was the son of Aurelius, but surely no mother, not even a Highland one, would allow her child to play with the creature that spawned this beast.

"What is strange about him?" she asked Sarah to get her mind off an uninvited Highlander and his devil-hound.

"Who?"

"Lucan MacGregor," Amelia reminded her. "Ye said he was a strange one. I find him very appealing."

"More appealin' than yer Edmund?"

"No one is more appealing than he." She didn't know why she admitted it; most likely because it was to Sarah, and Sarah knew everything about her. Perhaps, if she confessed to thinking him desirable, he would cease plaguing her. Besides, in the darkness beneath the blanket, her friend couldn't see the fire blazing Amelia's cheeks and bubbling up in her belly. "Of course, it doesn't matter what else I think of him, which is very little, I assure ye. I am promised to another and he is—"

"More virile than the chancellor is on his best day."

Amelia would have argued with her, but what was the point when Sarah was correct?

"He kissed me." She held her breath as Sarah gasped. They clasped hands, careful of Amelia's sore fingers. She wanted to tell Sarah everything.

"Och Amelia, when? Why did ye not tell me? How was it?"

Amelia closed her eyes, remembering, smiling. She would be logical in the morning. Tonight, she didn't want to think about consequences; a fault her mother would tell her was nothing unusual . . . or acceptable.

"'Twas divine. Never have I been kissed so." She sighed and then pulled the blanket down to have another look at him.

She didn't have to look far. Edmund stood over her, smiling like he'd heard everything. Amelia quickly realized that he had. Unlike Sarah, he had a perfect view of her flushed face.

"What..." She swallowed, mortified at what she had said, and took a moment to begin again. "What are ye doing standing over us? What if we were sleeping? Ye would have frightened poor Sarah to death if she—" Her face twisted with pain when Sarah poked her hard in the side.

"Ye know I don't frighten that easily, Amelia."

Amelia glared at her while Sarah turned her most radiant smile on Edmund.

"Don't mind her, m' lord," Sarah cooed. "We weren't sleepin'."

"I know," Edmund confessed with a grin that would likely cause Amelia a se'nnight of tossing and turning in her bed. "I wanted to make certain ye were both comfortable before the rest of us go to sleep."

"I would love it if ye would remove yer *dog* from my back. I don't mind sharing my patch of ground with him but he's gangly. As we speak one of his paws is pressed into my spine."

Amelia was impressed at how quickly Grendel sprang up at Edmund's softly spoken command that the beast go someplace else. She also felt terrible watching the mongrel slip away into the shadows beyond the fire. He turned to look at her just before he blended in with the darkness. She thought she heard a low whimper.

"Luke is taking first watch if ye need anything."

Amelia returned her gaze to Edmund and wondered if he thought her overly pampered and spoiled. It wasn't that she didn't want to sleep with a dog, it was because . . .

Edmund bid them good night and turned to walk away.

Amelia sat up, wanting to stop him from leaving just yet. Why? Did she care that much what he thought of her? She barely knew him and what she did know wasn't all that favorable. He was an outlaw from an outlawed clan. He'd kidnapped her from her home and if that wasn't bad enough, he did so directly after he kissed her. He'd threatened harm to her uncle's life and to the life of the lord chancellor. What then did it matter what he thought of her? But it did matter. Perhaps because somewhere deep down she didn't believe that he was cruel or callous, the way MacGregors were rumored to be. No merciless barbarian could take such pity on her while he mended her fingers.

"Mr. MacGregor?" She stopped him before she could give herself a good reason why.

He turned and managed to scatter her thoughts with a mere slant of his lips. "Edmund," he corrected.

She sighed and nodded, thankful for the extra moment to come up with a valid question for why she'd stopped him from leaving. "How did ye come by the name Grendel? I've never heard of it before."

"'Tis a name taken from an epic Anglo Saxon poem."

"About a hero of that name?" She almost smiled, guessing she was correct. Edmund was a patriot, loyal to Scotland's cause. Men like him sought heroes to remember.

"Nae, lass. Beowulf was the hero of that tale, Grendel was the fiend he slew."

"Fiend?" she asked quietly, looking into the shadows where Grendel had disappeared. Certainly the dog was no fiend. Aye, he was a beast, huge and furry, but... "Why would ye name him after a monster?"

Amelia's heart pounded violently when he made his way back to her. He squatted at her side, close enough for her to smell the scents of moss and burned wood on his plaid. His eyes, level with hers, appeared dark and fathomless in the dim light, tempting her to fall into them, to lose herself there, forget her father, Walter, everyone, save him. When he spoke, his voice caressed her in layers of sultry, spine-tingling warmth.

"He hates music."

She blinked out of the spell he'd cast over her. "What?"

"My dog. He hates music. His namesake hated it and became a fiend by killing men who pained his ears with their music."

It wasn't a humorous story, but she found herself wanting to smile nevertheless. "But he's a dog! How can he hate music? I don't believe it."

Edmund shrugged his shoulders. "Sing to him and find out."

"Will he tear at my throat then?" she challenged him, not believing the dog would harm her at all.

"That depends on how poorly ye sing."

"I sang fer the queen last spring and she voiced no complaints."

"I heard she has a deaf ear. Be assured that Grendel does not."

Against her better judgment, Amelia laughed and gave him a playful slap, then squeezed her eyes shut and brought her sore fingers to her lips. She opened her eyes an instant later when he took her hand tenderly in his and brought it to his lips.

"I should beat Darach senseless fer letting ye fall off his horse."

"I...I..." Oh, hell, what was she about to say? She had no idea. His warm mouth on her fingers thrilled the thoughts right out of her head. Still, she didn't want him to be angry with Darach. "I've fallen before. It wasn't his fault."

"Ye will ride with me from here on out. I'll not let ye fall."

She shook her head. That was a terrible idea. She didn't want to ride with him, feeling his body so close to hers. She didn't want to like him or think him kind. He wasn't. Everything he did, he did for a purpose. For Scotland. What would become of her and Sarah at this Ravenglade they spoke of? Would he ever let them go? What if her uncle signed the treaty? What would happen to her and Sarah then?

"Sleep now." He pulled the blanket up to her neck as she lay back down. "Ye'll be safe."

"He's verra charming."

Amelia closed her eyes at the sound of Sarah's voice.

"I can see how ye let yerself be fooled by him."

Amelia nodded. She would have to be more careful in the future. He'd abducted her. At this very moment her poor father was likely worried sick. That thought gave her the momentum she needed to continue disliking him.

She looked around the campsite. Everyone was lying down and still, save for Lucan. A forest creature scurried by her and nearly startled her out of her skin. She'd never slept out in the open before. Another sound from the shadows set her to prayer. Where was Grendel? She was sorry she'd had Edmund chase him away.

Perhaps she could get him to return. She whistled softly, drawing Lucan's attention and thankfully the dog's, as well. This time when Grendel lumbered toward her, tail wagging, she invited him under the cover with her.

She realized an instant later that her invitation might have been a mistake.

He smelled.

But he was big, and warm, and fierce looking. She felt safe lying next to him. She petted his head. Grendel. Not a fiend at all. She decided to put Edmund's words to the test, certain that he'd been teasing her. She'd never heard of a dog hating music.

She began to hum.

Grendel began to howl. And oh, if he had simply howled like a normal dog, it wouldn't have been so bad. His cries were agonized, loud, and harrowing. He didn't stop, even after everyone in the camp woke up and the sun rose over the hills.

Amelia felt terrible for everyone, even Grendel. She tried not to think about it too much while they made their way into Perth. Twice though, after Darach yawned, he turned to cast her a dark, accusing glance. She caught Malcolm offering her a pitying look and she guessed Sarah had told him about the unfortunate incidents that accompanied her.

Her mother blamed the incidents on Amelia's lack of self-control; her father chose to simply ignore whatever catastrophe she caused and paid for the damage without uttering a word to her about it. Dear Alice—and goodness but Amelia missed her—always assured her that her season of misfortune would end. No one but her uncle had ever declared what Amelia believed the trouble was.

Ill fortune followed her everywhere she went. Calamity plagued her, sometimes making her feel utterly hopeless, completely discouraged that anything wonderful would ever happen in her life. Most of the time she fought through her frustration and made the most out of what was given her, but everyone at home knew the truth. She was bad luck.

Unfortunately Edmund and his band of fearless, though tired, warriors were about to find out just how bad.

Chapter Eleven

Nothing moved beneath the pewter sky save for the four Highlanders, their large swords drawn. Seated in front of Edmund on his horse, Amelia felt a breeze cool the flesh of her nape, and it chilled her to the bone with foreboding. Grendel's low snarl rumbled in the morning silence.

They'd reached Ravenglade shortly after sunrise to find the castle drawbridge closed.

"Should the mercenaries ye hired be lowering the bridge by now?" Edmund asked Malcolm.

"Mayhap they fergot what ye look like?" Luke added, calming the restless stallion between his legs.

Malcolm shook his head. "The bastards know me well enough. If they dinna' answer m' call then they're dead."

As if to validate his statement, a crow cried out, breaking the ominous quiet.

Edmund wheeled his mount around, already looking for a safe place to deposit Amelia. "Buchanans?"

Malcolm nodded, following him with Sarah perched in his lap. "Aye. Buchanans."

An arrow pierced the air between Darach and Malcolm and hit a nearby tree with a loud thump. Everything happened quickly after that. The morning erupted with the sounds of Grendel's loud barking and the thunder of horses approaching from every direction.

Within seconds, Edmund and Malcolm left the women in a cluster of nearby bushes, ordering them to stay put. Grendel was also commanded to stay where he was, close to Amelia.

The Highlanders moved in unison, defending every side against the approaching riders. Edmund's stallion rose up on its hind legs while he cocked his bow, aimed, and fired.

A man went down! Amelia shook while her blood seared her veins. This was real. And more men were coming. She had heard tales of the strength of Highlanders in battle, but she'd never seen it before today.

She prayed to God never to see it again.

Metal clashed against metal in a grinding symphony of chaos and sparks. She turned away from the death she knew was coming for the fighters. She didn't want to see Edmund or his kin fall. She didn't want to think of what would become of her and Sarah if they did.

She felt like she was in a dream when Grendel broke free of her and raced into the fray, forcing her to gaze in their direction just as the skies tore open and poured rain down in icy sheets. The torrent distorted the air, but Amelia could make out Edmund and the others swinging their heavy claymores with terrifying accuracy. She thought she could smell blood, or perhaps because there was so much of it, she just thought the scent was saturating the heavy air. She tried to turn away again but she felt like she was no longer in control of her body. She watched, horrified and mesmerized, covering her ears at the screams of dying men.

She felt her heart pitch in her chest when she lost sight of Edmund. What would she do if he died? Would Malcolm and the others bring her and Sarah back to Edinburgh? Would Edmund's face, his smile, his kiss, haunt her for the remainder of her days? He came back into her vision a moment later, much to her traitorous relief, his sword flashing beneath a charge of lightning puncturing the clouds. Her gaze followed him as he yanked back his reins, heaving the stallion to an upward halt— high enough to place him above a man swinging an ax from his saddle. Amelia closed her eyes as the hooves of Edmund's horse came back down, crushing bone and silencing his opponent's battle cry.

It was difficult to tell how many men fought against the four, but numbers didn't matter. They were no match for the MacGregors and Grants. Edmund's claymore struck with merciless precision. Amelia watched, helpless and sick to her stomach from the carnage around her, but she managed a shout of warning to Edmund when another rider approached from behind. Engaged in battle with two men in front of him, he couldn't turn to defend himself.

He didn't have to. The attacker spun in his saddle to glare at the bushes where she and Sarah hid. He kicked his horse's flanks and lifted his heavy ax over his shoulder as he rode toward them.

Amelia clutched Sarah and shrank back. He was coming! He was going to kill them! But the man didn't waste time riding to them. He flung the ax and waited while it flew straight for her.

Lucan came at him from his left, passing the bush on his horse, putting himself in their path. The ax flew end over end and then hit something hard, stopping before it reached them.

The attacker came at them again but was halted this time by Edmund's sword across his neck.

Sarah pressed her face into Amelia's shoulder and wept when the man's body fell from his saddle. Amelia wanted to do the same but she couldn't take her eyes off Edmund. Sitting high in his saddle, his golden hair and his face spattered with his victims' blood, he looked like a lion wild to protect what was his. A moment passed and his expression changed, going soft on her and then on Sarah. He offered her a subtle nod, making certain she was not injured. When she shook her head, he called out to Lucan.

"Yer leg."

"'Tis fine."

Edmund nodded and turned his stallion back to the fight.

All around her the Highlanders' enemies fell. Some run through to the hilt by Malcolm's blade while others fell from their horses, broken and crushed beneath Lucan's mighty arm. Darach preferred to use a dagger and twice he leaped from his horse to his opponents' to kill them at a closer proximity.

Soon the fighting slowed, and with its end, the drawbridge finally descended. Edmund, Lucan, Malcolm, and Darach sat perched in their saddles, drenched with rain and blood, and watched the three riders approaching from the inner bailey. Malcolm waited until they reached him before he struck the first in the face with his fist and then ordered the other two to go back, get their comrades, and get the hell out of his castle.

"Mercenaries." He turned to Lucan with disgust. "Canna' trust a one even when it comes to keepin' Buchanans away."

Lucan nodded, then leaned forward on his mount and looked across the glen to where Amelia and Sarah were hidden. His eyes, like topaz flames, sparked and then faded as his eyelids closed and he fell unconscious from his saddle.

His three cousins leaped from their horses and ran to him, but Grendel reached him first, whining and sniffing Lucan's thigh. His plaid was cut. Blood saturated the wool and the ground where he lay.

"He's bleeding out!" Edmund tore a long strip from Lucan's bloody plaid and tied it tightly around his cousin's thigh. "We need to stop the bleeding. Help me get him inside."

"We shouldn't move him," Darach countered, swiping rain or tears from his eyes.

"We cannot leave him out here. Take the horses," Edmund commanded. "Malcolm, help me."

They picked Lucan up with exquisite care and carried him by foot over the drawbridge. Amelia clasped Sarah's hand and hurried to keep up with them. She heard a strangled cry from somewhere behind her and turned to see Grendel close his massive jaws around the throat of one of the Highlanders' dying victims. She looked away and swallowed back the swell of raw emotions that threatened to consume her. Lucan was hurt, possibly dying. Edmund didn't need to watch her fall apart. They needed her help.

"My nursemaid Alice taught me how to mix some poultices fer wounds."

Edmund turned to look at her over his shoulder. "Good. I would be in yer debt if ye help him."

"As would I," Malcolm agreed.

"And I," Darach echoed. "Tell me what ye need and I'll fetch it. There's an alchemist in the village."

Darach listened to every word she told him. She needed yarrow or agrimony to stop the bleeding. She also needed cinnamon or clove to reduce pain and disinfect the wound to avoid infection. She gave him a list and added a few things that Sarah requested in case of fever or infection and then sent him on his way.

She followed Edmund and Malcolm into an enormous room in the west wing and watched them as they set Lucan down in a bed that was so big it made the huge Highlander look small. They laid him on his side and set about examining his wound.

"His mother will kill us all if he should..." Malcolm's words faded and he looked away.

"He won't," Edmund finished after they all paused in silence.

The gash in his thigh, received from the ax he'd stopped from hitting Amelia, was about ten inches long and quite deep. He'd protected her and Sarah because she'd given away their position. She shook her head. She couldn't let herself think about any of that now. She had never seen a wounded man before. She prayed she didn't retch from the sight of his gaping flesh. She knew the wound had to be cleaned and likely sewn. The thought of it twisted her belly into a knot and produced beads of sweat along her brow. "We'll need fresh water."

"And clean rags," Sarah added beside her.

"I'll fetch them."

When Malcolm left the room to his task, Sarah turned to Amelia and offered her a comforting smile. "Ye clean him and I'll sew him, aye?"

Amelia nodded, loving her dearest friend for being able to read her thoughts and for helping her with this grim task.

"First though," Sarah continued, rolling up her sleeves and bending over Lucan's body, "we must discover if he still lives."

Amelia and Edmund watched and waited in silence while Sarah pressed her head to Lucan's chest. Moments passed, slowly, torturously, with Edmund running his fingers through his hair and finally turning away when Sarah said nothing.

"He lives," she finally announced, bringing such relief to Edmund that he fell back into a chair close by the bed. She touched the back of her hand to his forehead. "He's cool to the touch. We need to begin soon."

When Malcolm returned, she requested a pan and his and Edmund's removal from the room.

Amelia was glad to see them go. She didn't want Lucan to die, and she barely knew him. It was Edmund and Malcolm, and even Darach, when he returned sometime later with her herbs, who coiled her nerves into a knotted mess. They clearly loved him. She imagined the devastation of losing Sarah and had to push back her tears. She had to stay in complete control of her emotions and do everything she could to help Lucan. They couldn't let him die.

With that thought pushing her forward, she cleaned

Lucan's wound and applied her ointments, then aided
Sarah in repairing his sliced artery and stitching him up.
After three hours they were finally done. Amelia stood
back and cleaned the blood from her hands while the
Highlanders returned and took turns at Lucan's beside.
He still hadn't regained consciousness but they had done
everything they could. Now all they could do was wait.
The men all looked terribly worried and frightened for
their cousin, but Edmund broke her heart just a little
more. He stood by the bed, looking down at Lucan's unconscious body. Amelia couldn't read his thoughts, but
they were clearly fraught with despair. When he ran his
fingers through his hair and looked away, she wanted to
go to him. He appeared to be the one in charge of the
group, making the quickest decisions, ready for action an
instant sooner than everyone else. Did he feel responsible
the same way she did when people she loved were hurt?
Surely he knew this wasn't his fault. They were warriors.
Sometimes they died.

She caught Edmund's eye and held it for a moment,
unsure of what her reaction should be, but wanting to
somehow comfort him. A glance seemed to be enough.

"Thank ye," he said, moving around the bed to stand
before her.

Amelia felt her face go hot and looked away from him.
"Sarah did the more serious mending. Besides, ye've no
need to thank me. I'm fond of Lucan. I would not see him
perish."

She didn't realize her hands were shaking until he took
them and finished wiping them tenderly with a rag. Suddenly her knees felt shaky, too.

"I'm in yer debt."

"Nae." She shook her head and the room spun a little. "I—" She closed her eyes to clear her head but the room only reeled more.

"Are ye ill?" he asked her when she swayed on her feet.

Damnation, she wasn't prone to fainting spells like her mother and she certainly didn't want to faint in front of Edmund and his friends. She was made of stronger mettle than that, but the day had been so taxing what with all that killing, all the blood...so much blood...

"I'm fine," she assured Edmund, stepping away from him. "I simply need a bit of air. Would ye..."

She didn't realize she was falling or where she landed, or why she felt safe for the first time in two days.

✣

Chapter Twelve

Edmund watched Amelia's eyes flutter open as he set her down on a stone bench in Ravenglade's walled garden. He realized, standing over her while her lush black lashes rose slowly over the glory of her dark eyes, that she could be trouble. He liked her. He liked her more every moment he spent with her, especially after she saved his cousin. He would be forever in her and Sarah's debt for that. But he couldn't allow his feelings for Amelia Bell to go any further than this. He didn't have time for a lass in his life, especially not the Duke of Queensberry's niece, the Lord Chancellor of Scotland's future wife. He'd vowed to protect her and that's what he would do. And himself along with her. He hadn't expected to have to guard his heart from her. He'd never had to do it with any lass before her. But guard his heart, he would.

Though the idea of waking up to her slumberous face every morning was tempting, she was a dangerous distraction, and he'd been taught by men of honor to stay true to his course, wherever it led him.

Scotland would always come first. He didn't fight

alone. He had his cousins, more at home. His father and his uncles, all willing to die for their country or their name. He was one of them, their beliefs and ideals etched into his heart from the age of four.

But hell, he thought, looking down at Grendel's big head resting on her knee, even his dog liked her.

Her breathing quickened and she opened her eyes. He wanted to smile at her, but he didn't. "What happened?" She sat up, holding one hand on her head, and placing the other on Grendel's. She looked around. "Where are we?"

"Ye fainted. It stopped raining and I thought ye needed some air so I carried ye out here to the garden."

She spread her gaze over the tangled shrubbery and long weeds covering most of the ground. Though it was spring, most of the trees were bare and gray to match the sky. Still, when she scratched her head, leaving her hair bunched in that one spot, her eyes still a bit glazed and her cheeks flushed, he thought she looked like some delicate fairy queen who'd been snatched from her glade and dropped into a harder, uglier world where she didn't belong. A world inhabited by pitiful knights on quests to prove who they are and where they belong.

"'Tis sorely neglected, I know," he said, trying to lighten the mood that made him feel wretched because he couldn't have her. He shouldn't want her. "Ravenglade belongs to Malcolm now, but he spends much of his time in Skye."

She tilted her head and set those glorious eyes on him, rattling his head a bit. He sat down on the bench beside her. Her gaze followed him.

"I feel foolish fer fainting," she said, keeping her attention on his dog. "It doesn't happen often."

She was still angry with him. He understood but he wanted her atonement.

"Good, because I was beginning to think ye had some sort of sleeping disorder that plagued ye whenever I was near."

Her scant smile pricked his heart. She'd been through much since meeting him. The absence of her mirth was his fault and he felt the weight of it. "I wish I could take ye back, lass," he told her sincerely. "But I cannot. There is too much at stake fer too many."

"And I am the sacrifice."

For the first time he hated his task. He hated men who wanted power simply to take what others had, and that innocent people had to suffer for it. "I'll let nae harm come to ye, Amelia. Not from any quarter. But this must be done. And as soon as it is, I'll return ye into the hands of yer father."

She nodded, then angled her head away from him so he couldn't see her face. "I understand."

He didn't think she did. He waited a moment and when she remained quiet, he sensed something darker, deeper troubling her.

"Luke will recover, lass. He's strong and determined."

"I...I don't know." Her voice was a stark, strangled mess that drew him, along with Grendel, up.

"Amelia?" He sat forward. "I know ye did all—"

"This is my fault." Her eyes filled to the rims with tears that sparked in him a deeper purpose. "I called to ye and the man saw me, Edmund. Lucan saved us and he may die fer it." She covered her face in her hands and wept into them. Grendel whined. "Misfortune follows me. It always has! Ye should send me back before one of ye dies!"

Had he heard her right? Aye, he quickly realized he had. He remembered her father telling him how her "ill fortune" had driven off many suitors. Hell, even traveling bards sang of it. Edmund would have laughed at the idea of such a foolish belief, but Amelia believed it and he wouldn't mock her, so he merely smiled and moved closer to her.

"Listen to me, lass," he told her gently. "Ye called out trying to help me, and my cousin, who believes he lives in the time of Arthur, did what is in his blood to do. There's no shame in this day. No shame fer ye. Only gratitude."

"Ye speak of it lightly because ye don't know everything that's happened. I almost killed my father last winter when he nearly choked to death on one of my hair pearls that broke free and fell into his soup." She wiped her eyes and sniffed but her tears kept coming. "He sat there at our family table holding his throat, turning a horrible shade of gray, choking to death before my eyes. I didn't know what to do. I couldn't move, too afraid that if I touched him he would die quicker. Sarah saved him with a hard pound on the back."

"That sounds like an accident and nothing more," he said softly and smiled at her.

"It didn't matter what anyone called it when I dropped my baby cousin three days after he was born and brought on his madness." Her tears fell heavier as the true weight of her life came upon her.

Whatever Edmund convinced himself of earlier faded with the need to hold her. He wanted to comfort her and he wouldn't be denied.

Reaching for her, he pulled her in closer and closed his arms around her.

She sobbed against his chest. "My sister has already vowed that I may never hold my future niece or nephew."

He closed his eyes, angry. "Yer sister deserves her husband."

She laughed and he pulled back to see her and discover if his ears deceived him.

"There now, that's what I wish to see, yer happiness." When her smile remained, he considered it a great accomplishment, one that he wanted to continue striving to achieve. He ran the backs of his knuckles lightly over her cheek, vanquishing her last tear. "I'm certain ye are worth more to yer father than anything he possesses."

"I would do anything fer him."

Like marry the chancellor? He didn't ask her. He understood loyalty. He admired it. He would do anything for his own father.

"Yer fortune isn't really that bad," he told her instead.

She leaned in again and blinked her gloriously huge eyes at him. Edmund wondered how long it took a man to go mad with desire.

"I wouldn't get close to me, were I ye."

"I don't fear misfortune."

"How about ceilings falling down in yer bedchamber?"

He scowled, remembering that there was another man's bedchamber waiting for her. "'Tis good fortune, Amelia. 'Tis a sign from God not to marry the chancellor."

She tilted her face up to him and stared into his eyes for a moment that made him forget what they were talking about and filled his head with thoughts of kissing her. "I thought that at first but—"

"Ssh." He touched his index finger to her lips to quiet her. "Misfortune does not follow ye, lass. If it did"—he struggled to restrain himself from tracing the tip of his finger over the soft contours of her lips, leaning in—"my heart would not feel so light when I'm with ye. But if I'm wrong and misfortune ever dares come near ye again, I'll slay it like David slew Goliath."

Her smile widened into laughter. "Ye're quite audacious to make such a claim, Edmund MacGregor. But no one has ever promised me such a thing. I will hold ye to yer word."

He looked into her eyes and wondered if he'd gone mad. He shouldn't take interest in her life. A thousand times he heard his father's voice telling him not to allow distraction to veer him off course.

"I won't let ye down."

She thanked him softly and rose from the bench to leave him. Grendel stood with her. He had to have gone mad when he took her hand and stopped her, not giving a damn about distractions for the moment. "Remain with me a wee bit longer. At least until I can prove to ye that I'm more than just a thief."

"And a liar?"

He tossed her a smirk. "Ye ferget that ye already admitted that I did not lie to ye?"

She shook her head at him and didn't move forward or back to her seat. "I said ye hadn't been completely dishonest. But ye have nothing to prove to me. After ye saved my life today, I forgave ye fer all yer crimes against me, but I may make ye pay fer them yet."

His smile widened and then faded against the glorious vision of her swathed in warm, golden light as the sun broke through the clouds. For an instant or two he fell captivated by the sight of her with her damp hair curling softly around her shoulders. "Thank ye fer yer favor. 'Tis undeserved."

"Nae." She moved closer to him and patted his hand. He looked at her and then her hand. Hell, it was difficult to keep from kissing her senseless. "Truly, what ye did fer us today merits my favor. That man would have killed us. He almost killed Lucan with his ax. Ye may be an untrustworthy outlaw, but I don't feel unsafe with ye."

Should he thank her? He sure as hell couldn't seduce her now. "I'm pleased to hear it," he said, not sure if he was or not. And what did she mean calling him untrustworthy. It stung, but he *had* lied to her. Still, he didn't like that she considered him so despicable.

"I can seek yer fergiveness fer deceiving ye, Amelia, but not fer kidnapping ye. That I had to do and would do again."

She nodded and slipped her hand free of his. "I understand."

He saw her hand coming at him and braced himself for it. Her palm against his cheek didn't sting as much as he expected. He glanced at Grendel, relieved and a bit insulted that his dog was ignoring him.

"I cannot make ye pay fer what ye've already received absolution fer," she said, "so that was fer kidnapping me and turning my world wrong side up."

Edmund brought his hand to his face and watched her leave the garden with his dog under her palm. When she disappeared inside he closed his eyes and tossed back his head.

Hell. She was trouble.

Chapter Thirteen

Ravenglade wasn't the largest castle Amelia had ever been in; at least, it didn't appear to be on the outside. The interior was another matter. When they brought Lucan inside earlier, she had neither the time nor the inclination to look around. Now, left alone with Grendel close at her heels while Edmund and Malcolm were off speaking with the Buchanan chief, Amelia took in the grandeur of Ravenglade's Great Hall and tapestry-covered walls.

A single wooden table, long enough to seat at least fifty souls, sat in the center of the Hall. The table was bare now, save for two short candle stands placed at both ends and years' worth of nicks and gouges in the wooden surface. Amelia imagined it in its earlier days, surrounded by rowdy men slamming their daggers into the wood while they told stories of bravery and menace.

An enormous wrought iron candle chandelier hung directly above the table from the ceiling, ready to illuminate the cavernous interior when the sun went down. For now, though, sunlight puddled in from ten long, tapered mullioned windows set with clear glass. She guessed Malcolm's family must be quite wealthy to be able to afford such extravagance as glass.

Oddly, there were no drafts seeping in through the walls, thanks largely to the thick, colorful tapestries covering most of the walls. The simplicity of the scenes depicted in the art only served to accentuate the exquisite craftsmanship of the stitches, the consideration of every color and hue.

"The work of m' grandmother's fingers."

Amelia spun on her heel and found Darach leaning his back against the table, watching her. She smiled.

He smiled back. This time though, Amelia noticed the spark of flint within his emerald gaze. It made the backs of her knees tickle. She looked away, unwilling to succumb to his raw allure. She pitied the ladies who crossed this one's path.

"They're beautiful," she said, turning to admire the tapestries again. "Yer grandmother is a master embroiderer."

"Mayhap." He pushed himself up to sit on the edge of the table, his bare, booted legs dangling over the side. "But she prefers to be known as a master swordswoman."

Amelia shot him a skeptical glance over her shoulder. "Does every Highlander in Skye make the same boast? Even the women?"

"They might. But none of them are as convincin' in their claim as Claire Stuart is."

"Claire Stuart, Lady Huntley"—Amelia blinked at him—"cousin to the late kings Charles and James Stuart, family to the queen, is yer grandmother?"

He nodded, then hopped to the floor and joined her in

her stroll around the Great Hall. "M' grandsire Graham Grant aided her and the great General Monck in restorin' King Charles to the throne."

"He is a patriot, like ye and the others then," Amelia said, noting the measure of pride in his voice when he spoke.

"He didna' give a flea-bitten rat's arse aboot what was best fer the country. He was in love with his woman. He still is."

Amelia stopped and turned to him. "Still?" she asked him. Did men continue to love their wives after a long marriage? Was her father still in love with her mother? She didn't think he was. She didn't want that kind of life for herself. Her dear father. She missed him. Was he worried about her?

"Aye, still." The subtle change in the quirk of his lips when he nodded revealed that this proud, prowling young beast possessed a soft, romantic core.

She had judged both Darach and Grendel too hastily.

"What of yer parents?" she asked him on the way toward the stairs to relieve Sarah of watching over Lucan's bed. "Is yer father a warrior, too?"

"Nae, he's a bard. He's penned many odes to m' mother."

Amelia smiled to herself. Darach made better sense to her now. "Their love still burns strong, as well?"

"It does."

Lord, just what kind of men did they grow in those mountains of Skye, she thought as she reached for the door to Lucan's room. These Highlanders were different from the men she met at her uncle's balls. They didn't only dress differently, they seemed stronger, bigger, and

more confident, but less arrogant. They were rough and
hard on the outside, but deeper and more intense about
what they were passionate about.

Sarah looked up from the wet rag she was twisting in
her hands and glanced at the two people entering. She
should have looked tired after having spent her entire
afternoon at the wounded Highlander's side, but her eyes
still shone like sunlit fields behind strands of ginger
waves that had come loose from her plait.

"How is he?" Amelia asked, coming toward the bed.
"Thank God, his color is returning."

"Aye." Sarah leaned over Lucan and gently dabbed the
rag over his forehead. "He's strong."

He certainly was, Amelia thought, scanning her vision
over Lucan's long, lithe form on the bed. She folded back
the blanket that was covering him and sucked in a gulp
of air so hard it gave her the hiccups. He was naked! She
tossed the cover back over him, then stepped back and
looked over the bed.

"Sarah, where is his plaid?"

"'Tis there." Her friend pointed to the wool thrown
across his hips, not fully concealing his loins. "I had to
undrape most of him to make certain he was not cut anywhere else."

Amelia glanced at her beneath her lashes. "And was he?"

Her friend shook her head and then shot Darach a dark
look when he smiled. "Come over here and have a look
under them covers. Ye won't be smilin' long after that."

"I've seen gruesome gashes before, woman," Darach
informed her.

"I wasn't speakin' of his wound."

Amelia smiled into her hand and looked down to find

that Lucan had opened his eyes and was aiming a soft, intoxicatingly sweet smile at Sarah.

Her friend turned away from Darach in time to catch Lucan's appraisal. "Welcome back," Sarah greeted softly. "Ye had us worried."

"Fergive me," he whispered, his throat hoarse. He turned to grant his smile on Amelia next. His extraordinary eyes burned with residue from his fever, or anticipated dread to the reply of his next question. "Have my cousins minded themselves with ye both while I was away?"

"If they hadn't," Amelia told him with a wink, "they would be lying beside ye in that bed."

"'Tis aboot time ye opened yer eyes." Darach moseyed to the bed and sat at its edge. "I was beginnin' to think yer mettle wasna' as strong as mine."

"Och." Sarah swatted Darach with her damp cloth. "I suppose yer leg has been sliced down the middle before and ye almost bled out then?"

Amelia smiled; if anyone could give Darach a run for his coin, it was Sarah.

When Darach didn't answer her, she shooed him away. "Malcolm mentioned a cook. Go find her please and ask her to prepare something befittin' a celebration. Go on then," she added when Darach didn't move quickly enough.

They all watched him go, then Lucan's warm topaz gaze drifted back to Sarah. He licked his lips to moisten them, which prompted Sarah to pour him a cup of water. He accepted the offering and took a sip. When his hand trembled, Sarah reached for the cup before Amelia and held it to his lips.

"And Malcolm?" he asked Sarah directly once his thirst was quenched. "Has he treated ye with honor?"

Sarah stopped what she was doing and looked at Amelia first, then at Lucan. She laughed, but Amelia knew her well enough to know her humor was not sincere. When she spoke again, she proved Amelia to be correct.

"What is honor and what do I care of it?" She shrugged her shoulders and plunged her rag back into the bowl of water. "Ye needn't concern yerself with me, Mr. MacGregor. As ye just saw fer yerself, I can take care of m'self."

"I would prefer—"

He didn't get a chance to finish. "Now that I see ye're well"—Sarah abandoned the rag in the bowl, snatched up a dry cloth, and dried her hands—"I will leave ye to Amelia's care." She smiled, offered him a subtle bow befitting her station, then hurried out of the room.

Amelia looked after her, wondering what in blazes had come over her friend. This was the first time in Amelia's memory that Sarah actually ran from a handsome man. Could it be that she was losing her heart to Malcolm Grant? She would speak to her friend about it later and remind her that they could not have relationships with these men. She remembered with a regretful smile that Sarah was under no bounds. She could wed whom she wished.

She smiled at Lucan, pushing her thoughts aside. This man deserved her attention. She gave it to him, her smile wide with genuine happiness that he had recovered.

"She's correct. Worrying over everyone else will not aid in yer healing. I will prepare something fer ye later to help ye sleep."

"Ye have my gratitude," he told her. "I dinna' care fer being so helpless."

"Ye'll be up and about in no time at all," she assured him. She wanted to check his wound but she wasn't about to go under that blanket again.

"Would ye mind just adjusting yer plaid a bit so that I can have a look at yer thigh?"

He obliged and Amelia pulled back the covering again. Thankfully, everything was hidden, save fer his wound. Still, that didn't help her nerves when she touched him. Heavens, but the man was big. His thighs, dusted with black hair, were long and lean with muscle. His belly was flat and carved into small squares that rattled Amelia's nerves. However did Sarah work on him all day without being affected by his dark good looks?

"Sarah will need some protecting against Malcolm. She fancies him, but I fear he will leave her in a pool of tears and—"

"What's this?" Malcolm called from the door, about to enter with Edmund and Grendel behind him. "I give ye m' own bed to recover in and here ye are spreadin' heinous tales aboot me while restin' yer head on m' favored pillow?"

"I'd rather recover in yer barn than in yer bed," Lucan muttered.

"I could arrange it," Malcolm told him, then grinned and strode toward the bed.

Amelia watched Edmund make his way to the bed next.

Every assessment she'd made regarding the men here, and any other man in God's creation, seemed folly now. She filled her vision with Edmund, basking in the height

of him, the easy rhythm of his gait and the confidence
it exuded. He was everything she found magnificent in a
man, from the leisure of his smile and the slow, steady
gaze he spread over her to his anything-but-casual attention to her. Did he favor her? If he did, could she
resist him? She had to. For so many reasons, the most
important being her father. What would her uncle do to
him if she ruined his treaty? She couldn't think about it.
Her father would lose everything, including his wife, his
home, all his coin. It was one thing to get swept away
on silly, fanciful thoughts, but this was real. England's
enemy was holding her captive. The betrayal of caring
for him would destroy her family. And she could never
forget that because of her misfortune, it could destroy
Edmund, too.

"I never would have forgiven ye if ye left me with
nothing but him"—Edmund motioned with his shoulder
to Malcolm—"and his lazy-tongued cousin." He leaned
down and took Lucan by the shoulders. They shared a
smile. "I'm glad ye decided to stay with us."

He stepped away and made room for Grendel to rest
his massive head on the bed and stare at Lucan.

"Ye were supposed to have my back, Grendel," Lucan
told him. His voice was growing fainter. He needed to
rest.

The dog whined.

"Lucan needs to rest." Amelia shooed them all to the
door. "Ye can see him later."

She almost had them all out when Edmund stopped
and turned so quickly Amelia nearly landed in his arms.

He caught her and set her on her feet. "I don't know
about the past," he said quietly, standing over her and

looking into her eyes, "but ye've brought good fortune here, Amelia Bell."

Thankfully he didn't wait around for her to reply—since nothing at all came to her mind save to thank him and perhaps cry like a blithering fool. He left her wearing a worried smile, which prompted a grin from Lucan that was so resplendent it made her trip over the leg of a chair and crash into the table holding the bowl of water and wet rags.

Instinctively, Lucan moved to catch her and also to avoid the cooled water seeping into the mattress. He lost his balance and tumbled off the bed with a loud groan.

Fortunately, he landed on a thick plaited rug instead of a hard floor. She would need to call the men back to help her get him into the bed, but at least his stitchings hadn't come open.

Perhaps, she thought with a hopeful heart, Edmund was correct about her ill fortune.

Chapter Fourteen

W hen should we attack?"

"Who are we attacking?" Edmund asked Darach as he slipped into his seat in the Great Hall with Grendel at his feet.

"The Buchanans," Darach informed him and then looked at Malcolm, who was sitting next to him, for confirmation.

None came.

"Their burgh is but a few leagues away!" he insisted. "We could annihilate the entire clan and be back here in time to break fast."

"We spoke to William Buchanan."

"Who the hell is he?"

"The Buchanans' newest chief," Edmund told him. "His father, the previous chief, drowned in the Tay last month. William vows he knew nothing of the attack on Ravenglade and himself wants peace."

Darach laughed but there was no humor in the sound. "Of course he made such assurances, Edmund! He's the same as the rest. He doesna' want peace. They almost killed Luke! Such an offense canna' go unanswered."

"Fer now it must, Darach," Edmund told him. "Fighting between ourselves is foolish when we all have a bigger enemy out there."

"The duke didna' try to kill our cousin."

"Nae, he would only see us forbidden to practice what we believe. Right now, we should all have a common purpose and stand together."

Darach said nothing more and Edmund looked toward the entrance and wondered what the hell was taking the women so long to dress for supper. Malcolm had shown them a handful of gowns belonging to his mother and then led them to the private solar to dress. That was more than an hour ago. He'd never grown impatient to see a lass and he wondered if he should have Amelia check him for a fever.

He remembered Malcolm and Darach and blinked his gaze away from the entrance.

"What d'ye think would become of Amelia and Sarah if the four of us went to war with the Buchanans and they got their hands on them?"

"What the hell do I care what becomes of them?" Darach argued.

Malcolm finally looked up from his plate, prepared by his favorite cook. "How in blazes will ye ever be able to sing aboot duty and honor when ye dinna' possess a single strand of either?"

"Who said anythin' aboot singin', Malcolm?" Darach asked him with a murderous undercurrent deepening his voice. "Those lasses shouldna' even be here and they wouldna' be if not fer ye and Edmund."

Edmund stopped listening when he spotted the women standing beneath the entrance. Sarah saw them, smiled, then started over to the table. Amelia remained, hands folded in front of her, her gaze scanning the table, finally resting on him.

Edmund rose from his seat and went to her. Each step that brought him closer sapped him of his good senses. He didn't think she could captivate him any more than she already had, looking like a forest nymph in her nightdress and bare feet. But he was wrong. She'd chosen to wear one of Mairi MacGregor's slightly outdated corseted gowns. Edmund preferred the low neckline and dropped shoulders to the current style of mantuas and petticoats. This gown, cut from delicate coral fabric, accentuated Amelia's long waist. Her luxurious curls were pulled up and arrayed atop her head like an empress's crown. She wore no adornment on her neck. She needed nothing to add to her elegant lines and milky complexion.

"Ye look..." He paused, unable to find the right words to pay her the homage she was due. At his heels, Grendel barked as if to prompt him to speak. He obeyed. "...radiant."

"Thank ye." She accepted the arm he offered and rested her other hand on top of Grendel's head. "It smells wonderful in here."

"'Tis Henrietta's cooking. 'Tis French."

"My, no wonder the Buchanans want this place." She looked around, tilting her face to take in the high walls and carved ceiling. "Ravenglade is lovely, despite being uncared for. I can feel the medieval breath of it, and yet it fits perfectly in our era with its rugs and glass windows.

Malcolm says 'twas his father's doing. 'Tis a pity his parents left it."

"The Grants have remained at the MacGregors' sides since the first proscription. Also, Malcolm's mother is a MacGregor and extremely devoted to her heritage and to Skye."

She paused her steps and looked up at him. "Perhaps ye'll tell me about Skye and the other MacGregors after supper—in the garden?"

"Of course." He smiled. "And ye will tell me of yer affinity fer gardens."

"Gardens with statues," she corrected with an arched brow aimed at him.

They reached the table and Edmund was pleased that both Malcolm and Darach rose briefly from their chairs to welcome her. He winked at Sarah, who was already seated. She winked back.

"Oh, Darach." Amelia eyed the dessert he was bringing to his mouth. "Is that a tart?"

He nodded and much to Edmund's—and Malcolm's—shock, he broke off a piece of the pastry and handed it to her, then smiled at her when she bit into it.

"Good, aye?"

She nodded, closing her eyes with delight. Then she turned a mortified look toward Edmund. "Did I miss supper?"

"Nae," he told her. "They just like to eat dessert first."

"Etta's dessert," Darach corrected him.

Amelia nodded enthusiastically, then sat back in her chair and glanced around the Hall. "All we are missing is music."

He wanted to bask in her lovely features. He could

have stared at her all night, but hell, he wasn't one of those courtly, flowery types. Or mayhap he was. Mayhap there simply hadn't been any lasses in the past who compelled him to go soft on the inside. He wasn't sure he wanted that kind of lass around him now. He had a country to save. A country that came before all else. He would do well to remember that.

Malcolm finished off what was left in his cup and swung his arm around Sarah. "Darach plays the pipes, and we've a set in the garrison."

Darach aimed a murderous glare at his cousin and opened his mouth to protest. Amelia's plea stopped him.

"I love the pipes! Oh, play fer us later, Darach. I beg ye."

Poor lass, Edmund thought to himself, she didn't know yet what a stubborn bast—

"If ye truly want me to."

Edmund's jaw went slack for a moment at Darach's reply, but he understood it. None of them were safe around her. "No one plays the pipes as well as Darach," he complimented.

"Many have tried," Malcolm said.

"And failed," Edmund agreed.

Supper went on in much the same manner, with banter and laughter exchanged, and the men fawning over their lady guests. It didn't matter that they were kidnapped guests. The men of Camlochlin had been raised better than to treat women roughly or mercilessly. As long as Amelia and Sarah were with them, they would be treated kindly.

When supper was over, Sarah insisted on bringing a plate of Henrietta's delicacies to Lucan. With her gone, Malcolm excused himself and left the castle in search of easier pursuits, and after Edmund removed Grendel from the premises, Darach gave himself over to what Edmund knew was Darach's secret passion.

Edmund learned to play many instruments when he was a lad, but he'd never been able to master the pipes. He didn't need to when they had Darach to play the way he did. As much as he wanted to walk with Amelia alone in the garden, he knew she was enjoying the music by the tears streaming down her face.

"'Tis so haunting and beautiful." She sniffed quietly. "'Tis difficult to believe he could produce such a sound."

Edmund smiled. "Aye, he likes to play the death marches. It helps him believe he's not betraying his warrior instincts."

She smiled and clapped her hands when the tune ended, and Edmund wasn't certain—in fact, he doubted the good of his own eyes—that he saw a streak of crimson blushing Darach's cheeks. He looked around, wishing the others were there to see it. They would never believe him.

They shared another drink with Darach before Edmund rose from his chair and offered to escort Amelia outside. He wanted to be alone with her. He told himself he could resist her. He could be alone with her, even kiss her, without involving his heart. He wasn't the kind of fool who kidnapped his enemy and then fell in love with her. He made certain, walking with her to the garden, that his heart was properly guarded and remained separated from his desires.

The garden was quiet save for the sounds of a critter, finding its way in through one of the many cracks in the walls, and scurrying off into the tangle of bushes. The waning full moon cast its pale glow on an old stone fountain while deep shadows clung to gnarled trees and overgrown ivy.

"It must have been quite beautiful out here once," Amelia said softly, keeping her arm looped through his.

Edmund didn't remember Ravenglade in its grander years. By the time his father had brought him and his mother to Camlochlin, Malcolm's kin had more or less left Perth after living there for three years and Connor Grant had begun building his manor house beneath the braes of Bla Bheinn Skye for his wife and bairns.

"We used to ride here many years ago, when we were younger, me, Malcolm, Luke, and Adam, our chief's eldest son, after the Grants left it. We came fer hunting and lasses and to pretend that we were lairds of our own castle."

She smiled and moved a bit closer to him. "Ye speak as if ye are old already."

"I feel older," he said thoughtfully and covered her hand with his. "Mayhap I'm just more serious."

"About what?" she asked after a slight catch in her breath when their fingers touched.

"My duty."

"Then ye're correct," she told him, glancing up at him with the moonlight in her eyes. "Only a mature man can put away his selfish desires fer something greater than himself. Or have ye already mastered them, Mr. MacGregor?"

She was correct. He had to put away his selfish desires of being with her. He had to keep his eyes on his duty, his true passion. But looking into her eyes, he wondered if she was aware of the effect she had on him. What a successful assassin she would make had he an enemy intelligent enough to use her. She made him doubt his discipline, cast his concerns to the damn four winds, and ache to carry her to his room and kiss her out of her clothes.

He bent to her and pressed his mouth to the pulse at her temples. "Edmund, if it pleases ye, lass. And nae, I haven't learned to master them as well as I'd hoped."

She read his meaning and swept her head away, blushing. He stared at the throat she exposed to his hunger and was tempted to run his lips, his teeth, down the creamy length of it.

"Ye have a sweet nose, lass."

She met his gaze with a curl of her lips that, coupled with the beguiling curve of her of nose, nearly drove him mad with more than just desire. He wanted to spend more time with her, enjoy her company, bask in her loveliness.

"Ye have a strong nose, Edmund." Her smile widened along with his when she used his given name. "And a lovely mouth." She sighed close to his lips when he dipped closer to kiss her. "But…"

She moved away from him but remained fastened to his hand. "Tell me how I might trust a man who has already used me fer his own gain? Whether or not I understand yer duty, I prefer not to be manipulated because of it."

He slowed his steps, pausing to mull over her words. She had a valid point. He'd used her as a pawn in a dangerous chess match. He couldn't ever love her without giving up everything he believed.

His struggle with always doing the right thing was getting more difficult because of her. Hell, he was beginning to doubt what the right thing was anymore. They could all end up dead over this. Would he even care about laws and treaties if Malcolm and Luke or Darach were dead?

Aye, he did feel older than the rest. He'd put the weight of a country on his shoulders.

"There was no laughter in my life for the first four years of it," he began hesitantly. He never spoke of this to anyone. He wanted to tell her to help her understand what drove him. "When I first arrived in Camlochlin, I soaked up my childhood like dry soil after a drought. I played hard, and practiced hard, both in the list and in my grandmother Kate's library. I was accepted fully into the fold, but I felt I had more to prove because I wasn't born a MacGregor. Foolish, it might be, but sometimes I believe that doing my part in saving Scotland will prove my love and my commitment. I truly am sorry fer bringing ye into it."

She was quiet for a moment, pondering his words. Then, "Yer kin don't sound like they need proof from ye. In fact, from what I've heard of them, they sound like they would prefer it if ye lived a happy life, committed to a wife and children, not to dying young. Also"—she raised her head and looked at him—"if ye're trying to save Scotland to prove something, then ye're not doing it fer the right reasons."

When he remained quiet, she tugged his hand. "Are ye angry at my words?"

He shook his head and drew her closer. "I was wrong fer taking ye. But I don't regret it. I would keep ye here with me longer...to appease my own selfish desires."

She laughed and the sound of it was refreshing to his weary soul.

"'Tis a good thing really, that ye kidnapped me. Fer

Sarah would have come with or without me. And I would much prefer to be with her and watch over her."

"If ye remember, lass, I asked ye to come away with me and ye agreed. I wouldn't necessarily call it kidnapping." He smiled and winked at her.

She pinched his arm hard. "I am the Duke of Queensberry's niece. Ye kissed me and then smothered me with a rag and handed me over to be delivered here. How precisely is that not considered kidnapping?"

When he considered all his possible replies, none seemed worthy of her.

"Never mind it all." She grinned playfully up at him. "I will forgive ye for it all if ye promise not to harm Walter or my—"

Her words came to an abrupt halt as an arm appeared out of the bushes, followed by a big, muscular body, and took hold of her.

"Edmund!" she screamed, terrified, holding out her arms to him.

His thoughts fled, abandoning him along with doubt and hesitation. His dagger was out of his belt and hurling end over end before the bastard had time to react and hurt her. She screamed and leaped into Edmund's arms while her attacker crumpled to the ground, Edmund's dagger in his throat.

"I've got ye, lass," he whispered, lifting her to his pounding heart. "I'll let nae harm come to ye."

She smiled while he carried her back to the castle. "Edmund?"

"Aye, lass?"

"Now I trust ye."

He smiled and pulled her closer against him. Neither

of them heard the bushes rustle or the footsteps running away as the attacker's unseen companion fled in the darkness.

Edmund brought her to the solar. He sat her on the cushioned settee and covered her with a blanket when she trembled. Damn it, he thought while he started a fire in the hearth. This would not have happened if he hadn't put Grendel out while Darach played the pipes. Grendel had taken off, mayhap as far as Skye to get away from the sound. Had he been here, he would have alerted Edmund to the man waiting in the shadows. Edmund swore again. He'd done nothing but put her in danger since he took her.

He swallowed and turned to look at her.

She looked up from her silent appraisal of the flames sparking to life. "Perhaps," she told him quietly, "ye should be away from me before I get ye killed."

He blinked and then tossed her a disgruntled half smirk. "I think yer fergetting who flung his dagger and did the killing, lass. I'm a wee bit insulted that ye have so little faith in my skill."

He decided then and there that her wry smile was every bit as bonny as her sincere one.

"Truly, there isn't one among the bunch of ye who doesn't think his sword is the most deadly."

"Not as deadly as yer tongue," he countered, coming to sit beside her.

Their eyes met and they smiled at each other.

"There is nothing deadly about me, save the curse I bring to others."

He laughed softly, bending to her mouth. "I disagree, Amelia. Fer ye've brought nothing but light to me."

He cupped the delicate contour of her jaw in his hand.

He watched her with hooded, heated eyes as she parted her lips to receive him. When her body wilted against his, he coiled his arm around her waist and pulled her in closer. Her soft groan against his mouth made his body jerk as if a wet whip had been slapped across his back. The bewitching innocence of her tongue fluttering inside his mouth made every inch of him go hard as steel. He'd forgotten how damned good it felt to kiss her.

He'd been with a few other women, playful romps in the hay of his aunt's barn before he grew more serious about his love and his fight for Scotland. But none had ever tempted him to offer them anything more than pleasure. None of them enchanted him with their winsome smiles and restrained defiance—though the worst she had done was befriend a servant and fall asleep barefoot in a garden.

He pulled back slowly, reluctantly, knowing that if he continued kissing her it would only make him more desperate to carry her to the nearest bed and end any other man's claim on her. More desperate to keep her. And no matter what he felt about her, he could never do that without betraying his homeland.

Chapter Fifteen

Lucan MacGregor lay in bed and scoured his mind, trying to recall what he'd done to bring this misfortune upon him. To be in a sickbed, as helpless as a babe...He detested the thought of it so much that he couldn't finish it. How long would it take him to rise to his feet and fight for her properly?

"How badly does this pain ye?" Sarah looked up from examining his wound and poked his stitches gently.

Lucan had been sliced up a few times, both on the practice field with his uncles and cousins, and on the battlefield, upholding his name and his country. But no wound had been as serious as this one, none so deep that it grew infected. He knew it was by the red-hot pain coursing over his nerve endings. His breath faltered, and as it did, a ginger curl popped loose of her side braid and dangled over her eye.

He smiled at her. At least, he thought he did. His head still felt rather cloudy and to be honest, he wasn't sure if he was awake or dreaming. She looked like a dream working so diligently over him. She'd caught his eye from that first night in Edinburgh, when she stayed so closely by her dear friend. He'd tried to share words with her that night at the would-be celebration, but Malcolm had beaten him to it. Later, when his cousin brought her along, Luke had wanted to beat him senseless. Being attracted to her and then riding away from her forever was one thing. Having her around day in and day out to distract him and drive him mad every time she smiled at Malcolm was another thing entirely.

"Not so bad?"

He hadn't realized he'd started breathing, or that he was smiling like an imbecile now. "It feels hot."

He watched her while she returned her attention to his flesh. The span of her shoulders made him feel like a giant next to her. She would be easy to carry away . . . all the way to Skye if she asked him to take her.

She'd saved his life. She made him dream of her and dulled his pain. How was he supposed to woo her properly when he could barely sit up on his own?

It was bad enough that he couldn't save her from a bastard Buchanan waiting in the shadows, the way Edmund had saved Amelia the night before. But what made it all the more undignified was that, propped up on a silk pillow, he couldn't protect her from Malcolm.

"I think 'tis infected." She looked up and tucked her hair behind her ear. "I will have to get Amelia. She knows more about herbs than I do."

He stopped her when she turned to go, closing his fingers around her wrist. But when she turned to discover why he'd stopped her, he didn't know what the hell to say.

"Thank ye fer spending so much of yer time here."

Her eyes widened with surprise. She laughed, as if he were mad to make such a ridiculous statement. "How d'ye know how much time I spend here? Ye've been asleep fer most of those hours."

"But I know when ye're here."

Her laughter faded and she finally met his gaze head-on. "Ye do?"

He nodded. Damnation, this was the perfect moment to move closer to her. But he couldn't. "Ye wear a scent about ye of peat and morning dew. It makes me think of home. And of ye. I've dreamed of ye twice now." He looked away, not wanting to embarrass her when he quirked his mouth, remembering the images that were fired into his thoughts. "I'm grateful," he continued, capturing her gaze again, "fer yer attention."

She didn't blush like others might, but paled until her eyes shimmered in a dozen different shades of green.

"That isn't something ye need to thank me fer, Lucan. 'Tis m' duty."

"Why? Ye're not a servant here."

"It matters not." Her spine stiffened and she freed her wrist with a gentle tug. "I do it because I should, and fer no other reason."

"I see." He nodded. "Such dedication to yer duty is even more commendable."

She opened her mouth to say something but the door burst open and Malcolm, slayer of hearts, pestilence to purity, entered, all smiles and carefree abandon.

"Good day, Luke, 'tis pleasin' to see ye up and—" He narrowed his eyes and rethought his next description. "Ye dinna' look all that well in truth."

Lucan cut him a sharp smile, or he may have frowned.

He wasn't certain. The chambers didn't look so clear either, and hell, but when had it gotten so hot in here?

"Yer insults have no effect on me, Cal. Someday ye'll understand that 'tis what's inside of a man that makes him a man, not his appearance."

"And someday, Luke, m' courtly brother, ye'll understand that 'tis what a man conceals beneath his plaid and his skill at usin' it that makes him a man. Now dinna' vex me. I've had to withstand the company of eleven Drummonds this morn when they came to collect the dead fer the Buchanans. I've already warned Will Buchanan that if we are attacked again, the only peace his people will know is what is carved into their chief's headstone." He moved closer to the bed and touched his knuckles to Lucan's cheek. "When are ye goin' to— Hell, ye're burnin' up."

He turned to Sarah. "Where's Amelia?"

"Malcolm, don't shout at her," Lucan warned. Damn him for not being able to do more than that.

"She was in the garden this mornin'," Sarah's soothing voice flirted about his ears.

"I'll get her," Malcolm said. "Ye stay here with him."

Kind of his cousin for suggesting she stay, Lucan thought, drifting off. He would have to thank him later. "Sarah."

"Aye?"

"If I had legs I would kiss ye, lass. I'd make ye ferget him and anyone else." He closed his eyes, happy to be dreaming about her again.

She smiled and coiled her arms around his neck as he floated toward the ceiling. "Prove it," she teased, parting her lips.

He did, closing his arms around her, pressing her closer to his hot body. Hers was even hotter. Their tongues became flames that ignited passions yet unleashed for them both and consumed them in fire.

Scorching fire.

And then he stopped dreaming and clung, alone in the fiery darkness, to sanity.

Amelia spread the cooled cloth over Lucan's forehead in an effort to lower his fever. She'd done everything she could with the herbs at hand and with what she knew, but it was as if a fire raged within him. They reopened the wound and Sarah restitched it. Malcolm contemplated riding to Skye and fetching Lucan's mother, Isobel. According to Darach, she knew how to heal any affliction. But the men doubted they could get to her and bring her back in time to make a difference.

"As soon as he is well," Sarah said, more confident, or perhaps... more hopeful than anyone else in room, "I'm goin' to ask Malcolm to bring one of the gels in from the village to look after him."

Amelia looked up. "Why?"

Sarah took in the sight of him, the size of him lying in the bed, and her breath appeared to have been seized. "He makes me uneasy." She spoke so low Amelia almost didn't hear her.

But Amelia did, and she couldn't believe her ears. "How does he make ye uneasy? He's as helpless as a pup." She eyed the spot before the hearth where Grendel usually lay. He still hadn't returned to Ravenglade and Amelia was beginning to worry about him.

"Och, but he's not so helpless," Sarah whispered, star-

ing at him and sounding more defenseless than Amelia
had ever heard her sound.

"Whatever did he do?" Amelia went to her and took
her by the hands. "Edmund told me that Lucan would
never do anything dishonorable. He's been raised on tales
of chivalry and—"

"He's just so kind to me!" Sarah blurted.

"What in blazes is wrong with that?" Amelia frowned
at her, utterly confounded by this jittery, irrational side of
her best friend. "Here is a man who finally shows ye some
respect and it makes ye uneasy? Really, Sarah, I don't understand."

"Nor do I." Sarah stepped away, and out of Amelia's
hands. "But he makes me uneasy all the same. I would
prefer not to attend him anymore."

Amelia didn't realize why, but she felt like weeping
at Sarah's announcement. She almost reached out to stop
her when Sarah turned for the door, anxious to escape.

"May we speak further of this later, Sarah dearest?"

Her friend smiled before she left, and a flicker of the
flames that always shone in her eyes returned for an instant. "Of course."

Amelia stared at the door after it shut, wondering what
kind of friend she was that there was something about
Sarah Frazier that she didn't know until this moment.

She turned back to the bed and to the handsome face
as still as a mask. "Well, sir knight." She went to him and
smiled. "'Twould seem that yer influence on a lady in dis-
tress needs not the attention of yer body when yer words
are so powerful." She placed her hand atop his warm one
and patted it. "And fer yer kindness to my Sarah, I will
make certain ye live. I promise."

"And I bear witness to her vow, Luke." Edmund winked at her when she whirled on her heel at the sound of a voice behind her.

Oh, she knew what it was to fall entranced by words, a wink, a smile. To lose control over yer own thoughts and desires was a frightening thing, especially when she'd just promised to save someone's life. She couldn't let Edmund distract her, and there was only one way to stop it. If he intended on spending so much time with her as he had been, Amelia would have to make certain that time was spent keeping busy. "Will ye help me do it? Help me save him?"

"Tell me what to do."

"His body requires constant care. We must keep his fever down by preparing and feeding him special medicinal teas and keeping him cool with rags and baths. We must make absolutely certain that no part of the infection returns. To do that, we will need to keep the wound clean and dry. He'll need ointments applied and if he wakes with terrors at night, he must be kept calm and still."

"Let's begin then." The confidence in his tone and the set of his jaw made her smile.

Two hours later, they enlisted the help of Darach and Malcolm to stay with Lucan for a short time while they took their first rest from their toil. They left the sickroom and strolled the corridors, admiring the artwork along the walls. They stopped beneath paintings of some of the Stuarts and Grants in their family's history. There was a portrait of Admiral Connor Stuart, his stance straight and immovable.

A few smaller, but not by much, portraits lined one particular corridor leading to the master bedroom. Amelia saw the resemblance in Admiral Stuart and his sister, the infamous sword-wielding Claire. She was gloriously beautiful with pale, wheaten hair and the stature of a queen.

"I think poor Sarah is losing her heart to Lucan and she doesn't know what to do about it," she shared with Edmund while he pointed out Malcolm's parents on the wall. My, but they were handsome. Malcolm was a blend of both of them, with his mother's dark hair and his father's deep dimples. "That is why she has spent so many hours with him."

"I'm almost certain Lucan is suffering the same malady," he confided, escorting her back to the room. "I wish it weren't so."

"Why?" she asked, stopping to look at him. "Is it because of her station?" She couldn't imagine that it mattered to Edmund, but did it matter to Lucan?

"Nae, 'tis because of Malcolm."

"I don't think she cares for Malcolm," Amelia told him. "Sarah is…" She paused, trying to think of the kindest way to say it. "She is… not concerned with love. She enjoys the company of men but…"

Edmund smiled. "I know what ye're trying to say. I don't think Luke cares about her past."

"But I think Sarah does."

They reached the room and Edmund held open the door.

"What should we do?"

"Nothing," he said above her ear as she entered.

"I speak of after he recovers, of course."

"Even then, nothing."

She formed a word with her lips and then decided

against speaking it. "Ye're correct," she admitted after their helpers left the room. "We will be leaving yer company soon enough. No point in everyone getting attached."

She thought she might have heard Edmund swear, or perhaps chuckle, behind her.

"I think 'tis too late fer not forming attachments." He moved up behind her and swept her hair over her shoulder, exposing her nape. "Grendel likes ye." He kissed her once, twice.

She stepped away. "I think the beast loves me." She laughed over her shoulder at him. But her laughter faded all too quickly. What about the beast who kidnapped her? Was he growing attached to her? He certainly kissed her like he was. And she didn't mind his kisses. But she was a fool to think there could ever be anything between them. If her uncle didn't kill him, he would likely kill her uncle. She had to do something to stop it all. Even if she did and everyone lived, Edmund would ride back to his beloved Highlands and she...she would be returned to a life she didn't want. She didn't want to marry Walter. She didn't want to leave Sarah behind. No matter how she looked at it, her future appeared bleak. This may be her last opportunity to ever experience passion. Why should she deny herself? Still, it frightened her to think of what she was capable of feeling for Edmund MacGregor.

When he moved after her, she picked up Lucan's bowl of herbal water and shoved it against Edmund's chest, splashing water on him.

"We need fresh water."

His slow smile warned her that a simple bronze bowl between them wouldn't stop him.

"Thank ye, Edmund." She stared up at him, her smile slight but obviously still possessing enough power to bend him to her will and whim.

"Aye, lady," he relented with a chuckle. "Anything fer my cousin."

What about for her? Would he give up his fight for Scotland for her? Did she have any right to ask him to?

Chapter Sixteen

Ennis Buchanan, fifth cousin removed from the notorious James Buchanan, who once held court over Ravenglade and almost single-handedly ended the Stuart reign, trotted onward, toward Edinburgh. It didn't matter that he didn't own a horse to get him to his destination more quickly; soon he would have more gold than all his clan put together.

He laughed to himself at his good fortune. Imagine, the Duke of Queensberry's niece at Ravenglade, kidnapped by a MacGregor. Bastard outlaws. If he'd had a pistol he would have shot the miscreant who flung his dagger at poor George in Ravenglade's garden. He and George had gone to Ravenglade that night to finally kill Malcolm Grant, heir to the castle the Buchanans had wanted for so long. His clan had lost a lot of men upon Grant's return a few days ago and Ennis and George sought restitution. It wasn't difficult to get inside Ravenglade's fortified walls. Unbeknownst to the Grants, Ennis's kin had dug tunnels beneath the shallow moat, behind the castle, long ago.

His feet hurt. He'd been walking for almost two days

now. He could have made it to the city sooner, but he'd stopped to sleep and then to eat, and then for a bit of sport in the bed of a widow who had agreed to give him water as he passed through her village. He wondered what the duke would pay him for the return of his niece. He also wondered what the duke would think of his niece kissing a MacGregor. Heads were going to roll—MacGregor heads, and hopefully Malcolm Grant's.

He would be in Edinburgh tonight. By tomorrow, he'd be a rich man and holding court over Ravenglade castle. He began to sing while he strolled and looked up at the afternoon clouds. His luck couldn't get any better than this.

He heard a sound that gave his steps pause. A low deep-throated growl. He stopped singing and looked around. He saw no one and picked up his pace. Odd how the hairs on the back of his neck were standing straight up. It was as if he'd just walked over his own grave. He moved a bit faster, humming to keep his mind off the unnatural feeling of being followed. Leaves rustled to his right, nearly scaring him out of his skin.

"Who's there?"

The low-pitched growl again. It was terrifying to hear, like that of some hellhound come to exact punishment for his sins.

Ennis plucked a stick from the ground and held it up. "Come out!" he shouted in the direction of the tree line. "Before I..."

His meager threat was swept away with the breeze as something moved out of the shadows and into the sunshine. Ennis wanted to scream. What manner of beast was it? Fur as black as the devil's musings covered the enormous beast. Ennis recalled tales of wolves that were men at one time. He couldn't remember what they were called. Terror gripped him.

"What do ye want?" he shouted, holding up the stick as if to strike.

The creature settled low on its muscular haunches and skulked closer.

"Leave me alone!"

Ennis swung at the air and then turned to run for his life. He screamed as fangs sank into the back of his calf. He went down. The beast backed up and waited for him to rise up and run again. For the first time in his life, Ennis Buchanan began to cry.

Amelia opened her eyes and cringed when she straightened her neck. Sleeping in a chair for three nights was beginning to take its toll.

"Amelia, I think the fever has broken."

Her sleepy eyes widened on Edmund standing over Lucan's bed. He hadn't left her. Not for a moment. She sprang from her chair, the one placed beside its twin, where Edmund had slept when his shifts were done. When she reached the bed, Edmund smiled at her and she shared his satisfaction that they had done this thing. They had done it together.

Did she dare share his relief so soon? She looked down at the bed, and then she moved closer to it. Lucan's bedcovers were soaked. His color had returned, his breathing slowed. First she reached her fingertips to his face, then the back of her hand.

"He's cool." Her smile widened as she turned and set it on Edmund. "He will be fine."

All it took was the slant of his grin to make her leap

into his arms. He held her, his face pressed into her neck, silent with her, thanking God with her, basking in their relief. She thought that being with him under such trying conditions would have distracted her from everything she found so enticing about him. But she was wrong. Whenever she looked up and found him tending to his cousin, dedicating his time and his patience to Lucan's well-being, he grew even more attractive to her, if that was possible.

"We'll tell the others soon." He withdrew with heavy lids and the evidence of weariness thickening his voice. "Let us just take some moments alone without a dozen tasks on our minds now that 'tis over, aye?"

Amelia nodded and walked with him to the window. Dawn was just about to break over Ravenglade. She realized in that moment that Edmund had been the first thing she saw every time she opened her eyes each morning since the day they met.

She waited while he sat on the ledge of the alcoved window and took her hands to pull her in closer before she spoke. "I'm growing quite accustomed to waking up around ye, Edmund."

He arched a brow at her and swept his sultry grin over her face. "As am I to yer beautiful, slumberous eyes when ye open them."

She laughed with him, unsure of what they found humorous and not caring. His gaze narrowed and she thought he might say something. He paused, then let his eyes dip to her mouth. "Ye move yer lips when ye dream."

"I do?"

"Aye." He edged her closer between his knees. "Ye

do. Like ye're about to form a word, or blow out a candle. 'Tis most disarming. The new day beckons from the window, tempting me to gaze toward the north and the jagged landscape of my home. But I would rather look at ye."

Oh, was he so clever as to spin beautiful words around her like a web? If he wanted to capture her, he'd done it every time she watched him tending to Lucan. She didn't think about Walter or the fact that Edmund had kidnapped her, or anything at all. Those thoughts were obstacles to happiness. And she wanted to be happy. Even if it was temporary. She'd decided that this time was hers and she would enjoy it fully and with abandon.

"I don't recall my dreams," she told him softly, boldly inching toward his mouth. "But I was likely dreaming of ye. Perhaps of kissing ye." She puckered her lips the way he said she did when she slept.

He laughed softly against the seam of her mouth, then took it with more possession. Nothing Sarah had ever told her could compare with Edmund's kiss, or to the sensual flame of his tongue. He caressed her, claimed her with such exquisite care she went weak against him. The warmth of his lips, the tenderness in his hands while he tasted her, touched her face, her shoulders, her breasts, made her ache and grow wet and slick between her thighs. She knew, thanks to Sarah's instruction, that her body was readying to take him. The thought of it both terrified and made her burn to cinders. She wasn't shameless, but she had to fight the mad urge to tear away his plaid, stand him before her, and take in every inch of him before she climbed up all that muscle and begged him to drive himself into her.

Thankfully, someone knocked at the door.

Amelia broke away and was in the middle of straightening her gown and praying for her body to stop tingling when Malcolm charged into the room.

"Edmund—"

Malcolm stopped, took a better look at her, then cast her a knowing smile that made her go crimson.

"Darach's gone," he continued. "He's gone to Skye to fetch Isobel and her herbs."

"What?" Amelia asked, stunned and a little stung by the news. He'd had no faith in them. "He left? How do ye know?"

"He woke Sarah before he left and asked her to tell us after he'd gone. He didna' want to be stopped. No' that I woulda' stopped him. Nae offense to ye, lass," Malcolm offered, but the look in his eyes told her he didn't care if she understood or not, he would say what he had to say. "But Isobel MacGregor can just aboot bring the dead back to life. We dinna' want to take a risk, even the smallest one, and lose Luke."

He was correct, of course. These men loved one another. They would stop at nothing to keep the rest safe, as it should be.

"I just worry that Darach is alone," she told him in a softer voice.

"Dinna' be. Bein' alone is no' an issue fer the lad. Now"—he moved past her and the scent of Sarah's soap rushed through Amelia's nostrils—"how is he?"

"He's going to make it," Edmund told him, coming to stand beside him. "His fever broke earlier."

"Och, hell, that's good news." Malcolm sat on the edge of the bed and let his tense shoulders relax. He was silent for a while, just staring at Lucan, then he looked up at Amelia. "Ye have my gratitude, lass. I'll tell the rest of our kin of this."

"I couldn't have done it without Edmund's aid."

"Aye." Malcolm rose to his feet and took Edmund by the shoulders. "Edmund, ye're a good man. Too good to spend yer time aroond the likes of me."

"Och, hell." Edmund gave him a detestable look, then shoved him away. "Stop being a lass."

Malcolm adjusted his plaid and cast his cousin a sleek smirk. "Come to the lists and I'll show ye what a lass I am. We havena' practiced in weeks. Ye're gettin' soft."

"Give me a few hours to sleep and I'll be there," Edmund promised. "Ye need to be reminded who the better fighter is between us."

"I havena' fergotten. 'Tis Luke, but he's oot of the lists fer another se'nnight at least."

"Longer than that," Amelia told them. "And don't either of ye tempt him or lure him out of bed sooner or ye will suffer my wrath."

She knew Edmund's eyes were on her. She could feel them, alit, tender, captivated…amused. God help her, but loving an outlawed Highlander would likely send her mother to an early grave. Not to mention what it would do to her father.

A dog barked outside the window and all at once, Edmund and Amelia rushed to the ledge.

"Grendel!" Edmund shouted, elated at his friend's safe return. "Get yer arse up here!" And annoyed that the beast had worried him.

"'Tis a dog," Malcolm murmured as Edmund swept by him heading for the door.

Amelia hopped in place and stifled what would likely have sounded like a squeal when Edmund hauled back his arm and punched Malcolm in the guts, doubling him over.

"How many times do I have to tell ye? He's more than a dog to me."

Chapter Seventeen

The next two days were without a doubt the most wonderful in Amelia's life. She didn't fear or fight her attraction to Edmund. She knew deep down that she could never marry him, not while he fought against everything her family supported. Sadly, there were too many obstacles. She wouldn't lie to herself, pretending a happy ending with him. She would enjoy every moment with him before they walked away from each other when the time came.

She thought caring for him would be easy. But she'd never had genuine feelings for any man before, nor had Sarah, her teacher. She couldn't possibly know what she was getting herself into.

Amelia didn't care. There would be time enough with her mother later. Millicent Bell didn't understand passion because all she cared about was power and money. In that, she was very much like her brother. She loved her expensive statues, her servants, her jewels, more than she ever cared for her husband. Amelia would trudge through her mother's complaints about her the same way she did whenever she got caught spending her leisure time with Sarah. She did what she wanted.

Call her rebellious. She didn't care about that either.

The enjoyment she felt from spending time with Edmund was worth risking anything for. The best and most amazing thing of all, though, was that her season of misfortune seemed to have finally ended. In fact, things were beginning to go her way for the first time in her life. Her and Edmund's dedication to Lucan proved lifesaving. The giant Highlander was growing stronger every day, determined to rise out of bed as quickly as possible. She hadn't spilled hot water on herself, her patient, her helper, or the dog. Miraculous. The work she started on the garden with Sarah was coming along nicely and without a single prick to either of their bodies. She hadn't set fire to herself or anyone else, and twice she avoided tripping over her gown and tumbling down the stairs.

Who would have imagined that it would take her being kidnapped for things to start looking up? She wished Alice, her nursemaid, were here so she could rejoice with her. She could hear Alice's voice now, *I told ye yer season would end, sweeting*. Och, she missed Alice.

"D'ye realize how often ye smile?"

She looked up from trying to uproot the dead roots of a currant bush and squinted at Edmund. My, but he looked especially good all golden and dripping in sunlight. "Frowning creates deeper lines in the face."

He laughed and bent to take hold of the bush. "Ye didn't strike me as a vain woman."

"Ye should have examined me closer before ye took me," she teased, happy to be here, working under the sun with Sarah, watching him tugging at the root. He was incredibly graceful with supple, sinewy muscle rippling beneath his shirt. "I own at least one hundred gowns." She fought to master the uneven measure of her breath. Sarah would immediately sense any rapid changes. Passion was hard to conceal. "Isn't that correct, Sarah?"

"Aye," her friend agreed on the other side of a tangle of branches she was pruning. "But ye gave me more than fifty of them, so ye don't have a hundred anymore."

"Well then," Amelia said, moving on to the next dead root. "Tell Edmund of my terrible tantrums when I don't have my way. He seems to be convinced that I am some joyful cherub sent to brighten his days." She glanced up and cast him a fleeting smile she couldn't resist giving him.

Sarah thought it over, hacking away at a branch. "I don't know if stiffenin' yer spine, stompin' yer foot, and boldly defyin' yer mother and uncle could be considered terrible tantrums, but about brightenin' his day, he'd be the first to think so."

"True." Amelia stopped what she was doing and rested her hands on her lap. "Perhaps I should accept his assessment, since he is the only one who has ever made it."

"I've many more if ye care to hear them."

She turned to him and found him crouched beside her and smiling. "Many more assessments?" When he nodded, she beamed. "Aye, I'd like to hear them."

"All right." He shifted on his haunches and thought about it. "Ye're the perfect combination of innocence and mischievousness. I haven't yet concluded if ye're truly unaware of the effect of yer charms or if ye just use it all to the best of yer advantage."

"To what purpose would I use it?" she asked him, wide

eyed with surprise that he actually believed such a thing about her. "To persuade a man that I am worth the catastrophes that will befall him once he decides to court me?"

"No catastrophe has befallen me," he pointed out.

She shrugged and returned to her work. "Ye are not courting me."

"Och, fer heaven's sakes!" Sarah threw down her pruning knife and gave them both the same incredulous look. "Amelia, not only is he courtin' ye, but he kisses ye more than some married people do! And don't give me that stunned look. Everyone here, including Henrietta and Chester, the steward, knows about the two of ye. Why they—"

"What do ye mean?" Amelia threw her hands to her chest, sprinkling her bosom with soil. "What does everyone know about us?"

"That ye're both fond of each other!" Sarah shook her head with impatience. "Honestly, Amelia, I'm beginnin' to understand Edmund's confusion about yer innocence."

Amelia's mouth fell open. This couldn't be Sarah speaking. Sarah knew her better than anyone.

"At least," she retorted, angry in an instant at her best friend's words, "I'm not running away, hiding in fear, from the one man who treats me kindly. Ye're so used to being treated like an unimportant servant, even in bed, that ye don't know what to do or how to act with a man who is interested in ye fer more than just yer—"

"Amelia!"

"I'm incorrect, Sarah?" Amelia forged on, happy now to finally get this off her chest. "Edmund and I stayed with Lucan day in and day out until he recovered while ye were nowhere to be found. Ye didn't so much as ask about him! And now that he's awake, have ye visited him once? No! All ye do is trudge around here looking miserable. I told ye that Lucan asks fer ye and ye don't seem to care. And why not? Because he frightens ye. Ye're so terrified of feeling anything that ye would rather run away and be unhappy."

"Are ye quite done?" Sarah demanded. She didn't wait for Amelia to answer. "Of course I cared if he lived or died. He is a good man. Honestly, Amelia, it pierces my heart that ye would think such a heartless thing about me."

Amelia closed her eyes. She'd gone too far. She felt terrible. "Sarah, I—"

But her friend cut her off with an outstretched palm. "Please, hear what I have to say as I listened to ye. Aye, he frightens me and I don't care if Edmund knows it." She glared at him but his gaze on her remained soft. "But I'm not afraid of feelin', Amelia. I love ye, don't I? We are sisters. We've done almost everything together and shared all our hopes, our dreams, our fears with each other, but my dear, ye are not a servant. I'm quite at ease with my life. I do as I please and answer only to yer family. I'm not fool enough to believe that men like Lucan MacGregor would have anything to do with me outside of his bed. Those dreams are fer children, Amelia. They are not fer me. I would rather never love a man than give him my heart and have it torn to pieces."

Amelia swiped the tears from her eyes, repentant that she had brought up such a tender topic. "Lucan would not tear yer heart to pieces, Sarah."

"How do ye know that, Amelia? Ye don't know what he's capable of doin'. What if he takes hold of my heart and I . . ." She didn't finish but turned to leave the garden.

"Sarah," Edmund called out after her, halting her steps. "I know what he's capable of doing. If he wins yer heart, he will treat it with care and compassion."

She didn't turn to him to acknowledge what he said. She picked up her steps after another moment and left the garden.

Amelia felt awful. She wiped her hands and rose to her feet. Edmund stopped her from following after her friend. "Let her figure out what is best fer her."

"What if she doesn't know? I don't know what's best fer me. How can I trust that she knows what's best fer her?"

He pulled her into his arms and kissed her teary eyes. "She'll figure it out, lass. And so will ye."

She pushed away from him. "I don't know if I will, Edmund. I don't know what to do about Walter."

His eyes went a bit darker but he looked away and Amelia couldn't be certain. "D'ye love him, Amelia?"

"No," she admitted softly. "But that never had anything to do with it. Because of my mother's insistence that we live in Queensberry House, my poor father has had to bite his tongue while he grows deeper and deeper in debt to my uncle. He did his best trying to find good husbands for my sisters and me. Men who would add respect to my father's name. Is that so terrible?"

"Well," Edmund told her, reminding her of his last encounter with Eleanor's husband, Bedford. "When those men require dutiful wives who never give voice to their own opinions, then I would call it less than ideal. Is that what ye want fer yerself?"

"No," she assured him, twisting her skirts. He didn't understand and she didn't know how to help him. "But don't ye see? My father had very little before he wed my mother, and everything we have now, we have because of my uncle's grace."

"So ye're going to marry the chancellor because it will benefit yer father."

He sounded annoyed. But why should he be? Surely he didn't think they could stay together. They came from different worlds. He was indebted to Scotland and to his kin, giving him cause to hate her family and their allegiance to England. She was beholden to her father, dedicated to easing his life. Marrying the chancellor would replace the shame she brought to her father's name with status. Marrying a MacGregor would do the opposite. Of course, each day that she spent with Edmund made her realize more and more just how miserable she was going to be with Walter. Oh, but the day had started out so nicely. When had it gone so wrong?

"Edmund, there is no future fer us. Surely ye know that. There are too many obstacles in the way, like duty and family, and—"

"Aye, I know," he answered quietly, halting her words.

He knew. He didn't deny it then. Oh, what did she expect him to do? To say? Even if he wanted to fight for her, she couldn't destroy her father. She simply couldn't.

"And let us not forget my misfortune," she continued, more to convince herself than him. "Walter was the only man willing to overlook it."

He gave her comment the scowl it deserved. Then his gaze lowered, as did his voice. "Ye have thought of everything, then. What is there left fer us?"

What was left? Everything! Why was she saying all the wrong things today? Why were the two people she cared about forbidden? When he moved to turn away and leave her as Sarah had, she stopped him, taking hold of his arm. Forbidden had never stopped her before. She wouldn't let it now.

He turned and she looked up into his despairing gaze.

Did he care for her?

She reached her hand up to his face and watched his lids close as she touched him. "There is something between us, Edmund. It draws me to ye even when every thought in my head is shouting to keep my distance fer our hearts' sake. It tempts me to beg God that if this is a dream and I am still asleep at *David*'s feet in my uncle's garden, never let me wake. I don't want to contemplate my life. I want to live it."

She spread her thumb over his enticing mouth and inched closer toward it. "And all the pleasures of it. With ye. I know none of them and I want to learn with ye."

He pulled her in the rest of the way and covered her mouth with a hot, hungry kiss. She answered, rising up on the tips of her toes and plunging her fingers into his locks, then pulling him down to answer her passion. She felt engulfed in flames. Her nipples burned, as did the crux between her legs. Her lungs, too, so she didn't waste any breath speaking, except to say, "Take me inside."

Chapter Eighteen

They burst into the castle like a gust of torrid air. Grendel followed them toward the stairs, where they nearly mowed down Malcolm in their race to ascend.

"Luke was askin' fer ye both earlier," he called out on the way down.

"Thank ye, Malcolm, that's where we're heading," Amelia called back.

Malcolm paused and turned to look at them, his grin spreading over his handsome face. "Ye're no' goin' anywhere near his room, lass."

"Continue on yer way, Cal. We'll see ye later."

"Much later I'm hopin'," Malcolm murmured, doing what Edmund asked him to do. "Grendel!" He called out over his shoulder when he heard the door to Edmund's room shut and the mongrel whining on the outside of it. "Come to the Great Hall with me and I'll share my meal with ye."

He smiled as Grendel barreled down the stairs behind him.

* * *

Edmund looked at the woman sitting on his bed waiting for him. What was it that plagued him with the urge to smile like a fool every time he beheld her? Is this what became of a man when a lass began to chip away at his heart? Did he forgive every offense; choose not even to think on them, but rather on the indelible vision of his woman in his bed? He assumed it was by the odes Darach's father, Finn, sang to his wife.

"My heart is racing," she said, bringing her hand to her chest and looking up at him from behind long, thick locks of hair. Innocence and seduction. Her skin was pale, her eyes wide and sparkling in the candlelight.

"We can go back to the garden," he managed, moving toward her. He hoped she'd say no. He didn't want to leave the room...for a month. When she shook her head and shuddered on an anxious breath, he wondered again if she was aware of her power to seduce men just by sitting on a bed.

"Perhaps we can sit and talk for a little while?"

Did a man's heart give in to every request? "Of course," he granted, joining her on the edge of his bed. "Let me begin by asking ye a question."

"All right." She looped her arm through his and tucked one leg under the other. "What is it?"

"Why haven't there been a thousand suitors fer ye at Queensberry's door?"

"There were many, at first. But the more incidents I provoked, the fewer the visitors."

"But yer dance card was full the night we met."

She smiled, then shook her head. "No, 'twasn't. In fact, 'twas empty."

"Ah." He laughed. "A ruse well played if yer intent was to make me want to keep ye all to myself."

"No, 'twasn't that." She turned to conceal the scarlet streak spreading high across her cheekbones. "I was mortified by my empty card. Ye were the last person I wanted to tell."

He took her hand and kissed it delicately. "How could any man be unwilling to fight any foe, even misfortune, fer ye?"

"There was only one man, Edmund, 'twas Walter."

He doubted Walter would have cared if she had three eyes. Marrying her bound him to the Duke of Queensberry, who was, at the moment, one of the most powerful men in Scotland.

Edmund thought about the first time he was told of her misfortune by her father, and then again by her very own lips. He hadn't put much stock into it, not believing in such drivel. But how many times over the last few days had he saved her from catastrophe without her even knowing it? Yesterday when they were in the library, a heavy volume of *Hamlet* somehow fell from its shelf and set a course directly for her head. He managed to reach out and grab it before it struck her. Twice while they strolled Ravenglade's grounds, he veered her gently out of the path of a hornet's nest. When she nearly fell down the stairs—twice—he'd asked Henrietta to sew the hems of her gown a bit shorter to keep her from tripping over them, without her knowing, of course.

And those were only the times when she could have been hurt. He was still trying to forget how he narrowly avoided sitting on the garden mattocks she'd placed directly under him a little while ago.

"And now," he told her softly, "there is me."

She closed her eyes when he cupped her jaw in one hand and covered her mouth with his. He loved kissing her, taking his time, teasing her, biting her, tasting her, taking his fill.

"I think ye've conquered the misfortune in my life already," she groaned, drawing in a breath.

"'Tis what I do."

She giggled into his neck, then drew back to shine her smile on him full force. "Edmund, slayer of giants. Will ye stop at nothing and slay me as well?"

"I'll stop at nothing to protect ye."

Her eyes searched his, looking for something he hoped she found. "And what have I done to earn such a champion?" she whispered on parted lips.

"'Tis nothing ye've done, Amelia, and it can never be undone by ye." He bent to kiss her again. This time, she fell back on the bed, taking him along with fistfuls of his shirt in her hands.

Feeling her beneath him made him hard as steel. He wanted her, throbbed for her, and he was tempted to tear away the two flimsy layers of wool between them, spread her wide, and sink deep. The thought of it almost brought him to climax.

But she was untried and untouched. And though every nerve ending in his body burned for her, ached to be her first, he didn't want her to regret anything. She wanted to live her life and all the pleasures of it, and she would. He would help her, but that one pleasure would have to wait until he knew she truly wanted it to be with him and not just some memory to warm her while she lay in bed with her future husband.

"I fear if I take ye, I won't let anyone else ever do so." It was a statement of truth that pained him as it left his lips. He kissed her chin, the column of her neck, to redirect his thoughts.

"And I fear," she whispered into his hair as he bent his head to her throat, "that if ye take me"—she inched her thighs open wider and almost purred in his ear while she moved, a subtle shifting that pressed her crux to his hard shaft and ignited his passion into something he was no longer sure he could control—"I will never be satisfied with anyone else."

Aye, he wanted that. He wanted her to refuse the chancellor's hand, unable to marry him because of memories that plagued her. Memories of Edmund inside her, atop her, behind her, beneath her. He wanted to drive her wild, make her scream, and drench him in her desire. He smiled as he wedged his cock against her and she undulated her hips. She wanted him.

"Ye want to know pleasure, woman?"

She nodded, then laughed nervously when he began unbuttoning the front of her gown. She caught her breath when he pressed a kiss to the milky mounds of her breasts. Another button unfettered, more of her exposed, his hot tongue spreading like fire over her until her breasts spilled out into his hands. He groaned like the beast she set free and dipped his hungry mouth to her sweet coral nipple. He alternated between sucking her, laving his tongue over the small tight bud, and then grazing his teeth over it. She writhed in pleasure when he outlined her other breast with his finger. When she moaned, he tore the rest of the buttons away and kissed the flat belly he exposed.

He wanted to pleasure her but he wasn't certain he could do it without wanting her more than before. He had to stay strong. She'd already decided to go forward with her proposed marriage to the chancellor. The last thing he wanted was to lose himself to her completely... or to bring a bastard into the world. He wouldn't send her off carrying his child. He'd made sure that he'd left no babes behind after he lay with a woman. There weren't many women, but he used precautions. His true father hadn't cared about his bastard son or the lass he lay with and it had nearly cost Edmund and his mother their lives.

With that thought guiding him, he controlled his breath and his desire while he inched down her body, exposing more of her, kissing her everywhere, loving the sounds he dragged from her. He pulled her skirts up over her belly and basked for a moment in the sight of her gartered thighs and soft white hose covering her legs from the knee down. She looked like an enticing, intoxicating goddess lying there, waiting for him to continue undressing her. He did, taking his time, enjoying every inch of her.

He kissed the gooseflesh along her inner thigh. She trembled but he went farther, mindful of her short, shallow breath, of every quiver of her flesh. The scent of her so close drove him wild, but he took his time freeing her from each tied garter, rolling down her hose and plucking them from her feet.

She laughed when he kissed the top of her foot, her ankle. The slide of his fingers up the back of her bare calf made her arch her back and call out his name.

She was so lovely, so perfect. He rose up on his haunches, his cock stretching the wool of his plaid and making her large eyes even wider. He spread her legs. She closed them again.

"Lass." He smiled down at her. "Be at ease."

She nodded and at the gentle nudging of his fingers, she spread her legs wider.

When he bent to her and pressed his mouth to her warm, moist center, she cried out, then giggled and squirmed away. He laughed, watching her, but soon his intentions grew darker and this time when he moved to taste her glistening pearl he cupped her buttocks and drew her up, stopping her from moving.

He drank his fill, holding her steady, plunging his tongue inside her. Her groans grew louder, higher, until he thought Lucan would surely hear them. He didn't care. He wanted to bring her to the pinnacle of passion.

"Edmund, I can't…Don't stop. Don't stop." She gasped, then moaned, and then shuddered to her core.

He laved her engorged nub and suckled, his own blood coursing through him like the sea in the fury of a storm. He watched her lose herself, clutching fistfuls of his bed-coverings, grinding her hips into his face over and over until she collapsed, spent.

He sat back on the bed and swiped his hand across his mouth. Hell, she was irresistible lying there, out of breath, sleek with sweat. She looked at him and he smiled, satisfied with what he had done for her. Her eyes dipped to his erection jutting toward the ceiling beneath his plaid.

She reached for him, her eyes wide with apprehension. He wondered if she had ever seen a man naked before.

"'Tis all right, Amelia," he said softly, moving out of her reach. "This time was fer ye."

She nodded, smiled at him, and then closed her eyes. "I never thought anything could feel so good."

He moved along the bed to lie beside her and take her in his arms. "There are things that feel even better."

She leaned her head on his chest and wrapped her arm around him. "Sarah has always told me as much, but truly, I can't imagine anything feeling better than that. My body is still tingling."

He pushed himself down and pulled at his plaid. He wanted to show her, but it could wait.

"Thank ye, Edmund." She pressed a kiss to his chest, then snuggled closer to him, her bare breasts making it extremely difficult to rid himself of his erection.

He'd wanted to give her pleasure. He had. Why then did her gratitude feel the same as when he held the door for a woman? And why the hell did it feel so bad?

Chapter Nineteen

Sarah reached her hand out to Lucan's door for the fourth time in the space of ten breaths. Each time she retreated, not knowing what to say when she stepped inside. She had stayed away for days. What excuse could she give him? She certainly couldn't tell him the truth, that Amelia was correct about her. She was a coward. She'd always lived her life with careless abandon, never giving her heart to one man, but sharing it with many. Because she was afraid to. She was young, pretty, and unbound by the shackles of nobility. She could do as she pleased. And she did. She'd never cared what anyone at Queensberry thought of her, save Amelia.

The men who partook of her never cared what became of her afterward. She liked it that way. No attachments. No expectations. No heartache.

Malcolm Grant was the perfect man to give herself to. But she hadn't. And the reason was lying in a bed behind that damned door.

Her heart banged loudly in her ears as she reached for it again and this time the sound of Amelia crying out halted Sarah's movement. She turned, agape, and stared at the door to Edmund's room across the hall. Then she smiled.

"Well, good.fer ye, Amelia dearest. I'd love to see yer mother's face after she heard that."

She wasn't angry with her friend over the words they'd shared earlier in the garden. Sarah had been wrong to stay away from Lucan's bedside. The poor man had almost died. She intended to make up for her callousness by apologizing—no harm in doing that...if she could just open the door!

Girding up her loins one last time, she pushed on the door, then paused outside of it when it creaked open.

"Grendel?" a husky male voice called out. Damn it, but that voice plagued her dreams.

She stepped inside the room. "Do I look like a hairy, overgrown beast to ye?" She tried not to look directly at him, but her eyes had a mind of their own. And goodness, but he looked unforgettable!

It frightened her that for all of Malcolm Grant's charm and striking good looks, Lucan's was the face she thought about all day. His smile didn't beguile with dimples but with sincerity and with the kind of grace that only true beauty possessed. It didn't hurt though that his color had returned and his clean dark hair hung loose around his shoulders. Coupled with the gleam of his golden eyes, he looked more like a wolf lying there than a man.

"Sarah." He propped himself up higher on his pillow and smiled at her like nothing she could ever do could offend him. "'Tis nice to see ye."

He was not like any other man. He had touched her heart, and there was no sign of him letting up.

It was a mistake coming here. She nodded, then turned and looked at the door. Was it too late to turn and run out? Nae! She would admit to being afraid to feel anything for him but she wouldn't run away!

"How are ye feelin'?" she asked, strolling into the room and keeping a firm grip on what she was too scared to give anyone else. "Ye look fine...good...better." She wanted to bite her tongue off and then fling herself out the window for sounding like such a fool.

"I'm hoping to be out of bed in a few days."

She had only herself to blame for all the time she missed seeing him in it. She looked now, trying to take her fill in the quickest time possible. He wore a shirt or nightshirt possibly—she couldn't tell with half of him beneath the covers—but his covering did nothing to thwart the breadth of his shoulders. She remembered tending to his wound, removing his plaid to the vision of carved steel and thinking how ravishingly beautiful he was. But she'd been with beautiful men before. Lucan MacGregor was so much more than good looks. She didn't know too much about him since he'd been asleep for almost half the time she'd known him. But he'd been nothing but kind to her, and his cousins loved him very much. He'd told her that he dreamed of her. She dreamed of him, as well. She knew what he looked like in the throes of ecstasy thanks to the dreams that tormented her. He had a deep dimple in his chin that she dreamed of licking while he sank deep into her, stretching her to her limits, making her cry out with pain and with pleasure. She shook her head to clear it.

"Ye bring the sun with ye, lady."

"I am no lady, sir."

He smiled. "I am no courtly, well-bred man. I confess here and now that a few times when ye thought me asleep, I was in fact listening to ye sing while ye tended to me. I heard ye talking to yerself and to me while I drifted from this world to the next."

He heard her? What had she said? Her anger that he'd tricked her subsided in the next moment when he spoke.

"Ye captured my attention the first time I saw ye, and then my heart while ye brought me back to life."

Heaven help her, who taught this one how to put words together and strip a girl of all her defenses?

She didn't know what to do without them. "Ye embarrass me."

"Fergive me."

She thought in that moment that she could forgive him anything.

"I should go." She offered him an awkward smile, afraid that if she stayed she would never be rid of the thoughts of him naked and sweating over her...or even more dangerous, thoughts of him wooing her with flowers, pretty words, and tender kisses like the ones noble ladies whispered about at balls. "I'm verra' happy to see ye so well, Lucan."

She turned away. "Tell me," he said, stopping her. She returned her gaze to him to find him sitting up taller in the bed and folding his arms across his chest. "I feel like I havena' been fully awake with ye since we arrived. What do ye think of Ravenglade?"

"'Tis nice..." She gave the room a quick looking over. "A bit dusty."

"Aye," he agreed. "Ye would like Campbell Keep. 'Tis

more lived in. I'd like to show it to ye." He looked down at himself and then at her with a crooked grin she found irresistible. "As soon as I'm up and about."

She chose to ignore how rakishly handsome he was and give her attention to her skirts instead of him. "Ye called yerself a Campbell at Queensberry."

"My grandmother is a Campbell, as was my uncle. The keep was his."

"And is the keep now yers?"

"Aye, 'twill be when I take a wife."

She nodded but said nothing. *That* was a topic she didn't want to continue. She decided it best to shift it now.

"May I ask ye something?"

"Of course."

She turned back to him and even moved closer to the bed, to him. In all her days she'd never found it so difficult to speak to a man. She gritted her teeth and pressed onward, refusing to be rendered mute or witless by anyone.

"Why are ye bein' so kind to me yet again? I practically let ye die! Why, if it weren't fer Amelia and Edmund tending to ye day in and day out, ye likely wouldn't be here right now. I didn't bring ye back to life, they did. I didn't even visit ye and here ye are treatin' me like I did nothin' wrong. Why? What have I done fer ye that I should deserve such consideration?"

For a moment he simply sat there looking at her like he didn't know her or what to say. Then he cleared his throat. "I admit that yer absence troubled me. There were even days when I grew angry with ye, but 'twas because I felt hurt. But I decided that when I did see ye again, I wouldn't waste time clinging to those feelings.

I'm baffled about what I did to keep ye away, though. I've been worried that mayhap I insulted ye in my delirium."

She mulled over a few excuses as to why she'd stayed away but they all seemed so trite and made-up—which they were. Damn it, she couldn't lie to him, and that was just another thing that was so dangerous about him. She never had problems lying to other men.

"Nae, of course ye didn't insult me. Delirious or not, I doubt ye know how to be discourteous. I just...Well, I can't...Ye...Och, fer goodness sakes, I am fond of ye."

The room was silent save for Sarah's heartbeat thudding in her ears like a booming drum. For a moment, she couldn't swallow. Her head felt a bit thick and she feared she might faint. Did she just admit that she was fond of him? Was she mad? She laughed, praying that he would laugh, too, and they could chuckle over such a ridiculous statement. "What I meant to say was...I think ye're verra'...Well, yer thoughtfulness makes me..." She finally gave up and slapped her hands against her thighs. "Yer kindness makes me uncomfortable. I know ye're probably just nice to everyone but—"

"I see."

Nae! That wasn't what she meant to say.

"Ye prefer a man like Malcolm, who will use ye fer his satisfaction and then coldly cast ye aside."

"That isn't what I meant."

The wry quirk of his mouth was both heart-wrenching and irritating. "Ye may have found it somewhat troublesome to convey, but yer meaning was clear."

"Nae, 'twasn't." She left the window and marched toward him. "A man like Malcolm will never win m' heart.

But ye make me uneasy and I am not a fool to tempt fate and lose."

Sarah could tell by the glint of steel in his smile that he didn't understand her meaning. She was glad.

"So then, I make ye uncomfortable *and* uneasy. Anything else?"

"Aye, angry!" She turned on her heel to storm out of the room. And she wasn't running. She was leaving!

"Ye make me angry, as well," he confessed, bringing her steps to a halt. "Angry that a beautiful woman like ye would settle fer a man who couldna' be bothered to look at her—to look deeper than the shape of her bosom and the curve of her hips. Though there is nothing wrong with those either."

"Then ye've looked," Sarah said, turning slowly, arching her brow at him.

"I might not be a fickle rogue"—one edge of his mouth cocked upward—"but I'm a man."

She sized him up and remembered his body while she sewed him back together. He was a man all right. She would give him that. "Ye're not a rogue. Ye're more like a knight of old. I have never known one."

"Thank ye." He shined his smile on her full force, making her a bit weak in the knees. "I was named after one."

"A knight?"

"Aye, Sir Lucan from King Arthur and his knights of the round table. Sir Lucan was Arthur's butler."

"He was a servant?" Sarah asked, delightfully surprised. When Lucan nodded, Sarah did her best to keep her heart in check. She liked everything about this man and it frightened the wits out of her.

"What if I don't want a man to look deeper?" she asked quietly.

"Then ye haven't met the right man."

She laughed. "And how will I recognize this answer to m' dreams?"

He stretched his arms out to his sides, unwittingly inviting her to fall into them. "He'll make ye smile as much out of bed as he does in it. He'll come to know what makes ye happy and then do everything in his power to give it to ye. Ye'll find his interest in things that matter to ye and his protection from the things that dishearten ye. He'll see yer faults and love ye despite them."

God help her, she could love this man. Every nerve ending in her body went ablaze with warning. Run and to hell with what anyone thought! But she took a step toward the bed, and then around it.

"I don't believe in that kind of love, Mr. MacGregor."

"Well fortunate fer ye, he'll convince ye that yer wrong."

For some mad reason, Sarah felt like laughing and grinning like a loon. Was he that cocky? She hadn't thought so. What else was he hiding from her? She wanted to find out, but not now. Now, her heart was pounding too hard, and her legs didn't feel like they could keep her up another moment. Now she needed some fresh air.

"I will be sure to keep my eyes open fer this man," she promised and turned to leave.

"He'll be right here."

Sarah's blood rushed through her veins as she closed the door behind her and leaned against it.

She knew the right thing to do would be to stay away

from him. No good could come from this. He was the nephew of Clan Chief MacGregor of Skye. That likely made him something. She was a servant. If she wanted to protect her heart she should stay away.

The door across from her opened and Edmund poked his head out. When he saw her, he smiled and hopped out of the room, closing the door behind him. "Would ye happen to know where my aunt kept her gowns?"

She pointed right, then watched him go. She looked at the door, debating for only a moment before she knocked and plunged inside.

Amelia sat propped in the bed, clutching Mairi Grant's torn gown together at her chest. When she saw Sarah, her mortification subsided.

"I would speak with ye when ye're done," Sarah told her.

Amelia smiled—rather, she appeared to be bubbling over. "I would speak to ye as well."

Sarah went to the bed and kissed Amelia's cheek as she had almost every night since they were children. "I will be the one needin' advice on affairs of the heart this time, sister."

"Oh, Sarah." Amelia offered her most tender smile. "What do I know of love?"

Sarah smiled and then shrugged her shoulders on her way out of the room. "Then mayhap we will teach each other." She stopped at the door and turned to look at her dearest friend once again. "Lord knows 'tis a sentiment sorely lackin' in our lives. Mayhap 'tis time fer change."

Chapter Twenty

Darach hadn't gotten far when his trip to Skye was abruptly ended with the appearance of ten horsemen blocking the road.

Buchanans.

He could take them all, slovenly, unfit bastards that they were. But it would slow him up and he needed to get home and fetch Isobel.

"We have an agreement of peace with yer chief," he called out. "Let me pass before I kill every last one of ye."

Someone laughed at his claim, provoking a tight smile to curl Darach's mouth.

"Some of us dinna' want peace. We want blood and we want what belongs to us. Ravenglade!"

"Well, lads, I want three women in m' bed each night and I'd like to help in riddin' Scotland of Buchanans once and fer all, but we dinna' all get what we want."

He dragged his claymore free of its scabbard and readied himself for a fight. None came. Some heinous coward knocked him out and off his horse before he had time to swing.

Hours, or mayhap days, later, Darach cracked his swollen lids open a hair to see where he was. The searing hot pain in his face and his side helped him remember.

Lying prostrate on the ground, he moved, or tried to, and groaned as the pain of his wounds overwhelmed him.

There had to have been more than ten.

His ribs were broken, hard to tell how many. His nose, as well, for he could barely breathe through it. His eyes were nearly swollen shut, but he managed to discern that he was in some kind of barn. The only source of light came through cracks in the doors and walls. It wasn't much and Darach was grateful. Even with his broken nose, the stench of the barn threatened to overtake him.

To hell with peace. This meant war and Darach meant to see it come about even if he had to bring it himself. He tried to move again, just an inch at a time, toward the wooden doors and fresh air. Pain lanced through every inch of his body and he fought with every ounce of strength he possessed not to pass out.

The doors opened and sunshine spilled inside, momentarily blinding Darach. He was correct about the barn, unfortunately. Flies buzzed everywhere, searching out the dozens of mounds of manure left to decay in the dark. Or was it the carcass of whatever the hell died in here that they were looking for?

Someone stepped inside. Darach tried to sit up and realized that his ankles were secured to the stall. He reached, instead, for the handle of some kind of tool lying in the moldy hay and closed his fingers around it.

"Ah, the poet's son," said a male voice from the entrance.

Truly? Darach thought with disgust. After all the fights he'd won and all the Buchanans he'd left bleeding on the road, his distinguishing attribute was being a poet's son? This was something he was going to have to remedy soon.

"Are ye thirsty?" the voice asked.

"Fer yer blood, aye."

Laughter. Amused, mocking.

"I'll tell ye what, Grant. If ye ever gain yer feet again in this lifetime, I'll throw down my sword and let ye take a swing."

Darach did his best to focus on the man but all he could make out was a mane of fair hair and a medium build. He coughed and thought he tasted blood.

"Ye have a deal," Darach promised. "Only dinna' throw doun yer sword. I wilna' have it said that I killed an unarmed man. Nae matter what a low-born pile of shyt he may be."

The man tossed his head back and howled with mirth. "I like yer confidence, despite it being foolish. The thing that will end up killing ye, though, is not yer bravado but that ye care about what others think of ye." He moved closer to Darach and then crouched above his head. "Mayhap my being a low-born pile of shyt," he said softly while he pulled the weapon from Darach's hand, "is the reason I don't care about crushing yer skull when ye cannot even fight back."

"Or mayhap ye never want to see me fight back." Darach forced his eyes open as wide as he could. If it was his time to die, he'd wouldn't do it with his eyes closed.

The man laughed. "I dinna' want to kill ye. Scotland

is going to need young, fearless warriors like ye when we become subjugated to England."

Darach rubbed his head. "What d'ye know of the union?"

"Enough to know that we're all goin' to lose a lot more than castles we believe, rightly so or not, are ours. I've spoken with yer kin Edmund MacGregor at length about our troubles. We both believe the fighting between clans is silly and needs to end."

So this was the new chief, William Buchanan. Darach grimaced, since it hurt too much to laugh. "It seems the rest of yer kin dinna' agree, and after this, neither do I."

"Shame." The man moved to a stool and took a seat. "The ones who attacked ye have been dealt with by me. Some were sons of the men killed upon yer return. That's why they—"

"Those men lay in wait fer us to return. They deserved their deaths."

"Ye see, Will," came a voice out of the shadows. So unexpected was it that Darach almost leaped out of his chains. More surprising, it was a woman's voice. "We shoulda' just let him die."

Darach's eyes were still open, so he managed a decent look at the lass when she stepped into the light. A pale, round cherubic face eclipsed by mounds of tight golden curls that spread out like a blanket around her shoulders. How long had she been hiding there, watching him, before the chief arrived? He didn't like the fact that she wanted him dead and he was helpless at present to stop her wishes from coming to pass.

"Nonsense," William told her sternly. "The feuding

has to stop, Janet. Killing him would only keep the fighting going. And the next time ye ride out with Kevin and the rest, with trouble on yer mind, ye'll think again and return to me else I'll shackle *ye* to the stalls. I'm chief now and ye'll obey me. Understood?"

She glared at William first, then Darach, and stormed toward the doors. "I should have killed him when I had the chance."

William followed her departure with his troubled gaze and then turned back to his prisoner.

"Is she yer wife?"

"My sister. Her betrothed was among those killed at Ravenglade."

"My cousin…" Darach suddenly remembered Lucan and his reason for riding to Skye. He tried to sit up. "I have to get home. If Luke dies, I vow, I'll return here and kill all of ye."

William watched him struggle to rise and then sink back to the floor. "Ye're in no condition to travel, Grant. I can't let ye leave until ye're healed up anyway. Dinna' want yer cousins coming here to lop off our heads." He rose to his feet and headed for the doors. "I hope yer cousin lives, but men die in battle. 'Tis why it should end."

He stepped out into the light and closed the doors behind him, enveloping Darach in darkness once again.

Darach wasted no time. He felt around on the ground behind his head for the weapon. He found it and, grimacing with pain, swept it close to his side. He should have realized before that he didn't have the strength to swing it over his head. He needed to escape. He needed to recover a bit in order to do that. But he would. And then he was going to kill every last one of them.

He would begin with William.

Amelia squealed with laughter, passed Sarah, and burst into Lucan's room with Edmund and Grendel hot on her heels. Once inside, she realized her error in trapping herself within four walls. Her gaze darted about and laughter bubbled up to the surface.

"Ah, she flees to the knight fer aid." Edmund stopped beneath the doorway, a bit out of breath from the chase she had led him on. Grendel showed less reserve when he broke past his master's legs and leaped for her.

She squeaked, perking Grendel's ears, and twirled out of his path to the window.

It took a single, softly spoken command from Edmund to halt the dog's advance and resume his authority.

"But yer champion is abed, lass."

His deep, harmonic voice stopped her, too. She turned. Her eyes skittered to Lucan. She smiled when he winked at her and then turned to her pursuer.

"Even if he wasn't," Edmund continued, moving slowly toward her. "He wouldn't stop me from what I mean to do. Would ye, Luke?"

"Nae, brother. I wouldna' stop ye."

Amelia cut him a wounded look, knowing it would aid her to tug on Lucan's principles, but his eyes were already off her and on Sarah, who was entering the room with a stack of towels.

Everything happened so quickly just after Amelia turned her eyes toward her best friend that she knew if she replayed it all over in her mind for the next year, she wouldn't be able to tell the exact moment when misfortune found where she'd been hiding.

She'd already begun her step backward when Lucan vowed not to aid her. She looked toward Sarah, not for aid, but support, as one lass to another.

"Don't move, Amelia!"

As fate, horrible witch that she was, would have it, it wasn't Edmund's voice, but Sarah's that issued the command. Had it been Edmund's, Amelia was certain she would have obeyed.

Her arse hit the window ledge, or what she later found out was Lucan's bedpan. She knew she'd done something terrible when Sarah covered her mouth as the apparatus fell out the window. She knew it was the bedpan when Malcolm's voice boomed through the courtyard and everyone in the room, save her and Lucan, ran every which way.

"I'd hide were I ye," Edmund teased when she asked if he thought Malcolm would be angry with her.

She worried her lip and stepped away from the window, imagining that her victim was looking up and would see her.

"'Twas an accident." Lucan was a bit more reassuring. "If nothing else, we'll remind him of that."

"Amelia." Edmund came to her and she let him take her in his arms. "Do ye hear all that hollering, love?"

She nodded, feeling terrible for being the cause of something so vile.

"It means he's alive and the bedpan didn't kill him. It could have if it hit him at a certain angle. As irritating as he can sometimes be—"

"And that's often," Lucan interjected.

"—none of us want to see him dead. I think ye have it all wrong." He pulled back and looked into her eyes. "I think ye bring fortune to what would have otherwise brought calamity."

Amelia's heart welled up with a rush of warmth and worship so strong it nearly choked her. The only way to release it was through her eyes. She smiled through it, letting him know how he affected her. Every day she spent with him made it harder to envision a day without him, so she chose not to.

He didn't have to speak of his heart to her; she could see it in his eyes when he looked at her and in his smile when he spoke to her. He made her feel silly and sensuous and free to express both. After their first encounter in his bed a few days ago, he hadn't taken her back, but he wanted to. He told her he did.

He also told her that once he had her, he could keep her if he liked—something about a ridiculous Highland law she'd already forgotten. The true dilemma, though, was that she wanted to be with him. She wanted him to take her, to do this "claiming" he spoke about. But how could he claim her without causing ruin to her father? How could she tell her father that she would rather be the wife of an outlawed Highland patriot than to the chancellor of Scotland? She couldn't. She couldn't. Dear God, he would have seizures. Her uncle would likely bring an entire army down on the MacGregors.

Edmund broke away from her when the shouting below moved into the castle. He plucked a small chunk of soap from the table and went to the open door. "Malcolm," he called down the stairs to his cousin. "'Twas Grendel trying to look out. Apologies, brother." He tossed him the soap when Malcolm roared his way to the top of the landing. "Go wash in the river. Amelia and I were there a short while ago to clean some garments and I saw Meg Walker just arriving with her sister Mary."

The ruckus ended with a curt question and a mumbled oath about Grendel being a number of unmentionable things.

Amelia cast the dog a guilty look. He wagged his tail and saved the plaited rug from salvia falling from his jowls by lapping it up.

When he reappeared in the doorway, Edmund held his arms out at his sides. "Lady." His slow grin tempted her toward utter abandon. "Where is misfortune now?"

She moved toward him and turned briefly to Lucan as she went. "I wouldn't want ye to stop him."

Edmund took her hand and kissed it on their way out.

Chapter Twenty-One

The countryside swept past Amelia in a burst of color and the sweet spring fragrances of heather and pine. But she closed her eyes and pressed her cheek to Edmund's chest, preferring the feel of him while they thundered across the landscape on his stallion. He smelled like this place, with a trace of something else. Something she couldn't define, like wind across a loch.

"How long would ye have chased me today?"

Her cheek rose and fell with his breath and she fell like one under a spell at the cadence of his husky voice reverberating in her ear.

"As long as it took to catch ye."

She chuckled and ran her fingers over his corded belly. "My answer would not have changed. I cannot wed ye."

"It would have changed after I took ye back to my bed."

She lifted her head off him and poked him in the side.

"Ye're quite arrogant about yer skills."

"Nae, but ye would never be disappointed. Still, 'tis not about that. 'Tis because once ye consent to my body, the rest of ye is mine, too, if I so wish it to be. I told ye that."

She laughed. Honestly, he couldn't truly have such barbaric notions about marriage and look the way he did, or charm her senseless the way he had from the moment she first opened her eyes on him.

"'Tis all the truth."

"According to whom?" Her laughter relaxed into a smile. She almost wished it was the truth and Edmund would decide to have her for himself. This fantasy they were living was wonderful indeed, but soon it would all come crashing in.

"According to Highland law."

She rested her head on him again and closed her eyes to think about it for a moment to make certain she had it right. According to his laws, if she let him make love to her, she might as well be consenting to marriage.

"Then as I told ye this morning before ye gave chase, I shall resist ye until ye return me to Queensberry."

He turned slowly and eyed her over his shoulder. She did her best not to laugh. "Admirable," he drawled, surprising her.

He slowed their horse to a halt, slipped out of the saddle, and reached for her. "I want ye, Amelia," he told her while she slid into his waiting arms, down his hard body. "I want to explore every delectable inch of ye and set yer nerves aflame." He kissed her face, her mouth, and breathed fire into her, confirming his promise. She went weak in his embrace and victory sparked his eyes like lightning across the night sky. "I want to teach ye how to take me." He bent her over his arm and pressed his lips to her bosom. "I want to make ye wet and hot and ready with a few strokes of my tongue and the tight head of my desire." He grazed his teeth down her throat and slipped his hand under her skirts. She was wet and hot already, groaning like a siren at the mastery of his fingers. There was little left he needed to do to make her ready. "I won't hurt ye but I intend to make ye scream often."

The velvet tone of his voice down her spine and the way he petted and played with her made her want to scream now.

"Cease!"

He stopped almost immediately, pulling back his hand and setting her upright. He didn't look angry, but his eyes seemed to be cut from steel, as did the rest of him, she thought when he stepped away from her and she looked down. "I'm trying my hardest"—he took another step back and held his fingers to his nose and closed his eyes, lost for a moment in her scent—"to continue to give a damn about yer answer."

She chased him when he walked away. "That isn't true! I don't believe fer a moment that ye would take me against my will. Or trick me into belonging to ye. Banns must be read. We would need a priest."

He shook his head. "Banns are public announcements of a forthcoming wedding at a church. Many priests won't marry MacGregors as part of the proscription. So there is no church. No mass. When we want to unite, we only need consent. There are no banns and there need not be a priest, but 'tis all very binding."

"In what era?"

"This one. On Skye."

"Skye is barbaric then."

He took her hand and whistled for Grendel and his

horse, then led them all toward a grove of giant trees beside a waterfall. Amelia gasped at the beauty and the raw power of it—and of the man beside her, the soft breeze stirring his golden waves around his face.

"Skye is barbaric..." he said, staring at the woodland scene before him, "...and beautiful. I was a wee lad when I first saw it. I thought 'twas the Eden my mother taught me about from the Holy Book. But I knew 'twasn't. 'Twas too brutal, too inhospitable." He turned to her and smiled, wrenching her heart from its place. "But I loved it there from the instant I stepped foot off the ferry."

They sat on a sun-warmed rocky ledge and watched Grendel chase a small animal around a tree stump. They laughed about getting married, both admitting that it was impossible but pleasant to imagine. They were quiet for a bit, enjoying the day, but their words, though she laughed with him at them, weighed heavily on her. She was falling in love with him. She could no longer deny it. She truly wanted the things he jested so easily about. Oh, but her father had done too much to ensure her future—his and her mother's future.

Edmund cared for her, but she knew he loved his country and his kin so much more. It frightened her to think what he would do for either. Would he kill her uncle or Walter to stop the kingdoms from uniting? If he did, what would become of her father? What would become of his kin when war was declared on the MacGregors?

"When will ye contact my uncle about my ransom?"

"I already have," he told her. "The night we took ye I penned a letter to him with my demands. Of course, I didn't tell him who we are. No need to have him send an army to Skye."

"And yer demands are?"

"Stop the Treaty of Union from being signed. Draw up something new that will protect the men and women of Scotland against the whims of kings."

Amelia shook her head. "He'll never give up the influence and power he has with the English by doing either of those things."

"Even if he thought it would cost ye yer life if he didn't?"

"I fear not."

"And the man who is fortunate enough to be yer future husband?" He looked into her eyes and Amelia knew what he would do if he bore that title.

She smiled instead of giving him an answer right away. "'Tis not fair what ye do."

"What do I do?" he asked, hooking one corner of his mouth in a soft grin.

"Ye hold other men to yer high principles. 'Tisn't fair, because none of them can measure up."

He threw back his head and laughed. She basked in the sight of him, delighted in the sound of him. She wanted to look at him, hear him, touch him, and more for the rest of her days. Back there on the road, she was tempted to let him carry her to the closest bush and have his way with her. Never, ever in her life had any man made her feel such stinging passion. She ached for the hot stroke of his tongue…there. His big, broad hands cupping her buttocks while he lifted her hips higher so that he could drink her deeper.

She had to keep a clear head. She had duties to her family, just as he did.

"I'm pleased that ye think that way of me, lass." He

grinned, scattering her thoughts. "But there are men whose standards make mine look fit fer a fool. Men who would give up their lives fer what they believe in and fer those whom they love. Men who understand that nothing is more vital to their breath than protecting what is theirs, whether it be their family, their land, their religion, or their name."

She stared at him, loving his principles because she understood them. She would do anything to keep her father safe. And hating those same principles because they would keep Edmund from her, and she, from him.

"What do ye fight to protect, Edmund?"

"All of it. Scotland is my home, Amelia. The MacGregors are my kin—I am joined to them by more than the marriage of my mother or the love of Camlochlin. I am joined to them by blood. I mentioned my brother and sister to ye already, did I not?" When she nodded, smiling, he told her about them.

"Kyle is very much like my father. In fact, he looks almost exactly like him. He's quite stealthy and secretive and is very close to Caitrina, Malcolm's sister. He wanted to come with us but I don't want him fighting in my line of vision. 'Twould distract me."

"Ye love him."

"Very much, and Nichola, too. Ye would like her. She's full of life and joy. Everyone in Camlochlin adores her."

Amelia smiled, liking that he was so close with his siblings. "What is Camlochlin?"

He closed his eyes and inhaled as if he were just transported to another place. A better place.

"'Tis home."

She smiled, seeing the love for it in his eyes when he opened them and looked at her.

"We're outlawed, lass," he reminded her. "We prefer folks don't know where we live. Skye is a big island."

"The MacGregors remind me of Sarah," she told him, looping her arm through his and resting her head on his shoulder.

He laughed. "How?"

"People aren't allowed to associate with them. They are looked down upon as if they are worth less than others. Sarah is looked at that way because she is a servant."

He kissed the top of her head. "But ye defy the rules. Ye love her and stand by her side despite yer kin's disapproval."

She closed her eyes and nodded. "Aye. I do."

"'Tisn't just the MacGregors who suffer the scorn of others unjustly. 'Tis Scotland, as well. The English don't esteem our law or our Parliament. We are our own country. We don't need to unite with those who would subjugate us."

His words made Amelia angry, not with Edmund, but with her uncle and with Walter. She didn't pay much attention to politics, but hearing Edmund's side made her wish she had learned more so that she could confront the men who were making the decisions.

She listened while Edmund told her what he believed would happen to Scotland once the union took place. The more he shared his feelings on the matter, the more she was determined to stand on Scotland's side when he returned her home.

When would that be? She didn't want to return. Oh, she didn't want to marry Walter or return to her mother's constant criticism. She did miss her father and Alice though. And how they must be worried about her.

She didn't want to think about any of it now.

She wanted to remain there with him, kissing him, being held in his arms, for the rest of the day but Grendel's barking interrupted them twice.

Finally, with a muffled oath, Edmund left the ledge and called for the dog to come. When Grendel didn't return after another moment, Edmund turned to Amelia, a bit pale, then took off toward the woods. Amelia followed, calling Grendel's name and feeling sick to her stomach when they heard him whine.

They followed the pitiful sounds until they came upon him. But Grendel wasn't alone.

"What the hell do ye mean by not coming when I called ye?" Edmund demanded as if he expected the dog to answer him.

Grendel looked at the slightly smaller blond dog beside him and then back to Edmund, giving all the answer he could.

Amelia smiled and tugged on Edmund's sleeve. "She's very bonny."

"Grendel," Edmund demanded. "Get back to the horse."

"Edmund." Amelia pulled him away. "Give him some time with her."

"Amelia, I would not. She could be diseased—"

"She looks healthy enough. Now come on with ye. Leave the poor boy to his sport." Before he could protest any further, she pulled him away.

"If my dog gets his gel, then so do I."

Amelia laughed when Edmund reached for her. She

took off running but came to an abrupt stop when she hit a wall.

She looked up into deep, dark blue eyes and a sneer that could have frightened the sun from shining. When the brute closed his beefy fingers around her wrist, Amelia's breath stopped, along with her heart.

"Where is my dog, woman?"

"Let her go, Alistair," Edmund warned in a low growl behind her.

"Or what, MacGregor?"

"Or ye'll face the same fate as the rest of yer kin when they showed up at our door. This is Malcolm's land. Ravenglade is his. Accept it and be gone."

"I'll go as soon as I get my dog. Now where is she?"

Amelia turned and aimed an apologetic look at Edmund. This was her fault. Alistair was obviously a Buchanan and his dog was likely not going to be returning to him in the next few minutes.

"Better yet, keep the dog." Alistair grinned at her, exposing two missing teeth behind his dark beard. "I'll take this wee lass instead." He turned to go, yanking her along by the wrist.

"Amelia," came Edmund's silken voice behind her. "Cover yer face." The metallic click that followed was likely no louder than the snap of a twig underfoot, but it boomed and thundered through her ear and rattled her knees.

Alistair dropped her wrist as if it were on fire. He held up his hands and turned slowly to look down the barrel of Edmund's pistol.

"There's no need fer that now, MacGregor. I've not harmed her."

"Look at her."

Alistair obeyed Edmund's command and slipped his wary gaze to her. He squeezed his eyes shut when Edmund pushed the tip of the cool metal into his temple. The pistol was locked and loaded, ready to fire.

"Remember her. Warn yer kin of her. Fer if harm befalls her at yer hands or at the hands of anyone in yer clan, I will come fer ye first. Understand, Buchanan? 'Twill be me who ends yer life."

"Aye, I understand."

Amelia looked away, taking pity on the grimy would-be kidnapper. Well, the second kidnapper actually.

"Go then." Edmund dropped his pistol to his side. "Wait around the bend fer yer dog."

He didn't have to wait long. He hadn't yet made it to the curve in the road when both dogs barreled into the clearing, then raced toward Alistair on long legs and sleek muscles.

"Grendel!" Edmund shouted to him.

Grendel stopped with a whine. He cast a last, brief glance to Alistair's dog and then returned to Edmund's side.

Alistair stopped and looked behind him at the ruckus, and seeing his dog with Grendel, he deduced where she had been while lost.

He shouted something at her that was caught on the wind and carried away before it reached Amelia's ears. Then he kicked at her, provoking Grendel to take off again. Edmund held him steady.

"'Tis my fault he's striking her. I must help her." Amelia took off toward them, leaving Edmund to watch while Alistair picked up his head and saw her coming.

His face darkened into a mask of anger. "Ye thieving bastards ruined my dog letting her mate with that mongrel." He yanked a short sword from his belt and lifted it over his head.

Amelia screamed, unsure of whether he was going to kill her or the dog.

A pistol ball stopped him in mid swing as it shot into his hand, blowing away bits of flesh from his fingers and spewing blood onto Amelia's face.

She screamed again. And then she fainted.

Chapter Twenty-Two

Amelia opened her eyes on one of the plush settees in the private solar. A low fire burned in the hearth, warming the chamber just enough to make it perfectly cozy. She snuggled deeper into her blanket. A thought struck her. How had she arrived here? She sat up, eyes wide open.

She remembered. She closed her eyes, feeling queasy again. Alistair Buchanan's blood... She touched her face. Someone had cleaned it.

Something brushed against her hand and she looked down to see Grendel sitting at her side. She remembered the female and looked around. The dog wasn't with them. Had Edmund left her there, at the waterfall? Amelia would have to go get her if he had. She swung her legs off the side of the settee when the door opened and Edmund entered the solar with Grendel's girl hot on his heels and Sarah behind them, carrying tea on a tray.

"Thank God, ye're awake," her friend cooed over her. "I was ready to skin Edmund alive with fear that he shot ye."

"I'm fine, Sarah." Amelia smiled at her, then looked down at the dog. Edmund hadn't left her.

"She followed us home," Edmund told her, coming to sit beside her. "She hasn't left my heel since we arrived. She nearly tripped me down the stairs three times. I stumbled over her in the kitchen and fell into Henrietta, almost knocking the poor woman into her oven."

Amelia covered her mouth with her hand.

"Trying to avoid stepping on her toes," Edmund continued, "I dropped the tray of tea I meant to bring ye and burned my chest. Sarah finally took pity on me."

Amelia giggled, unable to help herself. Especially when she looked at Sarah, trying to conceal her grin.

"We have to send her back."

"What? Nae!" Amelia took hold of Edmund's arm. "Please, Edmund."

"What's all this talk of we?" Sarah asked, eyeing them both with a clever little glint in her emerald eyes, a glint Amelia knew all too well. "And why do ye care if he keeps a dog ye'll never see again, Amelia?"

"Aye," Edmund agreed, next to her. "Ye're returning to Seafield. What concern is the dog to ye?"

She blinked at him, then folded her arms across her chest. She wouldn't let him blackmail her with a dog. "I believe she was mistreated with the Buchanans. Look how bony she is. There is no shine to her coat. I'll not have her go back there."

"Mayhap yer husband won't mind taking her when he takes ye," Edmund mused.

"I'm certain that fer me, he would make an exception."

"What would the chancellor do," Sarah teased, pouring Amelia's tea, "with ye *and* a dog rainin' catastrophe down on his head?"

"It could prove to be the end of him," Edmund said

with a sinuous smirk creeping across his lips. "Mayhap ye should go to him and after a month, when he's likely dead, I'll come back fer ye and ye don't have to worry about yer father's ruin."

Amelia just stared at him for a moment, then she shook her head at him when he winked at her. "What makes ye think I would want ye to come back fer me once I'm a widow and free from the promise of marriage?"

"Because I would have yer dog."

Amelia looked at Grendel's girl, her tongue hanging out of one side of her panting mouth, huge, brown eyes fastened on Edmund. Amelia had to smile. He would have her dog all right. The beast loved him already. She sighed and smiled, letting Edmund have the win, for now. "She needs a name."

"Nuisance," Edmund supplied.

"Nae."

"Miss Fortune."

Amelia cast Sarah a dark look for her suggestion.

"Pest."

"Edmund! Stop that! She adores ye and ye're sitting here hurting her feelings! How could ye?"

"I don't need another dog, Amelia. Honestly. Grendel is enough to handle."

"How about Gazardiel?" Amelia suggested, ignoring him. "'Tis the name of the angel of new beginnings."

At the mention of her new name, Gazardiel wagged her tail. Edmund cast a glance heavenward, and Sarah offered him a pitying look.

Quite pleased with herself, Amelia leaned back in the settee and waved at Lucan and Malcolm when the latter helped Lucan limp into the solar.

"What are ye doing dragging him about the castle?" Sarah scolded Malcolm as he helped Lucan to a chair. "I told ye he's not ready to be up on his feet yet."

"He's strong enough to…" Malcolm began, then stopped when Gazardiel stepped in front of him and nearly sent him sprawling to the floor. "What the hell is that?"

"She's a dog, Cal," Lucan said, reaching for her shaggy head and scratching her behind the ears.

"I can see that. What's she doing here?"

"Her name is Gazardiel," Amelia told them with a happy grin. "We can call her Gaza fer short. Edmund saved her from Alistair Buchanan and we're keeping her."

For a moment, Malcolm simply looked at them. Then, "I must ask ye, Edmund, d'ye think all this is wise? I've said nothin'. How can I? But how far will this go?"

Edmund stared at him liked he'd just sprouted a tail. "How far will what go?"

"This." He motioned to Amelia. "Enjoyin' her is one thing—"

"Cal!" Lucan growled when Amelia blushed to her roots where she sat.

"Och, hell, she knows he must let her go," Malcolm argued with his cousin. "The days are gettin' shorter. Soon we'll know if the treaty is bein' postponed or not. If it's not—"

"Malcolm," Edmund cut him off with a quiet warning.

"Think clearly, Edmund!" his cousin continued. "She's too valuable to us right now. Ye've forgotten our cause."

"Nae, I have not." Edmund stood to his feet. "Not fer a moment."

Amelia listened with a heavy heart. She knew all of

this. She'd known about Edmund's cause and his devotion to it from the start. They'd pretended, lived like they had all the time in the world. But they didn't. Neither one of them wanted to forsake their responsibilities to their families by running away from them and into each other's arms. But she'd almost done it. She'd let herself care for him, perhaps even love him. She assumed he felt the same. But he'd stayed detached. He'd kept his feelings for her separate from his purpose. It broke her heart and made her wish she had been just as strong.

The truth hit hard, making her feel ill. She had to leave before she fell to the floor in a heap of sobs.

"Ye're lettin' her keep a dog, cousin," she heard Malcolm say. "How much more will ye grant her if she asks?"

Amelia didn't want to hear his answer. Either way, it was the end for them. She wasn't prepared for the pain. She took off with Grendel close behind. God help her, she loved his dog. She escaped into the garden and sat on the stone bench, hugging Grendel. All his talk of possessing her, about having a life with her and a pair of dogs, felt so right, like everything she'd ever wanted.

It hurt too much to lose.

But she knew it had never been hers to begin with.

Chapter Twenty-Three

Edmund watched Amelia flee the Hall with Grendel and he moved to go after her. Malcolm stopped him.

"She wasn't supposed to mean somethin' to ye." Cal took him by the upper arms and fixed his level gaze on him. "I thought ye understood that, Edmund. Ye're always the levelheaded lad of the bunch. Fall fer her, and our cause is lost."

Aye, Edmund knew his cousin spoke the truth. But... Ah, hell, there were so many buts. He wanted to be with her. He couldn't stand the thought of her marrying the chancellor... or anyone else for that matter. They'd played a dangerous game, pretending like they hadn't a care, or a purpose or duty. He'd gotten so caught up in it that he had forgotten... But he couldn't forget. Scotland needed him. Malcolm was right, she was too valuable to what they needed to do.

A year ago he was prepared to do anything to stop the treaty from being enacted. Twice, he'd managed to postpone the Acts of Parliament from being signed. He was so close now, and this time, it could work. But not if he threw it all away because of his heart. She tempted him beyond reason. But how could he bring her to Skye with him and still use her as ransom? Was he willing to give up his only means of getting her uncle to listen to him? Was he willing to give up his fight?

No.

He needed to get his heart back where it belonged. She would understand. She had her own loyalties to stand by and fight for. Her father's good name was a cause he admired, but he would have rathered it if marrying the chancellor wasn't part of that cause.

"We need her."

Edmund nodded at Malcolm, clearing his head. "I know."

From the corner of his eye he saw Sarah walking up to him. He turned to look at her and wished he hadn't. Disappointment tugged at her mouth while anger fired her emerald eyes. He didn't back up when she lifted her hand and slapped him hard across the face. Nor did he deny it when she called him a heartless bastard. She pulled her arm away from Lucan when he would have stopped her from leaving.

Edmund watched her go, most likely to her friend's side.

With nothing more to say to either of his cousins, he left them, with Gaza at his heels.

He thought about Amelia as he walked Ravenglade's halls. He could grow old happily with her. And if his years were not to be long ones, waking up to her for a few more of them would be all he asked.

If she weren't the Protestant niece of his greatest enemy.

He knew enough about kidnapping to know that if he

loved her, she was no longer leverage for his side, but for her uncle's, if the duke found out.

Thank the saints it hadn't gone that far. He didn't love her.

He slowed his steps when he came to the entrance of the garden and heard Amelia crying. He didn't go to her, determined to create distance between them. He leaned against the cool stone entryway and watched her weep into Sarah's shoulder. Twice, he stilled his feet from moving. But he couldn't stop his chest from aching with her. Every part of him ached for her. What had become of him, he agonized while her sobs reached his ears. He'd stopped thinking about Scotland and begun thinking about her. All the time. He missed her smiles, her touch. He missed everything about her and he felt lost without her at his side.

God help him, he thought, closing his eyes as the truth dawned on him. He was wrong. He had gone that far.

He'd been sitting so long his arse ached. Och, but what did he care? Soon, he'd have his weight in gold. His clan wouldn't need Ravenglade. He'd have something built that was even bigger. Buchanan Hall he would call it, and he would be chief over his kin instead of his dead brother's son, William.

Ennis looked around the private quarters of the Duke of Queensberry and tapped his finger on his knee. He wondered if the duke's butler repeated the message correctly. The duke's guest knew the whereabouts of someone who might be missing among them. Ennis mulled it over in his head and frowned. Now that he thought about it, it could easily be misquoted.

Surely if the duke understood it to mean the where-abouts of his niece, he would have rushed in straightaway.

No matter, soon the duke would know and Ennis would be rewarded. He could be patient and wait all night if he had to. He'd been patient at Jane Ogilvy's, hadn't he? After that hound from hell had attacked him, he would have perished if not for Jane. She took him and nursed him back to good health. He would remember her when he came into his fortune.

He'd been laid up for so long he worried that the duke's niece had already been found. If she had, Ennis prayed that the rest of his message would hold some value. Sympathizing with a MacGregor was a crime. He wondered what kissing one would be considered.

The wide doors of the chamber opened and Ennis stood to his feet when the duke entered with a host of other men and a woman behind him. Most of the men carried weapons.

"Remain standing, if you please." The duke snapped his fingers at Ennis, then sat down behind an enormous table that seemed to swallow him up. His chest barely made it to the table surface.

"Ye claim to have news on my daughter's where-abouts?" another man, standing off to the side, asked.

"Selkirk!" The duke's voice crackled with annoyance. He glared at the other man, waiting for the latter to back down. But Selkirk continued to wait for Ennis's answer.

"Well, did ye make such a claim?"

"Millicent," the duke growled, shifting his hard gaze on the woman present, "if your husband makes another sound, I will have you both removed."

Millicent reached out her hand and grasped her husband by the wrist. "Mind your mouth and let him take care of this, John," she commanded. "I don't want to be removed and miss what this man has to say. Do you?"

He shook his head and stepped back, into the shadows.

"Now you may speak," the duke told Ennis. "Tell me everything. Leave nothing out or it will mean your head."

Ennis rubbed his hand over his throat. This wasn't going to go the way he'd planned. But mayhap, he could change that.

"The MacGregors have yer niece."

Selkirk rushed forward but was stopped by a sword blocking his path. Millicent covered her mouth and then swooned.

"Kill this fool for wasting my time." The duke pointed to Ennis, rose, and moved to leave.

"James!" Millicent called out, stopping him. "What if they do have her?"

"Do you mean like the French had her?" The duke smirked. "You were certain about it, weren't you, Millicent?"

"In my defense, brother, the note that was left—"

Queensberry held up his palm, quieting her. "We already know that Lord Dearly, Viscount of Essex, and Lord Huntley, distant cousin to the Stuart queen, have taken her."

"I don't know who Lord Dearly is, but I know Edmund MacGregor," Ennis told them, clearing up the argument and hoping to save his life. "Huntley is Malcolm Grant. His kin, the Grants, are not only related to the queen but to the MacGregors."

"They are outlaws!" Millicent wailed, then wobbled on weak knees. Instantly, two older men from their train of followers stepped forward to aid her. "No, no," she cried. "It cannot be true!"

"I saw MacGregor with my own eyes," Ennis continued, "speaking to a lass who said she was the Duke of Queensberry's niece."

"They pretended to be—"

"Obviously," the duke snarled at his brother-in-law. When he returned his attention to Ennis, beads of sweat began to form on Ennis's brow. "Where is she?"

"I want coin fer what I am to tell ye."

The duke moved toward him, stopping a hairsbreadth away. He looked Ennis over from foot to crown, and then with an expression of pure disgust, he agreed.

"Very well, tell me where they are and I will repay you richly for the information."

Ennis smiled, letting relief wash over him. "Ravenglade Castle in Perth."

The duke smiled, then headed back to his table. He waved his hand at his guards. "Give him two gold and send him on his way."

Two gold? Was that all Queensberry's niece was worth? Ennis stopped when two guardsmen escorted him to the door. "There's more. I was hoping that this extra tidbit might sweeten my pockets a wee bit more."

"We'll see."

"Yer niece," Ennis said, casting a pitiful glance at the lass's parents. "She does not appear harmed."

Her parents visibly relaxed.

"In fact, she seems quite at ease with her captors. At ease enough to kiss one of them."

Millicent threw her shaking hands to her mouth.

The duke rose out of his seat again. "Which one?"

Now was a good time, Ennis decided, to put Malcolm Grant to a fitting end. A wee fib would ensure Grant's demise, and once he was dead, he or someone from his clan could take over Ravenglade. "Malcolm Grant," Ennis lied. "But it would be in yer niece's best interest to retrieve her before she becomes a sympathizer with the outlaws."

The duke scowled at his sister when she wailed, then he turned to a slightly smaller man stepping out of the shadows.

"Queensberry," the man said, his voice gravelly, like he needed to clear it. "I don't want a sympathizer for a wife. Do something about this liar."

Ennis's complexion paled. "My lord, I would never—"

"What would you have me do, Lord Chancellor?" the duke sneered.

"Captain Pierce," the chancellor called out to the guard nearest Ennis. "See that he never speaks poorly of my wife-to-be again."

"Wait! Please, my lord—" Ennis tried, but to no avail. He was dragged into the outer courtyard and shot once in the heart.

Inside, the duke rubbed his hand over his face. "Well, we know who has her and where she is."

"Ye cannot sign the act," John Bell said, anger clearly defined in his voice.

The duke laughed at him. "And what am I to do? Denounce the treaty I've spent the last year preparing? Give up everything I've been toiling over for years because of a letter promising to kill Amelia if the union takes place?"

"They are MacGregors." John Bell argued, pleaded.

"They will think nothing of killing her. Ye have to do as they say. Please, I will be forever in yer debt."

The duke was silent for a moment. Then he said, "I've already postponed the gathering of both Parliaments. I suppose a few more weeks to go fetch the girl won't make that big of a difference."

"Let us not forget that Miss Bell was seen in the arms of a MacGregor sympathizer," the chancellor added sourly. "I do hope 'tis just a rumor."

"Whether it is or it isn't," the duke said, turning to him, "you will fulfill the promise you made to her and her father to marry her or I will personally see to it that you are removed from office before the union takes place. You do still want to be the Lord High Chancellor of England, do you not, Seafield?"

The chancellor's expression went from sour to amiable in an instant. "Of course, my lord." He bowed to all, letting his eyes linger on Millicent. "If you will excuse me."

Millicent Bell smiled at him and watched him leave, then patted the duke's hand. "We owe you much, brother. Don't we, John? Once again he covers for our daughter's indiscretions. Oh, how could she do this to us? How could she sympathize with outlaws and give herself to them?"

"This is no fault of Amelia's," her husband snapped at her. "Stop thinking of yerself fer a bloody moment, woman, will ye? We have to get her back!" He turned to the duke. "We know where she is. When can we leave?"

The duke looked at him the same way he looked at his mad son. "Have you ever fought against Highlanders? History has been made on countless occasions because of the will and determination of these barbaric zealots."

"What do ye suggest, then?"

"I don't want to make war with my own countrymen just before I put my name to a treaty that half of Scotland is against. We need a show of force, but just a show. I think once these mountain men see our numbers they will hand Amelia over without a fight."

"Then let's do it," John said.

"We need the army, and that will take a bit of time."

"Amelia may not have time," her father argued.

"John may be correct," Millicent pointed out. "What if she shames us by falling for one of her captors? I met both of these men and they were charming and quite handsome."

"Amelia isn't such a fool to throw away a life with the lord chancellor, sister," the duke said. "She may be the bringer of black clouds, but she knows better than to go against our wishes and plans for her."

John Bell felt sick to his stomach. He hadn't slept, and he'd barely eaten since the night she disappeared. His poor gel. He hadn't known if she was dead or alive. Now that he knew, now that he had hope again, he was eager to save her.

Millicent Bell stepped out into the garden and looked around. When she found who she was looking for, his back to her, she smiled and headed toward him. When she reached him, she slid her palms up over his back. She wished he had more muscle, like her beloved statues, but one couldn't be too choosy.

"There now, all will be well."

"It better be." He turned to face her and she thought how handsome he was, how lucky her ungrateful daughter was.

"All you have to do is continue to prove to John how much Amelia means to you. He's already given his consent. Don't lose it, and don't let him know that my brother is involved in this. Do you understand?"

His smile chilled her blood. "Do *you* understand?" He pinched her face between his fingers. "If your daughter makes me a fool—"

"Walter, no—"

"I will destroy all of you. Beginning with your brother."

Chapter Twenty-Four

Darach sat with his back pressed into a corner of a stall in the Buchanans' barn, his legs outstretched before him and crossed at the ankles. His bruises, and there were many—in fact, he hadn't known until this point in his life that his body could hurt as bad as it did—was healing.

Healing. The thought of it brought images of Luke to him. Was he dead? Had Darach failed him? Please God…

Each passing day of his captivity found him growing stronger. More himself. Soon, he would escape this place and kill everyone who stopped him from helping his cousin and who had caused his pain.

"Ye associate with MacGregors. Ye know that's a crime, aye? Ye could be hanged fer it. I may just turn ye in before my brother returns. Better to watch ye swing from a noose than to have to sit here keeping an eye on ye."

Darach slid his gaze to his hostess, Janet Buchanan. He would like to begin with her. Twice now he cursed the shackles that kept him out of reach of her throat. He'd never throttled a woman before, but this wildcat tempted him sorely. "I find it difficult to believe that ye were truly betrothed. Ye're bonny, but I've seen bonnier."

"I should have hit yer head harder and killed ye, rather than leave the simple task to Kevin and his pathetic friends. The sight of ye repulses me."

Darach smiled in the shadows. The effort pained him, since his lip was still swollen, sliced in two places, and likely purple. With one eye still swollen shut, he guessed he was repulsive indeed.

"There's the door, lass. I'd kick ye in the arse on the way oot, but I'm restrained."

She laughed at him. Darach had to admit the sound of it warmed his blood. "Let me fill ye in, since ye're so helpless here. One of yer MacGregor friends stole my cousin's dog and blew off his hand. Tonight, they've gone to Ravenglade to get what is theirs. They will likely kill yer lads in their sleep."

Darach forgot for a moment that he was secured by the ankles and almost sprang to his feet. Ravenglade! He realized almost instantly that his cousins could handle any number of Buchanans who came against them.

"I hope ye bid yer cousin a fittin' farewell," he told her, sinking back into the shadows. "Ye likely willna' be seein' him again."

"He'll return," she corrected just as confidently. "Mayhap with a head or two that we could hang as decoration."

"Janet!" At the sound of her brother's voice, she and Darach both turned toward the barn doors. "Why the hell did ye not tell me what the lads were planning? They'll bring war on us, ye fool! Think of it. We kill them and then the rest of them come looking for us. We won't last a se'nnight against them."

Darach agreed, and as William dragged his sister toward the exit, he cast her an icy smile when she looked over her shoulder at him.

Normally, Grendel's earsplitting bark was enough to alert Edmund to trouble, but when Gaza joined him, they woke the castle.

Edmund was the first out of bed, since sometime during the night both dogs had managed to make their way inside his room.

"What is it?" Amelia asked, terrified, from her door when she saw Edmund in the hall.

Hell, he missed her. He hadn't spent more than an hour at a time with her since his eye-opening talk with Malcolm. He was miserable.

"I don't know," Edmund told her, draping the rest of his plaid around his shoulder. "Stay here. Don't leave yer room."

She nodded, watching him bend to fit various sized daggers into his boots, pistols into his belt, and his broad claymore into its sheath.

Lucan, Malcolm, a lass Edmund had never seen before, and Sarah were all exiting their rooms. Edmund pulled the women to him and then pushed them into Amelia's room.

"Someone's inside the castle," Malcolm said, following the sounds of the barking dogs below stairs.

"Ye left the bridge doun?" Lucan asked him in disbelief.

"I dinna' recall. I was drunk and Elizabeth was eager," Malcolm told him unapologetically. "Let's no' fret aboot how they got here but take care of them now that they are."

"Luke." Edmund stopped his limping cousin. "Why don't ye stay here until—"

Lucan shoved him out of his way and dragged a very long claymore from its sheath. "Ye stay with the women if ye're going to worry like one."

Edmund watched Lucan make his way toward the stairs, then followed him down.

Malcolm was correct. Someone was inside the castle. Grendel and Gaza were gone, their incessant barking ceased. Edmund knew Grendel wasn't injured but on the hunt for his prey.

As was he. As were his brothers.

They didn't have to wait long to find what they were hunting. Not a moment passed after they separated in the foyer when a man burst through the door to the servants' quarters with a weeping Henrietta under his arm and a pistol pointed at Malcolm.

"Is this what ye keep fer long, lonely nights, Grant?"

"That's my cook, ye bastard." Malcolm's voice rolled like thunder, chilling the air as he boldly stepped toward them. "Ye'd better shoot that weapon now, Andrew Buchanan, because if I get my hands on ye—"

Andrew fired, alerting everyone to them, including the dogs, and filling the foyer with smoke.

He missed his target, who never stopped coming at him until he reached him. Malcolm slapped the gun out of Andrew's hand as he was trying desperately to load another ball. He snatched Henrietta from the culprit's arm, then grasped Andrew by the back of the throat and smashed his face into the nearest wall.

Letting Andrew crumple to the floor, he turned to make certain his dear cook wasn't harmed. From the corner of his eye he saw three more men appearing from three different directions and another group of at least twelve exiting the Great Hall.

He smiled, his sword in one hand and a dagger in the other. A fiery woman in his bed and the challenge of a good fight after that. It was a good night, indeed.

Edmund would have agreed with his closest friend's sentiments, if he hadn't just caught sight of Grendel galloping up the stairs to the top, where Amelia stood looking down in terror.

Damn it! Why hadn't she stayed in the room?

"MacGregor!" someone called from among the intruders. "I want my hand and my dog back." Alistair Buchanan stepped forward and pointed with his only hand to the yellow dog that had sat down at Edmund's feet.

Edmund looked down at Gaza and felt his heart go soft. He shook his head in frustration with himself and with the Buchanans. When were these fools going to learn? And is this what loving Amelia turned him into? A pitiful sot with a weakness for a set of huge, brown eyes on a pretty female?

"Alistair, take yer men and get out before I rid ye of yer other hand, and mayhap yer empty head."

"I want my dog!"

Alistair's gaze rose at the sound of a slight moan from the top landing. Edmund didn't blink. If Alistair moved toward her, he would die.

"Call the dog, Alistair. If she comes to ye, ye can fight me fer her. Either way, she stays with me. If 'tis a fight ye want, I'll kill ye and every one of yer friends."

The one-handed Buchanan cast an uneasy glance at his

comrades. Empty-headed or not, Alistair understood his options were few.

A loud shout rang out, echoing through the halls, saving Alistair from having to make a decision. Grendel and Gaza remained at their posts, alert, ready to attack.

"MacGregor! 'Tis William," the voice called out from somewhere inside. "William Buchanan."

Edmund exchanged a glance with Cal and Luke. "Where are ye, Buchanan? And how the hell did ye get in here?"

The young chief appeared in an entrance to the foyer, leading to the kitchen. "The bridge was down; I came in through the rear bailey."

Edmund cast Malcolm an accusatory glare for leaving the bridge down.

"Will," Edmund reasoned, "what the hell are ye doing wasting yer time with petty clan grievances when yer country is about to lose its Parliament, its independence? Ye're fighting fer a castle that will likely be taken from ye the moment this union is formed."

"I didn't come to fight," the chief said, entering the foyer slowly. "I would appreciate mercy on my kin. I will repay ye by offering them to yer cause."

Scotland didn't need men who were forced to fight. She needed men who wanted to, who understood that they needed to. "My cause and yers are the same. If ye and yer kin understood what ye could lose, ye wouldn't be so eager to fight with us."

"Then tell us."

"Look, are we goin' to fight or not?" Malcolm rested the tip of his claymore on the floor and waited impatiently on it. "I'm not givin' up a warm bed and a warmer wench fer long speeches on things *I* already know."

"There will be no fighting," William announced, then turned to rake his eyes over his men. "But if ye will wait just a moment before returning to yer pleasures, Grant, there is something I must tell ye, as a token of my good will."

Malcolm glanced up the stairs to his buxom visitor and winked.

"Yer young Mr. Grant is in our care."

Edmund's heart pounded violently in his ears. Violence was what he recognized in Malcolm's and Luke's eyes. "Darach?" he heard himself asking.

"He's alive and well, I give ye my word!" William held his palms up when Edmund and his cousins moved toward him.

"Ye're lyin'," Malcolm growled.

"Nae. Against my will, some of the lads went after him and captured him on a road leading north."

"Was he harmed?" Luke asked.

When the chief didn't answer right away, Lucan lifted his sword.

"If any one of us doesn't return, my kin have command to kill him!" William held his hand to the hilt of his blade, but he backed away. "'Twas the only way to ensure our safety."

"Verra' well," Edmund said, sheathing his blade. "We won't kill any one of ye. Ye will all return alive, but I, fer one, intend on making ye all wish ye'd never set eyes on Darach Grant."

He moved forward with Luke and Malcolm at his side and Grendel returned to his heels, and the fighting commenced.

Chapter Twenty-Five

W e should go get him now," Malcolm insisted, and then cast an irritated glare at Amelia when she pulled the cloth around his hand too tight. "Two fingers are already broken, lass. Leave the other three intact, I beg ye."

"Fergive me," she answered quietly, keeping her gaze downcast.

"That's exactly what they're expecting us to do, Cal," Lucan said while Sarah tended to cuts on his face. "This entire thing could be a trap to get us to their holding. We may have sent some of them home with broken bones, but there are many more of them in their village. If they kill us all they dinna' have to worry aboot us bringin' our kin back fer them."

Edmund watched Amelia while his cousins argued about rescuing Darach. He already knew what to do about Darach. He didn't know what to do about her. That was an enormous problem, since he should know. Stick with the plan. Return her to her uncle once the treaty was dissolved, or kill her if it wasn't. Of course he couldn't kill her and neither could any one of his cousins. They'd never killed a lass before, and they never would. He'd never thought for an instant that the duke wouldn't do everything in his power to save his niece. Whatever the outcome, Edmund would lose her.

For the last two days she'd avoided him at every turn and he'd done nothing but sulk around the castle wishing for another way to have a future with her. One way in particular continued to invade his thoughts. It was something almost blasphemous to his heart, but relentless nonetheless. If the duke refused their demands Edmund could keep Amelia. He could keep her alive with him in Skye. It was blasphemous indeed, to hope the duke and the chancellor would go ahead with the treaty. Scotland would become part of the new United Kingdom. Everything he had fought for would be lost. He hated his traitorous heart for thinking it... for hoping for it, but he didn't want to let her go. When he thought about never seeing Amelia again... Saints help him, it was worse. She tempted him to give up all for her. It scared the hell out of him and stripped him of all his defenses, but he couldn't stop it. He didn't want to.

He caught her eye and smiled at her when she looked up. She didn't smile back.

The fight with the Buchanans was too much for her.

He would have preferred Amelia never to witness him in such a merciless state. She hadn't said a word since the fight ended and Edmund and his cousins tossed the Buchanans into the moat and then led the women to the solar. Mayhap she was not suited to the Highland life. It would be a good reason to let her go.

"Edmund, what is yer suggestion?" Malcolm asked him, drawing his attention away from Amelia.

"Luke's correct. It could be a trap."

"And if they kill him in the meantime?" Malcolm put to him.

"If they truly have him, they won't kill him," Edmund assured him and then watched Amelia rise to her feet and excuse herself. His gaze followed her out of the solar with Grendel at her side. Gaza remained at his feet but watched them as well, and then looked up at Edmund. He continued speaking. "Either Darach is already dead or William told the truth and he lives. I believe William told the truth. He wouldn't have taken such a beating if he was lying. As long as Darach lives, the Buchanans are safe from us. They know it. Their chief knows it. They won't kill him. We need to recover, regroup, and have a plan. They'll be expecting us when night falls. It'll unnerve them when we don't show up."

Malcolm nodded and ran his fingers through his dark hair. He glanced over at Elizabeth, asleep on his settee. "If we're no' goin' tonight, I'll be returnin' to m' chamber." He stood, went to the settee to pick Elizabeth up, then left the solar without another word.

"If ye will both excuse me," Sarah said next. "Amelia is troubled. I want to—"

"Nae, please, let me." Edmund rose before she could reply. Sarah was still angry with him and he didn't want to argue with her.

He didn't search long. He had a feeling where she might be, but Gaza led him straight there.

He didn't enter the garden immediately. Amelia's soft cries stopped him. For a good while he remained utterly silent and brokenhearted at the sound of her weeping. What could he say to her but beg her forgiveness for dragging her here, into a world of blood and gore no noble lady would ever be accustomed to seeing? To rough, brutal men, and dreary, dead gardens.

Another reason to let her go.

But none of his logic helped. When he could no longer breathe without holding her, he pushed through the gnarled tangle of bush and took her in his arms.

"Amelia, my love," he whispered, pressing her close, stroking her hair, breathing her in like she was all the air he needed to live. "Fergive me. Fergive me, I beg ye, fer my foolishness."

She looked up at him with tears misting her eyes to a rich mahogany. Gazing into them jolted his heart from its foundations.

"Oh, Edmund, ye were not foolish about the Buchanans," she said, more beguiling to his heart because of her sincerity. "What happened to Darach is not yer fault. If I hadn't pestered ye to leave Grendel to his sport with Gaza, then Alistair Buchanan would still have his hand and his dog, and..." She sniffed and tried to pull herself together. The strength she called up made Edmund adore her even more.

"Ye think this is yer fault?" he asked her softly, angry at the lies her family fed her about her bad fortune. "Love, Darach left fer Skye long before I shot Alistair. His capture had nothing to do with Gaza. In fact, if not fer them coming to get her, we might not have ever known what became of Darach."

She wiped her nose. "I did not think of it that way."

He smiled and wiped her tears. "Ye continue to bring us good fortune, Amelia. I was speaking about how foolish I was about us."

"And I understand about that as well," she told him. "I admit when Malcolm spoke about it I was hurt, but I know we can never be together, Edmund." She held her finger to his lips when he would have spoken again. "We are not children. I must wed Walter. I cannot bring shame to my father and you cannot give up yer fight fer Scotland. We would never ask such sacrifice of each other."

He sat there. Still. She was right. But he didn't want her to be. It sickened him. He had to find a way to keep her with him. Was it even possible? They both had so much to give up.

"What would ye have me do? How am I supposed to just walk away?"

She looked up at him through glimmering eyes. "How can I answer when I ask myself the same thing?"

"I cannot."

"Ye must." They had no choice. "But I don't want to return to Walter without knowing what making love to a man who truly feels something fer me is like. So tonight," she said against his lips, unable to keep a soft sob from escaping. "Tonight, ye will claim me, Highlander. But just fer one night."

"Nae." He shook his head. "If I have ye, I'll never—"

"If ye care fer me, Edmund, don't deny me this." She took his face in her hands and brought his mouth to hers.

He didn't.

Chapter Twenty-Six

Edmund pushed open the door with his boot and carried Amelia into his room. Part of him shouted to put her down and lock her away somewhere. But his heart pushed him ahead. He didn't think of how many nights they would have together. He cared only about this one.

He felt foolish and vulnerable at the way his heart beat over her, how his blood coursed like molten fire through his veins for her. He knew stories of great men who surrendered their hearts to their women. But it had never happened to him before. Thanks to his books... and Finlay Grant's poetic tales of Camlochlin's courtly love, he'd suspected it someday would. But he wasn't prepared for the full and utter change it brought in his way of thinking.

"I don't want to let ye go, Amelia," he told her, taking her to his bed. "What can I do to convince ye that ye would be happier with me than with anyone else?"

She clung to him as he lowered her to his mattress and dragged her satiny voice across his ear. "Ye can do nothing. My heart has already convinced me."

He pressed his lips to hers and fire scorched his mouth, the pit of his belly, below his navel.

Gaza's whimper at the entry pulled him away with an oath to ride to the nearest Buchanan holding and drop her at the doorstep.

After securing that they were alone and locked away, Edmund turned, stared as if stricken, and he was, at the goddess on his bed, and then returned to her.

"My dog loves ye already," she told him, then caught her breath while he undressed on his way back to her.

His plaid fell away as he lay beside her and took her in his arms. "If she loves me, how can I return her to the chancellor?"

"Let's not speak of him now," she whispered against his mouth.

He loved kissing her. He loved the taste, the feel, the scent of her. But he wanted more. He began unlacing her gown, taking his time, savoring each moment.

"I don't know what to do…about pleasing ye." Her voice quavered against his cheek when she broke their kiss.

"Ye can practice whatever ye want on me."

He felt her smile into his neck. "I can do anything?"

"Aye." He closed his eyes as she bit down on his neck and then traced her tongue over where she bit.

"I've never seen a man's naked body before." Her breath singed his chin. "But I've dreamed of a statue cool and hard beneath my fingertips."

He took her mouth with raw demand while she ran her palms over his hard angles. He wanted to rip her gown off her body and toss his garments to the fire and sink into her as deep as he could go. But he didn't want this night to end. Not ever, so he took his time.

But spurred by her desire to be ravished, he did get her out of her gown quicker than she'd ever gotten into it.

He wrapped her in his arms and legs, plundering her mouth and growing hard against her. When she scored her fingernails down his back, he lifted his head to look into her eyes, untangled their limbs, and straddled her in one fluid motion. His heavy cock rested on her belly while he cupped her firm breasts in his palms and traced her nipples with his tongue. Her body beneath him tempted him to madness. He need only spread her wide with his knees and thrust his cock deep.

She pushed him gently away, but only to lean up and feast her eyes on him hovering over her. And feast she did. Edmund felt her gaze as if it were a brand, burning him everywhere she looked. She smiled, her lids heavy, her hair tumbling about her face like some wanton garden nymph while she ran her fingers over the ridges in his belly, down his hips, and finally over his rigid shaft. She looked up from it, her gaze dark and glittering at the same time. "Ye're crafted like him, only bigger."

He angled his hips forward, offering her more of him. With her breath quick and shallow, she took him in both hands. He groaned and dripped onto her fingers when she squeezed him.

Gripped in passion's selfish throes, he bent to her and grasped her bottom lip in his teeth. He swept his tongue into her mouth, deep and wide, and lifted his hips up off her. She didn't release him but stroked his tender shaft in her small, hot hands until flames lanced his nerves.

He covered one of her hands with his big one and

guided her over him faster, harder. The urge to slip inside her, to be encompassed in her tight sheath, was maddening, but not yet. Almost.

Almost.

"Later, I will taste ye in my mouth."

Och, hell, how did she manage to speak words that made him cast his control to the wind? How could she be so innocent and so damned sexy at the same time?

He didn't know if it was her promise, the husky tone in which she spoke it, the rhythm of their hands, or everything combined that was his undoing. Scalding fire licked through him, bubbling deep within, building pressure until his muscles trembled with ecstasy and he moaned like some beast in pain.

He guided their hands to her entrance and ground himself against her one last time before his seed erupted all over her opening. She cried out as he released her and let her move him however she willed.

She coiled her legs around him and wiggled beneath him, against him, while the last of his cum shot out in a thick stream.

He spoke into her ear, telling her how good she felt, how he wanted to dip inside her and make her quake to her center. She smiled, a slow, languid smile, and guided his tip into her. She teased him, taking an inch and then retreating, anxious about the pain he would cause. When she did it three more times, each time taking him a little deeper, he nearly released himself again.

But now it was her turn.

Kissing her hungry mouth, he pushed deeper and deeper inside her until she cried out. He quieted her by remaining still atop her, looking into her eyes. Cupping her face in his hand, he spoke quietly against her rapid breath. "I love ye, Amelia."

Her eyes filled with large glistening tears while he began to move again. Slowly, meaningfully.

"Ye weren't supposed to seize my heart, lass. But ye did."

Like the first night they danced, he made love to her, caressing her in his arms as if she were everything to him. She was. He explored her, shared her intimate smiles, and kissed away her tears.

Later, when they rested, Edmund thought about what Malcolm had told him. His cousin was correct about their course. They'd veered off, and he led the charge. As precious as Sarah was to Amelia and Luke, she meant nothing to the two most powerful men in Scotland. But Amelia did. He knew how valuable she was. He didn't know what he would do about their course, but he knew that he loved this woman and he'd asked his best friend to stand with him. Of course, Malcolm vowed that he would.

"Edmund?"

"Aye, love."

"Is there a garden at Camlochlin?"

He moved in to kiss her. "Camlochlin is the garden, love. 'Tis only missing its angel."

Evening grew into the stillness of a night kept young by the laughter of a tavern wench while she traipsed around the lord of Ravenglade's bed, the quiet conversation of a servant and a knight coming to know each other over sweet wine and a warm fire, and the whispered promises of momentary lovers locked in passion's embrace.

"This is the third time ye have consented to me, lass." Edmund watched Amelia's lips curl into a teasing smirk while she wrapped her legs tighter around him.

"Do ye intend to have me then, Highlander?"

Her voice was thick with passion, her gaze on him smoky and sparked with the same hunger he felt coursing through him for her.

"I do, Amelia." He kissed her chin, her throat, and drove himself deep into her. He almost lost himself when she cried out. "But I would not claim a woman as mine without her consent." He bit her chin, then took her mouth with broad, slow strokes of his tongue that matched the rhythm of his thrusts.

"Do ye give yer consent, just fer tonight?" he asked, breaking their breathless kiss to look down into her eyes, slowing his movements and fighting the effect her tight thighs around his waist was having on him.

"I do." She nodded, tears welling up in her eyes, and arched her back, pushing her hips up. She moved in a little dance beneath him, against him, that shook him to his core.

He slipped his arm around her small waist and flipped onto to his back, bringing her over him. He smiled and drew in his bottom lip when she straddled him, bravely taking his full size.

Looking up at her, he knew that his heart was lost to her. Mayhap it had been from that very first night. He was in love with her.

Setting his palms on her hips, he guided her for a little while and then he drew her down on him, her breasts pressed to him, his breath becoming hers, his hands tight on her rear. He guided her up, down, once, twice, and then he felt her shudder and grow tighter around him. He slowed his thrusts, grinding her hips against his in a dance that pulled tight, short groans from her lips.

"Drench me, love," he whispered as she obeyed.

He watched her and did the same for her.

Chapter Twenty-Seven

By now, Sarah knew almost every curve, every arc, and every angle of Lucan MacGregor. But nothing was more perfect than his dimpled chin, she thought, wiping the last traces of blood from it, the decadent fullness of his lips, and the ease with which they curled whenever he looked at her. He was, she decided, the most perfectly formed man she'd ever met. She finished cleaning the last of the wounds on his face, a slight cut along his chin from the fist of a man even bigger than he was. Lucan had taken the blow straight on, shook his head, and then delivered a thunderous uppercut to his opponent that Sarah feared had killed the man. It hadn't.

"Ye're very dangerous without yer sword." She didn't move from her position standing between his knees where he sat.

"'Twas a good fight." He looked at her, his gaze level with hers. "I prefer it to more serious fighting."

She nodded, realizing for the first time, because of her closeness, that his left eye was slightly more golden and his right, a bit more green. "Ye're verra' handsome."

"Thank ye." His smile widened into a grin that snatched the breath clean out of her. "But I should be the one telling ye how bonny ye are. From the moment I saw ye, I didn't care if everyone else in the world vanished, as long as ye remained."

She shook her head and severed her gaze from his, still unfamiliar with such adoration.

He smoothed a lock of her hair off her cheek and traced her bottom lip with his thumb. "Ye're going to have to grow accustomed to such words, Sarah. Fer I wish to bestow them on ye until ye're old and gray."

She closed her eyes. Och, how could this wondrous man care for her?

"Sarah?"

She opened her eyes and set them on his and smiled. She had to smile, for he made her heart soar. She thought of the hours they'd spent together last night, talking, laughing, learning about each other. Never in all her life had she shared so much with a man... with anyone, save Amelia. She wanted to kiss him, to explore him, but she was frightened because unlike the other men in her life, Lucan meant something to her. She liked him very much... and she was tired of being frightened. Amelia was correct, Lucan was different. It was time to trust a man.

When she took his face in her hands and bent to kiss his bruises, he coiled his arm around her waist and pulled her against his chest. He opened his hand, spreading his broad fingers over the small of her back, and tilted his face to hers. She kissed his mouth, and her knees almost gave out beneath her. His lips were soft, temptation itself. He moved them with pure mastery of motion, opening his mouth and spreading his tongue inside her, withdrawing just enough to share her breath. Her insides burned with flames only he could extinguish.

He rose up out of his chair and led her to one of the settees in the solar. There, he sat and pulled her gently down with him. They lay, tangled in each other's arms, his long, muscular legs around her.

How safe she felt, cherished for more than the pleasures she could give him. For the first time in years she felt innocent, untried, vulnerable. Her heart beat madly, but she tried not to fight what he made her feel. His kisses were like the finest wine, smooth, warm, intoxicating. His fingers moved through her hair, over her throat, and down her hips until she felt heady with desire.

He held her face between kisses and told her how bonny she was and how she made him feel like a man. She laughed a little. He needed no help in being a man.

"How is it possible that no woman has snatched ye up yet, Lucan?"

"Some have tried, but none were right fer me. Until ye."

Her heart accelerated and she had the urge to run, to find the control she used to have with men that she seemed to have lost with this one. But she couldn't move. She didn't want to. She didn't care if she wasn't in control. Not this time. "What is it about me?"

He shook his head. "I admit yer beauty attracted me at first, but there was something else. Ye seemed verra' exposed, at risk to things around ye...like a wanderer in the lair of dragons."

"Ah"—she smiled—"so 'twas a knightly thing. Ye wanted to save m' from danger. What happens when I'm secure and no longer need a protector?"

"If ye let me"—his voice was low and rough along her mouth—"I will always protect ye from danger."

"That sounds permanent, Lucan."

"'Tis how I intended it to sound, lady. I want ye in my life. I want to make love to ye and watch ye grow fat with my bairns."

He kissed her and held her in his arms when she trembled.

Bairns? That was permanent indeed. Would she ever be ready for such permanence with a man? How would she know? She looked at him and he smiled. And she knew.

"So ye retrieved neither yer cousin's hand, nor his dog." Darach didn't care if he was beaten senseless for a second time; he had to gloat when William entered the barn that morning almost as bruised as he had been when they captured him. "I must tell ye, going to Ravenglade fer the hand was foolish. I'm certain m' kin had a good laugh over it. The dog..." He shrugged. "If 'twas Edmund who took it, ye likely willna' be seein' the beast again. Edmund has an affinity fer canines. Owns the ugliest one in Scotland."

"And *ye* might not be seeing Edmund again," William warned him and took a seat on a nearby stool, "or the rest of them."

"How many were there?"

"What? Ye know damned well how many there were. There were three! In my defense, I delivered a number of gut-crunching blows."

"Well then," Darach said while relief filled him. There were three. Lucan lived and fought. "Let me thank ye fer providin' m' lads with proper sport. Hopefully, when I am recovered, ye'll allow me the same pleasure. As fer that second warnin' ye're about to give me, I likely *will* be seein' them all. They didna' kill ye, nor even one of the others. That means a bargain was struck fer m' life." His mouth snaked into a smirk. "Ye knew ye couldna' take them on, did ye no'? We come from fightin' stock. Ye rode to m' cousin's castle and walked straight into hell. Did ye promise m' life fer yers?"

William stared at him for a long time. So long, in fact, that Darach thought he might have croaked in some kind of time-delayed consequence of having the shyt beat out of him.

"I had fifteen armed men at my side," William finally said. "Sixteen to start, but I'm told that Grant made a quick end of Andrew by smashing his head into the wall. Still, the Highlanders were outnumbered. I hadn't gone fer a fight, but even if I did, they weren't afraid, even with the numbers so stacked against them. 'Twas a wee bit intimidating, that." At first, the chief seemed to be speaking to himself, rather than to Darach, which would explain better why he'd complimented his enemies. But then he clearly looked at his prisoner and smiled slightly. "Neither Alistair's hand nor his dog are worth dying over, so I used ye as a pawn."

"That's no' always a good idea," Darach told him, with more respect for having been honest. "My kin dinna' respond well to Grants' or MacGregors' lives bein' threatened."

"Aye," William said curtly. "I surmised that much while they pounded our asses to the ground."

Darach smiled, making a mental note to remember William's words for a future ode he might want to someday write to the lads. "They're brutal bastards. Did ye lose any teeth?"

"Nae." William actually laughed, surprising Darach even more. "But Janet says my nose is broken and she had to stitch my brow."

"And he didn't yelp and whine the way *ye* did when I stitched that gash that wasn't closin' on ye last eve, Grant."

Darach wasn't sure if the sound of Janet Buchanan's voice made him want to smile or shout blasphemies. He looked up to heaven while she entered the barn. When would he be delivered from this sharp-tongued hellion?

"Did ye use a dull sewin' needle on him, too, witch?"

"Of course not, wretch. He's my brother." She tossed him a cool wooden smile. "His scar will be much straighter than yers as well."

"Pity fer him." Darach yawned. "We Highlanders take pride in our scars."

"I'm certain yer women don't feel the same way," she threw at him, then turned to William.

"Our women are no' sensitive barn wenches who recoil at the sight of a real man."

Her back stiffened. "Let me kill him, William."

"Don't touch him, Janet. I'm deadly serious. I wasn't thrown into a damned moat last night fer naught."

"Ye were thrown into the moat?" Darach asked him, doing his best to conceal his grin.

"Most of us were—"

"William, must ye tell him?" his sister complained. "He'll only wallow in it."

"I don't care. This feud is foolish. Mayhap MacGregor is correct and there are bigger, more threatening enemies waiting in our mist."

"He *is* correct," Darach said. "And there are."

William agreed. "But presently, yer kin are more dangerous than any laws. I intended all along to return ye to them. I just wanted to wait a few days until ye didn't look so beat up."

"I'll let them know that," Darach promised.

"Tell me, they will most certainly come fer ye then?"

"Most certainly," Darach assured him.

"When?"

Darach shrugged his shoulders. Even if he knew, he wouldn't tell him.

"Well, I should have told them I would return ye but the moat came quickly. If they don't come tonight, I'll arrange to have ye taken back in the morning."

He turned to his sister. "See that he eats and is cleaned up. I need to prepare everyone and see that there is no more bloodshed."

"I'm tired of looking after him, Will!" Janet called out to her brother, and then shifted her gaze to Darach when they were alone. "One more day and then I'll be rid of ye."

Darach tossed her a lazy smirk. "Ye'll miss me. What else will ye have to fill yer dull days?"

She laughed and he almost hated how beautiful she was when she did. He didn't like her, but he couldn't deny that no lass in England or Scotland was as bonny as she.

"I'll practice my skills so that if I am ever so unfortunate to meet ye again, I can kill ye properly."

Hell, she was a fiery wench. He offered her a cool smile that carefully concealed what he really thought of her. "If I'm ever tortured by yer company again, I'll gladly let ye kill me."

Chapter Twenty-Eight

The warm sun felt so good on Amelia's skin, though she was still slightly mortified by how much of her skin was exposed.

Edmund had taken her to a lovely loch just north of Ravenglade, surrounded on three sides by majestic willow and oak and leading out into smaller rivulets. Nestled within a glen of thick woodland, it offered the seclusion they desired to swim and make love in the cool water.

They had promised themselves only one night, but one night wasn't enough. Amelia wasn't sure if a lifetime would be enough. She knew they were foolish by continuing to be together, but she didn't care. Tomorrow would bring its own tears. She didn't want to dwell on the inevitable. What good would it do her to deny them these last times together?

She had never swum nude out in the open. At first, she thought they were mad for undressing outdoors. She'd already gone mad to continue this obsession with him. But when he stripped naked under the sun, she nearly fainted at the sight of him, all tall and golden against a backdrop of nature. When he beckoned her to follow him into the icy water, she followed, as naked as he.

She barely knew how to swim. Living in Edinburgh and being the duke's niece didn't afford her much opportunity to swim in a loch or anywhere else. Edmund held her while she floated on her back, gliding across the surface. He steadied her when she floundered at the absence of his hands and then dipped his mouth to her glistening nipples.

When he carried her out into deeper waters, she almost panicked, but he drew her body to his and held her aloft. She clung to him, not because she was afraid of the depths, but because she never wanted to let him go. How would she ever? She would rather die than live an empty life without him. It frightened her because she didn't expect to feel this way. She thought she could be strong and leave him when the time came. But the reality of it seeped deeper into her veins every moment that she spent with him. She was in love with him. Maddeningly and passionately in love with him.

She met the ardor of his kiss with equal measure. She wrapped her legs around his waist and beckoned him with her hips to guide his stiff sword into her. She cried out when he impaled her. She felt weightless in his arms and after a moment her body relaxed around him. Pressing her hands to his wet, hard chest, she pushed herself up and back, moving upon him while he cradled her rump in one arm and dragged her to him so that he could kiss her mouth, her throat, her breasts. He drove her mad and made her doubt that anything existed in the world, save him. She wished nothing did.

Later, they rested on the shore, in each other's arms,

while their clothes dried on the rocks. They shared childhood memories while Grendel and Gaza chased red squirrels and explored the surrounding area.

"I was in my thirteenth year when I and my cousins first saw battle. The Menzies had come to Camlochlin to reclaim some cattle they accused us of stealing."

"Did ye?" Amelia asked against his bare chest.

"Nae, though we had stolen cattle before. That time 'twasn't the MacGregors. My uncle Rob rode across the vast vale and tried to talk with them rationally, but from what I understood the Menzies and MacGregors have long been enemies, ever since the days when my grandsire made war with the Campbells."

"Highlanders remember wrongs done to them fer a long time, do they not?" It wasn't a question. Amelia and every Lowlander knew it to be true.

"Aye. But I aim to help change that. Our centuries-long divisions have made us weak against England. Feuds need to end.

"Anyway, some thought Rob should have used the cannons the instant the Menzies set foot on our land, but our chief is fair and not blood-thirsty, so he tried to speak with them first. But one man among the Menzies didn't want to talk and hurled his dagger into the small crowd that had gathered around our warriors. It struck young Hamish MacKinnon and killed him. That was when hell opened its fiery jaws and swallowed Camlochlin up for a wee bit."

"What happened?"

"They fought. My uncles, my kin, they took down men before my eyes, with sword and ax. They were brutal and merciless, as if every wrong ever done to them came afresh to the surface and gave them might to slay whatever they faced. I watched and also picked up my sword, as did my cousins Adam, Malcolm, and Luke." He smiled as if the memory were one that pleased him. "And wee Darach. 'Twas when we knew he was fearless, mayhap too fearless fer his own good. He was nine, I think, and he leaped into the melee with a battle cry that nearly made his poor mother fall over dead."

"Goodness, it must have been difficult fer her to realize that her boy had fighting in his blood so young."

"'Twas. And harder still fer my aunts Isobel and Mairi when their daughters, only a pair of years older than Darach, tried to fight as well. Although I think Mairi expected it of Caitrina, just not so soon."

"I never saw a dead man until I came here," Amelia told him, remembering her past with him. "I wasn't allowed inside my grandsire's chamber when he died of a sickness to his lungs."

"I feel responsible fer spoiling yer innocence."

She leaned up on one elbow and looked down at him. "Spoiling the innocence of my eyes or my body?"

He blinked, then grinned, looking unsure as to which answer he should give. "Yer eyes," he finally admitted. "I'm not done with yer body."

She shook her head at him playfully, then scooted out of his reach when he tried to keep her with him.

"Where are ye going?" he asked, watching her hooded, sleepy eyes while she slipped her chemise over her head.

"I saw lovely plump berries just over there." She pointed to a stand of willows when he looked. "I want to pick some fer us to eat."

"I'm perfectly content to dine on the plump berries before me."

"Och, fer goodness sakes, ye're beginning to sound like Malcolm. Close yer eyes and rest. I'll bring the dogs with me."

He nodded and closed his eyes. "Make haste, Amelia."

"I will," she promised and hurried off, barefoot.

Grendel followed her the instant she stepped into the woods. Gaza took off first toward Edmund and then back to Amelia when she realized her new and beloved master wasn't coming.

Amelia patted the dog's head. "I know, Gaza. I love him, too."

She walked farther along until she spotted what she was after. Fat, red currant berries grew in clusters, tempting her forward. She should have brought a basket with her from the castle. Henrietta could make some delicious pastries with the sweet berry.

"I don't like being pulled from my bed to go chasing after a lady. I don't care who she is."

Amelia stopped, quieting Gaza's low whine and keeping Grendel from rushing out of the trees.

"Well, you best care, Humphrey," said another, deeper voice. "She's the duke's niece, and soon-to-be wife of the lord chancellor."

Amelia didn't move. She didn't breathe. She was afraid that she might never move again.

"If Captain Pierce hears you speaking of your duty like that—"

Captain Pierce was here! Amelia looked longingly back the way she'd come, toward Edmund. She had to tell him, tell the others. If Pierce was here, then so was her uncle, possibly Walter—definitely an army. She wanted to move. But what if she cracked a twig or rustled the leaves? There were three men in Ravenglade, not including Chester, the old steward. She didn't care how skilled Edmund and his cousins were. They would lose against an army.

She prayed for the dogs to stay quiet. She didn't know that Grendel was trained to do just what she needed. Thankfully, Gaza followed his lead.

"Do you think the gossip is right, though?" asked the first man, a soldier most likely. "Do you believe she ran away with outlaws so that she could get away from the lord chancellor?"

"It's not our concern, Humphrey. Are you done taking your piss?"

"I believe it. She must know what a merciless bastard he is. Think you he has struck her yet?"

"Damn you, Humphrey, you're going to get us both killed."

Humphrey was quiet for a moment. Amelia prayed that he was done so he and his friend would leave. Then, "Remember that wench he nailed last winter on his visit to Edinburgh? The one he asked us to take from the local tavern? Perhaps Miss Bell knows how she was found dead the next morning."

Amelia didn't know. She clutched her belly and fought to keep herself upright. Walter killed a woman? It couldn't be true. That wasn't what they were saying.

"I asked around a little after the gruesome discovery and I learned that Lord Seafield enjoys some very perverse sexual desires."

"That doesn't make him a murderer, Humphrey."

Amelia thought she must be dreaming. How could she marry a perverse man after she'd been with Edmund? What if Walter murdered that woman? Did her father know? He couldn't know.

"And where in blazes is the duke? Why send us to Perth and then take his damn time getting here himself?"

"He'll be here in a day or two, Humphrey. Then we can get this business over with and return home. Now hurry up!"

Amelia waited for them to leave the clearing, and after making certain they were gone, she raced back to Edmund.

Chapter Twenty-Nine

Edmund sat in the solar with the others discussing what Amelia had overheard that morning at the loch. The duke had found them, and he was bringing his men, possibly his army.

"How did he find us?" Malcolm asked.

Edmund shook his head. "I don't know. Mayhap someone recognized us in Edinburgh. Most know that Ravenglade belongs to the Grants."

"Why aren't they here?" Luke tapped his boot on the floor. "What are they waiting fer?"

"Most likely fer the duke to arrive," Amelia told them. "The two soldiers I overheard discussed the duke's arrival in a few days."

"My guess is they won't attack until he arrives," Edmund said.

However the duke found them no longer mattered. They were found. An army was coming. Edmund and his cousins were going to need help. "We're going to need the Buchanans in this."

Malcolm threw back his head and laughed. "Ye're mad, cousin. I'd rather die in battle."

"Ye may get yer wish then," Edmund told him. "How do ye suppose we fight armed soldiers? We might manage to kill a dozen or so, but we are three, Cal. We don't stand a chance."

Malcolm closed his eyes and tightened his jaw. "What d'ye propose we do?"

"I think William is looking fer a way out of this mess with Darach."

"I agree," Luke said.

"We need to ride to the Buchanan holding today, while we still have time to leave the castle, and speak to William about his kin's duty to Scotland."

Malcolm shook his head. "William's new at being chief. He's young and doesn't yet command the respect from his kin that he's due."

Edmund disagreed. "After last night and the beating he took to save them, I think things will change. We will offer them something in exchange fer Darach and their aid with the duke."

"What do we give them?"

"Their dog," Malcolm suggested.

Edmund glanced at him with enough warning in his eyes to quiet him. "We'll offer them terms."

"Like what?" Malcolm asked, already sounding like he hated the idea.

"They want Ravenglade. We will offer them paid positions here. The place is empty fer months at a time. Ye keep yer steward, Chester, here and ye've offered Henrietta her own quarters if she agreed to stay. Why not take on more? Ye have the room."

Malcolm laughed and tossed his booted foot over the arm of his chair. "Ye think the Buchanans would stay as servants?"

"Nae. They wouldn't be servants. Ye'd be paying them in coin or in protection, whatever ye want to offer. They'd be living here. That's what they've always wanted. Ye need a gardener and ye could use a blacksmith and a bottler. How about a marshal?"

"A marshal fer what horses, Edmund?" Malcolm shook his head at him. "I have no carts or wagons. But while we're at it, why do I no' hire a few Buchanan minstrels to sing fer me? Och, I can also use a tanner and a soap maker and a porter."

"And a scullion," Sarah added. "Just this morn I heard Henrietta complainin' about cleaning the kitchen."

Malcolm stared at her for a moment, and then smiled indulgently. "I'm no' givin' any of this m' true consideration, lass."

Sarah smiled back. "I know ye're not, Malcolm. Ye only consider yerself."

Lucan's chuckle pulled Malcolm's hard gaze in his direction. "'Tis no' true."

"'Tis," Luke insisted.

Malcolm turned to Edmund and then rose from his seat when Edmund nodded his head in agreement. "What would ye all have me do, then?" He threw up his hands. "Invite the Buchanans into Ravenglade with open arms? Allow them to stay here in m' absence and then trust them to hand it back over when I return?"

"Why not?" Luke said. "Someone's got to make the first move toward ending this foolish feud."

"Writings will be drawn and signed," Edmund told

Malcolm. "I'll begin penning everything now. We'll send Chester an hour or two before we arrive to let them know we come with a peace offering. Ravenglade is yers, Malcolm, and always will be. If they try to take it again, they will lose their positions here and possibly their lives."

"Why the hell would I agree to any of this, Edmund?"

"Because, Cal, it gains us what we need and we get Darach back safely."

"Who says I want the hellion back?"

Edmund smiled at his cousin, knowing him better.

Malcolm tossed back his head and exhaled a gusty sigh. "All right then. Let's go do it."

Janet Buchanan stood in the shadows of the barn while her brother spoke to Darach about the afternoon's events. They'd received a visitor about an hour ago in the form of Chester, Malcolm Grant's steward. Chester was slightly built and of medium height, and no threat to her kin whatsoever. To Janet's estimation, he looked to be about the same age as her and William's father would have been.

The steward had been sent on ahead to prepare the Buchanans for the arrival of Malcolm Grant and his escorts, the MacGregors.

Her kin all listened quietly when he unfolded a parchment and began to read out loud.

"Malcolm offers us a place at Ravenglade," William filled Darach in. "We could make our home there and—"

"As servants," Janet muttered.

"As thieves who will pilfer everything they can get their hands on," Darach muttered back.

Janet glowered at him and opened her mouth to set him straight. William's voice stopped her.

"Grant and the MacGregors want to end the fighting and work toward peace. Some of us here want that, too. Either way, Darach, yer kin are coming shortly to discuss everything."

"Are they comin' withoot opposition?" their prisoner asked. "Or do they only think they are?"

"There's nae trap being set here," William assured him. "My father always knew that killing Malcolm or his father before him and taking Ravenglade by force would bring the entire Skye clan down upon our heads. I stand in his place now, and he didn't raise a fool."

Darach smiled at him and Janet's spine went soft. How was it possible that the bastard grew more alluring and virile every time she saw him?

His gaze found hers beneath the soft amber glow of a lantern hanging from the low rafters. She'd looked into the eyes of dangerous men before, but no one as perilous as Darach Grant. With his face less swollen and discolored, she had to admit he was the finest looking man she'd ever seen.

Janet knew she was mad and she would never admit to this aloud, but she didn't want his kin to come for him.

"What guarantee do I have that she was raised with ye, Will?"

Janet's fingers curled into fists and she remembered why she hated him. "I'm nae fool, Grant," she said tersely. "I think I've proven that to ye by not tripping over my feet every time ye look my way."

His emerald gaze glimmered as it came to rest on her again. "Ye have, indeed," he admitted softly.

Her belly flipped and she turned to her brother, only to

find Will watching her. She backed into the shadows once again.

"When they arrive," William continued on, "I'll speak to them and then bring ye to them."

Darach nodded. "Tell yer kin," he called out to William when he turned to leave the barn, "if anyone draws a weapon, I'll use yers to kill them."

William laughed but then let it fade with a nod, as if he suddenly believed Darach could do what he said.

"I will not miss yer brazen overconfidence, Grant," Janet told him when they were alone. She should have left right behind her brother.

"What will ye miss then?"

She shouldn't have looked at him. She heard the grin in his voice. She hadn't needed to see it.

Yer slightly sinister smile and the glint of something feral in yer gaze.

"The hope and expectation I experience every morn when I enter the barn that a horse somehow killed ye during the night."

He crooked his mouth. Mad as it was, he was going to miss this fire-tempered wench and her springy blond curls. "Ye have an acid tongue, Janet Buchanan." He went to her, but came to a harsh, abrupt halt, stopped by the restraints on his ankles. "I find it most appealin' and would like to—"

Shouts from outside halted whatever else he meant to say. Janet thought it best, but was a bit disappointed, though she would never admit to such a thing. His kin were here. He was leaving. The next time she saw him he would likely be married... or, more likely, dead. It didn't matter to her. As long as he was out of her hair.

"Farewell, Darach." She stepped back just as the barn doors opened again and Will returned.

Janet didn't look back as she left. She wouldn't think of him ever again. Nothing had changed.

She kept repeating it over and over again in her mind as she exited the barn and disappeared into the crowd of those who had come to see their enemies up close.

Chapter Thirty

John Bell paced a worn path in the grass. He looked off into the distance to where he understood Ravenglade Castle to be. He couldn't see it from where his brother-in-law's army made camp. Why were they so far away? What were they waiting for? He didn't care if the duke wasn't here yet. If Amelia meant more to her uncle than his position, he would be here by now, and so would her betrothed. How could Walter not be here? John closed his eyes to drive out the truth that Amelia meant little to her future husband. They should have charged forward and taken her with the force of their numbers.

Ah, he was normally a patient man. God knows he'd been patient with his wife for years, listening to her constant complaints about her life, and how she was forced to marry below her. He'd been patient when she arranged the marriages of their daughters Elizabeth and Anne to older, wealthy noblemen. He knew power was important to Millicent and she wanted her daughters to have it all, so he let her have her way. Besides, his two eldest daughters were exactly like their mother in that they sought power in their unions, not love. Amelia was different. She had always been different. He cursed himself, as he did every day, for not protecting her enough from her mother's critical tongue. He'd made many mistakes in his life, like agreeing to live in Queensberry House with his family, a place that wasn't his own, that he hadn't worked for, and could be taken from him at any point in time. He did it for his wife. But letting Millicent constantly berate Amelia was his greatest regret. If what that Buchanan man had said was true, that his Amelia had been seen kissing her captor, then he had no one to blame but himself and his wife. He'd been a coward, afraid that Millicent would have her brother toss him out on the street. There were many times when he'd wanted to leave on his own, but he'd taken vows and he couldn't leave Amelia. He'd stayed for her. He did all for her. He might not have protected her enough, but he was there to love her, and to remind her that she was a gift to him, a ray of sunshine in an otherwise gloomy hell. He wondered how his little girl was faring. He'd lain awake every night alternating between tears and rage. Would he ever see his daughter alive again? When he heard Buchanan speak of her, he almost fell to his knees with relief.

Had the outlaws hurt her? If they had, he would kill them himself. He knew how to fire a pistol and even wield a sword, though he hadn't wielded one in years. Nothing would stop him from ending the lives of anyone who put hands to his girl.

"There you are!"

John didn't turn at the sound of his wife's piercing voice. He closed his eyes and prayed for even more patience. When this was all over...

"What are you doing here all by yourself, John?" She walked around him so she could see him, or rather so he could see her when she shook her head at him. "Sometimes you are so odd." She blinked and then smoothed a wrinkle in his coat. "Walter and my brother have finally arrived and plans are about to be discussed on how to proceed. Do you want to be included or not?"

"Of course I do," he said, moving her out of his way. "What kind of foolish question is that? I've been waiting to proceed since Amelia first disappeared. Since we discovered where she was and yer brother took his damned time going after her."

"John"—his wife looked around nervously—"lower your voice before someone hears you!"

"Let them hear!" he shouted, frustrated and fed up at the slow pace of his daughter's rescue. He was tired of being a coward. He was going to fight for his Amelia. "I don't give a damn about politics or—"

"We already know that," Millicent hushed sourly.

"Good! Know this also. I don't care what people think about us killing Highlanders who have kidnapped my daughter. I don't care about which Parliament rules, or if Scotland and England unite. I care only about my Amelia, as should ye, woman!"

She pressed her hands to her chest in a display of utter shock and offense, a gesture John had seen on her as often as she breathed. "How dare you! Of course I care about her!"

"Aye, ye care that she marries one of the most powerful men in Scotland. Not because it's what she wants, but because it will benefit yer place in society. Aren't I correct, Millicent? Ye've always been hard on her, but after she caught the chancellor's eye, ye scrutinized everything she did, every move she made, even more than before, until ye likely have pushed her into the arms of a Highlander!"

Millicent looked so stunned and wounded that John almost relented and left her alone. But then she opened her mouth and he changed his mind. "With her natural tendency for disaster, her unladylike outbursts of laughter, and other emotions she has yet to learn to restrain, much like her father, not to mention her close alliance with a *servant*, could you blame me for worrying and trying to oversee her actions?"

"Aye, I could blame ye, but I blame myself as well, fer not getting her away from ye sooner." He had nothing more to say to her and stormed away, leaving her to look after him, speechless.

He entered the camp feeling like a new man.

"Bell." The duke barely looked up from a missive he was reading when John entered his tent. "Where's my sister?"

John didn't care where she was. He wasn't going to let another instant go by. He glanced at Seafield, who was sitting in a chair by the small table. "Are we going to get my daughter, or is her betrothed striking his proposal?" He turned to look more fully at the chancellor. "If so, I agree to it being stricken."

"John." His brother-in-law looked up.

"I'm her father," John reminded him. If he refused to give Amelia to Seafield, no one could force him.

"Lord Bell." Seafield snapped up from his chair. "If I've given you cause to doubt my love and devotion for your daughter, I beg your forgiveness. Let me do whatever I must to prove to you that she means everything to me?"

John looked into his eyes. "Go get her."

*   *   *

Amelia set the last cup in place on the long table in
Ravenglade's Great Hall and stepped back to admire their
work. She, Sarah, and Henrietta had stayed up all night
preparing a French feast for Darach's breakfast. While
Amelia learned how to make chocolate mousse tarts,
crème brûlée, and basil salmon pâté that almost made
Amelia cry it tasted so good, Henrietta talked about coming to know the Grants, and later, the MacGregors. She
told them about Edmund's and Malcolm's parents, and
hearing about them, Amelia felt closer to the outlawed
family. She already loved Luke, Darach, and even Malcolm.

How would she ever leave them? Leave Edmund? The
time was coming. It was just outside the door. How could
she marry Walter knowing what he may have done, what
kind of man he may truly be? She hadn't told Edmund
about the dead woman in Walter's life. Oh, how she
wished her father had come with the army. How she
wished she could speak to him. If he knew about Walter
would he ... And even if he did, Edmund would always
be her family's enemy. No, she wouldn't think of it today.
They had until at least tomorrow to forget the army that
had come for her. Today they were celebrating Darach's
being home. He'd arrived last night, looking quite well
save for the fading bruises on his face and the smell of
hay and other barn odors saturating his clothes. Amelia
hadn't realized how worried she'd been until she saw him
and felt the overwhelming relief of his safety and shared
the joy of his laughter.

She looked at the table now, arrayed with hot, scrump-
tious dishes, big cups of warm honey mead, and two

huge vases filled with bluebells and beautiful purple ling heather, obtained from the rolling hills just beyond Ravenglade's village.

"He comes!" Sarah called out from the entryway, then ran to stand with Amelia and Etta at the table.

They watched him enter the Great Hall, clean and beaming from ear to ear when he saw the table; Amelia caught Edmund's eye from his place beside his cousin and she smiled, pleased when the four big men entering the Hall closed their eyes and inhaled the delicious aromas of breakfast.

"Is that crème brûlée?" Darach asked, his voice quavering for the first time since Amelia had known him. "I love ye," he told Henrietta when she told him it was.

"The ladies helped me prepare it," the gracious cook told him.

He tossed Amelia and Sarah a grateful look. "I would kiss ye both but I dinna' want Edmund and Cal to accuse me of stealin' their women."

"Alas," Malcolm pined, "Luke already stole Sarah from me."

Darach winked at Sarah while he passed her to take a seat at the table. "I knew ye were an intelligent lass."

"Amazing," Lucan said, taking a seat. "What did they do to ye in that barn to make ye compliment me?"

"Presently." Darach closed his eyes and inhaled deeply. He groaned and reached for a tart. "I would compliment even that hideously homely dog that has taken up Grendel's place at Edmund's heels."

"Ye see?" Edmund glanced at Amelia while he dipped his bread into the brûlée. "I told ye to poison his tarts."

"Oh, we don't have to go to such extremes, do we?"

she asked, slipping into the chair closest to Darach. She rested her chin on her hand and smiled at him when he looked up, chewing.

"Her name is Gazardiel. We call her Gaza."

"Who?" he asked, taking another bite.

"Our new dog."

He cast Edmund a questioning look, then returned to his food.

"She used to belong to Alistair Buchanan." She nodded when the dawning light shone in his eyes. "Did ye see Alistair there?"

"Nae, lass, I saw only William."

"No one else?"

He looked at her. She quirked her eyebrow at him.

"There was no one else. May I commence eatin', then?"

"Edmund and the others told us that there was a girl at William's side who caught and held yer eye."

"So? I catch and hold the attention of many women."

"Nae, Darach, *she* caught *yers*. This one was...Edmund"—she turned to him—"who did ye say told ye that she was the chief's sister?"

"The chief himself as we were leaving, and I invited them here for supper."

"Ah, aye." She graced him with a smile she longed to bestow on him for the rest of her life. "Now I remember. Janet is her name."

"Whose name?" Darach asked.

Amelia blinked, turning back to him. "Janet's."

Across the table, Edmund smiled.

"What the hell are ye talkin' aboot, lass?"

"Very well, let me be clear." She moved forward and

patted Darach's arm. "We all want to know about this Janet, who, according to Luke, quipped about ye being impotent in her barn."

Sarah's laughter made the rest of them laugh with her. Darach kept right on eating.

"He has nae shame," Malcolm noted, then swigged his drink.

"Shame fer bein' shackled?" he asked, moving on to the brûlée. "That's what she meant."

"Then ye do know her."

"Aye, ye brought her back to m' memory. Janet Buchanan, a she-devil whose purpose on this earth is to make men wish they were never born. She's pig-headed and prideful and merciless. She stitched my brow withoot a drop of whisky to dull the pain."

"Hell, ye didna' weep, did ye?" Malcolm asked, digging into the salmon. "I mean, the lass stuck ye with a needle. I'm no' certain one can recover from that."

"I didna' piss m'self like ye did when Luke sealed that wound on yer shoulder last spring."

"He sealed it with a red-hot brand," Malcolm reminded him. "Ye would have fainted like a woman."

"Ha!" Darach countered. "I'll let ye cut me later and then let ye seal it with an iron just fer sport."

Amelia rolled her eyes when Edmund and Luke joined in on the conversation, jeering at one another and their weaknesses—which, of course, they all denied having. Was this what all Highlanders were like?

Grendel sat up on his haunches and growled. He waited a moment, ears perked, and then galloped out of the Hall. Edmund immediately stood from his chair and followed, knowing his dog well and knowing that something was amiss. Gaza took off after him. The Hall was silent for a moment. Amelia was about to leave her chair to find Edmund when Grendel's resonating bark shattered the morning peace.

Luke, Malcolm, and Darach were the next out, ordering the ladies to stay put. The ladies didn't.

She heard Edmund's shout like a rushing wind, bringing calamity and heartbreak.

"'Tis the duke! He's arrived."

Chapter Thirty-One

Edmund," Amelia said, heart racing, mouth dry, while she followed him between the garrison and the Hall as he gathered his weapons. Her uncle's army was camped well beyond the gate and drawbridge and out of range of any arrows or cannons, which Ravenglade did not have. "I don't want ye to die, Edmund. Ye must let me go."

He stopped moving and turned around to her, taking her in his arms. "I don't know if I can, Amelia." He looked deep into her eyes and she saw his purpose and his love for Scotland and for her fired from within. He must choose between the two desires of his heart. He couldn't win them both.

And what of her? She too fought a battle in which she knew the outcome—she would lose—but still had to fight, else her father would lose along with her, because of her.

"What about ye, Amelia?" he asked her. "Do ye truly want to go back? Tell me yer heart and I will honor it, if I must."

Of course she didn't want to go back. She *had* to go

back. Was she supposed to abandon her father? God help her, could she?

"But Edmund, what about the Union with England?" she asked him and felt a tear drop from her eye onto her cheek. "What about all ye've done? Could ye abandon it all?"

"There's nothing more to do," he told her. "I'll always fight fer Scotland's freedom. Whether 'tis now or five years from now, I'll fight with the rest, but in the meantime, I want to live my life with ye. I'll do what I must to bring ye with me to Skye, but I know the sacrifice ye'd be making and I need to know if ye want to make it."

Oh, she wanted it. What if what he must do meant killing her uncle? Walter? It would save her from her obligation to wed the latter.

Dear Lord, she gasped. She was becoming as savage as her beloved.

Tears slipped over her cheeks and he wiped them away gently. She would never be happy with any man, save him. She would never love another man, especially not Walter. Leaving Edmund meant sentencing her to a life of misery, but staying with him meant ruining her father. Her heart broke with the decision she had to make.

"I must go back, Edmund."

She thought she would weep for a year without ceasing at the memory of his eyes on her at that moment. She wished he knew her father so that it might help him understand why she couldn't leave him powerless in the hands of her uncle. 'Twas her father who brought her through her childhood a happy, well-minded lady. Without him, living under the weight of her mother's heavy words after the accident with her mad cousin, she

THE SEDUCTION OF MISS AMELIA BELL   275

would have crumbled and become a very dark, sad little girl.

"We'll speak more about this later," Edmund said, bringing her attention back to him.

He left before she could say anything else. She watched him leave. Would he let her go? He'd told her that he hadn't signed his ransom letter. He hadn't planned on fighting an army. Four men had no chance and no hope against a regiment. How long could they stay here? How much food was left? And when the two sides finally met, would she watch Edmund die? Panic sapped her strength. She had to do something. The army was here for her.

"The entrance is secure," Lucan called out when Edmund entered the inner bailey. He met Sarah on his way back and took her by the hand. "Tell Etta, we may be needing boiled tar and a source of fire."

"Ye four cannot hold them back fer long," Sarah spoke her fears out loud as Amelia entered the inner bailey.

"Just until we figure something out," Lucan promised. "Don't fear, lady. My cousins and I have gotten out of worse circumstances than this. Have we not, Edmund?"

"Aye," Edmund agreed. "We have."

Lord, how could they remain so calm, so confident, when they clearly would not see victory? Amelia wanted to weep for them, but they would find insult in it. They were proud and loyal to one another to a fault. Not one of them suggested the obvious: send her out. Lower the drawbridge and get rid of her and get the hell on with their lives.

It didn't matter whose fault it was, trouble followed her. And in this case, it came to the Highlanders in the form of the Royal Damn Army.

"We will see to what ye need," Sarah promised and hurried along.

Amelia went with her. She would figure out how to convince Edmund that he had to return her. She didn't want them all to die because of her. She would never let it happen.

"Sarah spoke true, Edmund. We cannot hope to hold them off fer long."

"Aye, I know, Cal."

"How long d'ye think 'twill take Darach to return with reinforcements?"

"A day, mayhap two."

Many clans in Scotland, Lowland ones included, were against the treaty and had already pledged their lives to fighting it. Stopping Queensberry was vital, and the MacGregors and Grants had him and his army sitting in one place, not suspecting resistance from behind. Darach needed to recruit those men now and bring as many as he could back.

They had lowered him from a window on the north face of the castle. With its boggy terrain and where the deepest part of the moat met the widest, no one was stationed there. Of course, it meant that Darach would have a difficult swim, but he had done it. By now, he was on his way to the next village.

"The Murrays and the Gordons will come fer certain."

Edmund agreed.

They stood together on the western side of the battlements with Luke holding the eastern wall. A light rain had begun to fall, making the walls slippery if anyone thought to climb them. No one did, for they would have to swim across the moat first, and Malcolm never cleaned the moat.

"I was careful not to pen any mention of who we were or in which direction we were heading with Amelia." Edmund racked his brain for the hundredth time, trying to understand how the duke had found them. He'd written only that he'd taken Amelia and if the treaty was signed, he would kill her.

"'Twillna' be enough fer them to have her back." Malcolm slicked his dark hair back to keep the rain from his eyes. "They will want our blood."

"I know."

"So dinna' return her. Use her."

Edmund looked up from across the moat. "As far as we've heard, the treaty hasn't yet been signed. As long as we have her, there's still time fer him to stop it."

Malcolm smiled. "Ye've thought this through already."

"'Twill buy us more time to figure out a way to escape."

"Is that the reason?" Malcolm asked him skeptically. "Or is it that even she canna' tear ye from Scotland, yer true love?"

Edmund shook his head and returned his attention to the army below. But he said nothing. He could not deny that he pondered ways to still save his country. Scotland had saved him, after all. But he had begun to doubt that Scotland was his true love. Amelia had stolen that title. He would do anything to keep them all alive. But for her, he would surrender anything, his life or his country. She didn't want to hurt her father and she was willing to sentence herself to a miserable life and a loveless marriage to the chancellor to prevent bringing shame on the Bell name. Edmund understood, and if the treaty was dissolved, he would honor his word. If it wasn't…

"Should we keep waitin' fer him, or send word first?"

Edmund found the duke among the men, doing what cowards tended to do—staying far behind his lines. "I'll get my quill." He sighed and set off to see his word done.

A short while later he returned with a missive of their terms. He rolled it, then tied it to one of Malcolm's arrows, lit the back on fire, and watched his cousin shoot it.

"Did ye remember to tell him that I enjoyed his wife?" Malcolm asked him.

"I'm saving that fer later."

"Mary, I believe is her name."

"Hell." Edmund laughed and shook his head at him. "Do ye speak in earnest? Is there a woman ye didn't sleep with in Queensberry?"

"At least two." Malcolm winked at him. "I knew Luke was attracted to Sarah. But I tell ye, cousin, ye're fortunate to have met yer Amelia before I did."

"Mayhap if ye had, we would not all be in this quandary."

Malcolm shoved him away. "Dinna' doubt what we did now. We did what we did fer Scotland."

Aye, and it put Amelia, all of them, in danger. He said nothing but rested his hand on Grendel's head and scratched him behind the ears.

The worst thing about being stuck in a castle was the waiting. The only strategic defense at Ravenglade was the drawbridge. If this were Camlochlin, cannons would have already been fired. His kin didn't need a moat and drawbridge when there were hundreds of men able to fight and only one direction from which to approach the castle.

"Ye need cannons."

"To use against whom"—Malcolm glanced at him—"the Buchanans?"

Before Edmund could answer, they spotted a fiery arrow sailing toward them. Before it struck a wall and fell harmlessly to the ground, Luke joined them and waited while Malcolm went to fetch it.

"Well, let's hear what he has to say then, shall we," Malcolm said, taking up the arrow and unrolling the missive attached to it.

"Gentlemen," he read out loud. "What ye demand is impossible. Actions regarding the great Treaty of Union are already set in motion and canno' be stopped, nor do I wish them to be. Ye have m' niece, Miss Amelia Bell. Ye have one hour to release her, unharmed, or I will set m' men loose on Ravenglade. I do no' care how many soldiers accompany ye, none will survive."

Malcolm looked up from the note. "He's an arrogant bastard," he said before continuing on.

"I prefer no' to war with the MacGregors or the Grants, so if m' niece is freed, we will take our leave withoot further quarrel."

"Not likely," Luke said aloud what the rest were thinking. "He gets her back and then he tries to kill us."

"I don't want to give her back." Edmund's confession drew their gazes. "But I can't ask any of ye to sacrifice yourselves when our cause is just about lost. We've run out of time, lads. I fear if we don't give her up, he'll bring a battle here. I don't want to risk her life."

"We'll figure something oot, Edmund," Malcolm told him. "We'll take her to Camlochlin."

She wouldn't want to go. Edmund didn't tell them about Amelia's choice. He should honor it, but how could he? It was like watching someone walk toward a cliff, someone he loved. Should he remain quiet and let her sacrifice her life, or shout for her to go the other way?

Edmund looked at Luke. "'Tis not just her, Sarah will not let her go alone."

Luke cast him a baffled grin. "Why d'ye remind me as if I might actually be considering lowering that bridge and letting either of them out of our sights? We haven't gotten what we wanted and at this point, even if we do, I still don't want to send Sarah back."

"'Tis settled then." Malcolm crumpled the note and threw it over the wall. "We're hunkerin' doun, lads."

Edmund nodded. He would speak to Amelia about her choice later. "We need to get the women up here, Chester and the other servants, as well. Disguised, the duke will believe them to be our soldiers. After they are seen, we can set them to safety again inside. Let's bring up all our weapons from the courtyard and keep them at the ready. I'm going to need to bring Amelia to the edge. Hold a blade to her throat, put a pistol to her head. Whatever needs to be done to make the duke believe we'll kill her."

Malcolm agreed it was a good plan and returned to his position. Luke moved a bit more slowly, eyeing Edmund from beneath the wreath of his dark lashes.

"Ye think the duke will believe our wee performance?"

"Why wouldn't he? He doesn't know any of us or what we're capable of." Edmund knew he had to *make* the duke believe it if they planned on getting out of Ravenglade alive.

"I'll get her," he said, turning to go. "I'll speak to her... to all of them before I bring them up. Aye?"

Lucan nodded and pounded his upper arm. "Aye."

As Edmund left the battlements, he thought about what his life would have been like without these men in it. Without his kin. He loved them and he missed the ones he'd left behind. His brother, who hadn't given up the skill of swordplay, but preferred perfecting the art of being indefinable and obscure, and discovering everyone's secrets. Nichola, his wee sister—well, not so wee anymore, he thought, reaching the second landing and heading down to the kitchen. At ten and seven she was blossoming into a beautiful woman and he should be home seeing to her well-being.

He stopped outside the kitchen, where the smell of burning pitch stung his nostrils, and thought of his father. Edmund missed practicing with him behind their manor house early in the morn, before the rest of Camlochlin woke. Like Malcolm's parents, Edmund's had chosen not to live inside the castle, preferring the intimacy of quiet mornings and warm, cozy nights over drafty halls and boisterous breakfasts. Not that they didn't spend time inside the cavernous fortress; Edmund and his cousins played in every chamber, explored every cave, while their clan came together and shared laughter and whisky.

He wanted to see everyone again. He wanted to make it out of this alive and go home. And he wanted to bring *her* with him.

He watched Amelia step out of the kitchen. He couldn't take his eyes off her. From the moment he first laid eyes on her, he didn't ever want to stop looking. He wondered if his father felt the same when he saw his mother.

Seeing him, she waved and made her way toward him.

Here it was, all that he wanted in life. He loved Scotland and everything it had given him, but he didn't want to die for it anymore. He wanted to live, and share it all with Amelia.

He took her hands when she reached him and pulled her closer. "Stay with me, lass. Make a life with me. Be the mother of my bairns. I'll give ye everything I have. I'll do everything in my power to make ye happy. I'll build ye yer own private garden."

She stared at him, her huge eyes growing even rounder, searching his. "Edmund, do ye know what ye mean to me? Do ye know that I love ye?"

"Aye, I do."

"But my father—"

"Is responsible fer his own life, Amelia. D'ye think he would want ye to be unhappy with a man who marries ye fer his own gain? If yer father loves ye, and I know he does, he wants ye to be happy with a man who would give his life fer ye."

When she seemed to be pondering it and said nothing else, he told her about the duke's letter and explained that they needed to convince him that they were sincere in their convictions. At least until Darach returned with reinforcements.

"Trust me, love."

When she nodded, doing as he asked without further question or quarrel, he wanted to carry her to bed and thank her properly, but that too would have to wait.

"From the moment ye first looked at me," he told her instead, "I knew my heart was lost."

"As did I," she whispered back, swiping away a tear.

Edmund smiled and kissed her, then set about to his task.

Chapter Thirty-Two

"My lords!" Edmund shouted from the lowest parapet around the gatehouse an hour later, when their time, according to Queensberry's note, was up. "Is this who ye wait fer?" Staying behind her, he shoved Amelia forward to present her to the men fifty feet below.

Amelia looked down. She saw her uncle and fought a wave of guilt and regret. What would he tell . . . her father? She saw John Bell standing off alone, to the right of the men. She should have known he would come. When she found him, pale and gaunt amid the others, she wanted to weep. Oh, what he must have gone through, worrying about her while she was happily falling in love. She felt heavy with guilt, burdened with sorrow over him. She had to speak to him. She had to let him know she was unharmed.

"Nae, it cannot be her," Edmund continued behind her. "Fer my first note to ye clearly stated that should the union take place, Miss Bell would die. Perhaps ye thought me insincere."

He drew the dull edge of his dagger against her throat. From below, her father shouted, a woman screamed.

"My mother?" Amelia's voice broke softly over the sudden silence. She found her below, saddled on a horse beside Walter's. What the hell was Millicent Bell doing here?

Amelia closed her eyes and leaned her head on Edmund, behind her. Her mother had come to see with her own eyes what trouble her daughter had gotten herself into this time so she could never let Amelia forget it. She'd let herself get kidnapped and held for ransom, putting everyone in danger. She was a fool, her mother would tell her. A shame to their family.

"Edmund, I..." She turned to tell him she couldn't do this. She couldn't let her father believe she was in so much danger, ready to be killed.

Her ankle twisted. She lost her balance and tumbled backward over the short wall. Edmund grasped her hand in time so that she didn't fall to her death.

She wished she had. Better death than tumbling head-first, toes pointed heavenward, skirts over her waist, and her hand clasped to Edmund's between her bare knees...

Her misfortune had returned.

Only this time she realized how much worse it was when an arrow cut the air and landed like with a sickening thud into Edmund.

He'd held on to her. He hadn't let her go even when the arrow pierced his shoulder. She wept while she tended to his wound. What were these men doing? How could they be so foolish as to believe they could get out of this alive? How was she going to leave him? She had to, for his sake and her father's. Dear God, her father was here! What would happen when Darach returned with more men? What if her father was killed? What if Edmund was killed? She had to stop it.

"'Tis just a flesh wound, love. A scratch." He took her shaky hand and kissed it. "'Twas good fortune that I caught ye and good fortune that yer father's arrow barely hit me."

Dear God, it was her father's arrow. She still couldn't believe it. She didn't know her father could even fire an arrow. "The sight of ye holding that dagger to my neck must have been too much fer him. I'm sorry he shot ye. He isn't usually—" She wiped her eyes but it was no use. "If ye would have dropped me, the duke and my mother would have blamed him and…" She couldn't think of it. "And my mother…she is here to make certain I'm returned and bring no shame to her."

"Why do ye care what yer mother thinks, Amelia?" Sarah stood by the doorway, arms folded across her chest, watching her friend. "She is and has always been a wretched human bein'. Ye are nae longer her responsibility. Ye're a grown woman who has been sharin' the bed of a Highlander and—"

"Sarah, please," Amelia groaned, finishing up her work on Edmund and bandaging him up.

"What, fer goodness sake?" Her friend stopped and came forward. "Ye could be carrying his babe. Ye could—"

"Ye don't think I know that?" Amelia ignored Edmund when he turned to smile at her. "How selfish of us to bring a babe into this."

"Nae, Amelia," Edmund said firmly, rising to his feet

and turning to take her in his arms. "Don't think that way. A babe between us will be a blessing, safe and sound and happy in Camlochlin." He kissed her and smiled against her mouth. "I need to get back to the battlements and show yer uncle that I'm not harmed. We will speak of this some more later, aye?"

She nodded, not really wanting to speak of anything at all anymore. She wasn't going back to Camlochlin with him and oh how it shattered her wretched heart. She wanted a life with him more than anything. But too much was at stake. Even if her father wasn't involved, her uncle would never let Edmund take her. If she was with child…Oh, saints help her, if she was with child hell would rain down on Queensberry House.

"Sarah," she told her friend after he left. "When I think of never seeing him again, never hearing him speak my name again, it makes my heart, nae, my soul, feel like 'tis dying."

"Ye don't have to leave him, dearest," her friend said gently. "Ye can have the life ye want. The life ye've always dreamed about. We can stay together, too, Amelia." Sarah took her hands. "I want to go to Skye with Luke…with ye."

Amelia closed her eyes. "My uncle will never let him live. Does no one understand that?"

"Amelia…"

But Amelia held up her palm when Sarah would have interrupted her. "I likened him to David. I flirted with him and let him captivate me, despite being promised to another. And now I've let myself fall in love with him and others will suffer fer it."

"Ye cannot live yer life fer yer father," Sarah insisted.

"He wants ye to be happy and ye're happy with Edmund."

She couldn't tell Sarah her plans. Her friend would try to stop her. "I am," she agreed instead. And she was. She was happier than she had ever been before in her life. "But I hate that my mother thinks me a fool. I hate that after everything else, I almost fell to my death in front of her."

"Yer mother is a miserable hag who would likely benefit from a stiff cock up her—"

"Sarah!"

"Well, 'tis the truth."

"Not one that I wish to hear!"

"All right then." Sarah smiled and moved in to kiss her cheek. "I'm going to change into men's clothing and then I'm going to the battlements. Ye're to remain here."

"Nae." Amelia stood up. "I'm perfectly capable of going up there and not falling."

Sarah passed her a doubtful look.

"We need it to appear as if we have more numbers than we do," Amelia reminded her. "Every head is important. I'm coming."

But Sarah wouldn't let her have her way. "I love ye, gel, and I'm not goin' to watch ye tumble over a wall twice as high as the one ye nearly fell from the first time. I know how ye get when yer mother is about. Ye're stayin' here. Ye're going to stay here and decide once and fer all which path ye will choose fer yer life. A path with Edmund and happiness, and at the rate ye both frolic in bed, a dozen bairns." She smiled when Amelia blushed to her roots. "Or a life with the chancellor, who is verra' much like yer mother when it comes to the less privileged. Not to mention that dead woman ye told me about. He will likely beat ye and make ye do all sorts of perverse sexual things. We will lose each other. More important, ye will lose yer happiness and everything else ye hold dear."

Her words brought tears to Amelia's eyes. She wiped them, opened her mouth, and then shut it again. Sarah was right. She would lose it all if she left Edmund. But she would lose much if she remained with him. She would lose her father and if her uncle attacked, she would likely lose Edmund. She had to find a way to return to her father and put an end to any further fighting.

She looked down and sniffed at Grendel at her feet. She sank to the floor next to him and closed her arms around his neck. "What I am to do, dear friend? I love yer father, but I love mine, too." She sighed and kissed his scruffy cheek. "Ye'll help me, won't ye?"

He lapped her face once and then resumed his panting.

"Ugh!" She wiped her face and stared at his disinterested profile while he kept his eyes on the door.

"Go to him then." She stood up and fell back into the settee. "And kiss him fer me."

She buried her face in Grendel's fur and wept when he returned to her and leaped onto the settee and into her lap.

Darach's good fortune put him in an especially pleasant mood on his way back to Ravenglade just a pair of hours after he'd left it. That had to be why he hadn't choked the breath out of Janet Buchanan yet. He had met up with William and his sister on their way to Ravenglade in answer to Edward's invitation yesterday. When Darach explained that the Duke of Queensberry and his entire garrison had arrived to take the castle and claim it back for the throne, William agreed to follow him back.

"Nae, wait fer me here," Darach had told him. "I'll return in a day or two with plenty of men at my back."

"Yer kin could be dead by then," William argued. "We'll go now. I'll send my most trusted men to gather the other clans."

That was when he told Darach about the tunnels. Hell, there were tunnels! The Buchanans had started digging them shortly after Darach's grandparents left Ravenglade. They'd had a damned long time to dig!

"That's how we got inside the other night," William had admitted. "The bridge was left down but we would be foolish to walk through the front doors of our enemy."

Bastard was right, and clever too. Tunnels! They could all fight about it later. Right now he had a way to get his cousins out without discovery. He wanted to shout with thankfulness. He loved a good fight as much as any other Highlander. But four against two hundred was hopeless, even for Grants and MacGregors. And William was correct. While Darach was out recruiting aid, his kin could die.

He was going to get them all out alive. It would have been one of the most perfect days of his life if Janet hadn't insisted on coming with them. He wasn't unsure if she could take care of herself if they came across a stray solider or two when they got closer to the castle. He'd seen her quick reflexes. He might have enjoyed her company, since her smile lingered in his thoughts when he woke up this morn. But so far, she had done nothing but argue with her brother and admonish him for telling Darach their grand secret.

"So yer plan," she asked William now, "is to get the rest of them out and then return fer our men and attack from behind?"

"That's correct, Janet," her brother drawled, beseeching the heavens. "I've already explained it. The duke's men will not be expecting any opposition from behind them."

"Hmmm, aye, I remember ye mentioning that already. What I'm still unclear about is *why*?" She shouted the last word and finally managed to anger Darach.

"Now that ye got that oot of yer system, can we have a moment or two of peace from yer viperous tongue?"

Janet narrowed her eyes on him and forced a tight smile. "I'll be silent. But first I want to know why we don't just let them kill ye all. Ravenglade would be ours."

"Aye, right after ye took down the army a hundred feet away."

"Why should we fight fer ye?" she asked him hotly. "If we are to be nothing but servants to the Grants, why the hell should we fight fer Ravenglade?"

"Fer the last time, ye willna' be servants." Darach shot her a dark look, then remembered why he was at this task in the first place. It may have been Edmund whose passion for it gave life to their cause, but Darach believed in it, too.

"Ravenglade is only the first thing they will take. The duke and the men with him wish to sell us all fer a price. And though noblemen like Queensberry and the chancellor will be collectin' the gold, 'tis us who will truly have to pay. Our country is aboot to be taken over by the English. They'll make decisions aboot our taxes, our duties and responsibilities to the throne, which will never likely see another Scottish king. Our land will be taken from us, especially if we own anything of value on it."

"We're with ye, Grant," William promised and cast his sister a chastising look. "They'll be no more talk of it."

Janet's cool glance caught Darach's, and damn him if it didn't make him smile. She was saucy, and he did like his lasses saucy. She wasn't the first lass he'd desired, but she was the first lass he wanted to bed and toss over the nearest cliff.

"What d'ye care about the laws here anyway? 'Tis not like yer kin obey them."

He could have ignored her—pretended he didn't hear her. She had mumbled her retort, after all. "What laws d'ye mean?" he asked, turning to look at her. "The ones that prohibit the name of a clan from bein' used or spoken? The ones that ferbid my kin from fightin' back, even if they are innocent?"

"I acknowledge that the proscription against the MacGregors is unfair—"

"Ah, ye acknowledge it," he cut her off momentarily to cast her a mocking smile. "There is hope fer our species yet."

She ignored his comment—which curled his lips with something more genuine.

"'Tis inhumane," she continued. "But the decrees against them are hardly ever exercised."

His gaze on her hardened and he liked the way it made her square her shoulders, like she was readying herself to take him on.

"How d'ye know what's exercised against us? Were ye there every time one of us was arrested? None ever return. They may no' hunt us with dogs and brand the faces of our women anymore, but we are considered the shyt beneath a nobleman's boots. And they dinna' just feel that way aboot us, but aboot all Scots. They will always seek to subjugate us. Always. If none of us fight back, 'twill nae longer be just the MacGregors whose rights are robbed from beneath his helpless arse."

Finally, he'd succeeded in silencing her. He wanted to shout a cheer of victory. But madly enough, disappointment seized him first. He wanted to tell her about his kin, about the deeds of men he considered far above any men anywhere else. Camlochlin bred great warriors, heroes who faced their enemies head-on and left respect and fear in their wake. He itched to tell her about his grandsire Graham Grant and his heroic deeds in aid of the Stuart throne. But his grandsire was part of the reason James Buchanan died. So he suspected she wouldn't enjoy hearing it.

"I'm turnin' into my faither," he murmured softly. He'd suspected it for some time now, tried to deny it. But he felt the pull of lyrics, the call of music in his blood.

"Is he that bad then?"

Darach blinked at her. "Who?"

"Yer father?"

Hell. Had he spoken loud enough for her to hear?

"He's worse," he answered. "He's a poet."

Chapter Thirty-Three

No one saw Darach and his two Buchanan guests enter Ravenglade since they did so from the north, and from a tunnel beginning at least a half mile away. They entered the castle through a secret floorboard inside a small storage room beyond the buttery, down the hall from the kitchen. Henrietta and Amelia discovered them first, thanks to Grendel's low growls and scratching at the door to be let into the small room.

Amelia was quite stunned to see the three of them step into the hall from another room thought to be sealed from the outside. She recognized William from his last visit here and guessed the girl with him was his sister, Janet.

"What are ye doing back here and how in the world did ye get inside?" she asked Darach, giving him a brief hug.

"Tunnels," he told her while she followed them to the battlements where Edmund stood watch with the others. They were all as shocked to see Darach and the Buchanans as she was. They all listened to William explain about the tunnels. Malcolm scowled during the entire rendition. His muttered utterings of words like "mole," "rat," "thievin'," and "bastards" brought a frown just as dark to Janet's face, but she didn't stare at Malcolm overlong. No woman did if she wanted to hold on to her good senses. Edmund appeared so relieved by the news that Amelia thought he might fling his arms around William, and perhaps Janet, too.

"Has the duke made any other move?" Darach asked after William peered over the wall and whistled at the amount of men below.

Edmund told them about the note attached to the duke's arrow. He also told him in brief detail about Amelia almost falling over the side and his being shot by her father. "They likely believe I pushed her and then dangled her above the ground as a threat. It has given us a bit more time, but I don't know how much. Once they start trying to get in, we won't have much time."

"What does her almost falling have to do with anything regarding the army?"

They all turned to Janet, who'd asked the question—all but Darach, who spread his gaze over the landscape, at anything but them, and inhaled a gusty breath.

"Miss Bell is the duke's niece," Lucan supplied.

"We kidnapped her," Malcolm added.

"So." Janet's eyes narrowed and darkened on Darach. "They have come fer her then and not fer Ravenglade?"

"Ravenglade?" Malcolm asked, looking none too pleased with her or her brother. "The only ones who want to try to take it from me are yer kin."

"Hell," Darach muttered and closed his eyes. When he opened them again he caught Amelia's gaze.

She smiled softly at him, understanding what he'd done.

"Not according to yer lying cousin Grant," Janet corrected Malcolm. "Ye see, Will?" She turned to her brother. "I told ye we shouldn't have trusted him."

"His intentions were not to deceive ye, Miss Buchanan." Amelia turned to her and wondered if the cool pewter skies had anything to do with the icy color of her eyes.

"And how d'ye know that, m'lady?" she asked Amelia, folding her arms across her chest.

"Because I know that he told ye whatever he needed to tell ye so he could find yer tunnels and get us out. If that makes him a scoundrel to ye, then mayhap ye need a loyal friend or two to prove ye wrong."

Janet found Darach's gaze and seemed to catch her breath. She returned her attention to Amelia and answered her warm smile with one of her own. "I'm not above admitting when I was wrong."

"Where does it lead?" Edmund's query drew her attention back to the men.

"About a half mile to the east, beyond the army."

"Impressive," Luke said.

"My kin had many long years to build it," William told them. "'Tis more impressive than ye can imagine."

"'Tis," Darach validated. "A man doesna' have to bend his head to walk through it."

"Show us." Edmund clapped William on the back and then handed him over to Luke. "If 'tis safe enough, we can leave tonight. I'll be along in a moment."

Before he left, Edmund walked back to Darach. "Ye'll keep watch fer a bit? Keep an eye on Amelia while she's up here?"

"Aye."

"I want to see the tunnel, Edmund," Amelia said.

"Ye will, lass," he promised her, touching her face with the backs of her fingers. "After I deem it safe fer ye."

She nodded. She would see the tunnel and use it later. Nothing had changed for her except that Edmund would be safe and she thanked God for that. But she still couldn't leave her father. Now, at least, she had a way to return to him. Her uncle had already stated in his letter that the treaty would not be dissolved. There was nothing left to be done. Would Edmund hate her for leaving him? She kept herself from crying and tried to concentrate on what she needed to do.

Edmund turned to leave and called out to Darach over his shoulder. "Ye saved us all, lad."

"Aye," Malcolm called, on his way out. "Ye'll be needin' an ode to yerself. Now there's a challenge."

Amelia smiled through her misery and turned to Darach while the others all left the battlements. "I like her."

"Who?"

She slapped him on the arm. "Ye know very well who." When he conceded with a smirk, she shook her head at him.

"I like her, too," he admitted. "But I dinna' want a wife yet."

Amelia pouted for a moment, knowing she couldn't argue his point. He was ten and eight, nine at the most. If he wasn't ready, it was good that he knew it.

"I hope I'm not interrupting," Janet said, reaching them. "I've already seen the tunnels, but never an army." She set her gaze beyond the moat and took in the sight, never once glancing in Darach's direction.

Amelia suppressed the urge to grin at them both and made her excuses to leave them. She would tell Darach later what she thought of Miss Buchanan. What did their age matter when there was so much charged power between them? The air smoldered and crackled and they both fought so hard to deny it. It was silly. Darach should allow himself the pleasure of loving one woman. Amelia would tell him that later, if she had time.

First she had to prepare for her escape. The thought of running from Edmund nearly brought her to her knees. He wouldn't understand why she left him. She should tell him, but what would she say? What if he stopped her by force? What would become of her father?

When Edmund returned from seeing the tunnels, she would retire to her room, claiming to need a nap after such a tiring, perilous day. She would leave shortly after that. Of course, traveling through the tunnel alone would frighten her but what else could she do? God help her, she would never be happy with Walter. She would never be happy with any other man but Edmund. She had tasted love. She'd been caressed by it.

Things were different now.

She had changed, but her future hadn't.

She went to the kitchen, where Sarah and Etta were preparing supper. Sarah. The thought of leaving her, of never seeing her dearest friend ever again, prompted more tears. She loved Sarah more than she could ever express, and she wouldn't express them now. She couldn't let herself be swayed. Sarah would have a wonderful life with Lucan. That's what mattered.

She reached for an apron and joined them at their task, keeping her mind off what she needed to do.

She thought about telling Sarah her plan, but decided against it. Her friend would try to dissuade her from going. Too many things could go wrong, but Amelia was willing to risk it. She needed to risk it.

With her decision made, she focused on baking shortbread cakes, a favorite of any Scotsman.

When an hour had passed, she left the kitchen without filling Sarah in on her plans. She returned to the battlements to make certain Edmund and the others had returned and the tunnel was clear and safe. After sharing a word with Janet, she looked out over the army of men below. Would she be able to find her father among them, especially with the sun going down? She would have to.

"Can we see where the tunnel will let us out from here?" she asked casually.

William gazed out, squinting against the setting sun. "Let me think." He measured distance with his fingers and pointed east, a good distance from the army. "Aye, I believe there is where we will come out. 'Tis difficult to tell from here. The woods look alike."

"By the time the duke knows we are gone," Edmund said, coming up behind her and closing his arms around her waist, "we will be halfway to Skye. We need to talk about this now, my love. Let's go inside, aye?"

She closed her eyes, afraid that if he turned her around to look at him, she would cling to him and never let go. How was she going to insist on leaving? Demand, if she must, that he return her or leave her here while he escaped? He wouldn't agree to it and she wasn't strong enough to resist him overlong. Could she truly leave him? How different would her life be now that she knew love? Could she live without it? Without him? He was her

David, her giant-slayer, only he didn't slay the giant this time. Was the difference that this time, she was in his life? What else would befall him if she stayed? She had to go. But if he knew, he wouldn't let her.

"There is no need to speak of it further," she said and dragged a breath into her lungs to help her smile when she turned in his arms. "I love ye and I cannot leave ye."

His relief was evident in his shaken breath, the warmth in his eyes, the handsome smile forming on his face.

After a kiss, he moved to return to his plans but she stopped him with a hand to his arm. "When will we be leaving?"

"We'll leave a wee bit before the midnight hour," he told her. "The tunnel is tall and wide enough for our horses to be walked out."

"Well then"—Amelia closed her eyes and prayed to just keep breathing a little longer when Edmund pressed a kiss to her temple—"I think I shall take a nap. I'm tired from the day and will need rest fer the journey. Edmund." She stopped him again when he turned to go. "Ye gave life to my dreams. I will love ye and no other fer the rest of my life."

His smile faded a little and he took a step back to her.

"Edmund?" Malcolm called. "William's agreed to bring Henrietta and Chester back to his village until the army leaves Ravenglade. Come, more preparations need to be made."

"Go, my love," she urged him. "I'll see ye after."

She watched him leave, calling out to Darach as he left the battlements. She musn't think. Just do. Move before she never moved again. She hurried to the buttery. On her way she picked up a meager candle to light her way inside the tunnel. She had to do it quickly, before anyone saw her. Before she listened to her heart and took her nap instead of running away.

Pulling up the floorboard, she said a quiet prayer and crawled inside. As she suspected, it was daunting being underground, surrounded by wooden beams and dirt. Thankfully, there were torches lit along the way, to light her path. The Buchanans had truly accomplished an impressive feat digging out this tunnel, but she still didn't like being in it. She pressed forward, refusing to think about what she was leaving behind. She didn't hear the low whine behind her, the heavy breathing following her. She heard nothing but the sound of her own heart beating...breaking.

Chapter Thirty-Four

Edmund looked into the face staring back at him and adjusted its left eye. He stuffed more hay into the Highland dummy's plaid and buffed it up a bit. It was supposed to be him after all, not a woman. There were eight hay figures in all, four of which were donned in the belted plaids belonging to Edmund and his Highland cousins. None of them minded leaving their plaids behind. They owned more at home and there were plenty of clothes in Ravenglade to wear, left here by Connor Stuart and the men who came after him.

Currently, Edmund wore a waistcoat, dark brown breeches, and a white ruffled shirt. The fit wasn't too bad, a bit tight, but Sarah whistled at him when she passed him in the hall and Janet stared at him in the courtyard behind the curtain wall where they dressed their dummies. Hopefully, his appearance would please Amelia as well. He looked around the torch-lit yard for her. He hadn't seen her in an hour and supper was almost ready. He'd checked her room but she wasn't there. He'd thought she might be packing a few things or helping Etta and Sarah in the kitchen. When he hadn't found her, he'd come out to the courtyard and found the others making their models. He'd decided to wait for her there.

"Has anyone seen Amelia?" he asked now, feeling a wave of sudden fear grip him at how dark it had become. He shrugged it away. She hadn't left the castle. Had she? When had he last seen his dog? He wanted to laugh at the silly fear threatening to grip him again. She was here, somewhere in the castle…doing something. Likely on her way to him right now.

"I thought she was in the kitchen," Malcolm said.

"She's not," Luke told them. "Sarah was looking fer her a wee while ago."

Edmund remained calm and turned to Darach and Janet. They both shook their heads. They hadn't seen her. He didn't run back into the castle. He wanted to, but he didn't want the others to believe he found her foolish enough to leave on her own. Or that he was the fool for believing her when she told him she loved him and that she wanted to stay with him. He made his way inside the fortress and then dashed to the kitchen and plunged inside. She wasn't there. The garden. He sprinted to it and entered the cool night air.

"Amelia!" he called out into the darkness. "Grendel!"

He turned when no answer came and sprinted across the long corridor and burst through three doorways, the last one being the one that led to the buttery.

When he saw the floorboard pushed aside, he knew. She'd gone. She'd left him, and without even a damned farewell.

He disappeared into the hole, leaving the floorboard where it was.

* * *

Amelia stopped and leaned her palms against the wall.
God help her, how long was this tunnel? She hated it.
She hated the shadows that danced along its walls and
ceiling. Twice she had to stop to close her eyes and
force herself not to panic. She couldn't breathe. She felt
like she was choking on the stale, hot air and she wanted
to run back. If it weren't for Grendel, she would have.
She spoke to him and watched him breathing without
struggle.

"I'm not going to tell ye that ye're a good boy fer
following me, Grendel, but I'm happy ye're here, dear
friend." She thought of how much Edmund loved this
worthy dog. She sniffed back another barrage of tears.
There had been two others since she'd entered the tunnel.
The first one came thanks to Edmund and the second,
Sarah. She doubted her heart would ever mend and she
would spend every night of her life weeping.

"I think I feel the slightest bit of a breeze." She stopped
and tried to concentrate on the whiff of fresher air she was
certain just wafted across her face. "I pray we're close. I
fear going mad in this place."

Grendel looked up at her, his dark eyes large and almost understanding. And then he pricked his ears, turned
his head to look forward, and took off.

"Grendel!" she shouted for him. She didn't want him
to leave her alone. She ran after him, her heart pounding
madly as she hurried along a crooked path cooled by the
night air. She was approaching the opening.

Thank God.

A pistol shot rang out close, stopping her dead in her
tracks. Another sound followed that fell so heavily on her

heart, she would have fallen to her knees from the weight of it if she weren't holding on to the wall.

A dog's cry. Grendel.

She ran toward the sound but stopped before she left the concealment of her hiding place. A soldier stood beneath a column of pale moonlight, a smoking pistol in his hand, and Grendel fallen at his feet.

Nae! Nae! Not Grendel! Amelia fell against the wall, and then to her knees. This couldn't be happening. Not to Grendel. *Oh, God, please, please not Grendel*, she prayed while the soldier shoved her beloved friend with his boot. Grendel didn't move. Amelia clamped her hands over her mouth to keep herself from screaming. Even in her torment she couldn't give away the tunnel. She couldn't go to him. She couldn't run out and let them see her. The army would get inside Ravenglade and kill everyone. She wanted to scream because this was her fault. The horrible scene before her was her fault. There was no denying it this time. She watched along the tunnel entrance, carefully hidden behind the thick brush and trees as more soldiers appeared, alerted by the pistol fire.

She forgot about her father, her mother, everyone in her life, while she waited hidden in the darkness, shaking, counting moments until it became utterly unbearable, waiting for the soldiers to leave.

What had she done? She tried as best she could not to sob as images of Grendel, ever at her feet, assailed her. She'd come to love the way one of his ears pointed upward while the other flopped over his brow. It made him look especially adorable. Aye, he may have been bred and raised to fight at Edmund's side, but around her, Grendel was a huge puppy.

"I come to take a shyt in private," the soldier told his friend, "when this mongrel come out of nowhere and attacks me."

The other one laughed. "Must have been that god-awful singing of yours."

Amelia sobbed quietly into her hands.

When they left the scene a few moments later, she left her hiding place and walked slowly to Grendel's body lying in the leaves, lifeless.

She fell to her knees.

"Grendel." She moved his head into her lap and ran her hand over his shaggy head, her tears falling into his fur. "Oh please, boy, don't go. What will I do without ye?" She had caused this. If she hadn't left Ravenglade, Grendel would likely be sleeping at her feet in the Great Hall right now, not dead in her lap. She thought nothing could ever happen after this instant that could be worse. She was wrong. She was so very wrong.

She knew that what had happened was tragic, a thing never to be forgotten. But when she heard Edmund calling her name, she remembered that the tragedy was not hers alone. Grendel was his.

She didn't want to look, to see him coming, to see the truth and the horror and the sorrow dawning on his face.

"Amelia!" he came out shouting, not caring whom he alerted.

Unable to stop herself, she turned to face him, to quiet him, lest they shoot him, too. His steps faltered when he saw her on her knees.

He moved to run to her but she held up her palm, stopping him. "Come no closer!" She wouldn't have him see. She wished he never had to see.

"Amelia, were ye shot?" His voice broke with emotion, and refusing her wish, he took a step closer. "Are ye hurt, my love? I heard a—" He ceased. That was a good way to describe what happened in those next few seconds. Edmund ceased.

His beautiful blue eyes welled in pools of tears as they fixed on the one she held in her arms. His head shook, denying what he saw. He took a step back, wishing, Amelia guessed, that he could go back. His mouth opened for air he didn't care about breathing. His legs suddenly moved, prompted, it seemed, by the tight groan that escaped his lips. When he stood over them, Amelia thought he would toss back his head and howl like some aggrieved beast, but his sorrow was far more heartbreaking.

He sank to his knees beside her and reached for his dog. Amelia surrendered Grendel without a word. She wanted to get up and run, run and never bring such misery to anyone again. But she couldn't move. She couldn't leave Edmund to this alone.

"How did this happen?" he asked quietly, trying to look at the gentle beast in his arms through his tears.

"He followed me. A soldier was singing."

But Edmund didn't hear. He'd closed his eyes and buried his face in Grendel's fur.

She did this to him. Who was next? Darach? One of the others? Would it be someone at Camlochlin when her uncle followed her there? Edmund's beloved father, perhaps? How long would she stay with him, risking his life and the lives of his family to her misfortune?

The others had appeared from the tunnel, alerted most likely by the pistol shot. Amelia didn't know how long they'd been there, but they stood back, giving Edmund his respect. She heard one of the men sob and another swear and storm away. Luke, Malcolm, and Darach had lost a friend and Amelia felt the weight of that loss more and more. But when she spotted Gaza a few feet away sitting between the trees, her eyes steady on Edmund and Grendel while a long, high-pitched cry left her body, Amelia finally rose to her feet and ran.

Chapter Thirty-Five

It didn't take Amelia long to find the army. Trying to remain hidden while she found her uncle was another matter entirely. There was no point in finding her father first. He couldn't stop the attack on Ravenglade. Her uncle could.

She was more certain than before that she had done the right thing by leaving Edmund. He would end up like Grendel. Deep down she always knew. Either her misfortune would get him, or her uncle's army would.

She was finally spotted and taken into the custody of Captain David Pierce, a man whom Amelia knew from the Queensberry garrison. He didn't treat her roughly while he brought her to her uncle's tent. Even when she tried to break free of him, he merely yanked her forward.

"The duke will be curious to know from which way you came."

Amelia's heart pounded. Good Lord, she hadn't thought of what to tell him! "I escaped."

"That's obvious," the captain said, his lips crooked into

a smirk that didn't reach his steely gray eyes. "But how? The bridge isn't down."

Amelia glared at him. "Where is my uncle's tent, Captain?" She remembered to breathe when he pointed to it. It was only a short distance away. She needed more time to think about how she had escaped her captors and gotten here.

"And my father?" she asked. "Where is he? I would like to see him first." Her father wouldn't care about how she came to be there, only that she was safe. Speaking to him would give her more time to think.

"I'm sure your uncle will send for Lord Selkirk after he speaks with you."

Damn it, but he was a stubborn man—probably why he never married—but thanks to Sarah's past instruction on how to get what you need from a man, Amelia knew what to do. "Captain." She sniffed and dabbed the corners of her eyes with her sleeves. "I have been through a tremendous ordeal. I honestly don't know how I lived through this night." It was easy to make herself cry. Grendel's death and Edmund's sorrow were still fresh in her mind. "'Twas the worst of my life," she sobbed, telling him the truth. "I want nothing more than to feel safe again in my father's arms."

He stared at her, trying to see more in her eyes than she cared to show him. When she thought he would refuse her, he looked around and then nodded. "You will have a few moments only. I will bring your mother to his tent."

"Nae." Amelia touched her fingers to his arm. "She will be angry with ye fer not bringing me directly to her brother."

Captain Pierce knew it to be true. Everyone who knew

Millicent Bell knew that her loyalty fell to her brother before her husband. If she discovered that the captain of her
brother's guard did anyone's bidding besides or before the
duke's, she would make certain the duke knew about it.

"Come with me then, lady." He tugged her forward.
"See your father quickly."

Amelia managed a soft smile and wiped her nose with
the back of her hand. The captain smiled back.

They moved quickly, quietly through the shadows until
they reached her father's tent. At the entrance, Amelia's
heart battered in her chest. She missed her father so much.
It felt like months since she'd hugged him, kissed him,
told him she loved him. She couldn't wait another second
and pushed aside the tent flap.

Amelia thought her well of tears had dried up, but she
was wrong. The instant her father turned in his chair and
saw her the floodgates reopened.

"Papa."

His dark eyes lit from within as if a flame that had died
was rekindled. He stared at her for a moment or two as if
she were a ghost and not real at all. Then his voice broke
on a ragged note as tears filled his eyes. "Amelia?" He
took a step forward. "My daughter?"

She ran the rest of the way to him and he caught her
in his eager, waiting embrace. "Are ye well, Mellie?" he
cried into her hair, holding her.

She was now. For tonight, at least. Oh, she had so
much to tell him. She would tell him everything, starting
with the night she went dancing.

Standing by the entry, Captain Pierce kept his stoic expression unchanged when Amelia smiled at him, thanking him silently for this time.

"I knew yer uncle wouldn't agree to the demands. I feared that whoever had ye would kill ye."

She shook her head, sitting at her father's feet a little while later. "I'm sorry ye worried so, Papa. I was well taken care of, well protected."

"We were informed by one Ennis Buchanan that he saw ye being kissed by Grant. I suspect after yer night of dancing, he meant Edmund MacGregor."

She didn't deny it but nodded her head. "Aye, he meant him," she admitted quietly. She looked away from his searching gaze, unsure of how to tell him the truth. That she'd fallen in love with a Highland outlaw.

"I see," her father said just as softly. "Ye care fer him?"

She nodded her head again and then dipped her face to his knee. "I am quite madly in love with him, Papa. And tonight, I killed his dog."

"The duke's tent?"

Edmund peered through the heavy brush partially blocking his view of the aforementioned structure. "It could be." He leaned back and rubbed his hand over his jaw. How the hell did he know whose tent it was? What did he know about anything? She tricked him. Why had she tricked him? Why not just tell him the truth, that she wanted to go back to her father, to Walter? Why had she lied straight to his face shortly before she left? The instant she had a chance to go, she fled without even a word. Twice! Was she so heartless? He didn't know. But he was going to find out.

"Edmund," the man to his right whispered. "This is a poor idea. We cannot fight all these men."

"What would ye have me do, Luke?"

"We would have ye use yer head," Malcolm said in a hushed voice. "No' lose it. We need to devise a plan. We'll get her back, but no' by dyin'."

"Go back then and devise something," Edmund told them both. "I'm not leaving."

"I'll stay with ye, Edmund."

Edmund turned to Darach. Any other time, he would have welcomed Darach's fearless loyalty. But not now. Not when they faced an army. Hell, he didn't want them to be here. When he noticed that Amelia had left after Grendel...he'd tried to go off on his own to find her but the lads had followed him. They had tried to stop him from getting close to the duke's camp, but Edmund knew that was where Amelia had gone. He would not be stopped.

He regretted his decision only because it put his cousins in danger. But now was not the time to doubt himself. He had to talk to her, to find out how she could leave him and how long she had been preparing to do so.

"This doesn't concern any of ye," he told them softly. "Go back to Ravenglade. Gather the others and go. I will catch up later."

"Nae."

"Darach, ye'll do as I say."

Darach chuckled. "Ye still like to think of yerself as m' faither then."

He was about to tell the young hellion that he would kick his arse like his father never had before when Malcolm folded his arms and settled into his position behind a thick tree trunk. Luke did the same, letting Edmund know that none of them were going anywhere.

Very well then. He was patient. He would wait until they were asleep and then he would find her.

It took longer than he expected. Three hours later, Malcolm and Luke sent Darach back to the castle to inform William and the others of their delay. Amelia had been taken out of the tent by the same dark-haired man who brought her into it, and then escorted to another, bigger tent behind the troops.

Edmund watched, alert and unwearied, while her mother was brought to her next, escorted by the Lord Chancellor of Scotland, Earl of Seafield, Amelia's future husband.

He almost left his concealment when he saw Seafield. Had Amelia chosen the earl over him? Was she kissing him right now, telling him how horrible these last few weeks had been for her?

He knew he was on the verge of madness to even consider such betrayal from her. He knew better, but he sill considered storming into the camp and taking her back.

After another hour passed, his cousins had finally begun to snore. Edmund said a silent prayer and then stretched his limbs and crept along the shadows to yet another tent where Amelia had been taken. There were still enough of Queensberry's guards awake to cause a problem. Edmund didn't want to cause a disturbance and bring the rest of them down on his head, so he was careful not to make a sound and slipped into Amelia's tent without being spotted.

She sat on the ground, amid blankets and pillows, her knees pressed to her chest. Illuminated by candlelight, she looked afraid and alone… and beautiful.

But she wasn't alone. She hadn't been alone all night. Her family and her uncle's guards were close by. He had to hurry.

"Amelia." His voice was low, quiet, anguished.

She looked up and gasped, then sprang to her feet. "Edmund, what are ye doing here? Ye must go! Someone will come and find ye here and—"

"What are *ye* doing here, Amelia?" he asked, cutting her off. "Why did ye run away? Is this the life ye want?"

She shook her head and tears fell from her face. "'Tis what's best."

"Best fer who?" he demanded, raising his voice and no longer giving a damn who heard him. "'Tis not best fer me or ye."

"Edmund." She reached for him. "I will only bring ye more pain. My father—"

"More pain than this?" He stepped away from her. Too much had happened tonight. He felt on the brink of breaking and doing something he would regret, like tossing her over his shoulder, carrying her the hell out of here, and killing whoever got in his way. "How could anything ye do cause more pain than what tortures me right now?" He watched her tears slip down her cheeks and felt the sting of his own aching to fall. "We made plans fer a future together, Amelia."

"They were fancies, Edmund."

"Nae, they were real. I asked ye to stay with me. To be the mother of my bairns..."

"I want that, Edmund."

He wanted to laugh, to mock her words. But he couldn't laugh. Not tonight. Mayhap not for a long while to come. "Is that why ye slipped out of Ravenglade by tunnel tonight? Is that why Grendel is dead?"

He hadn't meant for his words to bring such sorrow to

her face. He knew Grendel's death wasn't her fault. But it left him empty nonetheless.

"I had to go, Edmund. I owe my father so much," she cried. "I never meant fer Grendel to die! Don't ye see? This pain follows me, Edmund. Ye tried to fight it but it will never stop and yer demise will be next! Do ye truly believe that my uncle would have left us alone? He would have killed ye, mayhap yer family."

Someone made a sound outside the tent. Amelia lifted her hand as if to touch him. "Go! Leave here quickly."

"D'ye love me, Amelia?

"More than life. But—"

"Then come with me."

"Please don't be a fool, Edmund," she cried, pushing him now toward the opening. "Ye must go! 'Tisn't safe!"

"'Tis too late fer that," he told her as two guards rushed in and grabbed him. They yanked his wrists behind his back and shouted for more guards to come.

But Edmund didn't fight back. He let them take his weapons and then him without a word, keeping his eyes on Amelia as they pulled him outside. She followed, demanding that they let him go.

"Please, Captain, he meant no harm!"

"I've given in to your desires once already this night, my lady."

Edmund recognized the captain as the same man who had escorted her around the camp earlier. He paid the soldier little attention while the camp came alive around him. He looked toward the tree line, hoping his cousins stayed where they were. He knew they would. Luke, at least, was not impetuous. He would keep the other two safe.

"Why have ye done this?" Amelia's anguished voice

drew his attention back to her. "They will kill ye. Why did ye come here?"

"Fer ye," he told her softly.

They had stopped and Edmund caught the captain's command to alert the duke that a prisoner was being brought to him.

"Edmund MacGregor?" the captain asked him while they waited and more guardsmen were awakened.

"Aye, Edmund MacGregor," he told him, emphasizing his surname.

The captain didn't look impressed but sized him up from foot to crown with mild interest. "Do Highlanders wear English garb now?"

"Do captains in a traitor's army concern themselves with fashion as well as warfare now?"

The captain laughed, then pulled him along by the elbow. "You've got balls to stroll right in here when half my men are still awake. I'll give you that, MacGregor."

"Captain Pierce, please," Amelia cried, following them. "This is all my fault. Please let him go." She put her hand to the captain's sleeve, trying to stop him.

Behind them, another soldier who'd been poking Edmund in the back the entire time pushed her hand away roughly and was about to admonish her when Edmund pivoted on his heel and faced him.

"Touch her again," he warned slowly, his voice a deadly combination of silk and steel, "and I will crack yer skull in two."

The soldier laughed but didn't speak another word to Amelia.

Captain Pierce pulled him forward toward another tent, one that Amelia had been inside earlier. Edmund guessed it was the duke's. When he stepped inside, he saw that he was correct.

"Edmund MacGregor, my lord," Pierce announced.

The Duke of Queensberry turned from looking out beyond a large flap in the back of the tent and smiled. He was not an imposing man and Edmund couldn't help but wonder how he'd managed to get so many to agree to sign his treaty.

"You're cleaner looking than I expected."

Edmund looked him over. "Ye're shorter."

The duke glanced at Pierce and nodded. Edmund doubled over from a fist to his belly. Amelia screamed as three more people entered the tent.

"Which one is he?" A man whom Edmund recognized as the chancellor gawked at him and then narrowed his eyes on Amelia. "Is this the one who kissed my lady? Grant is it?"

"Walter," Amelia's mother fawned, "we don't know that she kissed any of them. Ennis Buchanan wasn't telling the truth. Isn't that correct, Amelia?"

"Aye, Mother."

Edmund looked at Amelia while she denied him. He didn't want to think about why she was doing it. He hoped it was to protect herself.

"I'm a MacGregor," he told the chancellor. "And I can tell ye fer certain that she didn't kiss any Grants."

The chancellor glared at him, then at the duke. "Did I invite this uncivilized criminal to speak to me directly?" When the duke shook his head, Seafield rounded on the captain. "Teach this savage his place."

The captain hit Edmund in the belly a second time and then in the jaw.

This time, Amelia shouted at him and grasped his arm to stop him from striking Edmund again. Someone shoved her out of the way and sent her sprawling onto the floor. Millicent Bell shrieked at the sight and John, Amelia's father, turned a deadly glare on the man who had struck his daughter.

But it was too late.

They all watched in disbelief as Edmund, bound at the wrists, spun on his heel and faced the soldier who had put his hand to Amelia for a second time. Before anyone could stop him, he reeled back his head then brought it forward into the soldier's forehead with a resounding crack. The soldier sank to the ground. His body twitched once, twice, and then ceased moving.

Chapter Thirty-Six

Amelia had never seen a man go down so fast. Even Captain Pierce took an involuntary step back when Edmund turned to face them. Everyone in the tent, including Amelia, shifted his or her gaze from the duke's prisoner to the lifeless soldier on the floor. Amelia thought she might just faint with terror for poor Edmund. If her uncle wasn't going to kill him for kidnapping her, Edmund would surely hang for killing one of his soldiers. She wanted to beg him to plead for his life. She would beg her uncle to spare him.

Surprisingly, it was her father who stepped forward first and spoke. "Mr. MacGregor, why have ye come here? Ye understand, ye are an outlaw."

Something passed between them that only Amelia noticed because she knew and loved them both so much. Her father knew about her and Edmund. She had told him everything. He'd reminded her then, as he did Edmund now, of the consequences that befell anyone who sympathized with the proscribed clan. He was afraid for her.

"After I let yer daughter go," Edmund informed him,

sensing the reason behind her father's words, "I realized she had stolen my dog."

Her heart plummeted to the ground, knowing that if Edmund lived, he would never forgive her.

"Gaza," he supplied and turned to cast his heavy blue gaze on her.

"Well," her father asked her, "are ye in possession of his dog?"

"Nae," she told them delicately, hating to have to inflict more pain on Edmund. "She ran away."

He caught and held her gaze, speaking to her as clearly without words as if he'd uttered them. *Same as ye.*

"MacGregor," the chancellor spoke up, not getting too close. Amelia hadn't realized how short Walter was—not as short as her uncle, but short. Neither had she noted how skinny his calves were in his hose. "I'm not surprised at seeing you murder one of the duke's soldiers, but I question your reason for killing him. Do you care for Miss Bell?"

Walter might be short and frail in comparison to Edmund, but he was clever. He moved closer to her, close enough to warm her cheek with his breath. "Did this sweet innocent slay your heart, Highlander?" He smiled at her, then smoothed a tendril of hair away from her cheek. He slid his dark gaze to Edmund and with a satisfying quirk of his mouth, turned to Amelia's uncle. "He grows angry. It's clear to see in his eyes that he didn't follow her here for a dog. I want the truth before I take her to my bed. I won't go where a savage has already been."

Amelia paled and slipped her gaze to Edmund. *Please, please say nothing*, she silently begged him.

He seemed to have heard her and let Walter pass him unharmed when he left the tent.

"Walter." Millicent Bell moved to follow the chancellor outside. "You can be assured that despite my daughter's faults, she would never share a bed with one of them."

Amelia dipped her gaze to her shoes. It amazed her how much worse her mother could always make her feel. Just when she thought nothing could get any worse, her mother proved her wrong. Amelia realized now that Millicent Bell would never change. She loved Amelia, in her way. But Amelia was too much like her father to ever gain her mother's respect. She didn't care anymore.

"My lord," her father spoke to her uncle, dragging her attention back up. "My daughter is fully aware of the impossibility of a union between herself and a man who has opposing beliefs."

"Is this true, niece?"

She felt all the men's eyes on her. Everyone waited for an answer. She wanted to look at Edmund, but she was afraid that if she did, she might fall to his feet and prove herself a liar.

"Aye, Uncle," she said, hoping that it wasn't too late to save Edmund. Her father knew she loved Edmund, but this wasn't the time to confess it. "I am fully aware. What the chancellor fails to remember is that I escaped and came straight to ye."

"I thought Mr. MacGregor let you go."

"I lowered myself from the lowest window," Amelia said, controlling the quaver in her voice. "He saw me making a run fer it and let me go without chase."

"Until he discovered his dog missing," her uncle reminded her.

Amelia nodded and turned to look at Edmund. She couldn't keep her eyes off him, but she had to. She ached to run to him, touch him, free him. And then run away from him. Leaving him was the only way to ensure his safety. Or so she had thought. She'd run away and he'd followed her and now he was in more danger than before. What could she do to help him? How could she save him?

"You have caused my family a great deal of trouble, MacGregor."

"Uncle, if I may—"

"You may not!" The duke didn't shout. He cut her off like a blade coming down. Clean, precise, final. He turned to his captain. "If she makes another sound, remove her."

Amelia didn't break eye contact with her uncle right away. She'd grown up watching him intimidating everyone around him. She'd had enough of it. She would not defy him as long as he didn't threaten Edmund's life. No one, especially Edmund, would lose his life because of her, again.

"You do realize"—Walter returned and set his attention from her mother to Edmund—"that you could be tried for treason?"

"Treason against whom?" Edmund asked. "Queen Anne?" He shook his head. "She favors moderate Tory politicians, as do I. Or d'ye mean to charge me against our Parliament, which is soon to be dissolved?"

"England's Parliament will be dissolved as well." Walter smirked at him, as if Edmund were too ignorant to know. "The two kingdoms will finally stand on equal footing."

Edmund's smile was just as mocking. "And we have reason to trust England because they've upheld every promise made in the past?" No one spoke, but they all knew the answer. "Ye will all lose yer power, and then yer rights, just as the purer Scots before ye will have already discovered. Chancellor," he said, returning to him, "'tis not too late to change yer mind. If ye decide in these coming days to fight fer yer country's independence from subjugators, ye would have the support of many."

Walter narrowed his eyes on him, and then laughed. "A zealot. Now I understand why your kind are always the first to die. You cannot control your passions. Tell me, Amelia." Unexpectedly he turned to her, catching her off guard. "How often did he speak to you about his opinions, and was he always this passionate about them?"

"Leave her, Seafield," her father warned. "It isn't too late fer me to refuse my blessing."

Amelia cast her father a proud, slightly surprised smile.

She knew what Walter was trying to insinuate and so did the others. She hardened her jaw against him. Would he charge her with treason as well? Threaten to beat her? She took her time speaking, wanting to show him how little he intimidated her.

"Mr. MacGregor has many opinions and is passionate about all of them. But he forced none of his beliefs on me."

"What did he force on you, dear?" the chancellor asked.

Edmund moved toward him but was stopped by Captain Pierce, who, upon a second order from Walter, punched Edmund in the kidney. Amelia fought desperately against the tears welling up in her eyes when Edmund doubled over. She glared at Pierce first, and then at Walter.

"He forced nothing on me," Amelia answered, glaring at both of them. She was telling them the truth. What she had done with Edmund, she had done of her own free will.

"Then you remain pure for our marriage bed?"

"Seafield!" Amelia's father intercepted. "This interrogation of my daughter has gone far enough. I will not stand here and listen to ye dishonor her with such questions. Have me removed. I don't care. In fact, throw us out of Queensberry—"

"John!" his wife snapped at him.

He ignored her and continued—or tried to. The duke's subtle nod to Captain Pierce ended John Bell's uncharacteristic tirade.

Amelia watched her father being escorted out of the tent and wanted to follow. But she wasn't about to leave when Edmund's fate rested in her uncle's hands.

"For my sister's sake, I will not allow you to be questioned further tonight, Amelia."

Amelia didn't thank her uncle.

"Let us turn our attention to the prisoner. Shall we? Mr. MacGregor, let me assure you that the union between Scotland and England will take place. Kidnapping my niece wouldn't have stopped it. The only thing you accomplished was wasting my time and the time of my army by forcing us to come here. You distressed my sister until I had to pay four more physicians to examine her and confine her to her bed."

Amelia looked at her mother across the tent and shook her head, answering her silent questions when her mother severed their gaze and turned away.

"And most important," her uncle continued, "you incurred my wrath by stealing from me. I don't care about your cause or your beliefs, MacGregor. There are hundreds like you whose voices will be silenced eventually, just as yours will be when we return to Edinburgh. You will become their example."

"Uncle—"

He held up his hand to quiet her. "Defend him and his death will be slower. Captain!" He shouted for Pierce, then ordered that Edmund be taken away. "We leave at first light," he announced to his men when he left the tent.

Amelia watched Captain Pierce lead Edmund away. She had to do something to help him.

She refused to speak to her mother and returned to her tent unescorted. When she entered it, a hand over her mouth silenced her scream.

"There now, lass, 'tis only us." Malcolm's hoarse whisper fell across her ear.

"Let her go, Cal," Lucan said, leaving the shadows. "She's not goin' to scream, are ye, Amelia?"

She shook her head no, so relieved to see them that she felt a little woozy. They would help him. They would save Edmund.

"Why did ye come back here?" Malcolm let her go and moved to stand before her, his eyes hard on hers. "Ye had to know he'd follow ye."

"I had to return for many reasons," she began, hoping they would understand. "I thought I was keeping destruction from Edmund and complete ruin from my father."

"How are ye keepin' destruction from Edmund?" Malcolm asked quietly and more meaningfully than she'd heard him sound since she'd known him. "We could have escaped the duke's army, lass. No harm would have come to any of us."

She shook her head and wiped her eyes, determined to keep her wits about her after such a terrible night. "Ye don't understand. Grendel. I...I bring disaster...I—" Nothing was coming out right and it didn't help that she had begun to sob. Lucan was staring at her with pity shining in his topaz eyes and Malcolm stared at her as if her head just rolled off her shoulders and hit the ground. "My father...he has been my source of strength fer so long. No matter how much I love Edmund, no matter how badly I want to live my life with him, I cannot simply abandon my father to—"

The tent flap opened again. The Highlanders drew their claymores, ready to fight. Amelia's father paled at the size and height of them but held up his palms and shifted his gaze to his daughter.

"Are ye in danger from them?"

She would have smiled at him if she weren't afraid for his life. She shook her head and placed her hands on the edges of Luke's and Malcolm's swords to lower them.

"Nae, Papa, and neither are ye."

"Well, we will see—"

"Malcolm!" she hushed him with a dark look. When they were quiet, she peeked outside to make certain no one else was coming. She turned back to the men and met her father's sorrowful gaze. He looked away before she did and her heart ached to run to him.

"We know ye loved Grendel, lass. What happened to him wasn't yer fault."

Amelia loved Lucan for trying to comfort her. He just

didn't understand. "And ye should know how much I love Edmund. But what happens to him is indeed my fault. My uncle wants to bring him to justice in Edinburgh. We must save him."

"We will," they assured her. "Darach has…" They paused and looked at her father.

"My loyalties belong solely to my daughter," John Bell told them. "Ye may speak freely."

Malcolm waited another moment, eyeing the baron carefully, then said, "Darach has returned to Ravenglade to get William and bring more men here. We'll get Edmund away from where they're holdin' him but I fear he may no' leave here withoot ye."

"I cannot go with ye," she wept.

"Of course ye can," Lucan corrected her.

"Lass." Malcolm took on a more serious tone. "He already lost Grendel. Dinna' put him through more fer some reason ye think is noble."

"Are ye suggesting," her father finally spoke up, narrowing his eyes on them, "that my daughter give up her life with the lord chancellor and run off with an outlaw?"

Amelia looked away. Here was her biggest obstacle. Even if fate wasn't against her, her father would suffer if she chose Edmund.

"Papa, I…"

"Because I think 'tis the best idea I've heard in a month."

Amelia blinked and let her jaw go slack at what she heard. "Papa, what are ye saying?"

His eyes fell on her, a loving, sacrificial gaze that pulled a small sob from her throat. "I heard what ye said before, Mellie. I've lived my whole life miserable because I wanted to please my father. I don't regret wedding yer mother because she gave me you, but my years...If I had to do them over again, I would. I saw how yer Highlander looked at ye, how he was willing to fight for ye. Ye didn't have to tell me ye loved him because I can see it clearly in yer eyes. Ye don't need to worry about me. I don't care about power and prestige. I want ye to be happy and if that means ye living in a hovel—"

"A hovel?" Luke laughed. "She'll be living in a misty paradise guarded by two hundred warriors."

"Papa, what about Walter? Mother will make yer life miserable if I don't marry him."

"I don't care." He went to her and took her in his arms. "I will be fine knowing my gel is happy."

"Papa." Her tears came harder now. "I don't want to marry Walter. I don't love him. But how can I leave ye to the duke's mercy?"

"Och, hell," Malcolm said, growing impatient and a wee bit sentimental, if the glimmer in his eyes spoke true. "He can come with us. But let's decide already and get the hell oot of here!"

Her father at Camlochlin? Living among hundreds of warriors? She looked at him, hoping he would consent. He shook his head and she covered her face against his chest.

"There now, my sweet daughter, I cannot leave yer mother, though..." He shook his head. "I'll be fine. Ye have my blessing to go."

She had her father's blessing but she still wasn't sure what to do. Did she dare put Edmund's life in jeopardy by remaining with him?

She listened while Luke and Malcolm discussed rescuing Edmund and then hurried them all out of her tent. What would she do? She knew one thing only. She missed Edmund already. Lord help them both, she needed to see him.

An hour before dawn Amelia left her tent and headed to the place where Captain Pierce had taken Edmund. She stepped across the grass and over sleeping bodies without crushing any fingers under her shoes or even snapping a twig. Fate, it seemed, was on her side tonight.

She spotted Edmund lying among a group of sleeping men and moved toward him. When he saw her, he came slowly to his feet, his body lean and tense in the firelight. She wanted to run to him and beg his forgiveness.

"My lady," a voice in the darkness stopped her instantly, only inches from Edmund. "I was correct then."

She spun around and faced Captain Pierce behind the flames. "Correct about what?" she whispered, hating him for being there and herself for being so predictable.

"You"—he turned toward Edmund—"and him."

"Please, Captain." Her voice remained controlled, save for a hint of breathlessness. "Please remain quiet." *Please*, she mouthed, praying that he would grant her wish as he had earlier.

He said nothing. She almost smiled when she caught sight of a shadow behind him.

A click of metal and a flash of steel against the captain's temple stilled her heart.

"Were ye expectin' us as well, Captain?" came the low growl and thick Highland burr that Amelia had come to love.

She met Malcolm's cerulean gaze over the captain's

head and held up her palm. The captain had been kind to her tonight. She owed him something for that.

"Captain," she said softly when he reached for the hilt of his sword. "I've seen what they do in a fight and I never want to see it again. Please, trust me. Ye will lose many men."

The captain was still for a moment, his lips curling upward the only thing moving on him. "If that pistol is fired, I may die, but so will all of you." He looked Edmund straight in the eye when Edmund stood before him. "You are all standing in the middle of my army. When it is awakened, the men will not stop to see who they are killing."

Edmund ground his jaw and looked at her. Amelia knew what he was thinking because she was thinking the same thing about him. She didn't want to see him die. She didn't let her tears fall. Now was a time to hold fast to her courage.

He looked at Malcolm next, holding the pistol to the captain's head. He nodded and then shifted his gaze to Pierce's. "Give me a reason not to give my cousin the signal to shoot ye, and make it a better reason than the threat of Miss Bell's demise. Since ye expected her to come to me, ye'll understand that fer us, death is a better alternative than being apart. If we die here, so be it." He turned to Amelia and set his eyes on her. "Aye, my love?"

"Aye," she said rather meekly. She wasn't truly ready to die, but she guessed neither was Edmund. It was a clever ruse to show fearlessness to his captor.

"What glory is there for you in your death?" the captain pressed on courageously. "In the death of a few Highlanders and a nobleman's daughter?"

"'Tis likely ye'll lose more men than I," Edmund promised. "D'ye think my rescuers would come alone? Look toward the tree line, Captain. An army of . . . How many would ye say, Cal?"

Behind the captain, Malcolm shrugged. "Two hundred, last I checked."

"Two hundred men await our signal to attack," Edmund told him.

Amelia peered into the distance but because the tree line was beyond the light of many campfires she could see nothing but darkness. Were there two hundred men standing at the ready? Malcolm and Luke had told her that Darach went to get more men. Could they be here already? She looked at the captain, wondering what he believed.

He showed her a moment later when he lifted his palms to the top of his head in surrender. "Tell me what you want."

Chapter Thirty-Seven

'Twill be light in an hour," Edmund told the captain. "Give us that hour to escape before ye alert the duke. Bring yer regiment to Ravenglade and then go east when ye discover the castle empty."

"Very well," Pierce agreed.

Intelligent man, Edmund thought. Brave, too. Pity he was a traitor to Scotland.

"One more thing."

"What is it?" Pierce asked.

"I'm taking her." He reached out for Amelia's hand and almost tumbled forward when she pulled away from him.

"What are ye doing?" he asked her, remembering somehow to keep his voice low. He'd had plenty of time to think about what she'd told him in her tent earlier. He understood now the reason she'd left him. He thought she was over this ridiculous notion of having to protect her father, and him. Wasn't that why she'd come to him in the middle of an army, to tell him she loved him? Or had she come to bid him a final farewell?

"Amelia." He said her name on a ragged breath. "I won't leave without ye, lass. Nothing else matters in my life but ye. I want to be yer husband. Sarah told me about the chancellor's sexual perversions. Yer father would not want that kind of life fer ye."

"I know," she told him. "He's given me his blessing. But…" She looked like she wanted to leap into his arms, but she shook her head instead. "I couldn't live with anyone else's death on my shoulders. I loved Grendel. I loved him so much. I fear ye would be next."

"Amelia, I told ye that I'd battle misfortune fer ye. I'll be safe, but I don't care if I am or not. As fer Grendel, I loved him, too," he told her on a broken sigh.

"I know." She tortured him further by letting her tears fall without a single swipe to clear them. "This night will haunt me forever. I want no more like it. I will not come with ye."

He felt his stomach tighten into a knot. He looked at Malcolm and then at Luke standing behind him, unnoticed until now by Pierce. Was he expected to leave her here? Leave her to wed the chancellor? Was she mad?

He knew what he was going to do, but the sound of her mother's voice shouting as she ran forward from her tent—or was that the chancellor's tent?—alerting the rest of the men propelled Edmund into action.

In one fluid motion he stepped forward, swooped down over Amelia, and snatched her up off the ground.

The captain reached out to take her back but collapsed to the ground when Malcolm struck him in the back of the head with the handle of his pistol. Edmund didn't wait to see what happened next. He tossed Amelia over his shoulder and took off running toward the tree line.

Twice the duke's guardsmen swinging at him with long rapiers stopped him. Thankfully, they were commanded not to shoot lest they hit the duke's niece.

When Malcolm tossed him his claymore, Edmund fought with one hand, parrying and jabbing and spattering blood onto Amelia's back. Malcolm shot a soldier who was about to come up on him, then tucked his pistol into his belt and pulled out another, ready to fire. Luke dragged a man at his side as he ran. Edmund realized it was Amelia's father and wondered what the hell his cousin was doing.

By now all of the duke's men were awake and scattering about, waiting for commands from their captain—which wouldn't be coming in the next few minutes at least. That was all the time they had to escape.

Edmund thought all was lost when what appeared to be more than one hundred men stepped out from beyond the trees, bows pointed upward and arrows ready to fly.

"Buchanans?" Edmund asked Malcolm as they raced toward them.

"Aye, William proved true. Darach also brought with him some MacLarens."

"And I thought we were bluffing with Pierce." Edmund smiled genuinely for the first time that night. The coming morning was already looking better.

"Release her!" came a shout from the duke riding up behind them, "and I won't carve your heart out and send it to your family on Skye."

Edmund stopped just before the trees and turned. He set Amelia down on her feet and his lips snaked upward along her temple. "I can tell ye with confidence," he called out, "that my kin would love to have ye fer a visit,

Lord Queensberry. Bring all the men ye have. My kin will return later to comfort those soldiers' widows and mayhap bring their bairns back home and raise them as Highlanders."

Standing at his side, Malcolm chuckled, then turned to him. "We should kill him now and the chancellor after him."

Aye, they should, Edmund agreed. The union might be dissolved without its two leaders' signatures. But it would only delay the inevitable again and killing two prominent men such as them would propel Parliament into war with the MacGregors and the Grants.

"Edmund." Amelia's soft voice in front of him pulled him back. "Ye cannot kill them. The duke is my uncle, and the chancellor…" She paused, her breath suspended beneath the curl of his arm. She turned to face him, offering him a view of the soft dip of her brow, the raw, real emotion that lit her eyes from a place he wanted to continue pursuing. He loved her. He didn't want anything but her. "As terrible as he is, I cannot have more blood on my hands."

"Their blood would not be on yer hands, lass. This is about the union."

"Please, Edmund," she begged. "No more killing. I will go with ye. Leave this place to live another day. I beg ye. I could not live knowing that ye were no longer here."

"Edmund?" Malcolm insisted.

Edmund held up his palm to silence him. He would do anything for her. But could he leave alive the two men whose names would set the union in motion? Ah, if he hadn't met her…but he had. He never thought anything or anyone could ever mean more to him than Scotland.

But she did. She was his everything. He remembered the stories about his father, and how he'd gone to Dartmouth on a mission to save King James from William of Orange. He hadn't planned on falling in love with Edmund's mother, or with Edmund. But he did, and ultimately, he gave up his battle with the Dutch usurper to keep Edmund and his mother safe. Love changed everything. Like his father, Edmund would do anything for Amelia.

"Call off yer men, Queensberry," he ordered, eyeing the men coming toward them, some on foot and some on horseback. "Too many will die here today if ye don't. Including ye. We will release Lord Selkirk once we—"

"Selkirk doesn't concern me, MacGregor," Queensberry called out, causing Amelia's back to stiffen against Edmund when she turned back to her uncle. "I want the girl. Or, should I say, the chancellor wants her. If ye release her now, I won't have your balls hacked off and presented to him as a wedding gift. I warn you—"

An arrow piercing his arm and Darach's voice shouting from the trees cut off the remainder of his warning. "I grow weary of yer threats, Duke. The next one enters yer heart," he called out his promise, another arrow cocked and aimed. "After that, I will take doun the chancellor and any other man who dares to move forward.

"Edmund." He turned his eye to his cousin. "Let's no' tarry. The army doesna' have their captain but soon they will. Horses are waitin'. Our friends will cover us. Let's get the hell oot of here."

Edmund nodded, thankful as always to have Darach on his side in a fight. By now, both of Malcolm's pistols were again ready to fire, as were Luke's. If the Buchanans and the MacLarens could hold off the duke's men for a little while, Edmund and his cousins would be able to get Amelia to safety. They knew enough families on the way to Skye who would give them shelter.

He turned to the duke. Hell, there were so many things Edmund wanted to say to him. Mostly, not to merge with England. He wouldn't listen. "Ye'll be a witness to the birth of a new opposition against yer united kingdom. Remember my mercy when ye speak of this day in the years to come."

"I will remember it, Edmund."

Edmund looked over his shoulder at the bard warrior Darach and smiled. "I'm glad to hear that," he said and hauled Amelia over his shoulder again. "Let's be the hell away from here then, aye? Cover us." He turned to run and almost tripped over a mound of blond fur, teeth, and worshipful brown eyes. "Gaza!" Edmund nearly shouted with gladness. "Amelia, 'tis Gaza!"

Darach watched them take off together and pointed his sword toward the heavens. "Archers ready!" he shouted, commanding stillness while his unhorsed cousins found their saddles.

"Where is Sarah?" Amelia asked Darach when he caught up with them a few moments later.

"Janet took her, Etta, and Chester to Killiecrankie," he told her, then turned to the others. "We will meet up wi' them there, at the mountain pass, and then continue on to Rannoch. Jack Robertson will be expectin' us."

"This is why we bring him," Edmund called out to his cousins, who all agreed wholeheartedly. "We owe the Buchanans much as well," Edmund told Malcolm, riding behind him.

"I know. I know," Malcolm muttered on the way.

They rode hard and fast for more than half an hour before stopping to rest their horses and part ways with John Bell and the Buchanans.

"Where do ye think she's been?" Amelia asked Edmund while she scratched the dog behind the ears and welcomed her back.

"I don't know, but I'm glad she returned." He watched her in the sunlight petting Gaza and smiling at her. His heart swelled with emotion. "Amelia..."

She looked up at him, her smile fading.

"I don't want to force ye to remain with me. I'm just not sure I can go on without ye in my life."

"Edmund." She straightened and lifted her palm to his cheek. "Ye told Captain Pierce that death was a better alternative fer us than being apart. 'Tis the truth. I don't want to live without ye but I cannot stand the thought of knowing that I brought ye more pain."

"The worst pain would be to lose ye," he told her, taking her into his arms. "I love ye, Amelia. I will never stop loving ye. If ye leave me—"

"Pardon me," Amelia's father interrupted them. "May I have a word with ye both?"

"Of course." How could Edmund say anything else?

"I'm sorry Luke took ye with us," Amelia said. "I don't know why he did."

In John Bell's smile, Edmund could see his love for his daughter shine from a light within. "I asked him to bring me a moment after everyone began running. I wanted my chance to bid ye farewell. He was very clever about it, making it appear as if I were being taken against my will. I'm in his debt." Her father cut a brief side glance to Edmund, who was listening. "I was fortunate to have some time to speak with Lucan about ideals long dead. Codes of honor to God, king, and the women they loved." He chuckled at himself. "Living so long in the manner that I have has made me forgetful of them. Do ye believe in these codes?" he asked, turning to Edmund.

"Aye, my lord. Everyone in Camlochlin does."

"I like these Highlanders," John told his daughter. "They put me in remembrance of this country's origins. When men took on giants like the Romans, the Saxons and Normans, and the English, for the land."

Amelia looked at Edmund and smiled. "Aye, Goliath himself couldn't stand against them."

Edmund shook his head at her secret insinuation of David.

"My daughter told me much about ye, MacGregor."

Edmund grinned at her. "Aye?" It was nice to know that she spoke of him. "Well, my lord," he said, returning his attention to her father, "not everything ye hear about the MacGregors is true."

"I don't know about all the rest of yer clan, but of ye," John told him, "she told me ye're loyal and kind, and ye don't always tell the truth."

Edmund laughed, and hell, it felt good to do so again.

"And that besides me, ye are the only man she will ever love. So, I wanted to give ye both my blessing. My only request is that ye give me yer word of honor that ye will always care fer her."

"Ye have it," Edmund promised.

Amelia flung her arms around her father and held him close. "Oh, Papa, how can I leave ye? What will become of ye? The shame of yer troublesome daughter riding off with…"

John Bell held his daughter at arm's length so that he could look her in the eyes. "Ye have never shamed me, Amelia. Never. Ye've done nothing but bring joy to my life. I regret not defending ye more strongly." When she tried to deny his words he quieted her with a finger to her lips. "Fergive me fer almost failing ye again by accepting Seafield's offer fer ye. But it seems yer fortune changed fer the better the night yer betrothal was to be announced but postponed because of a caved-in ceiling." The baron smiled over her shoulder at Edmund. "Come to think of it, that was also the day ye arrived at Queensberry House, aye, MacGregor?"

Her father drew her in for a kiss and then handed her over to Edmund. "Write to me, daughter."

She nodded, tears streaming down her face while her father left her and saddled his horse for the ride back to Edinburgh with the escort of a dozen Buchanans.

When they were ready to continue on toward the place Darach fondly recalled as being the sight where the Jacobites almost took down William of Orange's entire army at the Battle of Killiecrankie in '89, Edmund pulled Amelia close before they readied their horses.

"I like yer father."

She nodded and smiled against him. "I knew ye would."

Chapter Thirty-Eight

Edmund watched Amelia's tearful parting from her father and vowed silently to make it up to her someday. Somehow he would find a way to bring them together again, whether in Edinburgh, or on Skye. He was also gladdened by Amelia and Sarah's joyous reunion. He would see to it that they were never separated in the future. He smiled. It seemed he couldn't stop. She was his. There were no more obstacles.

Darach and Janet's farewell wasn't tearful, but interesting to watch just the same.

Edmund had often wondered what kind of lass could interest Darach beyond the bedchamber. Aye, the lad had an eye for lasses. Deny it though he might, he loved music as much as he cherished his quill. But it was fighting that fired his passion most. Janet Buchanan fulfilled all those desires in the young poet-warrior.

He inclined his ear to their conversation. Why not? He might hear something that could prove amusing to tease Darach about later.

"Yer cousin Malcolm asked William to oversee Ravenglade while he's gone," he heard Janet say.

Hmmm. Edmund turned to Cal and winked at him. He knew it was hard for his best friend to give in. It made the sacrifice more genuine.

"So ye'll be livin' there then?" Darach asked her. When she nodded, a rakish smirk curled the upper end of his mouth. "In m' bedchamber, nae doubt. Dreamin' of the man who countered yer blows and will someday return to conquer ye beneath him."

The wind pushed her curls across her face, eclipsing her confident smile. "Nae, and I'll leave the dreaming of the woman who wrangled yer patience and rattled yer heart just a bit, to ye. This is one lass ye will never win. Farewell, Grant," she sang, walking away from him and toward her brother, waiting to leave. "When I marry, I'll be certain to have my husband thank ye fer the use of yer bed, if ye ever return."

Darach stared at her back for a moment and then aimed his clenched fists at the sky. He caught Edmund's grin and shook his head as he went to him.

"D'ye ever want to kill Amelia?" Darach asked innocently through his clenched teeth. "I mean just…" His words trailed off while he wrung his hands together in front of him, like he was strangling someone.

"Ye're way ahead of us in that area," Edmund assured him. "How soon d'ye think before ye're back?"

Darach chuckled but his eyes remained cool. "Why? If I waited ten years she still wouldna' have found a husband with that viperous tongue. If she does, he'll likely kill her after a month."

"Darach, that's an awful thing to say." Amelia came up

behind them. "Janet's verra kind, and quite lovely to look upon. And once her brother takes over Ravenglade in Malcolm's stead, men will find even more interest in her."

Darach glared at her and then blinked. "Ye're no' much better than she is, are ye?" He spread his green gaze over Edmund and offered him his most pitying look. "And I thought I was in trouble. Ye dinna' have a chance, m' friend." He patted Edmund on the shoulder and strode toward his horse.

"He thought he was in trouble." Amelia smiled, catching the meaning in his words.

"I know." Edmund laughed, agreeing with her.

She took his hand and led him back to their horse. "He is correct," she said softly, looking up at him and setting his heart to ruin.

"Who?"

"My father, when he pointed out the change in my fortune. He was correct. It changed with yer arrival."

He took her in his arms and gazed into her eyes. "I told ye that I'd battle misfortune fer ye." They laughed together and he kissed her, loving her mouth, her taste, the tight little moan he pulled from her.

"How long will it take to get to Skye?" she asked, pulling back while she could still stand on her feet.

"Several days," he answered, his own breath heavy in his chest. "We'll ride east to Rannoch and then to Glencoe. We have friends with boats and we'll sail to Skye rather than ride north."

"But Rannoch and Glencoe are east," she reminded him while they continued on their waiting horse. "Ye told Captain Pierce to ride east when they didn't find us at Ravenglade."

"All the more reason he won't go east. Why would I tell him which way to follow us? He'll likely go north."

She smiled and kissed him on the mouth. "Ye're clever, Edmund." She remained quiet for a few moments while they rode, then said, "How long do ye think it will be before my uncle or Walter comes for me?"

"It doesn't matter. He won't find Camlochlin, and if any of them does, there will be cannons waiting fer him and any fool behind him. Don't fret over them, or about misfortune any longer, Amelia." He kissed her once and then again. "Neither will find us."

She heated his blood and melted his heart. He wanted to lay with her, hold her until the sun descended and then rose again, touch her, kiss her, thank her. There would be time for such things later. The thought of it lightened his mood and propelled him to get moving.

"Come," he told her, "let's be off. We can make it to Rannoch by nightfall and then I can tell ye what ye mean to me in the comfort of a soft bed."

Henrietta, who opted to remain in Perth rather than travel to the Highlands, would have scowled at the supper set down in front of Amelia and the others inside Jack Robertson's inn.

Amelia was happy for the warm food and even warmer lodgings. She ate to her fill, not realizing how hungry she was until she found herself cleaning her bowl with her bread. Edmund smiled, watching her.

"Am I being distasteful?" she asked him.

He shook his head. "I was just thinking how my kin are going to love ye."

"Because of how I eat?"

"Because ye're not ashamed or afraid to be who ye are."

"Ye both live the way ye want," Lucan agreed, smiling at Sarah. "Ye're goin' to be happy at Camlochlin."

Amelia couldn't wait to get there, despite the still, small voice telling her he wasn't safe.

Thankfully sharing supper with Sarah, four rowdy Highlanders, and a moody dog helped her forget her past. They laughed late into the night and when it came time for bed, Edmund followed Amelia to their room.

She was exhausted. Every muscle in her body ached from the journey, but when Edmund closed the door and took her into his arms she felt reborn.

"Do ye plan on wedding me, Mr. MacGregor, or are ye going to stick with yer barbaric principles of claiming yer wench in bed?"

His eyes glittered smoky blue with dark intentions. "Both." He dipped his head and brushed his mouth over hers. "My bairns won't be bastards."

"Do ye plan on having many then?" She giggled against his lips, then his teeth when he took her bottom lip between them.

"Aye, plenty." He cupped her rump in both hands and hauled her up so that she straddled him where they stood.

She gasped at the steel lance pushing against his breeches to have her.

"I want us to take our time and savor every moment of making them."

His voice was husky and raw with desire. The sound of it caressed and heated her belly, then below. She had no idea how simply looking at him, hearing the melodic lilt of his voice, could invoke images of his naked body and of her tongue licking every inch of him—but it did. She tunneled her fingers through his golden waves and flicked her tongue inside his mouth.

He groaned and carried her to the bed. He laid her down gently, then stood over her and began to undress. She watched him peel away his shirt to expose an upper body carved from granite. Her eyes traced the corded sinew of his arms and chest, then down, slowly, over his tight, washboard belly. She wanted to rake her teeth over the sensitive curve of his hips, down...

A knock came at the door.

With a muffled oath, Edmund strode to it and pulled it open. A serving wench stood on the other side carrying a tray. Atop it were two flagons of wine and some fruit and cheese.

"Courtesy of the proprietor, sir."

Edmund smiled and accepted the offering. "Give him our thanks."

Amelia leaned up on one elbow when he returned and reached for a cup. She held it up. "Let us drink to making a son or daughter tonight."

He took his cup, sat next to her on the bed, and agreed. "And to not stopping until we get one."

They drank with gusto to their mission and kissed the wine from their lips. Amelia couldn't wait much longer to have her way with him. She'd spent many nights talking to Sarah about different things to do to a man and she was anxious to try some of them out on Edmund.

She sat up and pushed him down on the mattress and straddled him. They laughed when their drinks spilled and then grew serious when she licked the droplets from his chest. She plucked a berry from the tray and placed it carefully on his nipple. She took another and set it on his belly button. Another she placed on his hip and the last, she slipped down his breeches.

"Ye're hungry tonight." His thick voice shuddered as her mouth traversed his torso, snatching up berries as she went.

"Sweet," she whispered with a teasing smile, looking up at him from beneath her dark, lush lashes.

She took another sip of her drink, needing it to boost her courage to do things to him that "ladies" probably never did.

The wine helped, releasing her from trepidation at the idea of taking him in her mouth. Sarah said men loved it. Amelia wanted to do it for Edmund. But first, she wanted to play with him a little.

My, but he was so big and so hard beneath the stretched fabric of his breeches. She ran her palm over him and watched his eyes darken. Blood stirred; she bit her bottom lip and pulled at the laces confining him. She smiled when she found her berry nestled in the crease of his upper thigh and dipped her head to snatch it up. He moaned and then said something she couldn't quite make out. She looked up only to discover that there were two of him. She blinked. Suddenly she didn't feel well at all. A fog was closing in fast. Her limbs felt heavy. Her tongue, thick.

"Edmund, I…" She didn't finish but collapsed on top of him.

Edmund used every ounce of strength he possessed to sit up. His head felt like an anvil. The wine. The wine was drugged or poisoned. But why? The duke couldn't possibly have found them already. Who else would do this? He looked down at Amelia, her head resting on his groin. Whoever did it would die. He pushed Amelia away and swung his legs off the bed. He had to get to the others but his legs wouldn't straighten. He looked longingly toward the door and pushed himself up one more time.

He went down hard and quick, fading into blackness. From somewhere far beyond he heard a dog scratching its nails against wood and whining to be let in.

Gaza.

Hell, it was fortunate that he'd kept her.

Chapter Thirty-Nine

Captain Pierce's boots clicked against the wooden floor of Jack Robertson's inn while he paced the downstairs tavern.

"We should go up and check, Captain. We're wasting time."

Without pausing in his gait, Pierce flicked his irritated glance at the chancellor. "MacGregor killed one of my soldiers with his forehead," he growled. "If you want to rush above stairs and take him and his friends on, be my guest." Hell, he wished he would. He hadn't wanted the Earl of Seafield to travel with him to Rannoch but he'd had no choice. The duke had insisted he bring the chancellor to get his woman back.

Pierce wasn't entirely certain the lady belonged with Seafield, but it wasn't his decision to make. He knew his place and he kept it. He didn't like the chancellor but he had his orders—bring the duke's niece back to Queensberry.

At least he knew where to find them, thanks to Alistair Buchanan. Seems MacGregor took Buchanan's hand...

and his dog. The man hated the Highlander despite a peace treaty between their clans. He wanted recompense. Buchanan had heard one of them mention Robertson's inn in Rannoch, and was quick to turn them in.

East. Clever.

The captain set out for Rannoch immediately with twelve of his best men and after establishing that they were in the right place, threatened the proprietor to taint the Highlander's wine or turn the inn over to the throne.

Terrorizing an innkeeper didn't trouble the captain. Wishing he had more men in his army like MacGregor did. Outlaw or not, Edmund MacGregor was dangerous and fearless when it came to what he wanted. Pity that everything he stood for went against Parliament. He would have made an excellent soldier.

The one who struck him though—Pierce recalled the fiery sting of his head wound from the Highlander who had come up behind him—that one would pay for Pierce's constant headache.

"I think enough time has passed, Captain," Seafield whined and tapped his foot at the bottom of the stairs. "I'm eager to be away from this establishment and those who frequent here."

He looked about to quiver in his hose, tempting Pierce to imagine what it would feel like to backhand the sniveling little worm to the other end of the inn.

He walked up to him and swept his arm across his waist instead. "After you, my lord."

They climbed the stairs, making little or no sound, save for the creak of the third and fourth step. The serving wench who had delivered the drinks to the four rooms paid for by the Highlanders waited at the top.

"Where is the lady?"

The wench pointed to the third door on the left.

Before Pierce could stop him, Seafield rushed forward and pushed open the door. He disappeared into it, then stormed out of it an instant later, before the captain could even look inside. He marched toward the tavern wench with tight, narrowed eyes. When he reached her, he took her by the face, clutching her jaw.

"The woman in that room is not a lady. She's a servant, like you!" he shouted at her. "Where is the dark-haired *lady*? Even a waif like you can tell the difference."

This time she pointed between sobs to a door directly to their right.

When he moved to go to it, Pierce held out his hand, stopping him. The fool would get himself killed and the duke would blame Pierce. "Wait here. I'll bring her out."

The captain swung open the door with more caution in case someone hadn't taken the drink. He stood at the entry, sword drawn, and looked inside.

Seafield wasn't going to be pleased.

They'd found Lady Amelia, but she wasn't alone. Her shirtless lover lay crumpled on the floor a few inches from the door. He'd tried to go for help. The lady lay strewn across the bed. She'd fallen under first.

"Is she—?"

Seafield's query came to an abrupt halt when he defied the captain and plunged inside. The silence fell like an eerie warning to ready himself for something.

"Kill her."

"That will not happen." Pierce turned to look down at him. "If you attempt it, I'll cut off your head and toss it at the duke's feet."

Seafield held steady for a moment and then cracked. "Collect her then. Kill him," he ordered sharply, then whirled on his heel and left the room.

Pierce almost wished MacGregor would awaken. He felt cheated out of what he was certain would be a good fight. He didn't agree with killing men when they were helpless to defend themselves, especially when those men were warriors. MacGregor deserved something better.

With the duke's niece over his shoulder, he raised his sword over his head in his other hand and was about to bring down the final blow when he heard an unholy sound.

A dog stood blocking the doorway, ears pinned, eyes wide, fangs exposed and dripping saliva onto the floor.

Pierce lowered his sword and held up his palm. "Easy, beast."

The creature wasn't soothed in the least and sprang, in fact, for the captain's throat. Pierce blocked the huge fangs about to close around him with his hand. Bone crunched against the hilt he was clutching. He cried out.

The beast turned to encounter a pale-faced chancellor, summoned back by the bluster.

Without provocation, the animal clamped its fangs down on Seafield's ankle, bringing the chancellor to his knees before it ran off down the stairs and out of sight.

"What in blazes was it?" the chancellor wailed. "A demon?"

"Perhaps," Pierce said. He tore a strip of fabric from the lady's gown and wrapped it around his bloody hand. "Can you walk?" he asked, coming to the door. When

Seafield shook his head, Pierce called below stairs for one of his men to come up and carry him.

"Wait!" Seafield called out when the captain turned to go with the lady still dangling over his shoulder. "What about him? I told you to kill him."

Pierce shook his head. He didn't want to kill Mac-Gregor in the first place. Now he had an excuse not to. "If he has demons doing his bidding, I want no part of putting harm to him. That thing attacked me only when I lifted my sword to its owner. You want MacGregor dead? You kill him."

He didn't wait around to see what Seafield did. He knew that leaving MacGregor alive was probably a mistake he would come to regret later, when the Highlander woke up and found his lady gone. MacGregor would come after them. Pierce was certain of it. He'd heard what the couple had spoken to each other on the field. There was love between them. He wanted MacGregor to come. Let him steal his woman back if he could. With two hands or one, Pierce was eager to discover if his opponent was as skilled with a sword as Pierce hoped he was. If MacGregor needed to die, then let it be in a good fight.

He left the inn with the bold arrogance of a man with an army at his back. No one stopped him, man, demon, or dog, nor was he questioned about where he was taking the unconscious woman in his possession.

He would have preferred more time in silence, time to ponder his next move, but Lady Amelia stirred when he deposited her in his saddle.

"Do yourself good and keep your mouth shut," he warned an instant before gaining his seat behind her.

"The slut is awake." Upheld by two of Pierce's men,

one on either side, Seafield snarled as he passed her. "I should beat you senseless for what I saw in that room."

Pierce tightened his wounded limb around her waist. She remained silent.

"I did what you failed to do, Captain," the little peacock called out shrilly over his shoulder while he was placed into his saddle. "I killed him. I killed MacGregor."

Nothing Pierce could do after that could stop the lady from betraying her heart. Seafield would make her pay later. Every soldier knew of the chancellor's preferences in bed. Seafield enjoyed striking his women. He wanted to strike Miss Bell now. Pierce could see in his eyes while his ears took in her hatred toward him and her adoration for her lover.

He would ask his men later if the chancellor spoke true and he had, in fact, killed MacGregor. He uncoiled the bloody rag around his hand and let it drop to the ground, in case he was lying.

Amelia stared into the flames in front of her and ignored the men eating and speaking around her. Why did she wake up that night in her uncle's garden? Why couldn't one of the guests have stabbed her in the heart? Why had she agreed to go to Skye with him? She didn't stop her tears from falling into her lap, but she made no sound in her sorrow.

Edmund was dead.

"You better eat something," Walter ordered, suspended from a stocky soldier appearing over her. When she didn't answer him, he poked her in the side with his good booted foot.

"Rot in hell," she obliged.

She didn't cry out when he grasped a handful of her hair and pulled her head back to make her look at him. "I'll rot there, love, with you right beside me."

She hated him. She hated the sight of him, the smell of him, the sound of his voice. "I would rather die than marry you."

He drew back his hand to slap her but Captain Pierce's voice stopped him.

"You are not her husband yet. Until you are, you will keep your hands off her while she's in my care. If you don't, I will cut out your heart and tell the duke you were killed in the fight to keep his niece safe."

"I treated her well, Captain," Walter argued. "I agreed to marry her when no one else would."

"I don't care." The captain shrugged and looked at his soldier. "Lewis, find the chancellor a tree to sleep under and deposit him there."

"Queensberry will hear of your defiance to your duties," Walter warned while he was carried away. "You will be stripped of your title!"

Amelia folded her knees to her chest and hugged them. "Will ye?" she asked the captain quietly.

"That's not your concern."

"I'll speak fer ye...to my uncle." She wiped her eyes but looked away anyway. She wanted to ask him what happened to his hand, to Walter's leg. But she didn't want to know the answer. Not yet. If they fought Luke or Darach and were wounded from it, how did her friends fare? Where was Sarah? What had these men done? She wanted to know, but her heart, her mind, wasn't prepared to hear it.

"How did ye find us?" she asked instead.

"Ennis Buchanan the first time and Alistair Buchanan the second."

She cut her gaze to him again, her heart pounding against her ribs. "Alistair? When did ye speak to him?"

"Right after you all left Ravenglade." He stood up and stretched and looked around for a tree. "It seems your MacGregor made a lot of Buchanan enemies over the years."

Amelia closed her eyes and gritted her teeth not to scream. Alistair. He was Edmund's enemy because of his hand, because of Gaza, because of her.

She knew it would happen. Edmund was dead because of her.

She didn't know she sobbed until the captain rested his hand on her shoulder. "Come, lady. Get some sleep. Things might be different tomorrow."

Chapter Forty

Edmund raced out of Jack Robertson's inn with his cousins and Gaza behind him. Jack had told him who poisoned him and who took his woman. Outside, he stared out into the coming dawn and took a deep breath, readying himself for what was to come. He tugged on the collar of his shirt. He missed his plaid. He hated wearing English or Lowland attire. He was a Highlander and today he was going to fight like one. Today he was going to kill like one.

He didn't speak to his cousins while they mounted their horses. There was nothing to say. They would return to the inn for Sarah later, after they rescued Amelia. And they *would* rescue her.

Whose blood had he found on the floor in his room when he woke from his slumber?

Edmund didn't want to ride slowly, but tracks were easier to find that way. He couldn't assume Amelia was being taken directly back to Edinburgh. That would be too easy. He knew who took her, and Captain David Pierce was no lackwit. Still, he had to know he would be followed. Why hadn't the captain killed them all when he had the chance? Why leave four angry warriors alive?

He shook his head, not really caring why. Soon, and likely sooner than later thanks to Gaza's picking up their scent and leading them forward, Amelia would be back in Edmund's arms and their enemies would be sprawled out in puddles of blood.

"What's that?" Luke pointed to something dangling off a bush.

It was a bloody rag, Edmund realized from his saddle when he came to look down on it. The sun began its ascent and spread a shaft of golden light on the fabric. He recognized it and leaped from his horse to snatch the rag from its place.

"What is it?" Malcolm rode close to him and peered at it.

"'Tis Amelia's," Edmund told them quietly. He held the rag away from him and let it uncoil in his hand. It was hers. The blood in his room. Now this. The panic he'd been subduing since he opened his eyes finally engulfed him. What had they done to her? Why was the rag left for him to find? He would kill them, however many there were, he would kill them all.

"It may no' be her blood."

Malcolm was correct. Edmund looked at him and nodded. It might not be her blood.

He shoved the rag beneath his belt and sprang to his saddle with renewed vigor. "Let's get her."

They were riding for a quarter of an hour when they came upon the captain's camp barely concealed within a stand of trees.

"'Tis a trap," Luke whispered, surveying the scene before him.

"Aye," Malcolm agreed. "They want us to rush in and—"

Edmund marched by him and straight into the camp, cutting off the rest of Malcolm's words.

Edmund heard his cousins call him back in hushed tones, but he ignored them. While they were standing around contemplating, he killed the first sleeping solider guarding her. The next guard roused from his sleep and clutched his severed throat before falling back to the ground. Edmund barely had time to gut his next victim when the rest of them began waking up. He took out two more with a half turn, a two-handed slice, and a backward jab that brought him to one knee.

Malcolm and the others had barely reached him when a shout halted everyone's movement.

"MacGregor!" the voice called. "Move a hair and I'll start shooting your relatives."

"Where is she, Captain?" Edmund called out.

"She is safe and in my care. If you ever wish to see her again don't kill another one of my men."

"Bring her to me!"

The captain turned to a man at his right. They watched him disappear and then return with Amelia in his grip.

"Edmund!" she screamed, pulling on her captor to get to him.

He didn't move to get her but flicked his gaze to the pistol pointed at Darach. "If ye've harmed her—"

"I said she was safe."

"The bloodied rag?" Edmund pulled the cloth free of his belt.

"Mine." Pierce smiled and held up his hand. "Your dog attacked me as I turned to kill you at the inn."

Edmund stared at him like his ears had just deceived him. "My dog?" He thought he'd dreamed her.

"Aye." Pierce pointed at Gaza. "You are fortunate to own the beast. It saved your life."

Edmund looked down at Gaza sitting at his feet and for the first time, he saw her. She'd hardly left his side since he took her from Alistair. Even when Grendel had abandoned him for Amelia, Gaza had remained at his feet.

He patted her head now.

"I would like to keep her after I'm done with you."

Edmund looked up at the captain again with a smirk curling his mouth. "Tonight I'll leave here with both ladies and your head."

Pierce shrugged his shoulders and laughed. "You might indeed." He lowered his pistol and tucked it into his belt. "Let's discover if you are correct." He pulled a sword free from a scabbard hanging from his side and called his men to stand down. He waited for Edmund to do the same.

"Captain!" Amelia called out. She glared at the chancellor when he finally roused himself from his sleep and came near. "If ye harm him, I will not return with you to my uncle, or to my former betrothed. In fact"—she pulled up her skirts, drawing all eyes to her bare knee and the small pistol secured to it; she freed it and aimed it at Seafield—"I will kill the chancellor and do my best to kill ye, as well."

Pierce narrowed his eyes on her as if trying to figure out if she would do it. Finally, coming to his conclusion, he lowered his sword.

Edmund thought he looked more disappointed than any man he'd ever seen.

"I don't do this for you, Seafield." Pierce sighed, putting away his sword. "I do it for her. If she is willing to hang to save MacGregor, then she deserves to save him."

"Keep the pistol on him, lass," Malcolm called out to her when she began to turn away from the chancellor.

It was too late. In the time it took her to form a single breath, Seafield leaped at her, knocking over the soldier who had brought her to them.

The pistol fired. Everyone froze save for Edmund. He ran to Amelia and reached her as Seafield slipped down her body to the ground.

"Walter!" Amelia cried out, clutching him. "I didn't mean to…"

He looked up at her. "You aren't done with me yet." He scowled for all he was worth and then he fainted.

Unfortunately, he was correct. The ball entered his side. Damage was minimal. He would live to see another day.

"Bring him to the horses," Pierce ordered his men. "Tie him to the saddle if you must." He smirked at Amelia when she caught his gaze.

"Ye don't like him," she said.

He shrugged, straining the shirt across his shoulders. "I still have to return him safely to Edinburgh."

"And me?"

"You, I like."

She smiled and opened her mouth to speak but Edmund beat her to it. "Ye like her, yet ye're willing to let her wed a man who faints at a flesh wound?"

Pierce walked around his horse and came to stand directly in front of Edmund. Confidence lit his flinty gaze and curled the tips of his mouth. "She's not my woman, MacGregor. If she were, I wouldn't let me take her."

"I don't intend to let ye take her anywhere, Captain."

Pierce beamed. "Good! A fight for her then. Not to the death." He turned and grinned at Amelia. "If you disarm me, she is yours."

"Are we simply to believe yer word, then?" Darach called out, listening to the conversation.

"If he's lying," Edmund assured them calmly, "I'll kill him."

"Ah, a confident man. I like that." Pierce drew his sword and ushered Edmund into the center of the clearing. "How long have you been wielding a sword?"

"Since I was four," Edmund told him, unsheathing his blade.

"Who taught you?"

"My father." Edmund faced him and eyed the captain's wounded hand. Pierce was either a terrible fool or one of the most confident—

His thoughts came to an abrupt halt when, using only one hand, Pierce swung and nearly knocked Edmund's sword out of his grip.

All right then, fighting with one hand wasn't one of the captain's weaknesses. Edmund repositioned and parried three successive blows to different parts of the captain's body in the space of two breaths.

"Though I hate losing men, I was impressed by your entrance."

Edmund didn't answer him but cut a swipe across the backs of the captain's legs, angling his blade at the last instant so that only the flat surface struck, doing no damage.

Pierce almost went to one knee as he spun in a full circle. He held himself upright by sheer force of will.

When righted, he paused with his back to Edmund and his front to Edmund's kin. Luke waved to him, and Darach chuckled.

Edmund waited while the lads had their sport. They deserved it for being so patient. Pierce didn't seem to mind; when he pivoted around he was already smiling.

"Speaking doesn't distract you then."

Edmund laughed. "Ye don't know Darach. He never stops talking."

He watched the warrior twirl his hilt about in his hand, end over end, making it flash beneath the sun and dance as if it were an extension of his arm.

"And ye're not disconcerted by having only one hand."

"Let us test your theory." Pierce came at him in a hailstorm of quick slices and jabs.

Edmund countered every swing raining down upon him, battering the strength of the captain's wrist, barraging him over and over with heavy, two-fisted parries. He couldn't give the captain time to launch a different assault and mayhap rest his arm a moment or two. Pierce was seasoned, like Edmund's father and uncles. His experience might save him the day if given the chance. Edmund couldn't give him the chance. He was fighting for Amelia. For her, he would beat Pierce into a living mound in the grass before him, begging for mercy.

Malcolm and the lads were roused and riled up by their cousin's skill and power. Their excitement fevered Edmund's blood, his determination to win.

He swung hard and was momentarily blinded by the sparks shooting down their grinding blades. Eyes closed, he dipped his knee and whirled his claymore beneath and parallel to Pierce's. Metal struck metal again. Edmund rose up with the force and power of his full body behind him and cracked his blade down on the other.

Pierce's stunned gaze followed his sword's decent to the grass. When he looked up again, he offered Edmund a nod with a hint of amazement widening his eyes.

"Fight for me," Pierce said, taking hold of Edmund's hand.

"I cannot fight fer what I don't believe in," Edmund told him. "Ye come fight with me."

Pierce laughed and shook his head, stepping away. "We'll meet again, MacGregor. For now, take your prize and go."

Edmund went to her like he had no other choice but to go. He didn't. Not since the night he woke her in the garden where she'd been dropped by God, and then again in her soup. "Not a prize but a gift," he told her, catching her in his arms.

"One more thing," Pierce called out, looking toward the chancellor. "He does worse than faint at a flesh wound. He also beds barons' wives."

Chapter Forty-One

A crimson shaft of light poured inside the room, casting the cavernous chamber in a cozy, rosy light. Not too bright for waking up to, but a soft invitation to begin another day.

Amelia opened her eyes and stretched. She ran her hand over the warm body beside her. When he moaned, she turned and curled herself against his back. Pressing her nose to his bare shoulder, she breathed him in. "How is it that everything in Camlochlin is perfect?"

"'Twasn't until ye got here."

She smiled behind him and kissed his shoulder. He wasn't telling the truth, of course. He was being kind. He'd told her much about his home on the way here, but nothing in her wildest imagination could have prepared her for this place. She wasn't sure which was more primitively beautiful, Camlochlin Castle, carved from nature, or the land that surrounded it. When she first laid eyes on it all, including the cliffs that were as beautiful as they were treacherous, she wasn't sure she would ever grow accustomed to the isolation of Skye.

Two months later, nothing could ever take her away. She was never lonely. Ever. How could she be when her dearest friend in all the world lived right down the hall from her? Married, on the same day as Amelia, equal, accepted, adored.

"I want to lie here for the rest of the day," she whispered.

"I like that idea," Edmund agreed quietly, half asleep. "Let's do it."

"I can't. I'm going hunting with Abby and Caitrina. After that I'm meeting Sarah and Mailie in the kitchens where yer aunt Isobel is going to teach us to cook another one of her delicious recipes. After supper I promised—"

He flipped over and switched their positions, cradling her against his naked, hardening angles. When he nuzzled his face in the folds of her hair, she lost her train of thought.

When he slipped his arm around her waist and pressed her buttocks tighter against his full erection, she remembered.

"—I promised Nichola and Violet I'd teach them how to make tarts. Darach has been driving me mad to make them."

"All these promises to everyone else. What of yer husband?"

"What about him?" she asked, doing nothing to hide her haughty self-confidence that her husband wanted for nothing.

"He hungers."

"Fer food?" she giggled, being careful to keep her voice low.

He scooped her hair away from her neck and kissed

her sensitive flesh. He pressed slower, more sensuous kisses along her throat until he came to her lobe. "Fer ye," he growled in her ear.

Her legs opened of their own accord while he pushed his cock against her. Her movement only engorged him further. When she lifted her arm behind her to tug on his hair, he dipped his head and closed his mouth around her tight nipple.

Her cry of ecstasy only provoked him into clasping her hands and pushing her belly down flat on the bed. He climbed atop her, his lance thick and hard and pulsating for her. He spread her knees with his and thrust his shaft deep. The more she cried out, the harder he sank into her. He took her in long, fiery hot strokes that drove him to the edge of madness with the need to come until he passed out.

But he didn't.

He slipped his hand beneath her and took her hot nub between his fingers. He tugged and rolled her until she panted under him. Then he turned them over one more time, and with him on his back beneath her, his hungry cock buried to the hilt, and his fingers working her hard, they came together in a symphony of groans and cries.

They lay there, done, breathing hard, relaxed, for a moment before the whining began.

"Do ye want to go?" she asked him, hoping he would say aye. She was so tired all over again.

She watched him rise out of bed, the sun, a bit brighter now, spilling gold down all the contours of his sleek body.

David.

She closed her eyes but was awakened a moment later by a cold, hairy mouth.

"Edmund, ye always pick up that one. What about his sisters?" When she left the bed, she turned and watched Edmund holding Gaza's only male pup in his hands. She smiled, knowing why he always picked up that one. It looked exactly like its father.

Bending to retrieve the gown she'd laid out on the chair the night before, she began dressing for the day and smiled when Gaza rose from her place with her pups and went to the edge of the bed next to Edmund.

"Gaza still loves ye best."

Edmund smiled. "Nae, she doesn't. She loves Goliath best."

Amelia went to him and pinched him and then kissed the pup in his hands. "Do ye think Captain Pierce received yer letter asking about the dogs? Do ye think he will want one? I do pray he sees to my request to offer my father a place here. Ye will love him as much as I do."

"I'm certain I will, love. As fer Pierce, aye, he'll bring yer father, and he will want a dog. Everyone wants one. They're Gaza and Grendel's. They come from excellent stock, aye girl?"

Gaza rested her head in his lap, happiest when he was petting her. Which he did all the time. She never left his side...until she had her pups.

She helped him heal from losing Grendel and she mended Amelia's heart, as well. Thanks to Gaza, Amelia never again considered herself misfortunate. How could she when, if not for her begging Edmund to keep Gaza, Gaza wouldn't have been at the inn to save his life. He wouldn't now have Grendel's scruffy, floppy-eared son to train up.

"Edmund?"

"Aye, my love?"

She stood over him and smiled with her hand on her flat belly. "Promise me that after our child is born ye will not chose fer it the name of a monster."

He laughed, set Goliath back on the ground, and then settled in for another few hours of sleep. "I promise."

"Thank ye." She bent to kiss his head and then slipped out of the room.

Edmund's eyes opened and he stared at the door his wife had just used to leave. A child? Did she say... Was she stroking her belly... smiling?

He sat up, numb for a moment, and then leaped from the bed.

The door opened again and she stood there, waiting... waiting for his reaction.

He smiled at her and then caught her in his arms when she leaped into them.

They fell back into bed, Amelia's promises forgotten.

Alexander Kidd vows to recover a treasure
buried by his infamous father, Captain Kidd.
But the map that leads to the fortune is in the
hands of the clan MacGregor—and specifi-
cally a bow-wielding, raven-haired beauty
named Caitrina...

Please turn this page for a preview of

*The Wicked Ways of
Alexander Kidd.*

Chapter One

Captain Alex Kidd hooked his sapphire-ringed finger into the narrow handle of his jug of rum and brought the spout to his lips. The woman spread on the table beneath him moaned. He wiped his mouth and looked at her. The hunger in the slow, salacious smile he lavished on her made her drip around the base of him. He ran his hand up her thigh, withdrew from her hot body, and then drove himself deeper into her, biting down on her pink nipple. Ah, but there was nothing better than warm rum and an even warmer whore. Plundering a ship was a close second, but he'd done that already this morning. He laughed and the wench tightened her legs around his waist. He tipped his jug and drizzled his rum over her breasts and her belly, watching with dark, hungry eyes.

He wasn't sure of her name. He didn't need to know it. He paid her to please him and she did.

He heard the sound of fighting from beyond the door of the candlelit room. Fighting was good, but now was the time for pleasure. He bent forward and drank from her behind his veil of dark hair.

He sank into her, deep and slow, then withdrew almost completely, teasing her with what she wanted before he spread his palm over her belly and pulled cries from her throat with the gyration of his hips and the smooth thrusts that arched her back and brought them both to climax.

Done, he pulled back, fastened his breeches, and took another swig from his jug.

"Will I see you again?" the wench asked when he stood over her, covering his tattoos of Neptune and Poseidon with his shirt.

He looked at her and shook his head. The last thing he wanted in his life was a woman. His father taught him to trust no man, but he'd learned firsthand not to trust a woman. He never returned to the same wench's bed twice, providing no hope in forming attachments.

Pity, this one was a lovely thing with eyes as dark as coal and long raven hair. She was likely a native of the Americas and brought here to New York as a slave to work in one of its many backstreet brothels like this one.

He plucked an extra coin from a small pouch tied into his sash and tossed it to her, then stepped out of the room and out of her life, and into a brawl that sent his quartermaster flying across the full length of the front room.

Alex downed what was left in his jug, then smashed the clay vessel over the head of the man who'd done the punching. He watched the culprit go down, then cupped his groin and readjusted. A woman at a table at the other end of the room smiled at him and waved. He returned the salutation but headed to a larger table, preferring, for now, to share drink and laughter with the drunken, rowdy seamen who helped him sail his ship. He tucked in his shirt, then slipped into a chair and ordered another jug of rum.

"Capt'n." His tanned, one-eyed first mate turned to him. "Tell this scab-pickin' bottom-feeder"—he hooked his thumb over his shoulder, pointing it at another sailor who looked insulted enough to start killing people— "who among us plays the better jig on the pipes?"

"I've already told ya, Mr. Bonnet," Alex answered, giving his attention to his brocade coat and feathered tricorn hat resting where he'd left them on a chair to his right. "I prefer Simon's jigs over yars. That's why he's the ship's musician and ya're me first mate."

Alex paid his one-eyed comrade no mind when Mr. Bonnet cursed him for breathing. He looked up instead at the man who'd sailed by him a few moments ago.

"I think me tooth came loose that time."

Alex had known his quartermaster, Samuel Pierce, for more than eight years now. Sam was with him when he learned of his father's arrest, at his side during his father's hanging, with him when Alex's heart was broken, the first and only time, by a woman. They'd plundered many ships together and fought many battles, watching the other's back. Alex loved him like a brother. "The gold one?" he asked, eyebrow piqued.

Three of his men who had been deep in conversation stopped talking and turned to eye Sam.

"Not the gold one," the quartermaster growled at them. "But if any of ya be wantin' to try to pry it loose from me jaw, just stick yer fingers in there if ya have the balls."

Alex laughed and swigged his rum. "Robbie Owens there doesn't have 'em."

It was true, poor Robbie had lost his balls two summers ago when the mother of two of his children caught him in her sister's bed. Fortunate for Robbie that the ship's carpenter, Harry Hanes, knew how to stop bleeding and sew a man up good as new. Well—

"Captain Kidd?" A stranger appeared at the table, drawing all the men's attention to him. Another man would have taken a step back, or at least reconsidered his decision to make himself known to them as their dark, wary gazes fell on him.

But not this man. He remained unflinchingly cool in his drab but costly attire, clean hands folded in front of him.

"Who's askin'?" Samuel said, reaching for the cutlass tucked into his boot.

"My name is Hendrik Andersen. I was a friend of the captain's father, William Kidd."

"Me father had no friends," Alex corrected, reclining in his chair and slamming his booted foot on the table. "None who were worth more than bilge rat shit."

"I've been looking for you for several years now," the stranger continued, as if Alex hadn't spoken.

It didn't bode well for Alex that he'd been searched for and found.

"What do ya want?" Alex asked him. "Make yar plea convincin' or I'll kill ya where ya stand. I should do it now fer claimin' to be a friend to me father. No friends watched him die. All had abandoned him."

"But not you."

Alex slowly removed his leg from the table and sat up in his chair. How would this stranger have known that Alex was there at his father's death? His movements caused Sam and several others to draw their daggers, others their pistols, and begged Alex to let them fire.

Andersen didn't bat an eyelash. "I would speak to you alone."

"Nay," Alex said, not risking a stab in the gut the instant they were alone. The Royal Navy likely sent Mr. Andersen. They believed Alex was in possession of a map to the treasure his father gave his life up for. "Say what ya would now and say it quickly. Ya're tryin' me patience."

The man cleared his throat and glanced at the others. "Very well then. May I sit?" When Alex nodded, he pulled out the chair nearest Alex's coat and hat and sat down on it. Alex watched him catch his hat before it hit the floor and then place it, with the due respect a captain's expensive leather hat deserved, back on the chair. "I was your father's boatswain. I was with him when he captured the *Quedagh Merchant.*"

Everyone at the table grew silent. They all knew about the rumors of the *Quedagh Merchant*, the infamous Armenian ship said to be loaded with gold and silver, gems of every size and color, not to mention satins, muslin, and priceless East Indian goods, including silks. It was a treasure any pirate worth his weight in salt would kill for...or die for. His father was rumored to have captured it shortly after Alex left him to begin his own life of adventure and piracy. Andersen would have had to have joined his father's crew right after he left.

No proof was ever discovered against William Kidd, but Alex didn't doubt that his father had indeed captured the ship. What he didn't believe was that his father had trusted anyone with its whereabouts.

"Ye're tellin' me ya know where the *Quedagh Merchant* is?" Alex wouldn't have believed him if Andersen answered with an aye. The first Captain Kidd had been tried and hanged for piracy and murder rather than give up the location of that ship. Since Alex hadn't been with him when he took it, nor had Alex seen him alive since, he didn't know its whereabouts either.

"I'm telling you nothing of the sort, but…" Andersen paused and looked around. When Alex nodded for him to continue, he obliged. "There is a map."

A map. That sounded quite plausible, Alex decided. His father wouldn't have gone to his grave without a map to his greatest treasure. What if somehow he had come out of the trial alive? His father would have made certain there was a map.

"Where is this map?" he asked his guest casually.

Still reluctant, Andersen looked straight at Mr. Bonnet's patched eye and the scar running down beneath it. "You trust these men?"

"Nay, but I need them, same as they need me. Where is the map?"

"Scotland."

"Where in Scotland?"

"I have a condition, Captain Kidd," Andersen was foolish enough to announce.

Half the men at the table readied their daggers and aimed their pistols again. Metal gleamed against the firelight coming from the hearth.

"If yar condition isn't that ya walk out of here alive"— Alex tipped one corner of his mouth up—"then I'm afraid I must refuse."

"I wish to sail with you."

Alex shook his head. "I already have a boatswain. I don't need any more men."

"You need me."

Alex laughed. "Kill him," he told Samuel, rising from his chair.

"You need me to find the people who have your map," Andersen exclaimed as Samuel's dagger edged along his throat.

Holding up his hand, Alex halted Samuel's next move. Not that his friend was truly going to kill Andersen. At least, not while he knew the whereabouts of this alleged map. After that...

"Ya're correct in callin' it my map. Fer that, I'll spare ya. But I was born in Scotland. I don't need ya to find me way 'round. Now tell me of these people who have it."

"Will I sail with you?"

Regaining his seat, Alex narrowed his eyes on him, wishing he hadn't just said he'd spare him. It was obvious that this man who claimed to be a friend to his father wanted the map for himself. But why not just go to Scotland and get the map himself if he knew where it was? Why did he need Alex?

"You will never find them on your own, Captain," Andersen forged ahead, undaunted by Alex's scowl. "And if you do, they will kill you before your feet touch land. They are hidden in the mists in the Highlands."

Ah, savages. That's why Andersen needed him, his ship, and his crew. He'd let Alex take the map and then try to kill him for it later.

"Your father knew the clan chief. He took me and a few others with him as witnesses when he brought the map to them to guard. The chief agreed to surrender the map to you...and you alone."

Alex smiled at him. "Bring to me mind the reason I need ya again?"

"Because the chief doesn't know you, or whose son you are. If you happen to find them on your own you will have no way to convince them of your identity. They'll kill all of you for finding them. They value their privacy highly."

"So ya intend on provin' me identity?" Alex asked him. "How?" he asked when Andersen nodded his head.

"A letter."

Alex cocked his brow. "A letter?"

"From your father to the chief, stating that you are his son and the map should be handed over to you. I have been made privy to things about you that can prove who you are. And because I traveled with your father and already met them, my word will validate."

Believable and clever on his father's part. Alex would take this Dutchman with him. He wondered how much Andersen knew about him. He hadn't seen his father in a little under a decade and he'd changed much in that time. How could anyone prove his identity?

"And what of these folks who have the map?" he asked. "How do ya know they haven't already looked fer the ship?"

"They are Highlanders, not pirates. Their island is their treasure and they guard it unceasingly."

Alex thought about everything he'd been told so far. He shared a look with Samuel. As his quartermaster, Sam had as much say in what treasures they sought and plundered as the captain. More than that, he was the only man

Alex trusted. If Sam didn't feel right about Andersen and his claim of a map, they would forget him.

Sam ran his fingers through the blond waves on his uncovered head and nodded.

"I'll let ya board me ship." Alex turned back to their guest. "But I have a few conditions of me own. First, ya'll take four successive watches fer the first three nights at sea while we travel to Scotland. The crew can use the rest to recuperate from our time ashore. Second, ya'll aid our navigator and cook, Mr. Cooper, in any way he commands to get us to our destination as safely and as quickly as possible. I inherited my father's enemies, from the Royal Navy on up to the throne itself. If word of a map...nay, a whisper of it, reaches their ears, we will have to fly over waves or hoist our flag and kill some soldiers. I'm prepared to do either. Are ya?"

"If you command it."

Alex grinned at him and sank languorously into his chair. "I'm almost certain that at some point in our journey we'll discover if ya speak true." He held up another jewel-encircled finger to quiet him when Andersen would have spoken. "Next, I want the letter and would hear of me father's adventures from ya. We parted long ago."

"I know. He spoke of you often," Andersen told him.

"He trusted ya then?"

Andersen nodded.

"Then why did ya betray him by not standing at his side while he hanged?"

Alex noted the stranger's shallow breath before he answered, his gaze that fell to the ground and didn't rise again while he spoke.

"They would have killed me and you never would have found the *Merchant* and your father would have died for nothing. But I was there and I saw what you saw."

He knew Alex had been there. Had his father known it, too? It didn't matter. It was long ago, when the time of dwelling was lost past. Now he wanted to get drunk. "I've one last condition before I allow ya aboard me ship."

"What is it?"

"Pay fer our drinks. Do ya agree to these conditions?"

"Aye, Captain."

Alex grinned at him. "Then welcome to *Poseidon's Adventure*. We sail at dawn. Now, tell me who the hell we're goin' to see."

"The MacGregors of Skye."

"MacGregors." Alex chuckled and shook his head. Of course his father would have chosen them. "They are outlawed, are they not?"

"King William re-enacted the proscription against them when he gained the throne," Samuel reminded him.

"Their reputation of savagery precedes them," Alex said, remembering tales he'd heard about them.

"That is why we will need patience and precaution when we approach," Andersen told them.

"Ya just worry about gettin' us there." Alex cut his dark gaze across the room, to the woman who had waved at him earlier. She crooked her finger at him now. He sprang to his feet with the grace of a great cat and smoothed back any stray strands of chestnut hair that had fallen over his forehead. "I'll keep us alive once we arrive. Fer now, Anderson, ye're in charge of me coat and hat. Guard them well, or it will cost ya a finger."

He turned to his crew before he left. "I'll meet ya all

in an hour to stock the ship. Until then, enjoy yarselves, men. Who knows when we'll be ashore again?"

He smiled at the woman rising from her chair at his approach. She was eager to be pillaged and he was willing to oblige.

THE DISH

Where Authors Give You the Inside Scoop

♥ ♥ ♥ ♥ ♥ ♥ ♥ ♥ ♥ ♥ ♥ ♥ ♥ ♥ ♥ ♥ ♥

From the desk of Vicky Dreiling

Dear Reader,

I had a lot of imaginary boyfriends when I was a kid. My friend Kim and I read *Tiger Beat* magazine and chose our loves. I "dated" David Cassidy, a yesteryear heartthrob from a TV show called *The Partridge Family*. Kim's "boyfriend" was Donny Osmond, although she might have had a brief crush on Barry Williams, better known as Greg from *The Brady Bunch*. I did a quick search online and discovered that *Tiger Beat* magazine still exists, but the stars for today's preteens are Justin Bieber, Taylor Lautner, and members of the boy band One Direction.

The idea of a big family and rock-star boyfriends really appealed to us. We traveled in imaginary tour buses to imaginary concerts. We listened to the music and sang along, pretending we were onstage, too. Of course, we invented drama, such as mean girls trying to steal our famous boyfriends backstage.

Recently, I realized that the seeds of the families I create in my novels were sown in my preteen years as Kim and I pretended to date our celebrity crushes. As I got older, imaginary boyfriends led to real-life boyfriends in high school and college. Eventually, marriage and kids led to an extended family, one that continues to grow.

In WHAT A RECKLESS ROGUE NEEDS, two close families meet once a year at a month-long house party. As in real life, much has changed for Colin and Angeline. While they were born only a week apart, they never really got along very well. An incident at Angeline's come-out ball didn't help matters, either. Many years have elapsed, and now Colin finds he needs Angeline's help to keep from losing a property that holds very deep emotional ties for him. Once they cross the threshold of Sommerall House, their lives are never the same again, but they will always have their families.

May the Magic Romance Fairies be with all of you and your families!

www.VickyDreiling.com
Twitter @VickyDreiling
Facebook.com/VickyDreilingHistoricalAuthor

♥ ♥ ♥ ♥ ♥ ♥ ♥ ♥ ♥ ♥ ♥ ♥ ♥ ♥ ♥

From the desk of Paula Quinn

Dear Reader,

As most of you know, I love dogs. I have six of them. I see your eyes bugging out. Six?? Yes, six precious tiny Chihuahuas and all together they weight approximately twenty-seven pounds. I've had dogs my whole life—big ones, little ones. So it's not surprising that I would want to write dogs into my books. This time I went big: 140 pounds of big.

In THE SEDUCTION OF MISS AMELIA BELL we meet Grendel, an Irish wolfhound mix, who along with our hero, Edmund MacGregor, wins the heart of our heroine, Amelia Bell. Grendel is the son of Aurelius, whom some of you might remember as the puppy Colin MacGregor gave to Edmund, his stepson, in *Conquered by a Highlander*. Since this series is called Highland Heirs, I figured why not include the family dog heirs as well?

I loved writing a dog as a secondary character, and Grendel is an important part of Edmund and Amelia's story. Now, really, what's better than a big, brawny, sexy Highlander? Right: a big, brawny, sexy Highlander with a dog. Or if you live in NYC, you can settle for a hunky guy playing with his dog in the park.

My six babies all have distinct personalities. For instance, Riley loves to bark and be an all-around pain in the neck. He's high-strung and loves it. Layla, my biggest girl, must "mother" all the others. She keeps them in line with a soft growl and a lick to the eyeball. Liam, my tiny three-pound boy, isn't sure if he's Don Juan or Napoleon. He'll drop and show you his package if you call him cute. They are all different and I wanted Grendel to have his own personality, too.

Much like his namesake, Grendel hates music and powdered periwigs. He's faithful and loyal, and he loves to chase smaller things…like people. Even though Edmund is his master and Grendel does, of course, love him best, it doesn't take Amelia long to win his heart, or for Grendel to win hers, and he soon finds himself following at her heels. Some of my favorite scenes involve the subtle interactions between Amelia and Grendel. This big, seemingly vicious dog is always close by when Amelia is sad or afraid. When things are going on all around them, Amelia just has to rest her hand on Grendel's head and it completely calms her. We witness a partial transformation of ownership in the small, telltale ways Grendel remains ever constant at Amelia's side.

Even when Grendel finds Gaza, his own love interest (hey, I'm a romance writer, what can I say?), he is still faithful to his human lady. We won't get into doggy love, but suffice it to say, there will be plenty of furry heirs living in Camlochlin for a long time to come. They might not be the prettiest dogs in Skye, but they are the most loyal.

This was my first foray into writing a dog as a secondary character and I must say I fell in love with a big, slobbering mutt named after a fiend who killed men for singing. I wasn't surprised that Grendel filled his place so well in Edmund and Amelia's story. Each of my dogs does the same in mine and my kids' stories. That's what dogs do. They run headlong into our lives barking, tail wagging, sharing wet, sloppy kisses. They love us with an almost supernatural, unconditional love. And we love them back.

I hope you get a chance to pick up THE SEDUCTION OF MISS AMELIA BELL and meet Edmund and Amelia and, of course, Grendel.

Happy reading!

Paula Quinn

♥ ♥ ♥ ♥ ♥ ♥ ♥ ♥ ♥ ♥ ♥ ♥ ♥ ♥ ♥ ♥ ♥

From the desk of Kristen Ashley

Dear Reader,

Years ago, I was walking to the local shops and, as usual, I had my headphones in. As I was walking, Bob Seger & The Silver Bullet Band's "You'll Accomp'ny Me" came on and somehow, even having heard this song dozens and dozens of times before, the lyrics suddenly hit me.

This isn't unusual. I have to be in a certain mood to absorb lyrics. But when I am, sometimes they'll seep into my soul, making me smile, or making me cry.

"You'll Accomp'ny Me" made me smile. It made me feel warm. And it made me feel happy because the lyrics are beautiful, the message of love and devotion is strong, the passion is palpable, and the way it's written states that Bob definitely has Kristen Ashley alpha traits.

I loved it. I've always loved that song, but then I loved it even more. It was like one of my books in song form. How could I not love that?

At the time, however, I didn't consider it for a book, not inspiring one or not to be used in a scene. For a long time, it was just mine, giving me that warm feeling and a smile on my face at the thought that there is musical proof out there that these men exist.

Better, they wield guitars.

Now, from the very moment I introduced Hop in *Motorcycle Man*, he intrigued me. And as we learned more about him in that book, my knowing why he was doing what he was doing, I knew he'd have to be redeemed in my readers' eyes by sharing his whole story. I just didn't know who was going to give him the kind of epic happy ending I felt he deserved.

Therefore, I didn't know that Lanie would be the woman of his dreams. Truth be told, I didn't even expect Lanie to have her own book. But her story as told in *Motorcycle Man* was just too heartbreaking to leave her hanging. I just had no idea what to do with her.

But I didn't think a stylish, professional, accomplished "lady" and a biker would jibe, so I never considered these two together. Or, in fact, Lanie with any of the Chaos brothers at all.

That is, until this song came up on shuffle again and I knew that was how Hop would consider his relationship with Lanie. Even as she pushed him away due to her past, he'd do what he could to convince her that, someday, she'd accompany him.

I mean, just those words—how cool are they? "You'll accompany me." Brilliant.

But Bob, his Silver Bullet Band, and their music did

quadruple duty in FIRE INSIDE. Not only did they give me "You'll Accomp'ny Me," which was the perfect way for Hop to express his feelings to Lanie; they also gave me Hop's nickname for Lanie: "lady". And they gave me "We've Got Tonight," yet another perfect song to fit what was happening between Lanie and Hop. And last, the way Bob sings is also the way I hear Hop in my head.

I interweave music in my books all the time and my selections are always emotional and, to me, perfect.

But I've never had a song, or artist, so beautifully help me tell my tale than when I utilized the extraordinary storytelling abilities of Bob Seger in my novel FIRE INSIDE.

It's a pleasure listening to his music.

It's a gift to be inspired by it.

Kristen Ashley

♥ ♥ ♥ ♥ ♥ ♥ ♥ ♥ ♥ ♥ ♥ ♥ ♥ ♥ ♥

From the desk of Mimi Jean Pamfiloff

Dear Reader,

When it came time to decide which god or goddess in my Accidentally Yours series would get their HEA in book four, I sat back and looked at who was most in need of salvation. Hands down, the winner was Ixtab, the Goddess of Suicide. Before you judge the title, however, I'd like to explain why this goddess is not the dreary soul you might imagine. Fact is she's more like the Goddess of Anti-Suicide, with the ability to drain dark feelings from one person and redeploy them to another. Naturally, being a deity, she tends to help those who are down on their luck and punish those who are truly deserving.

However, every now and again, someone bumps into her while she's not looking. The results are fatal. So after thousands of years and thousands of accidental deaths, she's determined to keep everyone away. Who could blame her?

But fate has other plans for this antisocial goddess with a kind streak. His name is Dr. Antonio Acero, and this sexy Spaniard has just become the lynchpin in the gods' plans for saving the planet from destruction. He's also in need of a little therapy, and Ixtab is the only one who can help him.

When these two meet, they quickly realize there are forces greater than them both, trying to pull them apart and push them together. Which force will win?

♥ ♥ ♥ ♥ ♥ ♥ ♥ ♥ ♥ ♥ ♥ ♥ ♥ ♥ ♥ ♥ ♥ ♥

From the desk of Katie Lane

Dear Reader,

As some of you may already know, the idea for my fictional town of Bramble, Texas, came from the hours I spent watching *The Andy Griffith Show*. When Barney, Aunt Bee, and Opie were on, my mom couldn't peel me away from our console television. The townsfolk's antics held me spellbound. Which is probably why I made my characters a little crazy, too. (Okay, so I made them a lot crazy.) But while the people of Mayberry had levelheaded Sheriff Andy Taylor to keep them in line, the townsfolk of Bramble have been allowed to run wild.

Until now.

I'm pleased as punch to introduce Sheriff Dusty Hicks, the hero of my newest Deep in the Heart of Texas novel, A MATCH MADE IN TEXAS. Like Andy, he's a dedicated lawman who loves his job and the people of his community. Unlike Andy, he carries a gun, has a wee bit of a temper, and is blessed with the kind of looks and hard body that can make a good girl turn bad. And after just one glimpse of Dusty's shiny handcuffs, Brianne Cates wants to turn bad. Real bad.

But it won't be easy for Brianne to seduce a little lawman lovin' out of my hero. Dusty has his hands full trying to regain joint custody of his precocious three-year-old daughter and, at the same time, deal with a con-artist television evangelist and a vengeful cartel drug lord. Not to mention the townsfolk of Bramble, who have suddenly gone wa-a-ay off their rockers.

All I can say is, what started out as a desire to give Bramble its very own Sheriff Taylor quickly turned into a fast-paced joyride that left my hair standing on end and my heart as warm and gooey as a toaster strudel. I hope it will do the same for you. :o)

Much love,

Katie Lane

♥ ♥ ♥ ♥ ♥ ♥ ♥ ♥ ♥ ♥ ♥ ♥ ♥ ♥ ♥

From the desk of Jessica Lemmon

Dear Reader,

I love a scruffy-faced, tattooed, motorcycle-riding bad boy as much as the next girl, so when it came time to write HARD TO HANDLE, I knew what qualities I wanted Aiden Downey to possess.

For inspiration, I needed to look no further than Charlie Hunnam from the famed TV show *Sons of Anarchy*. I remember watching Season 1 on Netflix, mouth agape and eyes wide. When Charlie's character, Jax Teller, finished his first scene, I looked over at my husband and said, "*That's Aiden!*"

In HARD TO HANDLE, Aiden may have been crafted with a bad-boy starter kit: He has the scruff, the tattoo, the knee-weakening dimples that make him look like sin on a stick, and yeah, a custom Harley-Davidson to boot. But Aiden also has something extra special that derails his bad-boy image: a heart of near-solid gold.

When we first met Aiden and Sadie in *Tempting the Billionaire* (and again in the e-novella *Can't Let Go*), there wasn't much hope for these two hurting hearts to work out their differences. Aiden had been saddled with devastating news and familial responsibilities, and Sadie (poor Sadie!) had just opened up her heart to Aiden, who stomped on it, broke it into pieces, and set it on fire for good measure. How could they forgive each other after things had gone so horribly, terribly wrong?

Aiden has suffered a lot of loss, but in HARD TO HANDLE, he's on a mission to get his life *back*. A very large piece of that puzzle is winning back the woman he never meant to hurt, the woman he loved. Sadie, with her walled-up heart, smart, sassy mouth, and fiery attitude isn't going to be an easy nut to crack. Especially after she vowed to never, ever get hurt again. That goes *double* for the blond Adonis with the unforgettable mouth and ability to turn her brain into Silly Putty.

The best part about this good "bad" boy? Aiden's determination is as rock-hard as his abs. He's not going to let Sadie walk away, not now that he sees how much she still cares for him. Having been to hell and back, Aiden isn't intimidated by her. Not even a little bit. Sadie is his Achilles' heel, and Aiden accepts that it's going to take time (and plenty of seduction!) to win her over. He also knows that she's worth it.

Think you're up for a ride around the block with a bad-boy-done-good? I have to say, Aiden left a pretty deep mark on my heart and I'm still a little in love with him! He may change your mind about scruffy, motorcycle-riding hotties…He certainly managed to change Sadie's.

Happy reading!

Jessica Lemmon

www.jessicalemmon.com

Find out more about Forever Romance!

Visit us at
www.hachettebookgroup.com/publishing_forever.aspx

Find us on Facebook
http://www.facebook.com/ForeverRomance

Follow us on Twitter
http://twitter.com/ForeverRomance

NEW AND UPCOMING TITLES

Each month we feature our new titles
and reader favorites.

CONTESTS AND GIVEAWAYS

We give away galleys, autographed copies,
and all kinds of exclusive items.

AUTHOR INFO

You'll find bios, articles, and links to personal websites
for all your favorite authors—and so much more.

GET SOCIAL

Connect with your favorite authors, editors, and
other Forever fans, and share what's important to you.

THE BUZZ

Sign up for our monthly romance newsletter,
and be the first to read all about it.